Scion

Scion

A NOVEL

Bryant R. Camareno

To order additional copies of this book, contact:
Xlibris
844-714-8691
www.Xlibris.com
Orders@Xlibris.com
819668

As always, this book is dedicated to my family. I do this for you!

Acknowledgements

I want to thank my publishers at XLIBRIS for allowing my story to be told. I would also thank Justin Jacobson and Darrell Curts for their input and guidance as well as the encouragement of my true friends John DeGirolamo, Jeff Morris, and Mike Giasi. Finally, my heartfelt thanks to my wife Raquel and my kids Bryant-Christopher, Alexa-Cristina, Michael-Anthony and Nicolas-Andrew for allowing me to run my ideas by them.

The purpose of all wars is peace.
— Saint Augustine

Prologue I

The Crusades were a time of savagery and death, all in the name of the Christian God. The Fourth Crusade had been inaugurated by Pope Innocent III in an attempt to recapture Jerusalem from its Muslim captors. By the second year though, the divine purpose was gone; the pope's men had been corrupted. The Crusaders made their way through Egypt toward their new goal, the capital of the Christian-controlled Byzantine Empire, Constantinople. The Crusaders were turning on their brothers in faith.

The Crusader knights began the siege in April 1204. After capturing a section of the city, the invader army, driven by lust and greed, set the city on fire, nearly destroying it. For three endless, bloody days, the men of Constantinople were slain, and the women were desecrated. The massacre rivaled only that of the First Crusade in its raid of the small city Ma'Arrat al Numan. The Siege of Constantinople was the culmination of the Fourth Crusade.

In the midst of the conflict, a solitary knight traversed the bloodstained streets. He forced his way past the clashing armies toward the last of the great libraries of the ancient world: the Imperial Library of Constantinople. The solitary knight was a virtuous man, not corrupted by greed and true to his oath. He had his mission, one given to him personally by Pope Innocent III, one that he proudly accepted. Inside the library of Constantine the Great, he knew, despite the mayhem outside, the entrusted scribes were arduously copying the volumes from the papyrus rolls to the more stable parchment and vellum in a vain attempt to preserve these pieces of literature for all posterity. He removed his sword as he began to enter the great library.

With great force, the knight pushed open the heavy doors and was suddenly confronted by two elderly librarians. Being the scholars that they were, they took one look at the warrior's sword and backed away. One of the other librarians hurriedly closed the large door behind him, silencing the screams from the massacre outside. The knight marveled at the ornate design of the interior columns and at the countless scrolls and codices neatly placed upon the many large shelves built against the walls. Knowing what the champion was seeking, one of the two elderly confronters pointed to an area in the far right-hand corner of the building. The knight, intent on fulfilling his goal quickly, hastened past the volumes of papyrus texts and went directly to his goal. Before he could reach for the item, he heard a loud boom coming from behind him; it was the sound of the great door to the library being torn off its hinges as his fellow Crusaders burst in.

The valiant knight hid from their view as he watched in horror as his brothers-in-arms murdered the librarians. When the chance came, the knight quietly grabbed the relic he sought, carefully rolled the item, and placed it into a piecemeal satchel. The soldiers were reveling in false glory as they began to set the place on fire. This was the end of the imperial library.

The knight casually walked toward his brethren as they joyfully destroyed the various texts. He feigned the same sense of joy as he headed out the door. Before making his way through the threshold of the door frame, he felt the full strength of an arm grabbing his own.

"Where are you going?" the commanding voiced asked in between bursts of laughter. His breath smelled of poor wine.

The knight recognized his aggressor as a member of a rich family, bestowed with the title of a general by virtue of his power and wealth. The good knight's voice was stammering in fear. "I need some air. The smoke is making it difficult to breathe."

The rich man laughed as he released his grip. "Go and take part in the revelry."

The good knight sighed with relief and turned to leave when the nobleman grabbed the satchel.

"What have you there, young man?"

The knight reacted by snatching the satchel back. The general, visibly angry, unsheathed his sword. The knight removed his own sword and placed it to the general's neck before the general could even lift his arm. The champion's sacred vow was paramount; he would die if needed, but more importantly, he would commit the mortal sin if warranted.

"You will die for this!" the nobleman raged. He then screamed out to his soldiers. "Seize him!"

The good knight carefully paced backward, sword in arm, making his way out the door, clutching the satchel ever so tightly. One of the general's dutiful soldiers took out a knife and lunged at the knight. He first struck him with his fist about the head and face before plunging the knife into the good knight's chest. Despite his serious wound, the knight's skills still outmatched his attacker, and he was able to thrust his own sword into his opponent's chest.

The virtuous knight sobbed in distress as he pulled out his sword. His victim appeared to be only about seventeen years old. The knight raised his sword again and paced backward, while the general and the other soldiers stood at bay. The knight made his way into the street and entered the mass confusion of the ongoing massacre. He ran toward his steed. The nobleman angrily ordered his men to take pursuit, but the knight was soon lost among the ensuing chaos in the streets. He was gone.

By nightfall, the entire city was aflame, and the sacking of Constantinople was complete, but the general's own personal crusade to capture the insubordinate knight had only begun.

The Dream

The good knight raced across the torrid desert on his sacred mission. He had been riding for hours, stopping only intermittently to give his horse a brief respite. The sun was about to rise, and heat, only in its infancy, would come with it. The ebony steed scurried across the sand, strenuously carrying the valiant knight on his back. The horse and rider struggled as they continued on their course. The knight bled from the mortal wound to his chest as dry air made it harder for him to breathe. The knight firmly held onto the reins with his left hand and tightly held onto a large satchel with his other. He screamed at his horse, urging the beast to go faster. The blood and sweat from his brow combined into stinging streams for his eyes. He glanced over his shoulder, seeing nothing but sensing danger in the distance. Worried that the enemy would soon be upon him, the champion turned his gaze to the horizon, hoping his destination would soon appear.

Al-Jawf, Yemen
Present Time

Inside a tattered tent, in the outskirts of the town of al-Hazm, the young man awoke from his dream. Even though it was in the middle of the night, the young man would not be able to return to his slumber. This reoccurring dream of a crusading knight racing toward an unknown destination had been the same since Yousef Malik Hasan was a child. When he was a young boy, the dream would cause Yousef to cry in the middle of the night, bringing his doting mother, Aamilah, to his bedside to provide him comfort.

Most of Yousef's teenage years were spent sleeping during the day and sleepless at night in a failed attempt to avoid the recurring nightmare. A decade of sleepless nights brought only angst to a teenaged Yousef. In his twenties, the sleep-deprived young man became despondent and turned to self-study to keep himself distracted and to hopefully garner some relief. He would read of American imperialism and the atrocities it committed upon innocent people throughout the world. He was bitter and angry at having been born into a violent world. At twenty-five, he would leave the comfort of his mother and join various militant groups throughout the Middle East. Yousef had never quite found the one group that he thought was sincere in changing the world.

Yousef was a man without a country and without a home until he found the man who would be the father figure whom he never had: Imam El Fazazi. The imam took Yousef under his wing and into his new home in Yemen. For the last five years, Imam El Fazazi had been grooming Yousef to be the leader of a new movement that would strike horror in the heart of the West.

Yousef had a newfound happiness that would only be short-lived once he started having the *dream* again. He would no longer fight sleep or avoid the dream; instead, with the help of his imam, Yousef would sadly learn to embrace it. The dream, they determined, could only be interpreted as a Crusader embarking on a mission intent on destroying Muslims throughout the globe. This nightmare drove Yousef to become a threat to the world.

Prologue II

Leonardo da Vinci–Fiumicino Airport
Rome, Italy
1978

A team of ten scientists disembarked down the mobile stairway out of the National Airlines Boeing 747 and were greeted by three Catholic priests. The smiles on the priests' collective faces did not give away the fact that they had been impatiently waiting for the scientists on the tarmac for nearly an hour. Of the three priests, one stepped out and greeted the scientists.

"Signore Allison, it is a pleasure to meet you," the senior priest said, his near-perfect English hiding his native Italian tongue. He extended his hand. "I am Padre Silvio."

Mathew Allison, the lead scientist, returned the handshake. "The pleasure is mine. Are the others waiting?"

"Yes, they have been here for several weeks, but—"

"Excellent," Mathew Allison said excitedly. "I want to get started right away."

"There is a problem." Padre Silvio was visibly nervous. "We might not be able to begin just yet."

"Why? How long are we talking about? A few hours? A day?"

"Perhaps . . . indefinitely," the priest replied.

"You've got to be kidding me." Mathew Allison glanced back at his team and inquired emphatically, "We had the pope's permission. We came all the way here from America."

"That is correct, but you had his permission *before* his death. The new pope . . ." Padre Silvio paused as he lowered his head in grief. "The new pope has been convinced to put an end to your efforts."

"Nothing should have changed. I need to meet with the pope immediately," Dr. Allison demanded.

"Meeting with the Holy Father is impossible. Besides, I don't think that would make a difference. There is a *movement* within the church that is against this whole . . . well, that is, against *your* experiment."

"*This* is not an experiment, and it's certainly not mine," Dr. Allison said angrily. "It's meant to be a validation of our—"

Padre Silvio interrupted. "I do not think that calling it a *validation* makes your current situation any better."

"Please, Padre. You have to help us accomplish this task," Dr. Allison begged. "We have waited so long. This project is intended to reaffirm our faith."

"You do not have to convince me. The new pope knows of the benefits behind this endeavor, but there are forces even beyond his control." The priest paused and extended his hand. "Let us at least let our driver take you to your rooms while I will continue to do what I can."

Dr. Allison objected. "There's no way that I can go with you? Perhaps I can make a stronger case."

"Impossibile!" Padre Silvio exclaimed. "Please forgive my outburst, but I too am under pressure. So please come with me. Let me take all of you to the hotel so that you can all rest. I give you my word that I will continue to do all that I can."

Mathew Allison reluctantly agreed.

Padre Silvio and the other priests led the group of Americans into the airport.

"Since the Holy Father died, there has been a growing force within the church to put a stop to your project." Padre Silvio resumed once the group was inside. "When the conclave discovered that the artifact had been secretly moved to the Vatican, there was a surge of protest. The *others* demanded that it be sent back. They are trying to convince the new pope to cancel this whole operation."

"*Cancel the whole operation?*" Dr. Allison blurted. "We have spent nearly a decade just to be where we are now."

The priest continued to lead the way. "I beg of you not to be angry. Anger will not get you where you need to be."

"Please don't quote me James 1:19," Dr. Allison quipped.

"You know your Bible," the priest said, impressed.

"We're all Catholics here," Dr. Allison emphasized. "We may be scientists, but we have not lost the faith. We were carefully selected because of our faith. We're not here to discredit the relic but to only validate it."

"You are preaching to the choir, as you Americans say." Padre Silvio chuckled. "I am here to help you, not obstruct you."

"Forgive me, Father—"

"Is this a confession?" the priest joked.

They both laughed.

"I'm sorry," Mathew stated sincerely. "I know that you're here to help us. Please forgive me."

The priest jovially made the sign of the cross. "You are forgiven."

Neither man realized that Mathew Allison's group was listening to their conversation until the scientists laughed—with the exception of one man.

After collecting their luggage, the entire group of men eventually made their way into a large van.

Padre Silvio turned to the driver. "All'hotel." Standing adjacent to the vehicle, Padre Silvio once again made the sign of the cross, this time more sincerely. "May God bless these men and their endeavors."

Mathew Allison smiled and made a silent prayer, hoping that the good Lord would grant his request.

As the vehicle made its way into the capital, the scientists gawked in awe from behind the van windows at the splendor that was Rome. As they drove into the heart of the city, they marveled at the dome of Saint Peter's Basilica in the distance. As young Catholics, they had only dreamed of visiting the outskirts of the Holy See, but if it all worked out, they would soon be inside the most secretive part of the Vatican. The jet lag did not deter them from feeling the surge of adrenaline of being in the Eternal City. The busy pedestrians mindlessly walking up and down the streets, coupled with the reckless maneuvering of the sports cars and scooters, only added to the uniqueness of the city. The scientists were awestruck by the monumental Il Vittoriano as the structure passed them as the van made its way to Via Nazionale. The sight of street panhandlers and beggars was juxtaposed with the vast richness of the Vatican, which was just a few miles away. Within a few moments, the scientists were dropped off at the Hotel Artemide.

Mathew Allison opened the sliding door to the van and led the other scientists out.

"Please make yourselves comfortable, and I will notify each of you as soon as I can confirm the pope's approval," Mathew said to his team of learned men.

The scientists said their farewells and checked into their separate rooms.

*   *   *

Among the group of scientists, there was one man who remained stoic and appeared to be the loner of the group. The lonely American entered his room and elected not to turn on the lights. He lay on the bed and stared at the ceiling. Despite the exhausting, nearly ten-hour flight, he could not sleep. After several hours of mindlessly gazing into the darkness, the lonely American finally reached for the room's telephone. He dialed a number he had committed to memory. It was a local call. The voice on the other end spoke with an accent that the scientist could not discern. The lonely American's voice trembled with trepidation.

"It . . . It . . . It's me, Connolly. There's a problem."

The other voice remained silent.

Connolly continued. "The . . . The new pope has, uh, put a temporary stop to the operation."

The other voice screamed in anger.

"What do . . . what do you want me to do?" Connolly asked.

There was more silence. Finally, there was a command.

The lonely American listened patiently. "I'll do as you say. I'll wait."

* * *

For the next three weeks, the team of scientists either remained in their rooms or explored the Eternal City. They were bored out of their minds. They had come to Rome to be scientists, not tourists.

At the end of September, there was an announcement that shocked the world: Pope John Paul I had died. He died thirty-three days after his ordination.

* * *

Mathew Allison was enraged. He had been screaming at Padre Silvio through the phone. "We've been here for a month! And it has been a week since the new Pope's ordination—and still nothing."

"You have been very patient," Father Silvio agreed, his voice clearly excited through the speaker. "But I finally have good news for you. The Holy Father has granted your request. You will begin this afternoon."

Mathew was overjoyed. "Excellent! I've got to go. I've got to tell the others." Mathew disconnected the call and immediately called the rooms of each of his fellow scientists.

* * *

Upon receiving the news from Mathew Allison, Connolly, the lonely American, made his own call. The man on the other end of the call listened as Connolly spoke.

"We are ready to proceed."

Il Vaticano
1978

Mathew Allison proudly led his team of American scientists through Saint Peter's Square into the basilica. The men were disciplined scientists but could barely contain their own excitement. This was a momentous occasion for them all. They were astonished by the grandiose architectural sculpture, the lavish marble, and the extravagant artwork. The amount of wealth that had to be put into this sublime ornament of the earth was overwhelming. *How many mouths could have been fed with all this wealth?* they each, in their own way, wondered. The scientists were led down into the *scavi*, the necropolis, beneath the basilica, into a vast hall of the inner sanctum of the Vatican. The group of men waited patiently for several hours in the large anteroom next to the various sarcophagi until Padre Silvio finally exited an inner room.

"You have been approved," the priest said to loud cheers. "But the Holy Father has only given you five days to complete your research."

"Five days?" The scientists collectively mumbled in protest.

"We've been here for over a month, and that's all the time we get?" Mathew said angrily.

The priest nodded. "And not a moment later. And you must hurry before His Eminence changes his mind."

"Well, then let's get started," Mathew directed the others.

Padre Silvio proceeded to lead the scientists to a larger room where there was a group of men waiting. These other men were made up of Vatican scientists and several more priests. The men assembled around a large glass encasement. The item itself was fourteen feet by three, but the enclosure gave it the illusion of being massive. Everyone stood and gaped at the relic, mesmerized by its appearance; even the lonely American was in awe. There was stunned silence in the entire room. Mathew Allison broke this silence and ordered everyone to work.

*　*　*

During the ensuing days, the team of scientists worked both diligently and tirelessly, examining the item, sleeping only in shifts of an hour or two. The excitement of their task had the effect of energizing the men to the point that sleep was not of any major concern.

Amidst the endless examination and the exhaustion, the lonely American worked as relentlessly as the others, but staying true to his nature, he worked alone. His colleagues had no idea that the lonely American was accomplishing his own sinister plan.

*　*　*

After five eternal days, Padre Silvio entered the inner sanctum. He was shocked by the scientists' dreary appearances. All the humor had left the priest, and he appeared grim.

"Mr. Allison, you have overstayed your welcome by several hours. You and your men must leave," Padre Silvio entreated.

"We need more time—"

"You must leave—now." Padre Silvio was surprisingly earnest.

Mathew knew enough not to protest; moreover, he was tired. "Despite wishing we had more time, my men and I are forever grateful for the opportunity we have been given."

Before exiting the inner room, Mathew Allison stopped to have one last look at the relic. He became emotional and fought back his tears. He knew his research would not have been in vain, and while it would take many more months before his results would be published, he knew in his heart that his beliefs would be confirmed. He looked at his team and thanked them individually.

Padre Silvio escorted the scientists into the van, and they were all driven back to their hotel. Flight arrangements had been made by the church; some were scheduled to leave that night, others the next day. The lonely American offered to take the latter flight.

*   *   *

That last evening, the lonely American, despite his exhaustion, once again had no desire to sleep; he had his mission to complete. He had not even bothered showering and had been wearing the same clothes for the last five days. His reflection, when he finally looked, disgusted him. He appeared frail, sullen, and unrecognizable even to himself. Connolly had been so distracted by his apparition that he had not heard the phone ringing.

The voice was disturbed by the lonely man's failure to quickly respond. Connolly did not bother to explain. He just listened. He was given a new set of instructions.

"Understood," Connolly said. "No, I won't be late."

*   *   *

About an hour later, the lonely American exited his hotel, making his way down Via Dei Serpenti. Connolly wandered about for an hour, practically walking in circles.

Suddenly, as if on cue, he changed directions and walked over to a side street, Via Cimarra, and walked straight into a little café. The café had been closed for hours, occupied solely by a single server, but the employee acted as if he had been expecting the lonely American. The scientist sat at a table, waiting patiently, saying nothing, until he noticed there was a man hovering behind him. The man was dressed in a black suit. He was a man in black—an MIB, as they would come to be known in popular culture.

The lonely American realized that the café server was no longer there.

It was past three-thirty in the morning, late even by European standards. Both the café and the streets of Rome were now empty. Connolly reached into his jacket and removed a large manila envelope. He slid the envelope across the table into the hands of the MIB. "Very good work, young man," said the MIB, with his very strong British accent. In turn, the stranger attempted to hand Connolly a large white envelope. It was clear that inside the envelope was payment for services rendered.

The lonely American waved it away. "No, you keep it. I don't want it."

"My employers will insist that you be paid. We had an agreement. Agreements must be honored. Otherwise—"

"I don't care what they think . . . or what *they* do." The lonely American was adamant. "Take it. I'm done." The lonely American walked out the door and meandered through the streets.

*   *   *

Hiding in the recesses of the night were two other MIBs, watching him silently. They did not bother following him. They knew his destination.

*   *   *

Mark Connolly had every right to be angry at the church. The Connolly family had been a well-known and well-respected family in the Archdiocese of Baltimore, and Mark had always been the good boy. He was the second youngest of seven children, and despite him feeling that he was lost in the mix, his parents knew that Mark would be the most successful of the Connolly children. They put a lot of pressure on him as a child, but they only wanted the best for him. Mark had been active in the church since he learned to walk and had always wanted to be an altar boy since he could remember. He dreamed of being a priest when he was thirteen years old and studied under the tutelage of Fr. Danny Markle.

Father Danny had been the youngest priest the parish ever had. The people of the parish had the privilege of watching the young priest grow old and become a father figure to the boys. At the age of sixty-two, the priest had somehow lost his faith, or maybe he never had it at all. He had become a slave to the desires of the flesh. He had become a monster. He would become Mark Connolly's monster.

Father Danny insisted on having mass rehearsals three times a week. Mark spent his childhood reenacting the Eucharist down to the last detail, including drinking wine from the chalice. The wine tasted good to Mark. He would continue drinking the wine with Father Danny long after his altar boy duties had ended. They would drink until Mark would fall asleep. Mark would eventually be violated by Father Danny.

After their first encounter, Father Danny gave a crucifix for Mark to wear. "This is *my* gift to you," Father Danny said ever so genuinely. "I'm really proud of you."

Mark agreed to wear the ornament around his neck; however, it only served as a constant reminder of the shame Mark had to bear alone for the rest of his life. Later in life, excessive alcohol would numb his senses, but it would never erase his pain.

His parents never knew of the crime, which made matters worse for Mark. He would become a cutter, scarring his own body, and he was just as adept in hiding physical wounds as emotional ones. Mark carried the agony with him throughout his young adult life, and his sudden desire to not attend the seminary but instead go to medical school went unquestioned. The family took pride in him when he had been accepted at the Georgetown University School of Medicine, where he chose to be an oncologist in the hopes of curing cancer. However, the pressure of medical school doubled Mark's burden. Suicide crept into his thoughts from time to time, but it was never an option. Suicide was a sin.

Mark's family noticed a change in his behavior but attributed his despondency to the rigors of medical school. Months would go by before Mark would visit home. In between those visits, he had virtually no contact with his family, but their love for one another still seemed unwavering. Mark always had one excuse or another for not attending mass until one day the first of his nieces was due to be baptized, and Father Danny was to be the presiding priest. No excuse would ever justify his failure to attend the family ceremony, and so Mark could not refuse to go—lest his secret be revealed.

Mark Connolly watched the procession from the back of the church, and from his point of view, he could not—and really did not want to—see Father Danny, but he could hear his voice. The very sound of Father Danny's voice made Mark's skin crawl, and as always, he made a conscious effort to contain his anger. At the end of the nearly two-hour event, it was time for family pictures. Mark had forgotten about picture time. Father Danny would be included in the event.

Mark watched as the church cleared, leaving behind the Connolly family with Father Danny. Mark was terrified, the same as he was when he was thirteen. The next thing he knew, Father Danny was standing in front of him.

"Mark," Father Danny said, extending his hand, "it's so good to see you. How's medical school?"

Mark was flabbergasted that the priest acted so calm and collected, as if nothing had ever happened. Mark, on the other hand, was speechless.

His mother chimed in excitedly, "He's in his final year at Georgetown University. He's going to be a great oncologist one day."

"That's great," Father Danny said with the same serpentine smirk he had whenever he forced himself upon him. "I'm really proud of you."

I'm really proud of you. I'm really proud of you. I'm really proud of you.

Those words echoed in Mark's head. He was taken back to when he was an innocent little boy, back to the time he had first been violated.

Mark did not cry when Father Danny hurt him. He would not ever cry. When Father Danny would finish his deed, Mark would watch as the priest dressed himself, putting back on his white clerical collar. "I'm really proud of you," Father Danny would say. In fact, he would say it after every single encounter.

I'm really proud of you.

Mark trembled and remained silent. He worked up enough courage to fake a smile and was about to walk away when he saw someone walk out of the sacristy. It was an altar boy. He had to be around ten years old. He recognized the boy's face. It was his face. The boy looked devastatingly sullen.

The priest turned to the little boy and patted his head. "You did a great job today. I'll see you Monday for rehearsal." Father Danny stopped the boy as he was about to leave. "Are you wearing your crucifix?" he asked.

The boy paused and nervously removed the cross from under his shirt. "Uh-huh . . ." the boy mumbled nervously.

"I'm really proud of you," Father Danny repeated as he patted the boy on his head.

The boy quietly walked out of the church and rode his bike home to his family, who, assuredly, had no idea of the pain their little boy was enduring.

Mark had been somberly watching the little boy when he heard the priest's curdling words again. Mark looked back at the priest and saw that the priest had been smiling. Father Danny then turned his gaze and was now smiling at Mark.

"You—you son of a bitch!" Mark exclaimed.

Mark's entire family was shocked.

"*Mark?*" they all said.

The priest knew it was time to leave but was blocked by Mark. "No, sir, not this time! You're not going to walk away from this one!"

Three of Mark's brothers tried to intervene. Mark pushed them all away. He grabbed the priest by the arms and pushed him back against a wall.

"I've been silent for far too long! You'll pay for this! You will never hurt a child again!"

"Ma-Mark, please!" the priest screamed.

"Shut up! Don't say a word!"

Mark did not realize that the ruckus attracted many of the parishioners back into the church. It took several people to force Mark off the priest.

For the first time in his life, Mark was crying. He turned to his shell-shocked parents. "Mom. Dad. He hurt me. He's been hurting many of us for years."

His mother turned to his brothers. "Is this true? Did Father Danny touch you boys?"

The brothers emphatically said no.

His mother turned back to Mark. "Why would you say these things?"

Mark was in tears. "You . . . You think I'm lying? Dad?"

His dad looked away.

His mother looked around at the crowd. "Mark, you're embarrassing us," she spoke in a low tone.

"*Embarr*—Mom? You d-don't believe me?"

"Let's go home, honey. You're tired." Mark felt lightheaded and wanted to vomit. He walked out of that church and out of his family's lives and never saw them again. On that day, Mark stopped believing in God.

* * *

Mark's newfound solitude made him aspire to be a doctor even more. He was going to devote his life to pediatric oncology. He would help children in any way imaginable. It was a chance encounter at an American Chemical Society conference in Albuquerque, New Mexico, that had brought him to Mathew Allison's team. Mark's specialty in biochemistry made him a perfect candidate for Dr. Allison's special team of scientists. Mathew was recruiting Catholic scientists and promised him an opportunity to participate in the event of a lifetime: an event that would change religion as mankind knew it. Mark Connolly's anger at the church did not stop him from accepting Dr. Allison's offer, but it did make him perfect for the scheme arranged by the "men in black."

A month after the meeting with Dr. Allison, Mark was studying in the library when he was first approached by the stranger. The man was dressed in a black casual style.

"Mark? Mark Connolly?" the stranger asked.

Mark was certain the man was hiding a British accent. "Y-yes. Do I know you?" Mark replied.

"I'm a little offended that you don't remember me. I'm Stan Waszorski. We went to grammar school together. I was a couple of years ahead."

Mark remembered Stan Waszorski, but this man looked nothing like him at all.

"Do you mind if I sit?"

"Actually—"

"It'll only be a minute," the stranger began to whisper. "I just want you to know—I know what *he* did to you."

"What are you talking about?" Mark knew what the stranger meant, but he was testing him.

"Father Danny. I know what he did to you. He did the same to me."

Mark's interest was piqued. "What do you want?"

"I have a chance to get back at him."

"At who?"

"Father Danny. For what he did to us and what he's still doing."

"How?"

"The church let us down. They let this happen and did nothing to protect us or to stop it. This is our chance at striking back at the church."

"*The church*? I'm not interested in bringing down the church. I don't even want to deal with Father Danny anymore." Mark was agitated. "I think I should leave."

The stranger motioned him to sit down. "The church has ignored its victims for far too long. If we don't stop them now, it'll go on forever."

"So what? I can't help those other children?"

"We . . . *I* know that you're about to embark on a mission, and there's a way that you can help."

"How did you know about . . ." Mark was perplexed but was intrigued to hear more.

"Don't worry about that. Focus on how *you* can help us . . . help the countless other victims."

Mark hesitated briefly but then asked, "What are you proposing?"

The stranger went on for several minutes explaining how a little innocuous action on the part of Mark could change the face of religion, which was exactly what Mathew Allison had promised—but with opposite intentions.

Mark listened carefully, and after deliberate contemplation, he reluctantly agreed. "I'll help."

"Excellent." The stranger stood up.

Mark acknowledged the stranger and watched as he walked out the library. Mark would never hear from the stranger again until the day before he took off to Rome, when he received a mysterious phone call with very detailed instructions.

Now, in Rome, the lonely American had been sitting alone in his darkened room, staring outside the hotel window. Lurking behind him was an MIB, an assassin ready to kill. To the assassin's surprise, the lonely American had his own gun.

"You can save your efforts," Mark Connolly uttered. "I knew that man in the library wasn't Stan Waszorski. His attempt to disguise his accent gave him away. I knew that I never would have survive this ordeal. I had my reasons for doing what I did." The lonely American placed the gun into his mouth and pulled the trigger.

The last thought Mark had was that he wanted to believe in God and prayed that suicide really was not a sin; another was that Father Danny had escaped justice. The brain matter sprayed against the MIB, and the release from his sphincter covered the floor.

The would-be assassin quietly walked out.

Prologue III

Present Day
London, England

At four-thirty in the morning, the London streets were empty except for a group of eighteen-year-old male prostitutes wandering the streets of King's Cross in the northern edge of the city. "Business" had been slow lately, and the lads were about to call it a night and go home. Sadly, they had no real home. They only made it a few feet to this non-destination when they were approached by a mysterious figure. The male figure engaged the boys and solicited one of them to walk with him to his small car.

The boy, Dorian, had always been eager to make an easy twenty-five pounds, but the lure of the one hundred pounds the mystery man offered him made it a no-brainer. The man entered the driver's side of his vehicle, while the young boy calmly sat on the passenger side.

"Not much of a talker, eh, mate?"

Dorian's attempt to flirt had no effect on the man. The man remained silent as he started the car. He continued to drive for several kilometers until they reached a small isolated series of buildings. The man stationed his car behind one of the buildings. He sat there quietly and gave Dorian a menacing smile.

"Shall we?" the man asked.

Dorian was trembling but quietly assented. His subconscious was pleading with him that no one knew where he was.

The man led the way as he lured the young boy inside one of the buildings. The building appeared vacant and abandoned. The two went up a flight of stairs. After that, Dorian lost track of how many flights they ascended; he was too scared to count. They approached a door, which the man quickly unlocked. The room was small but surprisingly had all the furnishings necessary for a person to live quite comfortably.

The man walked behind a bar and poured two cups of red wine, handing one of them to Dorian; he never touched his. The young boy had tasted communion wine before, but this one was bitter. The man waited for Dorian to drink the last drop and then led him into the only bedroom. Dorian felt faint and collapsed onto the bed. The two started to engage in sex, but the passion quickly turned to violence as the man proceeded to beat the teen into unconsciousness. He then carried the nearly dead lad into a secret room.

The stranger dropped his victim onto the ground and opened a freezer box. The stranger stared at the remains that were lying in the freezer. His ravenous urge began to rise. The stranger turned back to Dorian, reached down, and proceeded to choke the boy to death. Once the young man was dead, the man continued to desecrate the body in ways that were beyond human.

The man's dark desires had been satiated—for now. The man reached into the freezer, removed the body of one of his recently deceased victims, and placed what was left of Dorian inside. All that was left of that frozen victim were the sliced fragments in one large plastic bag. The man took the remains of that victim and carried them out of the apartment by way of a large duffel bag. He placed the duffel bag into the trunk of his car and drove for several blocks. The sun would rise in an hour, and he needed to act swiftly. He turned onto a side street and pulled over. The man quickly removed the duffel bag from the trunk and discarded the remains on the side of the street, doing so in a manner that ensured that they would be found.

Within a few weeks, he would lure a new victim into his evil sanctum, and when he was done, the man would pray to God for forgiveness.

*   *   *

Dorian and his predecessor were the first two *known* victims of the ruthless killer who would terrorize the streets of London, England. The headlines for the *Daily Sun* would read that the city was in a state of fear because a new "Jack the Ripper" had emerged, only this time, the lives of young, teenage boys were at risk.

Prologue IV

Present Day
Tampa, Florida

Seth Jacobson never really wanted to be a lawyer. His passion was photography, but his father was an Orthodox Jew who wanted his son to be a doctor or a lawyer. Seth's father could support that his son was gay but could not accept that his firstborn wanted to be photographer. Seth reluctantly went to law school, knowing that he could one day return to his passion, but for now, he was stuck serving the indigent citizenry of the State of Florida, most of which should be committed to a mental hospital. He made $35,000 a year, which was more than enough to pay for his small studio apartment, help feed his cat, and pay for his hobby. Still, he was miserable.

Seth was an assistant public defender who hated doing criminal defense work, and so he volunteered to cover the Baker Act hearings. The Florida Mental Health Act of 1971 was commonly known as the Baker Act, which allowed the involuntary commitment of individuals who were deemed a threat to themselves or to others. Under the statute, a Baker Act hearing required a magistrate to preside over the matter and to take testimony from a licensed psychologist or psychiatrist to render an opinion as to the mental stability of the patient. Because that placement occurred against the will of the patient, due process required that the patient be represented by a court-appointed lawyer. Most of these hearings occurred at one of the many state-designated facilities. St. Joseph's Hospital was one of those facilities. The hospital, situated in the heart of West Tampa, was founded in 1934 by the Franciscan Sisters of Allegany, and Seth spent way too much time there.

Seth made his way down the hallway of the hospital. The smell of disease and iodoform made his stomach churn. This made him hate his job even more. He stepped into the makeshift courtroom, which was actually a once-vacant office that had been set up with a long conference table surrounded by chairs. At the head of the table sat the magistrate.

On one side of the table, Seth sat next to his client of the moment, and opposite him on the other side were the prosecutor and the doctor seeking to commit the patient. The doctor, as customary, would offer a twenty-minute presentation, always opining that the patient was a threat to himself or to others, and as always, Seth argued vociferously against involuntary placement.

"Respectfully, magistrate, the doctor's testimony does not support a finding that my client is a threat to anyone," Seth said angrily.

The magistrate inquired almost instantaneously, "But what about the doctor's testimony that your client 'speaks' to God on a daily basis?"

"You can walk into any church on any day - or even this hospital's chapel - and you can find people 'speaking' to God, and we don't involuntarily place them in the hospital, do we?" Seth responded.

"That's different—"

"Why? Because *you* say so?"

The magistrate stared at Seth almost menacingly. "Counselor, you are out of line."

"My apologies," Seth said under his breath. "But you do get my point, right? It's such a ridiculous notion that *praying* to God is socially acceptable but *talking* to God is not!"

"You don't believe in God, do you?" the magistrate asked.

"Not that that question is relevant to this proceeding—nor is it any of your business—but if you must know, I'm a Jew who doesn't believe in God."

The magistrate was visibly embarrassed by his own question. "Well, then you wouldn't understand. But nonetheless, it is not just that your client talks to God but—"

"But that 'God' talks back to her." Seth completed the sentence.

"Exactly," the magistrate said. "This court is fearful that with her claim of hearing voices and her 'accidental' overdose, greater weight should be given to the doctor's testimony. Therefore, as a result, I find that she is a risk to herself. I hereby order her to be involuntarily placed here at the hospital for a period not to exceed twenty-one days."

"Your Honor, she has a family," Seth pleaded earnestly. "Her husband and her children need her home."

"She won't be any good to her family if she is successful in killing herself, will she?" the magistrate retorted.

"But, Your Honor—"

"My decision is final."

Seth stood up and clenched his briefcase tightly. "I pray that you never 'hear' God talking to you during a time of need."

He stormed out of the room and shared the bad news with his client's family. As he had expected, the family took it out on him. They berated him for his ineffectiveness and questioned his qualifications. Seth stood there and accepted the scolding for a full ten minutes. Getting no reaction from Seth, the family irately walked away.

The young lawyer stood there quietly for several moments and then aimlessly wandered down the hospital halls. He continued on his way, not realizing that his name was being called by a nurse.

"Mr. Jacobson, can I bother you for a second?" the nurse pleaded.

Seth did not want to be in that hospital a moment longer. "I'm really pressed for time."

"It's about one of your old clients."

"Not right now." He tried to walk past her, but she stood in his way.

"Please," she begged. "It's about the Jane Doe."

"Jane Doe? She's still here?" Seth asked. "After all these years?"

The nurse led Seth down the hallway. "We've never been able to identify her. No one has ever claimed her."

Seth could barely keep up with her. "What's going on with her?"

"In the last few days, she's not been responsive to any of the medication, and I feel that she's gotten worse."

Seth followed the frantic nurse down the long hallway and rushed into the isolation room, where he approached a bedridden, demented elderly woman. The silver-haired woman lay strapped to the hospital bed. She bore horrific scars on her face. She reeked of filth. Seth could barely stand the sight—or the smell—of her.

She was mumbling. Seth could not make out what she was saying. He leaned forward to hear her better. The foul stench from her mouth was almost unbearable for him to tolerate, but still, he drew closer, trying to make out her words.

"Fee-o . . . f-f-fee-o . . . rell . . . feo-rello . . ." She whispered her words ever so slightly that Seth could barely understand.

Seth turned to the nurse. "What is she saying?

"I'm not sure," the nurse answered, staring down at the patient. "She's not getting better, and no one can understand her. It's been several years, and all the doctors do is continue to pump drugs into her. Her condition has been getting so bad these last few days that I became worried. I have been trying to call you, but I couldn't reach you. She's continuously kept in this catatonic state, and that cannot be healthy for her. There has to be something we can do for her."

"I can file a motion to have her reevaluated," Seth responded. "But I don't expect much from this magistrate."

"No, no . . . trofio . . . fee-o-rello . . . orfano-t-trofio . . ." Jane Doe continued. "Fee-o-rello . . . fi-o-rello . . . *Fiorello.*"

"*Fiorello?*" Seth asked. "What is *Fiorello?*"

The patient grimaced in pain and passed out from her pain. Seth was troubled by her discomfort.

"I'll see what I can do for her. See if you can find someone who understands her," Seth ordered.

"Okay, Mr. Jacobson, and thank you." The nurse was crying. "Please do something to get her out of here. She has been here too long. She has no one to help her."

Seth tried to console the nurse. "I'll do what I can."

He walked out of the hospital dejected, with no faith that he had the ability to do anything for the deranged patient—or for any of his clients, for that matter.

Book One

Chapter One

Al Jawf, Yemen
Present Day

The desert windstorm blew heavily against the tattered tent in the arid plateau of the southeast Yemeni desert. Inside the tent, Yousef Malik Hasan slept restlessly on the ground. It was the infernal dream of the medieval Crusader that was giving him his terrible night. Yousef awoke as he always did, drenched in sweat.

Yousef opened his eyes to see his imam, El Fazazi, sitting on the ground beside him. Yousef arose and struggled to sit upright. He reached down to massage his weak leg. A birth defect had left him with his left leg shorter than the right; he had to limp his entire life and did so as he made his way to the basin to wash his face.

"The dream, my son?" the imam asked.

"Yes," Yousef answered. "It was troubling, as always."

"Why does it still frustrate you?"

"It has been the same dream since my mother first held me in her arms, and I wish it to be gone," Yousef replied.

The imam rested his hand on the young man's shoulder, bringing him some comfort. "But why does it still bother you so?"

"The dream is so vivid, so real," Yousef said as he exited the tent and stared into the sunrise.

"So your frustration stems from your confusion?"

"Exactly, my teacher."

The imam took Yousef by the hand and sat him on the ground. "My son, let me ease your frustration once again. Remember, it is neither a dream nor a memory. It is a vision from God. It is a sign from God that you are to strike back at the infidels."

"But why me? I am not worthy."

The imam continued, "We do not question God's will. The Crusader in your vision symbolizes the malefactor who began the legacy of violence against our people. And for almost a thousand years, we have been at war with the infidels. The time has come to end their evil reign. And you, my son, will be the sword that will rid their filth from the earth."

"I do not question God's will." Yousef lowered his head, keeping his doubt to himself. "I . . . I am at His mercy."

The imam smiled confidently. He knew that Yousef was to be God's newest—and perhaps greatest—martyr.

Chapter Two

The average cost of an MQ-9 Reaper drone is \$12,548,710.60. The U.S. government ordered hundreds of these drones in support of its war on terror. One drone in particular took several weeks to manufacture. For this one drone, Nestor Rios was the engineer who had developed its internal combustion engine, Carol Stone and her team developed the program that operated its satellite data link, Blake Alscot modified its multi-spectral targeting system, and Adam Guyer cleared it for use. There were countless other engineers and specialists utilized to make this one piece of war machinery. This one drone was only one among scores of others as they sat silently on the aircraft carrier, making their way to the Middle East. This one drone made its way to Camp Eggers in Kabul, Afghanistan.

From that American military base, the drone was let loose into the night sky for testing. Eventually, it began its first round of reconnaissance. Using highly advanced night vision, the drone captured in its view a small village of suspected Taliban militants. Night after night, this drone continued the same covert surveillance. Later, a special operation demanded that the drone's surveillance be conducted during the day. Visual confirmation was necessary.

It was in this small village that a young Yousef lived with his uncle, having been sent there by his mother when he had just turned eight years old. His mother knew that Yousef craved the attention of a father figure, and "Uncle Mustafa" would be the closest thing he would be able to get.

At the time the drone was focusing on the settlers, Yousef was nine years old. In this little village, Yousef played with his best friend, Khalil. Khalil taught him to make the best of his limp and treated him like the other boys. Here, in this village, Youssef felt at home; moreover, he felt safe. He had not had his dream since coming to the village.

Thousands of miles away, sitting in a trailer in Nevada, a twenty-three-old American soldier sat behind a control panel, maneuvering that very drone. The soldier intently listened to the orders of his commander through the headset. The soldier received the order to zoom in on the village, looking for the intended target. The camera found the suspected target. The target's identity was confirmed: Mustafa Saed. *Uncle Mustafa.*

"Okay, *ladies!*" barked the commander through the headset. "Target has been confirmed—"

"Wait," the drone operator interrupted as he squinted at the video monitor. "I think . . . I think I see a kid. Wait. I see two of them. Two children in vicinity."

Another drone operator sitting next to him concurred. "He's right, Commander. There's two kids down there."

"They're all terrorists until they're not," added a third operator.

"Commander, what're your orders?" the first operator asked.

At that moment, a CIA operative sitting comfortably—miles away at CIA Headquarters at Langley, Virginia—spoke through a telecom speaker. "I say fire at will."

However, back in the shed in Nevada, the commander struggled with his decision. He glanced back and saw the judge advocate general (JAG) who had been assigned to supervise this special mission. Col. Wayne Coleman would be the final authority on the legality of the current missile strike. Without hesitation, the JAG officer gave the thumbs-up signal.

The commander acknowledged the signal and gave the directive: "Fire at will."

"God, please forgive me," the young drone operator prayed as he let loose the missile.

The villagers had no warning that terror was about to strike. Young Yousef's last memory was kicking the flattened soccer ball to Khalil. Yousef proudly summoned all his might to use his weakened leg to lob the ball over his friend's head.

"Goal!" Khalil cheered for his friend as he turned to fetch the ball.

The flattened ball fell close to Uncle Mustafa. Mustafa laughed as he motioned to kick the ball. Khalil held his hands up, beckoning the old man to kick it to him.

Yousef smiled as he had not done in a long time. He glanced up into the heavens, about to thank God for this joyous moment. For a brief instant, he saw a glimmer in the sky. He had no memory of the fiery destruction that would soon engulf his newfound home, killing nearly every person in the quiet little village. Only a handful of survivors remained. Uncle Mustafa's limbs had been ripped apart; Khalil had been incinerated. On that day, even though Yousef almost died, he had been reborn.

Back in the military shed in Nevada, everyone applauded and cheered the drone pilot for a job well done. The pilot faked a smile as he removed his headset. His shift was over, and he asked for permission to call it a day.

"Permission granted," the commander said cheerfully. "Go home to your wife and family. You've earned it."

The pilot walked out of the shed and over to his car. As he turned on the ignition, his cell phone began to buzz; it was a text message from his wife. He looked down at the message and began to sob. He was crying uncontrollably. He sat there for over thirty minutes before making his way home. The message read, "Don't forget to buy milk for the baby."

Chapter Three

Years later, Yousef would make his way throughout the Middle East, ending in Yemen, where, by chance, he would meet up with his imam. They met at a prayer service, and the imam was immediately impressed with Yousef's eloquence and confidence. Except for the noticeable limp, Yousef had all the trappings of a leader. The imam took Yousef under his wing and eventually introduced him to his ragtag team of young militants in training. Within a few months, Yousef was overseeing the small handful of young acolytes.

"These men are training hard, and it is pleasing to God," the imam boasted.

"You have been an inspiration to them and to me," Yousef said with pride. "But any one of these men would have been more qualified to lead the movement. Why me?"

"You humble yourself too much. Our people must not see that as a sign of weakness. *You* are their leader. *You* are the one they look up to, and *you* are the one who inspires them. *You* have the vision."

Yousef placed his right hand over his heart. "Once again, you are too kind."

"Now we must prepare our warriors in the field. The cameraman is ready. Are you prepared for the speech?"

Yousef hesitated. "I . . . I am not a good speaker. Is there no one else who could speak? Perhaps you?"

The imam reached out to Yousef. "You do not realize your potential. You have the skills to inspire. I have seen you teaching the children. They listen to you. They look up to you."

"I was not trying to be a cleric . . . I was simply trying to teach the children to read."

"But you did so much more . . . You inspired them."

"Imam," Yousef hesitated, "it is important that I tell you that I no longer have the faith—"

The imam hastily interrupted him and led Yousef away from the others. "Yousef, my son, you were always an avid reader. You have read way too much as a child. Those books, those newspapers—they have all been written by nonbelievers, and they only served to corrupt your mind. You must not let the others hear you speak this way—"

"Imam," Yousef interrupted, "but it was not just the books and the newspapers. It was all the death and the killing. No *God* would ever let that happen."

The imam was visibly angry. "Yousef, I implore you to think carefully about what you are saying. The world is watching you. You can make a difference. You want revenge for what happened to Uncle Mustafa and your friend Khalil? For the hundreds and thousands of children slaughtered every day by corruption and greed? God has given you this opportunity."

"I want to make a difference, but there has to be another way," Yousef pleaded.

"Name it. Name any other way, and we will do it together."

Yousef knew of no other way. "I understand. I'll do as you ask."

The imam smiled. "I cannot help you find your way back to God, but I can help you succeed in fulfilling *his* mission. We can do that together."

The men embraced.

"Do you have the speech?" the imam asked.

"I do." Yousef pointed to his temple. "I have it memorized."

"Very good, but remember, it must be recited exactly, word for word. Our people will be listening. The world will be listening," the imam lectured.

"I will not fail you."

Yousef led the way as he walked into a bunker where a teenage cameraman stood obediently, setting up a cheap handheld camcorder. The camera was facing a small table placed in front of a dark blue curtain. Yousef stood before the camera and spoke. He was passionate in his daily instructions, but now he shone brightly in his memorized speech.

"Our people have suffered from aggression, iniquity, and injustice imposed on them by the Zionist–Crusader alliance. Our blood has been spilled throughout the world, and the world did nothing to prevent these atrocities. There was further insult when the United States and its allies, under the cover of the iniquitous United Nations, dispossessed the people of arms to defend themselves. Our people have awakened and realized that they are the target for the aggression of the Zionist–Crusader alliance. All the false claims and propaganda about 'human rights' were exposed by the massacres that took place against our people in every part of the world. From here on, today our people will no longer sit still and stand silent to these atrocities . . ."

Yousef continued speaking for several minutes. At the end of his twenty-minute presentation, his speech was eventually disseminated to the world.

Yousef's initial video created frenzy throughout the world; it was not so much what he was saying but how he was saying it. He spoke of all the injustices going on in the world and how, with a collective effort, the world could change for the better—but it was his warm smile, his soft voice, and his piercing blue eyes that garnered most of the attention. Yousef would produce one inspiring message a week. Gradually, word of mouth spread. People were taking the time to watch his videos, but more importantly, they were listening.

Chapter Four

Al-Jīzah, Egypt

Moments after viewing one of the videos, Abdullah Abulateen turned off his computer and reached into his pocket to take out a set of keys. He exited his home and entered his barely functional 1967 VW van. Abdullah quickly drove through the narrow streets of al-Jīzah; he was calm and yet determined. Twenty minutes later, Abdullah stopped at a cheap hotel, where he picked up a group of four Japanese tourists for a private tour of the pyramids.

Abdullah smiled, introduced himself in broken English, and invited the tourists to get as comfortable as they could for the brief jaunt to Giza. During the ride, the group of Japanese men engaged in small talk. Abdullah continued to smile but said nothing. When they arrived, Abdullah drove the men to the unloading zone of a small hotel and watched as they disembarked. Abdullah observed as his passengers mingled with other tourists from other countries. From there, Abdullah was to act as a private tour guide for the Japanese tourists. He did not speak Japanese, but his English was adequate for the job.

Abdullah had been desperate for a job and was blessed to have his cousin turn him onto this opportunity; all he had to do was study a few books on the pyramids and know just enough to be qualified as a "private Egyptologist." As he waited for the tourists to prepare for the trek, he stood outside of his van and basked in the hot glistening sun.

Abdullah closed his eyes and thought of his baby daughter—his infant daughter, A'shadieeyah, his little princess, with her perfectly bronzed skin, silky dark hair, and beautiful large almond-shaped eyes. A'shadieeyah was the love of his life. She was his life. His wife had died during childbirth, and the baby was all he had left. Abdullah had traveled to the Gaza Strip so that he could seek the assistance of his aunts in raising his daughter. He travailed to protect his daughter during the arduous journey to Gaza, and with the mercy of God, he made it safely. He had only been there a few days when the war between Hamas and Fatah began.

After a series of violent skirmishes, Hamas took control over the Gaza Strip, and ultimately, an Israeli blockade kept Abdullah and his daughter trapped. For several months, the Palestinian rocket attacks and Israeli raids ravaged the countryside. The bombings and raids continued for nearly a year, and at the end of the Gaza War, over a thousand Palestinians had been murdered. A'shadieeyah was among them.

Abdullah returned to his home in Egypt, alone and distraught. His family had bought him a secondhand computer with the idea that this would distract him from his sorrow. The internet exposed Abdullah to a whole new world, a world full of new ideas, a world of hate, a world of anger and of violence—violence that was regularly inflicted by the West upon innocent women and children, innocent children like his beloved A'shadieeyah. The internet brought him new friends who lived very close to him and who shared the same views as he did. These new friends shared in his anger.

Meetings were held regularly, where his newfound friends spoke of a voice that promised hope and justice, but more importantly, this voice spoke of retribution. They introduced him to the teachings of Yousef, and Abdullah was revitalized. He would come to learn that this circle of friends extended to a network of people all over the world. They taught him to carefully study Yousef's videos because they contained secret messages that only they would understand.

This day was the day Abdullah had prepared for the last several months. He walked over to the hatchback, reached beneath several sheets, and removed an AR-15. Three of the other tour guides were in a circle and had their own assault weapons. Without any warning, all four men let loose their assault weapons, killing eighteen tourists.

The Egyptian military had very little time to react, but in the end, all four would-be terrorists were gunned down. On that day, Abdullah was reunited with A'shadieeyah.

Chapter Five

Mahmoud al-Assad was a second-generation Syrian American whose grandfather had come to the United States in 1941 after the British and French occupation of Syria, bringing with him his young bride and settling in New York. His grandfather eventually moved his family to New Jersey to get away from the insanity of New York City. Mahmoud al-Assad's father was born in Patterson, New Jersey, and when his father turned eighteen, he was drafted into the Vietnam War. After serving two years, his father relocated back to New York City.

Mahmoud al-Assad was born in 1971 and grew up an all-American boy. By the time he had turned sixteen, he went by the name Billy Assad. He played baseball and football and eventually fulfilled his dream of being a cop. He graduated from the NYPD Academy to his beat on the streets of Manhattan. Billy realized quickly into his tenure that the daily grind of the beat was never going to be good enough. The FBI sought people who were fluent in Arabic, and Billy was the perfect recruit. He had graduated from Quantico at the top of his class.

Mahmoud was never really a practicing Muslim but would attend the Friday prayer sporadically. It was after one such occasion that he ran into his high school sweetheart, Samina Pal. Samina was a first-generation Lebanese American. Her family was progressive but true to their Muslim faith. They were married when they were nineteen and had their first child at twenty-three and their second child a year later. They planned on having many more, but for now, his career got in the way.

Billy Assad was assigned to the Manhattan division of the FBI as an intelligence analyst. He and his team were responsible for monitoring the social media of the unlimited number of suspected "terrorists" scattered throughout the northeastern part of the country. His team spent countless hours reading and analyzing suspicious postings and viewing countless videos. Billy was shocked at the number of disenfranchised Americans who were either angry at their government or who hated this country. Within a few years, Billy Assad was promoted to special agent in counterterrorism. His work hours, long and hard, left him no time for his family. By the time his second daughter was born, he was only home on the weekends.

In recent months, his specialized team of intelligence analysts had been monitoring the social media of an individual who went by the name "anarkist.prime." Each day, the subject's posts became more aggressive and angrier and pleaded for a jihad in America. It was anarkist prime's promise that he would blow up the Statue of Liberty, which made him the primary focus of the FBI. With that threat, Billy Assad immediately applied for a subpoena to trace the IP address.

Eventually, the IP address led to an Abebe Abdulmaid, a black middle-aged Ethiopian single mother with a nineteen-year-old son named Abshir residing in Brooklyn. Billy ordered his agents to conduct surveillance of the apartment where she resided. Abshir never left his apartment, and school records revealed that he had been expelled from school in the tenth grade. He had no job and no friends—except the ones he made on the internet. He fit the profile.

Chapter Six

An array of FBI agents and New York police officers converged in the Manhattan office of the FBI at 0300 for a debriefing. Billy Assad coordinated the meeting and delegated the responsibilities for each team member. By 0400, the crisis management and SWAT team entered with their heavily armored tanks. By 0415, the caravan of vehicles was racing toward Brooklyn—their destination apartment 3B of the Tompkins Houses in Bedford-Stuyvesant, their target Abshir Abdulmaid, the radicalized nineteen-year-old Somali American.

Living at the Tompkins Houses in Bedford-Stuyvesant was so horrifying that all of New York considered it the most dangerous housing project in Brooklyn. Someone's worst enemy would not wish living there upon them. Violence and crime was a way of life. There was an average of at least one murder a week. The caravan of police vehicles stationed themselves a block away from the apartment. A team of agents ran stealthily toward their target. They entered a side door and made their way up the stairs to apartment 3B.

"FBI! Search warrant!" yelled one of the agents, simultaneous with a series of knocks.

Within three seconds, a battering ram was forced against the door, knocking the door off its hinges and onto the ground. An agent threw a flash grenade into the apartment, which detonated a bright light and emitted an earsplitting sound. A woman started screaming from within. A few moments later, an agent forced a Somali woman wearing her hijab from out of the back room.

"My son, p-please . . . Careful with my son!" the woman screamed out in her broken English. "He's a sick boy!"

The woman was forced out of the apartment.

"Abshir!" Billy yelled out as he charged down the corridor in front of the SWAT team. "This is Special Agent Assad with the FBI! Come out of your room with your hands up!" He approached the back room and reached for the doorknob. "Abshir! This is your last warning! Come out now!"

A moment passed, and Billy motioned for one of the agents behind him to charge in. The bedroom door was violently kicked open, and the team of men barged in. Sitting on the bed with a laptop on his crossed legs was their target. The young man was visibly startled and began to yell.

"This is my room! My room! You aren't allowed in my room!" the young man screamed as he was yanked off the bed and taken to the ground. He began to wail like a child. "Mama! Mama! Mamaaa!"

Billy Assad casually walked into the bedroom and looked down pathetically at the target of his investigation. He was perplexed. "This can't be right," Billy muttered. "Get him off the ground!"

The young man was lifted onto his feet, taken into the living room, and thrown onto the sofa. "Mama! Mama!" the man bellowed.

Billy kneeled before him. "Abshir, stop. Stop. Listen to me."

The young man continued to wail.

Discouraged, Billy Assad spoke into his radio. "Bring the mother back in here."

"Roger that," an agent's voice responded from the radio.

A few moments later, the weeping woman was brought back into the room. Billy Assad removed her handcuffs, and she was permitted to care for her son. As he stared at the weeping mother and child, it had become abundantly clear to Billy Assad that Abshir was not well—but more importantly, the boy was no terrorist.

Chapter Seven

"*You let him go?*" screamed Manuel Ortega, the Manhattan FBI's special agent in charge. Manuel Ortega was a hulk of a man who had also been a New York City cop and who had not lost one bit of his street-level personality. "What a monumental waste of time and resources."

"The boy is sick," Billy Assad defended. "He's autistic."

"I've arrested perps with mental illness before. They're all sick in the head. And for every perp *I've* ever collared, the courts have upheld their competency."

"He had the mind of a thirteen-year-old."

"I don't care. We're at war. And if you haven't read the reports, thirteen-year-old boys are committing acts of terrorism. We've got attacks going on in Europe, a looming threat in the form of an upstart terrorist running loose in the Middle East, and cells here in New York, and you just let one of them go."

"It was the right thing to do."

"You're not paid to do the right thing. You're paid to get these guys off the streets." The SAC rose up from behind his desk. "The press is having a field day with this story."

"I'll take full responsibility. I'll own it. It was my decision, and I'll own it. I'll go out there and give a statement—and hand in my resignation."

The SAC pounded his fists. "Bullshit! You resign, and that'll be deemed as an admission of negligence on the FBI's part. No, I've got our communications director out there spinning a story that'll make the FBI look like a hero. No, sir, you're not resigning, I might even promote you to save face. Everyone fails upward around here."

Billy was frustrated. "So what do you want me to do?"

"Keep your team monitoring the web and get me something."

"Yes, sir," Billy replied.

"And stop doing *the right thing* and do your job—or you'll go back to being an analyst."

Billy turned to leave when the supervisor suddenly handed him a file.

"Wait. Take this with you."

"What's this?" Billy Assad asked, looking at the folder.

"*That*," the SAC said, pointing at the file. "That is your next assignment."

Billy Assad opened the file and read from a single sheet of paper. "I don't understand," he said with a puzzled stare.

"That guy is going to be your new confidential informant."

Chapter Eight

Abu Ahmed had been arrested for immigration fraud by creating false driver's licenses and fake green cards. He was so desperately trying to avoid going to prison and deportation that he begged his federal defender to get the same agents who had arrested him to visit him at the detention center. After several weeks of begging and, as his federal defender would describe, kissing a lot of ass, his lawyer finally got an INS agent to debrief his client. Within a few moments of the interview, the INS agent knew that he had wasted his time. The inmate knew of a few Mexicans for whom he had personally manufactured and sold fake IDs. did not know their names, but he knew which restaurants in Manhattan they bussed tables for. The INS agent cursed at the federal defender as he walked out from the interview room.

"Wait! I have one more thing!" Abu Ahmed bellowed.

The agent ignored him and kept on walking; he was halfway down the hall but could still hear the desperate cries from the inmate. He continued his pace until the voice was barely audible, but there was one word that sounded very clear to the agent. This one word was enough to make the agent stop and turn around. That word was *terrorists*.

The agent raced back into the room and slammed his fists down onto the table. "This is your last chance. This better be worth my time."

The inmate was taken aback but spewed out what he had to say. The agent listened intently. From the information, the agent knew that what Abu Ahmed had to offer was way above his pay grade: a terrorist cell in New York City. The INS agent contacted one of his colleagues with the FBI, and a meeting was set to take place right away.

After a round of meetings with the FBI, Abu Ahmed officially became an informant. Within two days, a U.S. district court judge signed an order releasing him. Ahmed was told to produce results or else face prison *and* deportation. But even after six weeks, Ahmed still had not provided a single bit of information. The FBI was beginning to question his veracity. His FBI handler had promised that Ahmed would be back in jail by month's end.

What the FBI did not know was that Ahmed had lied about his knowledge of terrorist cells. He was desperate to produce anything— or anyone. After the stern warning from his handler, Ahmed began attending weekly Islamic services, alternating among the various mosques in New York, frantically trying to make some sort of illicit connection. Finally, within a day of his impending rearrest, Ahmed encountered Frankie Smiley at a bodega around the corner from the Masjid al-Farah on West Broadway.

Ahmed had seen Smiley once before in the small one-room place of worship, but that had been two weeks ago. At the time, Smiley had been a delivery man for a small produce company, but that was not nearly enough to support his wife and their two-year-old daughter. He found himself selling marijuana on the side. He applied for better jobs and government assistance, but there was never enough money. His wife soon took their child and left.

Deep inside, Smiley was seething with anger. Ahmed and Smiley quickly became friends, and they each started sharing their own "hatred" for the government. The excessive combination of alcohol and marijuana served to lower Smiley's inhibitions. He confessed that he was not a Muslim yet, but his disdain for America made him yearn for something more meaningful. Ahmed's feigned interest in Smiley made him feel special, like he had a friend. Their quips of destroying America quickly turned into actual discussions of a plot to bomb tourist attractions.

Eventually, their personal conversations evolved into a plan, and Smiley ultimately needed to recruit two other men.

One of them was Nestor Mitchell, who needed cash to get his ailing mother into a convalescent home. Mitchell's mother had been suffering from Alzheimer's for years, and he struggled in providing care for her. His repeated requests for government assistance went unanswered. Videos and images of false promises by politicians for universal health care only caused Nestor to become bitter.

The last to join their group was Ricardo Parrocha, an undocumented Filipino immigrant. Parrocha had only been in the country for a little over a year, overstaying his H2B visa. He knew enough English to get by and to make friends but not enough to get a job. The brain damage he had suffered from a car accident as a child made him susceptible to following orders.

Ahmed promised the men $100,000 if they successfully blew up a car in the heart of Times Square. After the trio had agreed to the plan, Ahmed was handed over to Billy Assad as CI #133578.

Chapter Nine

When Billy Assad was handed the file that day, he balked at the idea of a $100,000 payoff.

"Jesus," Billy said. "For that kind of money, I can get my mother to blow up a car."

Billy Assad was immediately, offhandedly dismissed by his SAC and told to get the job done. Billy left the office with an uneasy feeling. Billy Assad met with Ahmed, the informant, at a safe house to prepare him for the operation. They spent four hours going over the game plan. Billy implored Ahmed time and time again to stick to the guideline he had been taught.

On the first day of the operation, Billy Assad personally fitted Ahmed with the monitoring device. Ahmed had a hidden camera on his cap and one installed inside his car. He was tasked with making certain that all three conspirators repeated their desire to blow up the vehicle into one of these monitoring devices.

"Don't fuck this up," Billy Assad warned. "I don't need to be cleaning up any of your bullshit on the back end."

"Trust me. These guys are the real deal," Ahmed responded. "I'll be a hero."

You'll never be hero, Billy Assad thought.

Chapter Ten

Two weeks later, Ahmed was driving his car down 129th Street to pick up his crew in the heart of Harlem. It was uniquely hot that July, the kind of hot you only get by mixing ninety degrees Fahrenheit with urban overdevelopment, and Ahmed was sweating like a stuffed pig. It may have been more from the fear of being discovered than from the heat, but in either case, there was no disguising his discomfort.

"Guys, it's boiling in here." Ahmed spoke loud enough to be picked up by his handlers, who sat remotely inside a van in a parking lot on Forty-Seventh Street.

"Then turn on the air," Billy Assad said into his mic.

Ahmed adjusted the small earpiece hidden in his ear. "I thought I wasn't allowed to—"

The technician sitting next to Billy shook his head. "Leave it off. It'll interfere with the reception."

"Shit!" Ahmed had heard. "I guess I'll tough it out."

Ahmed reduced his speed as he saw his three targets standing outside the coffee shop, as they had been directed.

"Guys, I'm going into radio silence. I have a visual on my targets," Ahmed whispered.

"Roger that. Say the safe word at the first sign of danger," Billy commanded.

Ahmed waved at the crew to get into the van. Smiley sat in the passenger seat, the others in the back. Ahmed greeted them all one by one. Billy Assad listened intently. Smiley was shaking nervously.

"Why are you shivering? It's freaking one hundred degrees outside," Ahmed joked.

"I'm just a little scared is all," Smiley said.

"Dude, relax. This'll be a piece of cake," Ahmed responded as he made his way down to Times Square.

Traffic was at its usual gridlock. *Fucking tourists!* Ahmed thought. He predicted that it would take at least an hour to make the journey, time enough to get the guys to incriminate themselves, but no matter how much Ahmed tried to get the others to talk, Mitchell and Parrocha said nothing. Smiley, the talkative one, barely uttered a word. Ahmed knew that if he was going to save his ass, he needed more.

"Gentlemen, this is the moment we've been waiting for. Everything is in place, and the bombs are in the trunk. All you guys have to do is load the car, move it from its current location to Times Square, walk away, and detonate the bomb. Easy."

"We don't want to hurt nobody," Smiley was recorded saying. "We want to just destroy property. We don't want to take no lives."

Ahmed laughed. "Not at all. The explosion is just enough to set the car on fire, bust a few windows . . ."

"You sure?" Smiley asked, almost pleading.

"Trust me."

Chapter Eleven

Trust me. Billy Assad had heard the informant say those same two words weeks before the impending operation.

"*Trust me. These guys are the real deal.*"

"If these guys are the *real deal*, then why can't they supply their own bombs?" Billy questioned.

"I don't know. They're fucking idiots. That's why," Ahmed responded.

Billy dismissed Ahmed and made a call to his SAC, Manuel Ortega. "Manny, I really don't like this whole thing."

"And why the hell not?" Ortega asked.

"It stinks. These three targets cannot even supply their own bombs. We have to supply them with the duds.'

"So?"

"I just don't like it. Shouldn't these guys be able to make their own bombs? I'm no lawyer, but it just doesn't seem legal."

Ortega chortled condescendingly. "Well, I am a lawyer, and this is perfectly legal. It's no different than a *reverse* drug sting, and I know that during your early days, you did plenty of reverses." Ortega paused. "Billy, I can't emphasize enough how important it is to make this operation a success. The president is putting pressure on the DOJ, and the DOJ is putting pressure on me. Public perception is that we are losing the war on terrorism, and the president's poll numbers are down. We all need a win." The SAC paused again. "And do you really want these guys with live bombs? Look, Billy, if you can't—"

Billy Assad relented and sighed in frustration. "I'll get it done. I'll keep you posted."

Two weeks later, Billy listened as the *terrorists* agreed to the plan. Of course, none of these men had the means or the ability to carry out their threat, but in the eyes of the U.S. government, their actions would be enough to bring forth an indictment.

Billy Assad moved his unmarked vehicle to get a better position. He observed as Ahmed dropped off the men at the corner, a few feet away from the target vehicle. Ahmed watched as the three men loaded the duds into the car. Smiley got behind the wheel, and the other two piled in. The agents laughed as they watched Smiley drive around aimlessly.

"Son of a bitch can't even drive!" Billy Assad screamed into Ahmed's earpiece. "Where the fuck are they going? All they had to do was drive it down a few feet and abandon it."

Ahmed was quiet. In reality, Smiley really did not know how to drive and was lost. Somehow he managed to take the car to Fifth Avenue and West Fifty-Sixth Street and parked it onto the corner. The three men jumped out of the car and ran in separate directions. The army of agents who had followed the car rushed the men and arrested them with maybe more than necessary force.

The would-be terrorists cried and begged for forgiveness. They would have done or said anything to go home. As a result, confessions came before the agents were even ready. The team of agents cheered as they congratulated themselves with a series of high fives.

Billy Assad, on the other hand, remained stoic.

* * *

Six months later, the trial of the three would-be terrorists commenced in the U.S. district court for the Southern District of New York. The court-appointed lawyers each argued that while their respective clients were not the best of society, this government operation was specifically designed to turn them into terrorists. It was a classic case of entrapment.

The jury of eight white men and four white women listened intently, but they were not convinced by the defense counsels' argument. The trial lasted four weeks. The three men were easily convicted, and each was sentenced to twenty-five years. The editorial section of nearly every major newspaper ran a variation of the same headline, *"FBI Foils FBI Terror Plot,"* on a page that nobody read.

The U.S. government had their win. The president's poll numbers were up, and for his efforts, Billy Assad was promoted as the new SAC of counterterrorism. Manuel Ortega was promoted to a job overseas in a different department. Abu Ahmed was given a green card and $30,000 and quickly went back to committing more crimes involving immigration fraud.

Chapter Twelve

For the next year, Billy Assad, the new SAC, and his team of dedicated men and women devoted their time to monitoring suspicious emails, postings, and videos. Billy's team was overwhelmed but devoted nearly every waking hour with social media from all over the world that made known their dedication to advocating terrorism on U.S. soil. Billy directed his agents to engage in chatter with these newly discovered targets. The team soon became aware that these targets had one thing in common: they were influenced by an upstart named Yousef. The chatter became more and more intense. Billy had a feeling that something dangerous was looming. He would need to find out more about that "Yousef."

Chapter Thirteen

Munich, Germany

The teenage boy closed his laptop and began to cry. Videos of the multitude of dead children from all over the world scorched and ravaged by war always made him upset. He would spend his free time looking at these videos, up to several hours at a time. He came across a video of the White Helmets as they vainly tried to rescue the infant victims of airstrikes; these would always make him angry.

Then he came across one of Yousef's videos. Yousef spoke of the injustices throughout the world that were intentionally inflicted on the young, the weak, and the oppressed. Yousef spoke of the hypocrites in world governments who pretended to care and who promised change, but the change was only an illusion; the promise was only a lie. This young German boy watched Yousef's most recent video at least twenty times. He found Yousef's messages to be inspiring and emotional, bringing him to tears.

The young boy removed the nine-millimeter Glock handgun from underneath his mattress—the gun he had stolen from his best friend's father—and took the box of ammunition from his closet. He walked by his mother. She had been cooking in the kitchen and had not seen him leave their home. He walked a few blocks to a mall and started shooting. By the end of the twenty-minute ordeal, he had killed eight other teenagers, and then in front of two police officers, he killed himself.

Chapter Fourteen

A group of five Tunisian males met each Saturday. They would meet at the local pub, watching football and discussing politics in between matches. When they had come as refugees five years ago, they were welcomed with open arms by the good-hearted relief workers, but within months, they found themselves without work, begging for relief, while the rich and elite lived lives of obscene luxury. Their meetings were filled with talk of discrimination and abuse. They spoke of the injustice that permeated throughout the world and of a new voice that promised a new revolution. *Yousef* was that new voice.

His message was clear and promised change in the world, but it was not without sacrifice. They knew that one of them would have to be that sacrifice. The oldest of the men made it clear that he would be the one. There was no debate. Within a week, the plan was in motion. That week, he drove a cargo truck through a large crowd of people.

* * *

During the ensuing year, Yousef produced videos on a biweekly basis. The world was on the precipice of chaos. The worst was yet to come.

Chapter Fifteen

Al Jawf, Yemen

The sound of a radio announcing various terrorist strikes throughout the world startled Yousef awake. He was surprised to hear the mention of his name as the cause of the destruction.

Yousef barged into his imam's tent. He was angry. "My messages were meant to inspire revolution, spread reform, but instead, they are inciting hate and violence. That is not my way."

"My son, we do not question God's will," the imam replied. "Revolution is violent. I have been your teacher since you were a young man. I would never lead you astray."

Yousef was tearful. "But people are dying!"

"It is God's will—"

"It cannot be!"

The imam attempted to comfort his pupil. "It is. The dreams. Remember the dreams."

Yousef was stoic; he could not forget the dreams.

The imam led Yousef out of the tent. "Just think about all the women and children who are dying at the hands of the oppressors. They speak of peace but never produce it."

Yousef relented. "It is true. I cannot disregard the dreams. The world must understand that the people need a change."

The imam was visibly pleased. "Now go, my son. You must deliver your next message."

"So soon. Now?" Yousef asked as he was being led into a far tent. "I just made one this week. There is not another due for—"

"Yes. We must increase the frequency of your message. People are thirsty for change. You are the vassal for change. From you, they must drink. The more videos we produce, the more your message will be drunk."

Yousef was distressed but quickly composed himself. He made himself prepared to deliver a new message, and that very night, a new message was spread throughout the world.

Chapter Sixteen

Every server working at the restaurants along each side of the Las Ramblas strip always found it a challenge to exit their respective cafés, cross the streets, and evade vehicular traffic to cater to their customers, who were sitting patiently in the wide center promenade.

On this beautiful Thursday afternoon, the sun was at its brightest, and the heat was bearing down on the people. Raoul Julian Esparza looked across the street from a window to see that his customers at table 2 were apparently ready to order. He removed his notepad from his back pocket and placed the pencil in his ear.

As he crossed the street, Raoul Julian heard the loud screams of people, and to his left, he saw the rows of people scatter along the busy promenade. He also heard what sounded like the acceleration of a motor engine. Then Raoul Julian watched in horror as waves of people were being mowed down by a vehicle. Before he could react, the white van was upon him.

Raoul Julian was only twenty-three years old when he died. He was one of thirteen people killed. There were over a hundred injured.

The driver would later abandon the vehicle and be gunned down by the police.

The driver was of Moroccan descent. He was also twenty-three years old. Authorities would later find out from his parents that he spent a lot of time watching videos on his cell phone. He had become reclusive and despondent. Their son would only speak of vengeance for the violence inflicted by the devils of the world. They loved their son; he was a good boy. They had never thought that their son would become responsible for one of the deadliest terrorist attacks in Spanish history.

Chapter Seventeen

The Dream

The heat was unbearable, but the knight was grateful that the sun had shifted. The sun was slowly setting behind him, and in just a few long and agonizing hours, the sun would be setting. He struggled to keep from blacking out; the blood was beginning to gush from his wounds, but he would not fail his mission. He would not violate his oath. The knight looked behind him and could see the sand rising in the distance, which only meant that the enemy was closing in.

The knight seemed no closer to his destination than he was hours ago. His horse had been running tirelessly, and yet the desert ahead of him seemed to extend even farther. His destination was nowhere in sight. Still, he clutched the satchel ever so tightly. The knight's wounds opened wider, and he was bleeding more profusely. The knight looked behind him once again and saw the funnel of sand rising even higher. He looked ahead and saw nothing; he was losing faith in his mission.

Chapter Eighteen

Yousef awoke from his dream and was even more bothered. He was drenched in sweat, and the stain of tears had covered his sheets. Yousef knew that *he* was the person behind the pursuit of the knight, and eventually, Yousef would catch him. Yousef gazed at the numerous newspaper clippings he had been collecting, clippings of the innocent civilian casualties that his reign of terror had created. He wanted no more dying, no more killing in *God's* name. He wanted it to stop.

However, comingled with the newspaper clippings were other articles, articles he had been collecting for years. These articles were stark reminders of the other atrocities that had taken place around the world. The more he thought of the people dying at his hand, the more he thought of the hundreds of civilians who had died in the U.S. airstrike of the Jidideh neighborhood of Mosul, Iraq, the thirty civilians who had sought shelter in a school hit by the U.S. airstrike in the town of Mansooura in Raqa Province, the thirty-seven civilians killed by the United States in their airstrike of the mosque in the village of Jina in Aleppo Province, or the four million casualties killed by U.S. interventions in Iraq, Afghanistan, Pakistan, and Yemen. He also thought of Vietnam, Cambodia, and Laos and the more than twenty million people killed in thirty-seven "victim nations" since World War II.

He recited his prayers, and like an epiphany, he suddenly realized that his actions were, in fact, against God's will. It was then that he decided to stop praying. He would no longer pursue acts of violence in the name of God, but he would never stop his war—and he would never stop his pursuit of the knight in his dreams.

Chapter Nineteen

The following morning, Yousef strolled into his tent and watched as the teenage boy behind the camera turned it on. Yousef proceeded to speak. Within a few minutes, his speech was over, and now it was his imam who was angry.

"You deviated from the script!" The imam threw the written manuscript to the ground.

"The substance has not changed," Yousef defended. "The message was still very clear."

"You are disobeying God's will?"

"I am no longer doing *God's will*." Yousef was brazenly defiant. "I am doing what needs to be done to save mankind from itself. I am going to release more messages on a more frequent basis—but I will no longer do it in the name of God. Now please take leave so that I can prepare my next message."

The imam was speechless as he exited the tent. He stepped away to ensure his privacy and retrieved the satellite phone from underneath his robe.

"Yes, it is me," the imam announced as he glanced over his shoulder to be certain no one could hear him. "We may have to change our plans.

He is rebelling. He is deviating from our operation. We may need to terminate it."

The imam stepped closer to the tent and began to listen to Yousef as he made his presentation.

The imam spoke into the phone. "Wait a minute. He's filming a new message. Let me hear."

The imam pressed his ear closer to the tent, and as he listened to Yousef's message, the imam realized that Yousef was even more impassioned and much more effective.

The imam returned to his call. "Let us wait for a while. The young man may still be of use to us."

By night's end, scores of Yousef's new messages were being seen throughout America.

Chapter Twenty

Fort Hood, Texas

Major Ameen had been a loyal soldier, but loyalty to his family was more important. He grew tired of what his country was doing to his people in the Middle East. There were promises of peace to Muslims throughout the world—a Nobel Peace Prize had even been awarded to his president—but the bombing of the innocent only increased. It was his own country, his own military, that was committing the genocide. He felt that his country had betrayed him, and he fought back the only way he knew how—the way Yousef had taught him.

Major Ameen walked into the medical deployment center and stood at the doorway. He gazed at the group of dutiful soldiers. No one had realized he had been standing there for several minutes. He took his weapon and indiscriminately opened fire on the scores of unarmed soldiers. Then he took his sidearm and shot himself in the mouth. American history would record this as the largest mass murder at a military installation, but most Americans would soon forget this massacre.

Chapter Twenty-one

President Nicolas Adams was visibly upset. Standing behind his desk within the Oval Office, he was yelling at his chief of staff.

"This terrorist, *Yousef*, has inspired a *U.S. citizen?*" the president exclaimed. "What is the plan to stop him?"

"Yemen authorities won't do anything," the chief of staff responded. "They won't arrest him. They won't support us in any way."

"This is utter bullshit! Why are we even talking to that shit hole country? Is there nothing we can do?" the president asked.

Standing in the back of the room was the head of the CIA, a remnant and perhaps the last surviving member of the Cold War era. He was in his late seventies and had served at the pleasure of six different presidents in nearly every cabinet position. He stood there quietly until the president called upon him.

"We can have him assassinated," the CIA director said ever so confidently.

"We can't. It's illegal," the president asserted.

"We can utilize our drone operations to bomb him to death."

The president sighed. "That's illegal too."

The chief of staff chimed in. "Then we'll make it legal."

Chapter Twenty-two

Billy Assad walked into the FBI headquarters and into his office. His phone rang, and he instantly recognized the number. It was the director of the FBI. Billy took a nervous swallow.

"Director. How can I help you?"

"Billy, how are you this morning?" said the director.

"I'm doing well, Director. How are you?" Billy Assad heard the anxiousness in his own voice.

"Please, call me Sam."

"Yes, S-Sam. To what do I owe the pleasure of this call?"

"I need you on the next flight to Washington."

Billy was even more nervous. "Washington?"

"That's right," the director answered. "Right away. We're having a Joint Special Operations Command meeting, and we want you to be part of it."

"*JSOC?* Me?"

"Yes, you. We are reassigning you for a special mission at SOCOM."

"I'm so honored. That's great! If you give me a few days, my family and I—"

"No," the director interrupted. "I mean *right away*. We need you here tomorrow."

Billy was pleasantly shocked. He paused for a moment and then said, "Yes, sir. I'll be there tomorrow."

Billy replaced the phone on the receiver. He could not contain his own excitement. He immediately thought of his wife and how he wanted to share this news with her. Billy removed his cell phone and thought twice before he called her. He thought of his daughters, of his family, and of how much he would miss them. His instinct was to refuse the offer and to call the director back, but he knew that would be the death knell of his career.

I need to let Samina know right away, he thought, but he knew Samina would be upset. She would bring up how he had not seen the family in weeks. *Or has it been months?* Either way, she would not be happy with this news. He thought against that too. He set his cell phone down and made arrangements to fly to Washington, D.C.

Chapter Twenty-three

The Dream

The knight stared into the horizon. His destination was still not in sight. The sun was setting, but the heat was still too much to bear. He continued to bleed from his wounds. He felt faint; he was ready to die, but he would not let go of the satchel. He was too weak to look behind him, but he knew the enemy was closing in.

Chapter Twenty-four

MacDill Air Force Base
Tampa, Florida
United States Special Operations Command
(USSOCOM)

It had been three weeks since his arrival at his new position, and Billy Assad was now the top expert on Middle East terrorists, and on his list of priorities was Yousef. Yousef was now perceived as a growing threat.

Billy had made the flight to Washington, D.C., following the phone call with his director but without saying goodbye to his family. He called his wife soon after he landed and told her the news. Her disappointment was painstakingly obvious, and Billy was heartbroken. He promised her that this operation would soon be over and that he would take his family on a long, well-deserved vacation. From Washington, D.C., he flew to Tampa, and now Billy Assad walked down the corridors of central command, missing his family but determined to serve his country.

The last three weeks had been uneventful. There were a lot of daily meetings but very little action. All the action was back at the FBI/New York. *Thank god for the daily briefings from my old team*, he thought. For the first time in his career, he was bored to death.

As he turned the corner to make his way to his office, he saw a commanding military veteran walking toward him. The man's name was Gen. Lance Norton. General Norton was a career military man. He was a man who had no wife and no children and who only lived for the military. His only obligation was to serve and protect his country.

The general stopped Billy in the middle of the corridor.

"Mr. Mahmoud Assad?" asked the general, shaking Billy's hands with hands that could break concrete.

Billy Assad nervously answered, "Y-yes, sir."

"I've got good news," said the general. "You're going to meet and brief the president."

Billy Assad took a big swallow.

Chapter Twenty-five

Nicolas Adams-Patiño was destined to become president. He had gone from being a Miami-Dade county commissioner to a representative with the Florida House and then to governor of Florida, where he had made a name for himself by spearheading education funding, welfare reform, and affordable health care.

His grandfather Benjamin Adams was an evangelical missionary who had done charity work in Guatemala and who worked his way to Costa Rica, where he met Nicolas's grandmother, Hilda Patiño. Hilda was a dark-skinned mulatta from the town of Puntarenas on the Pacific side of Costa Rica. They had met at a church gathering and got married within six months. They had their first child after a year, and their second was born eleven months after that. Nicolas's father, Juan Miguel Adams-Patiño, was their third and last child.

Juan Miguel was an unexpected pregnancy, born nearly twenty years after his parent's last child. He practically grew up an only child. His parents were both too busy doing their missionary work and too old to rear their son. Juan Miguel was always respectful but was quite rebellious; he had always felt that because he was not planned, he was nothing more than a burden to his parents. He also resented the fact that his parents spent so much time at the church. Juan Miguel refused to go to school and decided to leave the comfort of Costa Rica. He had dreams of becoming a lawyer and wanted to live in America.

In June 1961, Juan Miguel arrived in New York City. Despite having an American father, Juan Miguel struggled to speak English. It was difficult for him to find a job. Luckily, he found one at a drapery factory in Brooklyn, making a dollar twenty an hour. He convinced himself that his situation was only temporary. Soon, he would complete his high school equivalency and go to college and eventually law school—or so he believed. Time and fate would prove otherwise.

Life in New York was not easy for Juan Miguel. The work was hard, the living conditions bad, and the winters brutal. Juan Miguel, about to give up, was forced to return to Costa Rica after the death of his mother. At his mother's funeral, he met a seventeen-year-old local girl from San Jose. Her name was Ana Cecilia, the granddaughter of the pastor of the family's church. Perhaps it was because of the grief of his loss that Juan Miguel had become enamored with the young girl. He felt committed to marry Ana Cecilia.

Benjamin Adams—who was eighty-six, sickly, and far too grief-stricken to go on living alone—asked Juan Miguel to stay. Even though Juan's elder brothers were in their late fifties and busy with their own families, Juan Miguel rejected the old man's plea, and on December 31, 1963, he returned to New York with Ana Cecilia. Upon arriving in New York, Juan Miguel and Anna Cecilia rushed to Our Lady of Guadalupe and begged a kindhearted priest to officiate an impromptu wedding. They married minutes before the new year. Benjamin Adams died the following day.

In 1966, Juan Miguel received his green card and a draft notice from the U.S. Army. Juan Miguel contemplated returning to Costa Rica but decided against it when he found out that Ana Cecilia was pregnant. He wanted their child to be born a U.S. citizen. They named their U.S.-born son Nicolas.

The young soldier went on to complete basic training in Fort Benning, Georgia. Fearful that he would be sent to Vietnam, Juan Miguel made arrangements to send his wife to Costa Rica immediately after the birth of their child, but as luck would have it, the U.S. Army did not send him to fight in Vietnam. Instead, they assigned him to military intelligence and shipped off the young soldier to Fort Huachuca, Arizona. He fulfilled his two-year obligation, and instead of returning to New York, he moved the family to Miami, Florida.

In Miami, Juan Miguel set up house in the roughest part of Hialeah. Anna Cecilia cleaned houses, and he earned a living as a mechanic, never achieving his dream of becoming a lawyer. Despite wanting the very best for their son, Nicolas's parents could not afford private school for him, and the young man attended public school. He later attended Broward Community College before gaining admission to the University of Miami on an academic scholarship, where he majored in political science. From there, Nicolas felt obligated in fulfilling his father's dream of becoming a lawyer.

While he had more than others, he believed his life was never easy. Even though he had anglicized his name to Nick Adams—or "Nicky," as his mother used to call him—he identified himself as a Latino. His first language was Spanish, and before he had attended school, he learned most of his English from watching public television and reading comic books. He struggled in trying to hide his accent, but he never shied away from his Hispanic roots. After the arrival of the *Mariel* refugees in the eighties, Nicky assimilated himself with the Cubans. He grew to identify himself more with them than with his own Central American culture. Most people assumed that Nicky was Cuban, and even though he did nothing to perpetuate that falsehood, he did nothing to change it.

Once accepted into the Miami School of Law, he wasted no time in studying his course books. Not wanting to burden his family with the expenses of his education, he worked three part-time jobs to support himself. He excelled and rose to the top of his class. At his graduation, his parents beamed with joy and were proud of his enormous accomplishment. Before he had even graduated, he was getting job offers from various law firms, but he had his eyes set on only one job: prosecutor for the Miami-Dade State Attorney's Office.

During the ensuing five years as a prosecutor, Nicky Adams made a name for himself as one of the toughest (but fair) litigators in the county. He worked his way from misdemeanors to homicide and organized crime within a year. His trial techniques once again caught the eye of many of the more prestigious law firms, but instead, he vied with countless other young lawyers for a job with the U.S. Attorney's Office.

While most young lawyers took years to secure even an interview, because of his reputation, he was hired with very little effort. As an assistant U.S. attorney, Nicky Adams handled the most serious white-collar offenses, and his reputation skyrocketed even higher. After five years with the federal government, Nicky Adams finally gave in and went to work for a multinational law firm that specialized in banking, tax, and government affairs. By his fourth year, he was literally the face of the firm. His likeness was plastered on billboards, buses, and park benches and in all the local periodicals. His very presence brought to the firm an average of tens of millions of dollars a year to the average growing revenue of $2.1 billion. Nicky Adams took great pride in being a Latino minority and worked harder than any other lawyer in the firm. He earned his way to the top.

On the tenth anniversary of his time with the firm, he announced his candidacy to run for the state legislature. He was a state representative for two years and then chose to run for governor. He served two terms as governor and was considered one of the greatest in Florida history. He led the country in job and economic growth, but his legacy was in education. As governor, he signed into law the first state income tax ever imposed in Florida history. It was met with much controversy and resistance but added so much revenue to the state's coffers that Florida had an enormous budgetary surplus. Within three years, Florida had the highest ranking in education—another milestone in Florida history.

At the age of fifty-four and with his elderly parents by his side, he made the surprise announcement that he would run for president. His primary opponent was a long-standing member of the U.S. Senate and was expected to win the election. However, his opponent was not well-liked as a career politician. The primary battles had been nasty, and because Nicky had never been married, his opponent made the insinuation that he was gay. Nicky made the wise decision to not dignify the insinuation by responding. That stance only enhanced his image. He was making great strides in the polls, and there was speculation that he would easily steal the election.

Three months into the campaign, the heads of their political party called for an emergency closed-door meeting between the two candidates, and it was agreed that all negative campaigning had to cease. It was making the party look disgraceful, the party bosses said. At the meeting, the party heads made the surprise request for Nicky to concede to his opponent in the primaries with the promise that he would be given an important cabinet position or an ambassadorship, and then in eight years, he would have the full support of the party, and he could run for president himself.

When Nicky asked why they would not offer him the position of vice president, the party heads replied that the position had been offered to another career politician. He asked if the putative vice president decided to run for president himself in eight years, then what would become of him? With that question, the party leaders remained silent. Nicky Adams politely rejected their offer. The party leaders were not happy, but Nicky Adams's popularity with the electorate tied their hands to showing nothing less than full support lest they lose the general elections.

Nicky Adams went ahead, full steam, with his campaign. At his party's national convention, with his parents again by his side, he joyfully accepted his party's nomination for president of the United States. His primary opponent retired into obscurity.

The contest for president became heated during the general election. His opponent was a retired military general and a veteran of the endless war on terrorism. The retired general preyed on America's fear of the unknown and the perpetual terror that America's enemies would strike again, but that attack never came, which the general cited as the very reason for electing him. There was no doubt as to his patriotism, but he was already in his late sixties and offered no real plan as to how to bring prosperity to the American people.

Nicky Adams's repeated mantra was that he would "lead with a conservative mind but be guided by a liberal heart." He slowly but surely won the hearts of the American people. His years of public service spoke for itself. Ending poverty, homelessness, and unemployment was his promise, and he had a plan to fix it. He highlighted the ever-increasing expenditures to the military budget for weapons that were either never used or not functioning properly. Nicky Adams also pointed out that those costs did not take into consideration the perpetual funding of Western European nations or the cost of the endless war on terrorism fought overseas. All those expenditures amounted to billions a year, while the rest of the Americans suffered. He proposed a gradual cut to the military budget over the course of ten years, applying that to funding education, infrastructure, and the eradication of poverty. He also proposed that by cutting wasteful funding, he would lower taxes on the middle class. These were radical ideas, but the country was desperate. Most people cheered him, but there were a few who watched in disapproval.

Nicky Adams would win the election by a landslide in both the popular and the electoral vote. He would later be sworn in as the first Hispanic American president. Since he was a single man, his parents were there by his side every step of the way. His first one hundred days were uneventful, but he was surprisingly awarded the Nobel Peace Prize for his "extraordinary efforts to establish peace and prosperity throughout the world." After three months into his presidency, it was time for him to start fulfilling his campaign promises to the people.

When the time came for him to lobby to put his policy in place, he received a visit from some of the most influential corporate leaders and billionaire financiers. These were the rich elite. That visit came during a formal White House dinner he had put together to convince the private sector to do more to contribute to the needs of the people. As the night progressed, he was unwittingly being led into the Diplomatic Reception Room. It was there that the cadre of corporate leaders and billionaire financiers enjoyed fine brandy and Cuban cigars with their president.

The conversation began cordially, but Nicky Adams soon noticed that the atmosphere in the room had become tense. He noticed that his secret service detail were no longer with him. The White House staff and servants were also gone. Nicky Adams looked around the room as each of the rich elite surrounded him. He was in the middle of an unwelcomed circle. One of the leading billionaire philanthropists broke the silence.

"Mr. President, on behalf of all of us here," he said, raising his glass in a toast, "I want to personally congratulate you again."

The circle of billionaires cheered. Feeling uneasy, Nicky Adams reluctantly raised his own glass. He motioned to break through the circle, but it was clear he was to remain right where he was.

"We all want to wish you much success during your presidency and are hopeful you will serve two terms and that your legacy endures," the billionaire said to more cheers.

"Well, t-thank you . . . again." Nicky Adams fumbled with his glass, losing his grip. It shattered on the floor. None of the others moved.

"But, Mr. President," the billionaire continued, "we are all worried that your ideals and your expectations are unrealistic."

"How so?" Nicky asked.

"Your proposal to cut the military budget is dangerous."

"*Dangerous?* How?"

"It's dangerous to our national security."

"My proposed cuts are only gradual," Nicky defended. "And it wouldn't affect—"

The billionaire interrupted. "It's too dangerous."

"You say that, but I've consulted with the brightest military experts—"

"Those were just false opinions just to help you get elected." The billionaire drank from his brandy.

"You *are* wrong," Nicky interrupted. "I've seen the reports—"

"*Nicky*, I don't think you understand. It's too dangerous – dangerous for *you*."

Nicky Adams was shocked at the informality and at the lack of respect for the Office of the Presidency. He was never one to back down from a fight, and despite his apprehension, he was not about to start. He stood face-to-face with the billionaire. "Are you threatening me?" Nicky said, clenching his fist.

The group of men broke into laughter.

"You see, that's why America loves you." The billionaire chuckled. "That's why *we* love you." The billionaire placed his hands on each of Nicky's shoulders. "You remind us of so many of our past presidents who were tough and tenacious and willing to stand up for their beliefs. Sadly, for them, their political careers were cut short by controversy, scandal . . . death."

Nicky stared at him defiantly.

The billionaire stared back at him, unmoved. "Yes, indeed. You *are* being threatened."

Nicky swiped the man's arms off him and was about to call for the secret service, but before he could do so, the billionaire interjected with a quick remark.

"Don't bother screaming for help. How do you think we got you alone in here? They're not going to come in here and rescue you. They work for us. *You* work for us."

"If you ever threaten me again," Nicky said angrily, "I swear on my mother, you will face the full power of the federal government."

"Your mother?" the billionaire asked. "How is she?"

"M-my . . . *mother?* What do you mean?"

"I've just heard that perhaps she wasn't feeling well."

"How could you . . ." Nicky was flabbergasted. His mother had been ill lately, and the doctors had not yet been able to pinpoint the source of her ailments.

The billionaire handed him a piece of paper. Nicky opened it, and on it was the name of a well-known oncologist in South Florida. Nicky recognized the name. He had researched the name himself, dreading the worst and hoping not to need the specialist's services. Nicky hesitantly took the paper and said nothing.

"I'm sure the good doctor will help your mother."

"I-I think it's time we call it a night," Nicky said.

The others all agreed.

"Yes," said the billionaire, "it's getting late. And you, my friend, Mr. President, have a lot of work cut out for you."

Like clockwork, the doors to the room opened, and all the servants and secret service agents made their way in. Within moments, the room was cleared of everyone except for Pres. Nicky Adams. He stood there silently in the center of the room, and for the first time in his career, he felt powerless.

*   *   *

The following day, Nicky Adams took Air Force One to Miami and surprised his parents with a visit. They easily noticed his distress. Nicky attributed it to the stress of the office. He held onto the name of the doctor in his breast pocket, eager to take his mother to see the specialist. He would not be bullied, but his mother's health was paramount. Nicky talked her into visiting the doctor. She was seen that very day. After a multitude of tests, their worst fears were realized—cancer.

The doctor had had remarkable results with many of his other patients; her prognosis was good. No one was told of her illness, and the public was ignorant to her condition. Still, the media noticed that the president appeared distracted.

Nicky Adams returned to Washington and resumed his work. He was determined to keep his promise to the American public. His mother was under the best medical care, and so he would be resolute and steadfast. He would not be intimidated. His approval ratings were at a historical all-time high. Two years into his administration, he was on the verge of passing nearly every one of his policies. He ignored all calls and refused all visits from the billionaire financiers.

The night before his mother's monthly checkup, he and his team of security detail reserved the private room of a swanky restaurant in South Miami Beach. Nicky wanted to celebrate his mother's well-being with both his parents. The paparazzi crowded the entrance, fighting one another to take the best picture. Moments later, the paparazzi cleared the way as a group of men made their way into the restaurant.

At first, Nicky struggled to see who the men were, but once the group was inside the dining room, Nicky's mouth dropped. Standing before them was his mother's oncologist. The doctor was surrounded by the team of billionaire financiers. The secret service cleared the way for the men.

Nicky was trembling inside. Nicky's mother was oblivious to her son's strife and was elated to see her doctor. As she rushed to embrace the doctor, the group of financiers stared at the president. The one billionaire in particular was staring at the president with a stark grin.

The billionaire spoke. "Mr. President. It's always a pleasure to see you."

The president simply nodded in return. He rose from the table and greeted the doctor. "Doctor, what a pleasant surprise."

"It is a most pleasant surprise, Mr. President," replied the doctor. "These men were kind of enough to make a gracious donation to our hospital, and the least I could do is accept their invitation to dinner."

President Adams gently grabbed his mother and returned her to her seat at the table. The president shook the doctor's hands and said to him, "We will see you tomorrow."

"Yes," the doctor said. "I look forward to seeing you both."

The doctor and his company sat a table at the opposite end of the restaurant. The billionaire made it a point to be in the president's line of sight. For the rest of the evening, President Adams could not take his eyes off the man. His parents did not know what was wrong, but they knew enough not to say anything.

*   *   *

The next morning, the president and his parents had been kept waiting in the sitting area of the doctor's office for nearly an hour. When the doctor finally walked in, he had a somber look on his face. The doctor stared at the medical report in his hand. He looked up, and his sullen gaze said it all. The president and his family broke into tears. The bad news destroyed his mother emotionally. The chemotherapy and radiation treatment destroyed her physically. She was dying.

Somehow news of the president's mother had made the headlines. When news of his mother's illness was finally out in the public, President Adams announced that he would take a few days to care for his mother, but he assured the American people that nothing would stand in his way of leading his country. A few days turned into a few weeks, but the Americans supported their president and worried for him.

As his mother got progressively worse, Nicky realized that his father had begun to deteriorate. He wanted to chalk it up to grief, but he knew better. Nicky became desperate, and in that desperation, the president swallowed his pride and made several attempts to reach out to the financiers, but this time, it was the rich elite who ignored his phone calls. He was sickened by the idea that there had to be a sinister connection between the billionaires' discontent and his mother's decline. As several days went by, the president expended all his resources and connections to try and get the cadre to return his calls, but the response never came. His mother died nearly four weeks after the encounter at the restaurant.

The whole world grieved with him. To the president's disbelief, the billionaire and the other financiers had the audacity to appear at her funeral. The president was visibly withdrawn and could not muster any strength to object to their presence. The billionaire approached the president and wrapped his arms around the grieving man in a feigned attempt to appear as if he were comforting him. The president did not resist.

Nicky Adams remained emotionless as the billionaire whispered in his ear, "Now you must care for your father."

Nicky pulled back, quivering in fear. "My condolences, Mr. President," mocked the billionaire, saying it with an acerbic smile.

Nicky Adams escorted his father to the presidential limousine. The driver and the rest of the motorcade were directed to drive to his father's home. Nicky and his father chose not to have a post-funeral gathering and opted to spend it in solitude. The secret service was ordered to wait outside. They sat across from each other and cried in unison.

The following day, they awoke to the sound of the phone. It was the doctor. Evil had turned its gaze in his father's direction; the test results were in, and the doctor wanted to discuss them in person. The two men wasted no time in getting dressed, and they made their way to the doctor's office. They were personally greeted by the doctor himself. They had seen his dire look before.

"The results are grim," said the doctor, "but I'm confident this time, we can have better results."

The president glared at the doctor. "That's what you told us before."

"True, but I guess it will all depend on—" The doctor stopped himself short.

"It will depend on what?" the president hesitated to ask.

"I guess it'll depend on . . . you."

President Adams was too exhausted and emotionally drained to be angry. He knew then and there that the doctor had been bought. "What . . . Whatever I can do to help my father, you can count on me." The president's voice was wavering.

"Good," said the doctor. "All of America is counting on you."

They shook hands, and the president walked his father out of the office.

During the drive to his father's home, President Adams's mind was racing. His father was speaking to him, reassuring him that everything was going to be okay, but he was not listening. All he could think about was the promises he had made to the American public. Nicky Adams was an idealist, and the Office of the Presidency stood for something far greater than all else, and a promise made was a promise kept—but he looked at his father, sitting across from him. The old man looked frail, weak, and, more importantly, terrified, and Nicky Adams was scared for him.

President Adams had been so rattled by the last few days' events that he had not realized that the limousine television had been on. A cable news network had breaking news: the mysterious terrorist known as Yousef had inspired another attack, and this time, it was on U.S. soil: the attack at Fort Hood. He immediately called his national security advisor.

"Mr. President," the advisor said.

"Summon the entire cabinet. I'll be flying back to D.C. tomorrow."

"The entire cabinet? Tomorrow is Sunday."

"*Sunday?*" The president had no idea what day of the week it was. "We're under attack. We need to reassess our policy, our strategies. We have been attacked, and now we need to strike back."

The president could sense that his national security advisor was smiling. "Yes, sir. I'll rally the troops. We will all be there."

"Very well. I fly in tonight, and I'll see you first thing in the morning." Just before the president disconnected the call, his advisor uttered a comment. "Mr. President, one more thing—how's your father?"

Nicky Adams looked at his father, who was gleaming with joy, watching his son—the first Latino president of the United States—at work.

"My father? My father is just fine."

Chapter Twenty-six

With time, Pres. Nicky Adams's original plan to reduce the military budget was gradually phased out. As he had expected, the American public protested and became outraged, but fear kept the public in line—fear of another terrorist attack.

President Adams stood before the American public, and he explained that the rising threat of Yousef caused him to modify his promise. National security was always a priority, but the change in circumstances placed a moratorium on his promise. The war on terror had to be his priority, and he promised that as soon as Yousef Hasan was brought to justice, he would reinstate his original promise.

Some of his supporters were disappointed, but the majority of Americans were too distracted by reality shows, Hollywood movies, and football games. In the ensuing months, the president's primary obligation (and his subsequent new slogan) was to "keep America safe." With the exception of a very few, all his campaign promises were soon broken and forgotten.

The corporate leaders and financiers were pleasantly pleased with their president. The president's father would soon be cured of his disease.

Chapter Twenty-seven

The president was the last to enter the Situation Room. Sitting around the entire table were his chief of staff, Gen. Lance Norton, the head of homeland security, representatives of the CIA, and the sole FBI representative, FBI agent Billy Assad. They all rose to their feet as the president took his place at the head of the table.

"Please sit," the president requested. "Now where are we on this Yousef guy?"

General Norton made it a point to be the first to respond "Mr. President, we have been tracking Yousef Hasan throughout Yemen. He travels from camp to camp and is very seldom in one location. But we have human intel that may help us narrow his location."

"What's your estimated time before we can confirm his location?" the president asked.

"Not sure," the general responded. "But as you can see, we have a joint task force working tirelessly on finding him."

"How secure are we on American soil?" the president continued. "I don't want another Fort Hood."

"For that question, I'll turn you over to the FBI." The general gestured to Billy Assad. "Mr. President, I introduce you to Mahmoud Assad."

Billy was still awestruck by the presence of the president. He quickly composed himself. "Pleasure to meet you, Mr. President, but please call me Billy."

"And you can call me Nicky—but not in public."

Everyone in the room chuckled.

"Please, Billy, tell me—what do you have to add to all this?" the president pressed.

"All our FBI offices are closely monitoring websites and chat rooms," Billy said confidently. "We also have informants who have infiltrated various radical groups that have been deemed 'high risk' for attacks."

The president folded his arms. "Are we any closer to a real cataclysmic attack?"

"There's plenty of chatter out there," Billy said. "There's a lot of anger and dissension. But nothing formulative to the point where we can secure FISA or search warrants or much less an arrest."

The president had a look of consternation. "I'm really worried that we may be too late—"

"Mr. President," Billy interrupted, "I assure you that we are doing all we can to prevent anything further happening on U.S. soil."

As Billy was finishing his thought, the collective phones in the room were sounding off; they were the sounds of an alert. Each person in the room gathered their phones and gawked in horror.

Just then, the door to the room opened. It was the president's assistant chief of staff. Her face was ashen white.

"M-Mr. President." She struggled to speak. "W-we've had another attack!"

Chapter Twenty-eight

A twenty-seven-year-old Bangladeshi man came to America on an F43 family immigrant visa by way of the extended family chain migration. He eventually became a lawful permanent resident. He married his Bangladeshi girlfriend, and they had a little girl a year later. Despite having traveled overseas to his native country five times in the short time he had been here, he never raised any red flags with the Department of Homeland Security. No one thought it to be suspicious that the Bangladeshi took his wife and child to his native country and returned forty-eight hours later without them—because no one was looking.

It was a chilly December morning, so no one in the walkway below the Port Authority Bus Terminal in New York took notice that a man was wearing extra layers of clothing. Underneath his clothing was an improvised low-tech explosive device, made up of a foot-long pipe, black powder, wiring, and a countless array of nails of different sizes. Video surveillance would show the man as he made his way up the Eighteenth Avenue F train platform from Brooklyn and exiting the A train at the Port Authority Bus Terminal stop in Manhattan. Not long after that, he attempted to detonate the makeshift bomb. There was a loud noise and a burst of smoke, but there was no explosion. The commuters ran for cover in a panic, but no one was hurt.

When arrested, the man's only words were "President Adams, you failed your country."

A search of his home computer's hard drive revealed a cache of Yousef's videos. A suicide note pinned to his living room wall read, "Allegiance to Yousef."

*   *   *

At that very moment, in Yousef's sleeping quarters, a middle-aged woman covered in her hijab watched as Yousef tossed and turned in his sleep, restless from his dreams. The woman watched in great discomfort as Yousef appeared to be writhing in pain. The woman had been accustomed to witnessing the young man's distress. She had seen it firsthand since he had been a child, but her personal torment never diminished.

Aamilah held her prayer beads firmly and prayed for peace. Her prayers were for her son. She also thought of the mystery that had brought Yousef into her life and how the curse that followed his birth had haunted them both ever since. She prayed harder as she thought of the evil that was to be known to her as *Fiorello*.

Chapter Twenty-nine

The Port Authority attack was embarrassing for the FBI but particularly embarrassing for Billy Assad in that it had happened in his own backyard. Those ensuing days at SOCOM were extremely stressful; the entire staff was on high alert. There was little or no time to sleep.

Billy determined that the cache of videos seized from the Bangladeshi's computer naturally had to be the key to the way Yousef's message was being spread. While Yousef's spoken words were incendiary to be sure, there was never an overt call for violence. *There had to be something more,* Billy Assad surmised, *something hidden within the messages.*

His team there at SOCOM and back in New York devoted their time in carefully reviewing and analyzing every video, examining every hand gesture, counting every eye flinch, and studying every background. For ten straight days, their investigation went as such, and yet nothing could be found.

Billy must have dozed off because he had not heard his cell phone ring until the caller called him a second time. It was General Norton.

"I want you in the debriefing room right away. I want an update—and you'd better bring me something good." With that, the general disconnected the call.

Billy eyed the other agents surrounding him. They looked at Billy pathetically. They knew they had nothing to offer.

Chapter Thirty

Billy Assad stepped into a debriefing room and encountered a room filled with the usual military commanders, FBI agents, and CIA analysts. Commanding the room's attention was General Norton. The men in the room were viewing the most recent tape made by Yousef except the general, who was momentarily preoccupied with a phone call.

General Norton disconnected the call and directed his attention toward Billy. "So, Mr. al-Assad, what have you come up with?"

For reasons known only to the general, he refused to call him Billy. Billy was always taken aback by the general but pressed on. "Our intelligence was correct in that this most recent tape was made and released the same morning. Our analysts are convinced that there is a hidden message within these videos. We've seen this type of coded messages before. We are convinced that the messages are hidden within the very words he uses, his eye movements, his hand gestures, the color of the background. With each of the previous videos, we surmised that the intended recipients would piece the messages together to tell them the when, the where, and the how."

"And you reviewed all the tapes that preceded the attacks in Egypt, Spain, France, and Germany and here in the United States?" General Norton asked, pointing to the video that was currently on display.

"Yes, we have," Billy answered.

"And has your team been able to break the code and identify how the messages were conveyed to the different sleeper agents?"

Billy hesitated; his face gave away the answer, but still, he responded, "No."

The general and the others in the room had a look of regret.

Billy resumed, "But we're convinced that this video, along with the others, are preparing the sleeper cells for an attack here in America."

"How can you be certain?" the general inquired.

"We saw this with Osama bin Laden's videos leading up to 9/11, and so it's not a new concept. The frequency of Yousef's videos corresponded with the frequency of the attacks. It cannot be a coincidence."

The room became uneasy.

Billy continued, "The messages have always been loud and clear to his followers. We just can't read them in time. And there are more videos coming in daily." He paused to catch his breath. "I am convinced that we're at a point where it's not just a matter of 'is' something going to happen, but it's just a matter of 'when.'"

"How long before we decipher this one video?" General Norton asked emphatically.

"Days. Weeks. Not sure, but I can tell you that between the intelligence we've received thus far and the little bit we gathered from this video, Yousef's assuredly telling his operatives that the plan he's had in store is about to take place. He's letting them know he'll release another video shortly with the specifics."

"The when, where, and how?" The general was noticeably upset.

"I can't be certain of the where and the how. That may have been set in motion a long time ago. This Yousef character is a smart guy. He may have been expecting a leak down the road, and the where and how may have already been predetermined. The only thing left to convey is the when."

"But by then, it may be too late!" the general shouted.

"Exactly," Billy Assad agreed.

The general looked Billy in the eye with a furled brow. "So what do we do?"

"We keep analyzing all the videos, twenty-four hours, nonstop." Billy answered.

"But there's a new video coming out all the time."

Billy scowled. "Then we can't waste time."

"These videos have been plastered all over social media and have made all the news outlets. It's gone viral. It's only a matter of time before these sleeper cells act on them. I say we put the country on alert—and now!" the general barked. "Something is about to happen, and it's going to be huge, and America cannot be caught by surprise."

Billy was reluctant to protest but was compelled to do so. "General, respectfully, we can't tell the country to be on alert."

"And why the hell not?"

"Because without knowing any more details, it'll cause mass hysteria."

"I don't give a shit! I think the public has the right to know. They need to be vigilant and prepared."

"I think most Americans already are. I think we should contact the president right away and—"

"Sir," the general interrupted, "*that* directive came from the president himself. That was the national security advisor himself I was talking to as you came in. The president feels compelled to alert the nation."

"I have to protest," Billy said adamantly. "Any change in the conditions will cause the sleeper agents to go deeper underground. That will only impede our investigation."

"I have discretion to give you a few days, but that's it." The general was livid and stared at all the personnel in the room. "I suggest all of you intellectuals to get me something substantive right away—or the blood of many more Americans will be on your hands."

Chapter Thirty-one

In the first few hours past midnight, the empty halls of the White House seemed eerily silent, which was contrary to the normal hustle and bustle of its daily routine. The various secret service agents stood and kept vigil as the silence was broken by the hurried pace of a solitary man. The agents spoke to one another by their radios as they watched the man pass them by; he was heading toward the Oval Office.

A few moments later, the national security advisor barged into the president's private office and approached the president. "Sorry to interrupt you, Mr. President, but we have an update from SOCOM and the Yemeni government."

The president had been in his office for the last twenty hours, reviewing the countless intelligence briefings, and had a look of sheer exhaustion. The president motioned for the gentleman to sit down. "Please take a seat."

"General Norton reports that the analysts at SOCOM may have gotten a break in their investigation."

"That's good news—I hope."

"It can be. He just needs more time."

"What is the nature of this lead?" the president asked.

"The analysts believe they have discovered hidden messages in all of Yousef's video messages," the national security advisor answered.

"Have they been able to decipher them?"

"No, not yet. But they are pretty sure they are about an imminent attack, but General Norton needs more time."

"Do you mean . . . delay public notification?"

The national security advisor nodded. "Correct."

"By how long?"

"A few days, maybe a few weeks."

The president looked at his national security advisor for guidance. "What do you think?"

"I think we should give them more time. The FBI thinks that if we make a public announcement of any imminent attack, it will create mass hysteria, and it will compromise their investigation."

"That's fine. Tell him to take as long as he needs." The president sat back in his chair. He appeared more relaxed. "What's the news from Yemen?"

The national security advisor handed him a dossier. "It's official. The Yemeni government has tried him in absentia. A Yemeni judge ordered that he be captured 'dead or alive,' and the president of Yemen approved foreign military raids to apprehend or execute the terrorist."

The president smiled. "Excellent news. Now what do we do?"

"Now we place Yousef on a 'kill list.'"

"I thought that we had to make it legal first?" the president asked.

"He's not a citizen, so all you will have to do is name him a threat to national security, and that will make our execution of him legal."

"O-okay . . ." the president stuttered.

"Oh, and we need to make sure the press is notified. We're going to scare the shit out of this guy and maintain the public's confidence." The national security advisor had turned to leave and then stopped and chuckled.

The president was bewildered. "What's so funny?"

"We cannot torture suspected terrorists, but we sure as hell can use a drone to bomb the shit out of them."

The national security advisor continued to laugh. The President did not.

*　*　*

Later that morning, the president made his public announcement on national TV, and with his articulate skills, he was able to convince the nation and the whole world that without the benefit of a judge, a jury, or a trial, Yousef deserved to die—and that he would die.

Chapter Thirty-two

Al-Jawf, Yemen

Yousef's mother, Aamilah, ran across the terrain of the hidden camp, desperately looking for her son. She was a tall and slender woman in her late fifties, but her hijab and the scarf around her face hid her beauty and elegance. She found her son as he came out of one of the tents. "My son, did you hear the news? The American president is looking to kill you."

"I have heard," Yousef replied. "But you mustn't have any fear. America has threatened to kill me for some time."

"Yes, but this time, the American president himself has made the threat." She rushed into his arms. "I am afraid for you, my son."

Yousef kissed his mother gently on the hijab over her forehead. "You have always been too worried for me. You must be strong for me, as I will be strong for you."

"I have always been strong for you, my son," she replied.

He embraced her. "That is true. You have been stronger than any son can ever hope for. But you must be even stronger now."

His mother was shaking nervously. "Why? What is happening? What is going to happen?"

Yousef's body tensed. "There are things I must do that I cannot share with you. But to keep you strong and to keep you safe, my men will take you away from here. It is no longer safe."

His mother was more furious than confused. "What do you mean for my safety? Where am I going?"

"I cannot tell you," Yousef answered. "But you must leave as quickly as possible."

"Now I am really afraid for you," she said, grabbing her son's arms. "My place is by your side."

"Please don't make this harder for me. Go with my men, and they will keep you safe, and in turn, it will make me safer. I can protect myself better if I am not worried about you," Yousef said, holding back his tears.

They embraced each other, and Yousef walked away without saying another word.

His mother held back her own tears, and after whispering a silent prayer, she murmured to herself, "I have always been by your side, even on that day when you were an infant and those evil men came to kill you. Even if I cannot be physically by your side, I will never stop protecting you . . ."

She finished her prayer, and two of Yousef's most trusted bodyguards hurriedly placed his mother inside a SUV, and she was driven into the horizon.

Chapter Thirty-three

Yousef's mother had been safely escorted to one of the countless tower houses in Sana'a, in the heart of Yemen's capital. She would be safe, hidden among the crowded buildings. Upon arrival, she climbed four flights up the stairs to the *mafraj*, the highest level of the home, the room with a view. Her son had given her a satellite phone to be used only during emergencies, and in her mind, this moment clearly qualified as an emergency. She made a desperate call to America.

Chapter Thirty-four

A young staff attorney answered her phone at the New York office of the American Civil Liberties Union (ACLU) and listened as the caller identified herself as the mother to Yousef in broken English. The young attorney was about to dismiss the call until she felt the desperate plea of the woman on the other end of the line. After a series of questions, the staff attorney believed the woman she was talking to.

The ACLU had long been looking for a test case to challenge the validity of warrantless "kill lists," but not a single case was ripe or newsworthy—until now. A few days after the call, at the request of Yousef's mother, the ACLU filed a lawsuit challenging the government's authorization of the use of drones for the expressed intent of executing a foreign national far from any armed conflict zone. The ACLU argued that the U.S. government's targeting of Yousef violated the constitution's fundamental guarantee against the deprivation of life without due process of law. It was a long shot by legal standards since Yousef was not an American citizen and there was no formal declaration of war, but the ACLU was eager to take on the task.

The ACLU's argument that the operation was a "targeted killing" by the United States outside the context of armed conflict was based on vague legal standards, a closed executive decision-making process, and evidence that was never presented to the courts. The ACLU filed its lawsuit in the Southern District of New York and, because of the likelihood of irreparable harm and loss of life, petitioned the court to place the case on the "fast track" docket. The United States responded by filing its motion to dismiss. Oral arguments were scheduled to take place before a federal district court judge.

Two weeks later, lawyers for the United States argued in courtroom 443 of the Thurgood Marshall United States Courthouse that even if it were established that Yousef was a U.S. citizen, Yousef presented an imminent threat against the United States, and as a result, the fact that he was overseas did not give him sanctuary from being lawfully attacked. The ACLU, on the other hand, argued that because the United States was not involved in any armed conflict with Yemen, the use of military force to carry out Yousef's death violated international law.

After three hours of vociferous oral argument, the court published a twenty-page order dismissing the case, and the United States was free to kill Yousef as a military target. The hunt was on.

*   *   *

By the end of the short-lived judicial process, Yousef's name became even more infamous, and he was the darling of the antiwar left. For the right, he represented a shining example of the current administration's inability to keep their country safe, and for the rest of the world, he was becoming a popular figure and a cult hero to many.

Chapter Thirty-five

Those who knew Temir in New York and in Shahrisabz, Uzbekistan, where he had lived before coming to the United States seven years ago, said they saw no warning signs of radicalization. As a result, his friends and associates were surprised to hear that he had chosen a truck as his weapon to "inflict maximum damage." A few days before the incident, Temir rented the truck and practiced making turns. The day of the attack, Temir raced this truck into pedestrians on the West Side Highway and continued all the way to the Brooklyn Bridge. He killed ten people and injured twenty-five others in the process. The deadly ordeal ended when Temir collided the truck into another car. He was finally brought down when he was shot by police and taken into custody.

The FBI and the New York Police Department would later execute a search warrant of Temir's one-room apartment off Bryant Avenue in the Bronx and found that the young man lived in complete squalor, with no electricity, no water, and virtually no food to eat. The young man had been fired as a dishwasher in a local diner because of his erratic behavior and inability to keep up with his work schedule. His neighbors never saw him, but a check of the local public library revealed that Temir spent most of his free time using their computers and free internet. Video footage would reveal that the young recluse would spend many nights sleeping in the rear of the library. Nearly every computer of the Hunts Point Library had evidence of Temir's state of mind. The browser history revealed his obsession with the radicalized groups living both in America and abroad, but more importantly, law enforcement found proof that Temir had viewed every single one of Yousef's videos.

Chapter Thirty-six

"I want him dead!' the president demanded, slamming his fist onto his desk. "We've got midterms coming up, and I promised America that Yousef would be brought to justice by now. More Americans died yesterday!"

"Calm down," his national security advisor demanded and whose rudeness caught the other people in the Oval Office by surprise. Quickly changing his tone, the national security advisor pointed to the chair behind the president's desk. "Please sit, Mr. President."

The president acquiesced and managed to ask, "Why haven't we killed him yet? We got the approval from a U.S. district judge."

"Our intelligence is narrowing down on his location," the national security advisor continued, "but there are things that are left to be done."

"*Things?* What *things?*"

The national security advisor patted the president's shoulder as if he were soothing a crying baby. Using his soft, cooing voice, the trusted advisor beckoned, "Please try to relax. Soon, the American people will be safe, our party will win the midterms, and Yousef will be dead. Let me . . . Let *us* work out the logistics. Now you and your father have another vacation to prepare for."

Chapter Thirty=seven

Al-Hazm, Yemen

Distraught by the news of the ACLU's battle in court, Yousef's mother decided to turn to another outlet that might save her son: the media. Yousef's mother had one of her bodyguards drive her into the town of al-Hazm, where she was scheduled to appear remotely on international television. She had reached out to several news sources, identifying herself as Yousef's mother, and it was not until one German network had verified her claim that they agreed to hear her story. They would meet her at the outskirts of the al-Hazm airport at an abandoned television station.

The German cameraman politely asked her for permission to place the microphone on her dress. She refused and placed the microphone on her own. The reporter was appearing remotely on a small screen placed before her. It was agreed that the interview would take place in English. Her hijab covered most of her face, but her broken English was comprehensible, and her point was very clear. She was pleading for her son's life.

"This message is for the American president," she said, staring straight into the camera. "Please, good sir, I beg—do not kill my son.

You claim you are a president defending human rights, and yet you continue war atrocities, hunting my son like an animal. You speak of truth, but you hide behind 'national security.' My son is no threat to your country. He is no threat to your country's national security. There have been enough killings. Please, in the name of *God* and in the name of peace . . ." She began to cry and unexpectedly removed the scarf from her face. She looked directly into the camera and made one final plea: "Mr. President, I beg—spare my son."

*   *   *

At the very moment of the live interview, the president was in Ireland, drinking a cold beer at a very old but quaint little pub. Secret service saw to it that he would never see the telecast.

Chapter Thirty=eight

In the ensuing months, America would continue its reign of terror, conducting more than thirty airstrikes against suspected Yousef strongholds in three Yemeni provinces. As a result, over a thousand "militant" operatives were killed for the cost of over a hundred civilian deaths, but still, Yousef remained at large.

During that time, the U.S. media either downplayed or completely ignored any incident that occurred both here and abroad that was in any way related to or influenced by Yousef, but the news outlets could only hold out for so long. The midterm elections were only a few months away, and the administration agreed that only after the president's party was able to maintain its power would the terrorist experts and pundits be finally allowed to discuss the subject matter. For now, America was repeatedly assured that Yousef's threat and might had been diminished.

The Americans were never told that Yousef was producing an average of two videos a week and that his influence was growing exponentially around the world. The analysts were clear in their reports—a massive terrorist act on U.S. soil was imminent.

Chapter Thirty=nine

Billy Assad had been locked up in his small office for the last six hours and had reviewed as many video messages produced by Yousef as he could. He had given up looking for clues; he would leave that to the codebreakers and the mathematicians. Instead, he was looking for something else. Billy knew some Arabic, and there was something about Yousef's speech pattern, his dialect, and his accent that Billy always found odd. Billy was also fixated on Yousef's facial features. None of this lent him any clues as to what region of the Middle East Yousef was from.

Billy recalled that Yousef's mother had been recently interviewed, but since the terrorist's mother was of no military or national security interest, she was virtually ignored. Billy quickly logged into his computer and began doing an internet search focusing on the woman. He found her recent German television interview and played it over and over. He repeatedly paused the image when she removed the covering from her face. Billy then began rummaging through a pile of file folders, desperately looking for one file. After a few minutes, he found the one he was looking for, and he carefully perused every word of it, line by line. He stopped reading and stared at the still image of her face on the computer.

After several hours, Billy Assad came to a surprising conclusion.

Chapter Forty

The CIA analyst dropped another stack of DVDs onto the conference room table. "Here's the latest batch of videos," the analyst said, fearing he would draw the ire of General Norton, who had been sitting at the head of the table; in the same room, there were two other CIA analysts and a few military personnel.

"Yousef made all these?" the general inquired, smirking in disgust.

"Yes. Each DVD represents just one of his twenty-minute presentations."

"And what's the total now?"

"A hundred and fifty . . ." the analyst said almost fearfully.

"And Yousef is making more videos every day," the general said angrily, scattering the DVDs across the long table while staring at the analyst like it had been his fault. The general continued yelling. "I've got the national security advisor up my ass wanting results! We have no idea where the hell this guy is, and there is chatter that the sleeper cells here in America are activating."

It was at that moment that Billy Assad walked into the room. He had a look of fatigue and desperation.

"Where the hell have you been?" the general demanded to know.

"Well, actually—" Billy attempted to answer.

"I need an update on this mess now!"

"Um, okay. My agents are telling me that there's a lot of chatter, but nothing seems organized—yet." Billy's fatigue was starting to show.

"*Yet?*" the general barked. "So what do we do? Wait until *after* an attack to do something?"

The room went silent.

General Norton rose to his feet and stood up straight. "I've given you enough time. I'm going to recommend to the president that we make a public announcement. I can't just sit here and wait while all of you Ivy League analysts do your work and accomplish nothing. I will not let another 9/11 happen on my watch."

"You know my objection, and I implore you to avoid that at all costs. Don't you recall the danger of mass hysteria?" Billy Assad reminded. "I need a little more time."

"*More time?*" The military veteran was aghast. "I disagree. I think we should alert the country before—"

Billy Assad was polite in his interruption. "Sorry, but publicly broadcasting this news would only throw the country into chaos."

"Mr. FBI, I know the fucking risk, and that's a risk I'm willing to take."

"Wait a minute." Billy stopped as he contemplated a thought.

"*Wait? Wait for what?*"

"Maybe this is what Yousef wants from us," Billy suggested.

The general grew impatient. "Explain yourself—and quickly."

"Maybe Yousef wants the president to make a public announcement and throw the country into chaos. Perhaps he would like the president to declare martial law. Curfews. Internment camps. What greater way to terrorize our country by depriving us of our civil liberties?"

The general appeared to be resigned. "That's the smartest thing you've said since I met you."

"Making a public announcement could fit squarely into Yousef's plans."

"Is Yousef really that smart?" the general asked.

"Yes, I believe so. Maybe not formally but definitely self-taught."

"Why don't you *intelligence analysts* finally tell me what you know about this guy?" The general directed the question to the analysts, but Billy Assad did not waste any time responding.

Billy was prepared, and he handed out dossiers to each member of the meeting. "That's actually what I was working on, which is why I was late to this meeting."

The general was impatient. "Just tell me what you know."

"He's about thirty years old, speaks about four to five languages, and walks with a distinguished limp. Not much is known of his past after his youth, but we do know that he's wandered from one militant group to another, apparently never feeling at home with any one of them. As a result, he's started his own movement."

"His own *movement?*" the general asked aloud.

"Yes, he's created a movement of followers who are disenchanted, upset over the status quo."

"*Terrific,*" the general said sarcastically. "Just what the world needs—another idealist, Islamo-fascist terrorist."

Billy Assad abruptly corrected the commander. "I'm not so sure of that now. In the beginning, his messages were clearly supported by a distorted view of Islam—but now not so much. Now he seems to have dropped the religious tone, and that's what is making him even more dangerous. Because his philosophy is becoming secular based. His appeal is quite broad."

"Well, that's a new one—a Middle Eastern terrorist who's not *religious,*" the general said, scratching his bald head.

"That's just it," Billy Assad said. "I don't even think Yousef is Middle Eastern."

The entire room stood silent and in complete awe.

The general looked perplexed. "What? I'm afraid to ask, but if he's not Middle Eastern, then where's he from?"

"It's all preliminary," Billy Assad continued, "but I think he's European."

Chapter Forty-one

The Dream

His enemies were gaining ground. The pain from the knight's wounds made his journey unbearable; he was bleeding profusely. He noticed that his horse had also been injured during the battle, but still, his steed valiantly raced across the sand. The gallant knight was losing faith that either he or his horse would be able to complete their mission, but the knight prayed for God's help. As if God had heard him, the knight could faintly see his final destination looming in the horizon—but his enemies were not far behind.

Chapter Forty-two

MacDill Air Force Base
Tampa, Florida

General Norton cleared the room of the nonessential personnel, leaving behind the CIA analysts and Billy Assad, the only FBI representative.

"What do you mean he may be *European?*" the general reacted. "He's a Muslim terrorist."

"He's definitely a terrorist," Billy replied. "And while he may have once been a Muslim, I don't think he was born in the Middle East."

"You'd better explain yourself right now. You aren't making any sense at all," the general ordered.

Billy Assad had one last dossier that he held in his hands. It was labeled *Yousef.* "Well, let me explain." He took out the documents and spread them across the large table. "When I was originally assigned to this joint task force, I took the liberty of reviewing all the CIA's files that were privy to me. My colleagues in the CIA did an excellent job of compiling a considerable wealth of information on Yousef, ranging as far back as his youth."

The CIA analysts in the room smiled almost arrogantly.

"But," Billy Assad continued, watching as their smiles turned to frowns, "the CIA missed something very vital." Billy Assad pulled out a series of pages and held them up. "While it's true that as a young man, he traveled across the Middle East, very little is known of where he was born. I came across one intelligence report that identified his mother as possibly Aamal or Aamilah, but there's virtually nothing on her. Nothing."

"Get to your point, son," the general demanded impatiently. "Quickly."

"However, one field report drafted over ten years ago revealed an interview with a villager who remembered her when her son was a toddler."

"What village?"

"Somewhere in Nangarhar Province."

"Did she have family at this village?"

"Well, the villager who was interviewed seemed to remember that this woman, Aamal or Aamilah, was related to one Mustafa Saed."

The general was racking his brain. "*Mustafa Saed* . . . Didn't we have him killed?"

"Yes. A drone strike killed both Mustafa Saed and one of Yousef's childhood friends. Apparently, Yousef himself was there in the village at that time. He survived, and our intelligence surmises the death of Mustafa Saed and his friend sparked Yousef's anger."

"How did his mother meet Mustafa Saed?"

Billy was reading from his notes. "This was before my time with foreign intel, but apparently, Ameen was known for recruiting teenagers from all over Europe, mainly young children, both boys and girls. He would indoctrinate them, convert them, and then strap them with bombs."

"Yes," the general added. "He was responsible for some of the most horrific suicide bombings in Europe in the 1990s and 2000s. He was on the run for a decade before we finally killed him. He must have recruited Yousef's mother, and either was about to put her to work or perhaps didn't want her. What else did the villager say?"

"The villager had no idea where she came from but remembered that she and her son appeared practically out of nowhere. He remembered that she struggled to speak in Arabic and relied on the old man to teach her to speak."

The general was intrigued. "And what does all that mean?"

Billy Assad paused as if for a grand effect. "According to this report, the old man remembered that she was fluent in . . . Spanish."

"*Spanish?*" The general was shocked. "So who is this lady, Aamilah?"

"Well, I tried looking for pictures of her in the files, and there is nothing on her from that time frame."

"Nothing?"

"Nothing. But I started viewing all the various news stories of Yousef, and one story in particular had a video of him as a young man, and for a brief second, in one of the many montage footages, there is a woman standing beside him." Billy Assad removed a still photograph from his folder. "I had that old photograph blown up, and then I took a snapshot of the recent German television interview of the same woman, whereby she was pleading for Yousef's life, and I'm pretty confident that this is, in fact, his mother."

"I still don't see how you came to your conclusion that Yousef is European."

"I had forensics run a diagnostic on the facial features on both Yousef and his mother."

"*And?*"

"Forensics are pretty certain they are both of European descent."

Once again, the room was silent.

The general turned his attention back to Billy Assad. "I want you to run these faces on every single database in the world. I want a real name to those faces."

"I'm already on it," Billy Assad said proudly.

The general then pulled out another still photograph of an older Yousef and his imam. The military vet pointed to the cleric in the photograph. "Who is *this* man?"

"That's El Fazazi, his imam," Billy Assad replied. "He's been his mentor and teacher since Yousef was a young man. There is virtually nothing on El Fazizi. But I believe he's the key. You eliminate him, and you pretty much cut off the head of the snake."

"Why haven't I been briefed on him before?" The general shook his head in disbelief. "Why haven't we targeted him?"

It was then that one of the senior CIA officials jumped in. "I wouldn't worry about him."

"Why not?" both the general and Billy Assad asked.

"That imam," the CIA analyst said ever so strangely, "El Fazazi—he's one of ours."

Chapter Forty-three

Yousef awoke from his dream in his usual cold sweat. He rose from his floor mat and exited the tent. He watched as the sun rose; there was a time he would have praised God for letting him witness another glorious morning. On this day, he said nothing and thanked no one.

He walked over to the wash basin, where he cleansed his face. The cold water quickly revived him and made him forget his dream, albeit only for the moment at hand. He walked into a larger tent, where a group of young disciples had been waiting patiently. He was driven by his dream to produce more videos.

Chapter Forty-four

In Mesquite, Nevada, a real estate investor took his laptop, stuffed it into one of ten ranger bags, placed them into the trunk of his car, and headed for Las Vegas. A nurse in Chicago, Illinois, viewed a series of videos on his iPhone as he commuted home on the L train. An assistant public defender in San Jose, California, spent his lunch break behind closed doors, looking at videos on his state-issued computer.

Throughout America, people from all walks of life and in nearly every profession spent their days and nights watching Yousef's messages. They all had things in common. They were all hardworking, middle-class Americans, driven by the same level of frustration and, more importantly, anger. They got up early every morning with the promise of a better life, a piece of the American Dream, a pot of gold at the end of the rainbow. Instead, they became deeper in debt, living in substandard conditions, and their retirement investments lost to Wall Street greed. Their anger peaked for those politicians with big pearly white smiles and empty promises. It was these same meaningless promises, election after election, that motivated these people throughout America.

If only we could direct our wrath at the politicians was the thought they all shared, but the politicians were out of reach, so for now, these irate denizens would be forced to take out their frustration on the innocent.

The government analysts soon identified that there was one new demographic that Yousef's videos were reaching: fourteen-to-nineteen-year-old white males. These boys had an eerie similarity in that they were victims of bullying and suffered from depression, anger, and rage toward others. They were loners, quiet—the unassuming kid who lived next door. Yousef's messages had reached the heartland of America, the suburbs, the young men who were too young to know about the stress of bills, burdening debt, and high taxes. Many of them were too young to vote and could not tell the difference between a Republican and a Democrat, a liberal and a conservative; if anything, to them, politicians were all the same because that was what Yousef had taught them. However, the most important thing they learned from Yousef's messages was that there were other victims of bullying all over the world, bullying at the hands of the U.S. government, and it was their time to stand up to their aggressors the only way America could comprehend. These young boys listened intently to Yousef's messages, striving to work up the courage to stand up for themselves and the meek of the world once and for all.

Chapter Forty-five

"Wait. What?" Billy Assad asked, shocked. "The imam is a CIA operative?"

"Yep. Been one for a long time," the CIA analyst said casually.

"Do you mean to say that one of our CIA operatives is responsible for creating one of the world's most wanted terrorists?" Now it was Billy Assad who was outraged.

"I wouldn't say that he created him. Perhaps he molded him. But he's getting paid handsomely for it."

"This is unbelievable!" Billy Assad exclaimed, rubbing his temples.

"And he'll be greatly rewarded when he helps bring Yousef into custody—dead or alive."

Billy looked at the general. "Did you know about this?"

"No, son. I didn't." The general looked at the CIA operative disapprovingly. "But I can't say that I'm surprised."

"If the imam is your operative, then why hasn't he told us his location?" Billy Assad demanded.

"You really want to know?" the CIA operative inquired.

"Yes, goddammit!"

"We aren't ready to kill Yousef yet. He still serves a greater purpose."

The general and Billy looked at each other in astonishment.

The general stood in the face of the CIA operative. "I'm commanding you to tell me the location of your operative and Yousef right now."

The operative stood defiant. "Sorry, sir, but no can do. This operation is way above your pay grade. If you need us to help you review the video messages, then my team is at your disposal. But telling you Yousef's location would be a violation of *my* orders. You keep doing your analysis and keep our Americans safe. You do your job, and we'll do ours. Now if you'll excuse us, we have to update the national security advisor." With that, the senior CIA analyst and the other operatives walked out of the room.

Billy Assad looked at the general for guidance.

"Don't even think about it, son," the general said, attempting to calm Billy. "This is how *we* do things now. I'm not surprised. I don't like it, but I've learned to accept that is the new way."

"But how? Why?"

"It can only mean one thing, son," the general said to Billy.

"What is that?"

"It's as the CIA said. Keeping Yousef alive serves a higher purpose."

"And what would that be?"

"A political purpose. Keeping the president and his lackeys in power."

Billy Assad had never felt more disappointed in his life. The only consolation was that he maybe had a newfound friend in General Norton.

Chapter Forty-six

The national security advisor barged into the president's bedroom. It was 4:00 a.m., and the president had been awoken from his deep slumber.

"Sorry to disturb you in the middle of the night, but you wanted to be briefed as soon as we discovered anything. Well, sir, I think we have bad news. Our analysts have deciphered enough of these messages to confirm that the terrorists have broken up into different cells throughout the United States."

The president rubbed his eyes. "Any idea as to when the next attack may be?"

"Still no idea."

The president threw the bedsheets aside and walked into his study. The national security advisor dutifully followed. Both he and the president exchanged commentary for several minutes.

The president listened carefully, and after several minutes of contemplation, he issued his directive: "I want to intensify monitoring and scrutinizing of all possible targets, including FISA monitoring, surveillance, and the use of informants."

The national security advisor was more than glad to follow those series of orders. As he was about to turn and leave, the president bellowed one final command.

"One more thing," the president said. "Any update on Yousef's whereabouts?"

The national security advisor paused before answering. "No, sir. But I'm sure we will find him soon."

*   *   *

The advisor stepped into the hallway and made a call to Langley. The CIA director herself answered the phone.

"The president is getting restless, but the good news is that he's authorized FISA surveillance and greater electronic surveillance," the advisor said.

"That's good news." The director sounded pleased. "This will help us crack down on these fringe groups that are waiting to blow up in our faces."

"I also think it's time we pull the plug on Yousef."

"Already?" she said, surprised. "Isn't he more of use to us alive than dead?"

"I think Yousef has outlived his usefulness." The advisor was blunt. "The polls are down, and the president and the party could use a boost. This will be his rallying call during the midterms and his reelection campaign."

"Understood. I'll contact my team at SOCOM."

Chapter Forty-seven

The Dream

The good knight sensed that his journey was about to draw to an end, just short of his destination. His horse was struggling to maintain his course. His destination was less than a league away. The knight felt that if he extended his hand, he could reach out and touch his coveted destination, but his horse was slowing down.

The Crusader spotted something from the corner of his eye. It was *them*. It was the enemy. *They* were quickly approaching. He could not—*he must not*—slow down, but he knew that the steed could not survive much longer. The Crusader knew this, but his mission had to succeed. The relic in his satchel had to reach its destination; it had to be protected. The good knight realized that his steed was about to die; it was on the verge of collapse. He prayed to God that his horse would not die . . .

God must not have been listening.

Chapter Forty-eight

Yousef had done something he had never done before—yell at his mother. He was speaking to her through his satellite phone. "Mother, *why did you do that?* Why did you give that television interview? The whole world was watching!"

"That is precisely why I gave the interview," his mother replied through her phone, "because the whole world was watching. I may be old, but I am not blind. I have been watching the news. I know that your life is in danger. I did not raise you to be a terrorist."

"Mother, only in the eyes of the infidels am I a terrorist," Yousef answered. "I am a shepherd to my people. They are lost lambs that need guidance. Our people have endured so much."

"But must you sacrifice yourself for them?" his mother pleaded.

"If that is to be my destiny. But, Mother, you need to be taken away for safety. My enemies now know where you are. You must leave."

"I cannot tolerate being away from your side. I need to come back to you as soon as possible."

"I can better protect myself traveling alone. I cannot protect us both."

His mother was hysterical. *"Traveling?* Where are you going?"

"Mother, I've said too much already. I will be leaving very soon. Now go with my men. They will take you to safety."

"I would rather die than be without you!"

"If I die, it is God's will. You taught me that. And you always taught me that we cannot change God's will. Now my men have been instructed to take you to a village, the location of which will be discussed only in person—"

"No," his mother interrupted. "If I am to go, I will go to a place of my choosing."

Yousef breathed out a sigh of relief. "Very well. My men will take you to a place of your choosing. But you must promise me to not talk to any more reporters."

His mother was not so relieved. "You are my son, and I will always protect you. But I fear that my attempts were in vain. The American president wants you dead."

"I do not fear death," Yousef said both proudly and defiantly. "But I do fear for your safety, and now the whole world knows who you are."

His mother was now making the demands. "I will relocate only if you do the same."

Yousef was silent. Suddenly, the imam walked in but did not want to interrupt. Yousef pointed to him to wait, but he knew from the imam's face that the cleric had dire news.

"Mother," Yousef continued, "I give you my word that if you relocate, I will do so as well." He could finally sense his mother's relief and imagined her smile on the other end.

"Thank you, my son. I hope to see you soon."

Yousef smiled and disconnected the call.

* * *

At that very moment, CIA analysts at Langley received a phone call from the national security advisor. The analysts, in turn, contacted General Norton at SOCOM. Within moments, an MQ-1 Predator drone changed its course and began its hunt for Yousef.

Chapter Forty-nine

After disconnecting the call with his mother, Yousef turned to his imam.

The cleric wasted no time to speak. "The cells are responding accordingly. There are various random 'isolated incidents' occurring throughout the world. The American cells are awaiting your command."

Yousef was both content and upset at the same time, but the look of despair on his imam could not be ignored. "Then why are you so sullen?"

"My son," the imam said, "our sources tell us that you are no longer safe here. Your mother was correct in that you must leave this place. The Americans and their drones are closing in on you. They could strike at any moment."

"I think it is important that I stay here with my men." Yousef continued his defiant stance, disregarding the promise he had made to his mother.

"Your safety is paramount. Without you, our people would no longer be useful. You must leave now," the old man insisted.

"Very well," Yousef relented. "I am glad you offered to stay here. If something should happen to me, I want my mother taken care of."

"Of course." The old cleric responded reassuring his young student.

Yousef called out to several of his loyal men who had been waiting outside his tent. There were a total of nine men. Yousef gave them all brief instructions, and they were asked to prepare for their evacuation of the camp. The imam took his leave and exited the tent.

Yousef spent the next twenty minutes packing his essential belongings. Outside his tent was one of three SUVs that were prepared to leave at a moment's notice.

*   *   *

Moments before Yousef's anticipated departure, the Predator drone twenty thousand feet above followed his movement. It was the dead of the night, but the thermal imaging camera from the drone twenty thousand feet above easily captured everything.

At Langley, the CIA analysts watched carefully, trying to identify which of the several men seen exiting the tent was Yousef the terrorist. At that very moment, Billy Assad and his team were watching the same image at SOCOM, and on the West Coast of the United States, a drone operator sat watching from the small shed in Nellis Air Force Base in Las Vegas.

One of the analysts at Langley moved the cursor on the large screen, placing it on one of the infrared figures. "Yousef has to be the tall man in the center," said the analyst's voice from the sound speaker in the center of the conference table.

"No," Billy Assad said. "Remember, Yousef has a noticeable limp. Look for anyone with a limp."

"They all seem to be walking normally," the same voice said.

"I say we take out the whole group," General Norton's voice said, booming, startling everyone at SOCOM.

Billy Assad was no longer fazed by the general's bluntness. He knew the general to be frank, but Billy never doubted that the general's true intentions were to protect his country. After the general had made his comment, he heard a voice direct a comment to him.

"Not legal," said the attending JAG officer, standing in the rear corner of the room. "We need confirmation of identity."

"Just keep your eye on the group," Billy Assad ordered. "He should stand out any minute now."

Everyone in Nellis and SOCOM kept their eyes on the group of men displayed on the large screens. There was an eerie silence as they all watched as the suspected terrorists congregated on the ground for several minutes. Billy Assad prayed for some movement among the men so that the drone operator at Nellis would not be forced to bomb the entire group; he held his breath for several minutes as the scene remained the same. Finally, three different SUVs pulled up, lining up one behind another.

"Oh shit!" Billy Assad and several others said simultaneously as they watched the nine men separate and enter the three different vehicles in groups of three.

They are all now doomed to die, Billy Assad thought.

General Norton walked to the center of the room. "I'm superseding all command now. Langley? I'm taking over."

"Yes, sir," said the voice from Langley.

The general looked at the JAG officer. "Are we clear for a good kill?"

The JAG officer gave his usual thumbs-up. "We are a *go*."

"Okay, Nellis, on my mark," the general ordered.

At that moment, the drone pilot zeroed in on all three vehicles.

"Wait!" Billy Assad screamed. "There he is!"

At that very moment, a tenth man was seen limping out of the tent and entered the second vehicle. The drone's camera captured the scene as all three vehicles took off in three different directions. Billy Assad breathed out a sigh of relief as the drone began to follow the target SUV.

*   *   *

A moment before departing for one of the SUVs, Yousef was collecting his belongings. He abruptly became ill and lightheaded; he started hallucinating. The image of the crusading knight had always haunted him, but he had never dreamt of the knight during the day, much less while awake. He was recalling the dream from the night before.

Yousef was surprised at how vivid the vision was even at this most stressful moment. He became lucid enough to notice that his loyal men had loaded themselves into the three SUVs; they were waiting patiently for Yousef to choose which of the vehicles he would enter so that the other two vehicles could serve as decoys. Before deciding to exit his tent, Yousef walked over to the computer, where he released his most recent recording into the internet for the whole world to see.

Suddenly, the images from his last dream were replaying in his head. He suddenly paused, and his sixth sense was telling him not to leave. He carefully stuck his head out of the tent, and he knew that the Americans were watching him from above. *But how? How could they have found me?*

Yousef knew that if he stepped into any one of those vehicles, it was certain doom. He also realized that if he stayed, they would all die. He was not afraid to die, but he knew it was not yet his time. He could see his band of loyal men waiting inside each vehicle. Each vehicle had a different and secret, predetermined location; only he knew where it would take him. All he had to do was choose which of the vehicles to enter. If he was correct in his premonition, he would never reach his destination, and everyone in the car he chose to get into would die. He did not want to waste another prayer seeking heavenly guidance, but he so desperately needed it now.

In his mind's eye, he had another sudden image of the knight failing to reach his destination—failing to complete his mission.

Maybe it is my time to die. He could not shake his foreboding feeling, but he now had the nagging feeling of wondering *how* his enemy knew of his location. *Maybe a little prayer? Maybe a little guidance.*

His vision was interrupted by the entrance of his imam.

"You must leave now!" the imam said emphatically.

Yousef stood there and smiled as if he had had an epiphany. It was as if his prayers had, in fact, been answered. He looked at the three vehicles idling outside the tent. It was time for him to make a decision that would alter his life forever.

Chapter Fifty

In the vast terrain of the desert, Yousef's caravan of three vehicles left the area and made their way from his camp. The drivers of the three SUVs were instructed to travel as quickly as possible in three diverse directions. Each driver knew that the Americans had their sights on one—if not on all three—of their cars. Each driver said a silent prayer; they knew they had a one-in-three chance of getting blown up but they were willing to die for Yousef. It would have been a greater honor to die with Yousef. They each pressed the full weight of their body on the gas pedal.

At that very moment, at SOCOM, General Norton and the others followed a singular car through the "eyes" of a military drone flying miles above. The drone soon lost sight of the other two vehicles. Unknowingly, at that moment, the men in those two other cars had made their escape.

The target vehicle was now making its way through a small village. There were women and children scattered throughout. Thousands of miles away, at Langley, CIA operatives had the very same image displayed on their large screen. A CIA operative issued the command to strike.

Within moments, General Norton received the directive through his headset. Billy Assad was at his side. The general looked back at his attending JAG officer. The JAG officer paused to reflect and then gave his own legal assessment by lifting his thumb in approval.

"What about the casualties?" Billy Assad asked.

"They are all terrorist operatives," the general responded.

Billy Assad was vexed. "And if it is found out that they are *not?*"

"Then they will all be posthumously exonerated."

"Target on sight!" the twenty-three-year-old drone pilot in Nevada shouted.

"Fire at will," the general ordered.

The drone unleashed its weapon, appropriately named the Hellfire missile. The bomb violently incinerated the car that carried Yousef, engulfing the surrounding people in a fiery hell.

After watching the billowing smoke fill the screen for several moments, the drone pilot said, "Good kill."

"Good kill," repeated General Norton.

The whole room broke into cheers. Billy Assad, on the other hand, was somber, distraught. He had just witnessed an entire village—civilians, women, and children—decimated in the blink of an eye.

Chapter Fifty-one

At 9:59 p.m., Eastern Time, the president of the United States paced along down the Cross Hall on the first floor of the White House, following the red carpet to the lectern situated in front of the news camera. He reached the podium and waited for the signal from the director.

Three, two, one . . .

"Tonight I can report to the people of the United States and to the people of the world that the United States has conducted an operation that has killed the terrorist known as Yousef. The collective forces of our military, the CIA, and the FBI exhausted all their resources and spent many months searching and hunting down this criminal. At approximately 11:00 p.m., Yemen time, and 4:00 p.m., Eastern Time, a military drone successfully brought an end to this man's reign of terror."

The president went on to speak for several more minutes using the same charm and charisma that had gotten him elected. Yousef was dead, and the president's party would later win the midterm elections by a landslide, and history would show that on that night, by virtue of his announcement, the president was virtually reelected at the next general election.

Chapter Fifty-two

In the ensuing days, television networks all over the world devoted every single minute of airtime reporting on Yousef's death. To many of the pundits' collective surprise, despite the president's overwhelming support, the reaction to Yousef's death was mixed.

How can we lawfully invade sovereign territory and kill one of its own citizens? How can we kill a foreign national without due process? How can we justify the use of military force without a formal declaration of war? The silent majority were all asking the same questions. The pundits were caught off guard, and it took them a whole week to be able to spin this in the president's favor. By week's end, any doubts that Yousef's death was illegal was eradicated, and the president was once again a hero.

As for the rest of the world, the response was not so heartwarming. There were many people mourning Yousef's death, but the greatest impact was felt by his followers; he had become a martyr for many of them. His acolytes throughout the world began to view his collection of recorded messages, attempting to decipher their secret meanings. In turn, self-appointed cell leaders sent out their own coded messages to the countless followers spread out internationally. Soldiers, police officers, pilots, doctors, and everyday citizens from every nation were told to prepare for the final attack.

Those messages made their way to America and were received loud and clear.

Chapter Fifty-three

At SOCOM, Billy Assad and his team of operatives cut short their celebration when one of the CIA operatives grimly notified them of a slew of newly intercepted messages. The agents surmised that a large wave of attacks was going to take place soon.

Billy Assad excused himself and returned to his office to momentarily compose himself. He was exhausted and had not slept in days. This new batch of messages was not something Billy wanted to hear. He closed the door behind him and sat at his desk. He rested his head on his forearms to take a brief respite. On his far wall, he had four television screens, each on a different network. They were all airing the news story of Yousef's death, but on one of the screens, the words *Breaking News* interrupted the current story.

Billy Assad was fast asleep, oblivious to the alert. The scene on one of his screens changed to a news reporter who was reporting live from London, England. Behind the reporter, crime scene tape surrounded a body covered by a white sheet. The reporter gazed into the camera and delivered his story.

"Reporting from Sussex, law enforcement officials have found the body of a young teenage male. While the preliminary results are still pending, sources indicate that this is the work of the same serial killer who has been plaguing the streets of London for the last several months . . ."

The citizens of London were affixed to their television screens and would live in fear for the next several weeks, but for Billy Assad and the majority of Americans, this news was a nonissue in that this serial killer was wreaking havoc over three thousand miles away.

Book Two

Chapter Fifty-four

Present Day
London, England

Charlie Murphy was born in the West End of Edinburgh, the child of two wealthy parents. His father was a banker and his mother an accountant; money was never an issue in his household. He was an only child and was spoiled to be sure.

Life was good for Charlie up until he was ten years old. His father was embroiled in a scandal and was accused of embezzling nearly a million pounds. Although never formally charged, his father was forced to resign from the bank he had worked in for the last twelve years. For the next year, the threat of being charged with a crime loomed over his father's head. The elder Murphy was forced to short-sale their home to pay for the city's best lawyer. The family had to move to a one-bedroom apartment.

Depression forced his father to drink. One day he took his car for a drive and was never seen again. Rumors abounded that he had secretly chartered a boat to Costa Rica. Officially, he had committed suicide by drowning in the Water of Leith, a few kilometers from where his car was last seen. His mother became despondent and relied on antidepressants.

Eventually, protective services were forced to place Charlie in a foster home. His mother would later slit her wrists.

By eleven, Charlie had become depressed himself and became a truant from school. Up until he was sixteen years old, he was placed from group home to foster home and then back to group home to start the cycle again. He found heroin and alcohol. He prostituted himself to support his habit. He wanted to change, but he had no one left to help him.

At eighteen, he wanted to leave Scotland and start a new life. He hitchhiked and train-hopped all the way to London. A trucker was kind enough to take him on the final leg of his journey into the city, dropping him off a block away from St. Ermin's Hotel. He had only been in the city for a few hours when he ran into the dark stranger.

Charlie last remembered panhandling a fifty-pence coin from a friendly tourist, and he wandered around, looking for a convenience store in the hopes of buying a soft drink. It was his first time in London, and he had no idea where he was going. He wandered on until he made his way to St. James's Park. He perched himself by a tree and fell sound asleep.

He had no idea what time it was, but it had to be past midnight when he awoke. The streets were quiet, and it was cold. He struggled to work up enough energy to make his way down the streets. Charlie had not touched a drug in over two days, but his anxiety was building up, and he was craving some relief. He did not want to prostitute himself, but he knew he would not be able to survive with only fifty pence.

That was when he first saw the dark stranger. The stranger was tall and handsome, and they had a clear attraction to each other. No words were exchanged, but the kindness in the stranger's eyes brought Charlie some comfort. Charlie took the man's hands and followed him to a car.

*　　*　　*

Charlie had no memory of the blow to his head, but when he awoke from his unconsciousness, he could feel the blood oozing from his temple. His left eye was swollen shut, and his other eye could only see in various states of blur. He was lying naked on the ground, feet bound together, handcuffed to a metal cot. There was a singular light hanging from the ceiling. It barely lit the room.

He knew he had been violated. He could feel the blood seeping from his rectum. With what was left of his good eye, he could barely make out a figure moving around in the adjacent room. The blurry figure was moving back and forth through the door frame. It was the stranger. He was naked. He had shiny metal objects in his hands.

Charlie started to wail. "P-please, mister! Please let me go! I won't say anything."

His cries went unheeded. The stranger continued to pace back and forth within the other room. Charlie continued to cry. He soiled the floor from fear. The stranger stopped pacing. There was silence, not even a sound from the other room. Charlie held his breath, hoping to hear something. There was nothing.

Please, God, make the bad man go away.

Charlie caught his breath and heard some rumblings in the other room. It was the sound of metal banging together. Suddenly, the light in the other room was off—more metal. Charlie saw a hand come from around the corner and turn off the light switch. The entire place went dark. It did not take very long for Charlie's eye to adjust to the darkness. He had never been more terrified. The stranger rushing toward him was the last image he saw before blacking out again.

*   *   *

The last time Charlie woke up, he was lying inside a bloodstained bathtub. He knew the blood was his own. The pain from breathing was unbearable. He looked down to see that he had stab wounds all over his body. Blood was dripping from everywhere. Charlie was too weak to cry. He was about to pass out again. His final vision was of the stranger hovering over him, naked, about to violate Charlie again.

Chapter Fifty-five

Nothing could have prepared the Scotland Yard police officers for the sight. The officers surrounded the remains of the young man and were disgusted. One of the officers vomited his breakfast; the others felt lightheaded. The body had been dismembered and clearly violated in ways in which only the most perverse would take gratification.

The young officers had not been trained in how to investigate this kind of murder. All they could do was cordon off the area until more seasoned detectives could take over. Dawn was about to break, and the rising sun would not bring any comfort to the young men but would only fully expose the brutal massacre that had occurred.

* * *

Moments before dawn, a black stretch limousine was pulled over by the London police. The driver lowered his window and addressed the constable.

"Good morning," greeted the driver. "Is there a delay?"

"Excuse the interruption. The road ahead is the subject of an investigation," the constable answered. "I suggest you take the alternate route to the left."

The driver was about to protest when he was interrupted by the passenger, seated in the back seat.

"Driver, I suggest that you follow the command of the good constable."

The constable recognized the passenger as James St. John-Smythe, a thirty-two-year-old aristocrat. St. John-Smythe lowered the window, allowing the constable to gaze inside the back seat. The constable poked his head through the window to see that St. John-Smythe was surrounded by two sleeping women. Based on their formal dress, it was clear that they had come from a night of formal dining and excessive drinking.

The constable smiled at the young aristocrat and pleaded his apology.

"Nonsense," said St. John-Smythe ever so eloquently.

With that, the aristocrat was allowed to leave. The chauffer dutifully drove the large sleek limousine down the streets of London, making his way to the M5 and taking the exit leading to Gloucester Hill. The driver continued to make his way to an exorbitantly large home situated on over four hectares of land: Wyndham Court. The driver parked the vehicle at the end of an elongated driveway, where they were immediately confronted by a group of men in black suits. *MIBs*.

St. John-Smythe exited the vehicle, leaving the sleeping women inside the car. One of the MIBs escorted him into the mansion and then into a large study. Standing in the middle of the study were two elders, dressed similarly as the men who had escorted St. John-Smythe. Naturally, these two men were much older than the rest and were regal in appearance and in demeanor. They also appeared much more menacing.

One of the two elders was at least seventy years of age, but his strong physical stature made him appear much younger than his true age. His name was Sébastien. He spoke angrily at St. John-Smythe. "They found another dead body. What do you know about it?"

"Sébastien, what are you implying?" St. John-Smythe appeared taken aback and was just as angry in his response. "I've been out frolicking with my companions. Ask the chauffeur if you don't believe me."

It was at that moment that the other elder stepped forward and spoke. "We did. We called the driver earlier this morning, and there was a four-hour gap where he had not seen you." This man was named Ducard, and he was equal in size as the first elder and perhaps just as old but carried his intimidation out in front of him.

"Ducard! Really? The chauffer said *that?* I want him fired immediately!" St. John-Smythe screamed.

Sébastien reacted violently by grabbing St. John-Smythe by the throat. "You are an insolent whelp. Don't you realize how important you are to mankind?"

"I do," St. John-Smythe wheezed, "and that is why you should unhand me."

"You're disgracing your bloodline!" Sébastien barked.

"What are you talking about?" St. John-Smythe asked.

"*The body!*" Sébastien screamed. "They found the dead body! This is the third one in six months!"

"The authorities cannot prove anything. Now unhand me!" St. John-Smythe forced Sébastien's hand from his throat.

Sébastien quickly composed himself. "I'm not the only one you need to worry about. *We* have spent decades painstakingly sorting through the bloodline to find you. And don't you think for one bloody minute that *we* have not spent another decade to find another suitable replacement."

St. John-Smythe was no longer recalcitrant. "I don't doubt that, but I know exactly what my role is for mankind. I certainly don't think you want to have to wait another twenty to fifty years to find someone who can fulfill his destiny to mankind." St. John-Smythe straightened out his suit and began his climb up the long stairs to his room. "I'm tired. I have a full day of festivities and functions ahead of me, and I need my rest." He took his time walking up the extravagant staircase up to his bedroom but suddenly stopped at the top and turned to the elders. "Oh, and I want that chauffeur *terminated*."

Within moments, Sébastien and Ducard were joined by the other elders, who had been observing from the darkness of another room. The group of elders moved into a large hall and converged at the center of it.

Sébastien spoke. "This is not at all what we expected. After all these years, we've failed. He doesn't even care that we know all about him."

"The world need not know of his . . . *imperfections*," Ducard replied.

"He's a disgrace to the bloodline," Sébastien protested. "I want nothing to do with his *presentment*. I would rather he die by my hand—"

"We mustn't be so brash, my brother," Ducard interrupted. "He's far more important than you seem to realize."

"I will never forget the importance of all this," Sébastien defended. "Like you, I made a blood oath since I was a young man to protect the bloodline. But the bloodline was meant to bring salvation to humanity and not shame. We should not have abandoned our *original* plan. With more time, we could have made it work. It's not too late to seek out the others. He cannot be allowed to continue."

"*More time?*" Ducard inquired. "Have you seen the state of the world? There is war, hunger, poverty, and terrorists threatening the world. Every day we are one step closer to self-destruction. Your *plan* was doomed to fail from inception. James will fulfill his destiny, and I will not let anything or *anyone* stand in his way." Ducard's anger was seemingly directed at Sébastien.

"You dare threaten me?" Sébastien asked.

"You are an elder, a brother. There's no threat. I am simply reminding you of our sacred vow. You would have said the same."

"I will not stand in your way," Sébastien said reluctantly. "But I cannot and will not tolerate his *imperfections*."

"Very well," Ducard said, heading out of the hall. "We are in agreement then. We do nothing to alter the presentment." Ducard continued on his way, but before exiting through the door, he looked at the others, "And don't forget. Terminate the chauffeur—and the two girls."

Chapter Fifty-six

James St. John-Smythe had been confined to his room of Wyndham Court, the outside of which was guarded by two burly MIBs. The directive from the elders was twenty-four-hour watch in shifts of twelve. Until the hysteria of the most recent discovery of the body subsided, James was not allowed to leave his room under any circumstances. His room was the equivalent of a hotel suite—rooms within rooms and a large bedroom, with its own bathroom and kitchen, all the amenities and sustenance needed to keep James comfortable for a month—but there was nothing that would satiate James's desire for nearly that long.

James paced around his room, sulking like a petulant child. He fell back on his bed and turned on the television. The only thing that he found worthy to watch, albeit for a few moments, was a new story on an international terrorist who went by the name of Yousef. Someone identified as the terrorist's mother gave an impassioned plea for her son's life. After those few moments, he became bored again.

He elected to give one last channel a try when the local news was warning the denizens of London to be wary of a suspected serial killer roaming its streets. This brought a smile to James's face. However, there was one aspect of the story that did bother him: the killer was being compared to Jack the Ripper.

"No, no, no!" James reacted angrily, punching his fist against the wall. He yelled into the television screen. "Jack the Ripper was a novice compared to me! How dare you compare *him* to me!"

He went over to his study and removed a sheet of stationary. He had on his desk an old-fashioned typewriter; he had envisioned that one day he would need it for this very purpose. He sat down at his desk and began to type. Within a few minutes, he was done. James was smiling again. Images of his victims began circle the edges of his vision, and he was becoming aroused. He needed to go out again. It was time.

Chapter Fifty=seven

The homeless man had been offered one hundred pounds if he delivered a letter to Portland Place, the broadcasting house for the BBC. The vagabond did as he was paid to do; then he returned to his bicycle and rode off. The receptionist at the front desk was not sure what to do with the unmarked envelope and called for her supervisor. The supervisor held it to the light and saw that it simply contained a harmless note. The supervisor, in turn, handed it to the on-duty producer.

Betty was a twenty-five-year-old communications major who had landed the career of a lifetime: a BBC producer. When she read the contents of the letter, she knew she was sitting on the story of the decade—if not of the century. She reached over to the receptionist's phone and called her executive producer.

"S-Sally," Betty said nervously, "I have something in my hands that will blow your mind." She listened to her boss. "No, it cannot wait 'til later. It has to air tonight! I'll meet you in your office and summon one of the writers. Oh, and, Sally, cancel the top story."

Betty made it to her executive producer in less than a minute. Sally was surrounded by a team of producers and writers.

"This better be good." Sally read the letter to herself, and two minutes later, she cried out in joy.

"How do we know it's legitimate?" one of the producers asked aloud.

"It has to be," Betty responded quickly. "It has one or two details that the public at large doesn't know about."

"Like what?"

"That the killer had sex with his victims *after* he killed them."

Sally was visibly shocked. "And how would *you* know of these details?"

Betty blushed. "Let's just say I have been having intimate conversations with an officer working on the case."

"Well, this intimate secret better be true. We don't have time to verify this letter." Sally took a moment to read the letter once again. She looked up and said to the producers, "Run it."

*   *   *

By the six o'clock airing, the top story of Yousef's death had been bumped for a new story. The BBC had in their possession a letter written by London's own serial killer. The letter was typewritten and was only a paragraph long. The news anchor spent nearly the bulk of the program summarizing the killer's victims for the last six months and then discussed the contents of the letter. By the end of the program, news sources all over the world had received photocopies of the same letter. The letter would only bring more fear to the good people of London:

> To the journalists of the world,
>
> Greetings and salutations. You have witnessed my master work and know that I am not to be trifled with. You have taken great joy in comparing me to the antiquated Jack the Ripper, and while his work has been the subject of folklore and legends, his actions do not compare to mine. While his victims were dissected for nothing more than a great curiosity, I, on the other hand, have taken the time to eviscerate my victims for nothing more than simple pleasure. I take great joy in violating my victims both before *and* after. While Jack the Ripper may have said that he gave birth to

the twentieth century, I will bring about death and destruction to the epoch of man. And as a result, I ask that you kindly refrain from comparing me to—and naming me after—a pale version of what I am. If you grant me this one wish, no harm will ever befall you or your loved ones. Henceforth, call me *the Sinner.*

Yours sincerely,

From that moment on, the killer was given the nomenclature of his choosing.

The Sinner.

Chapter Fifty-eight

The wretched London fog was unusually thick on this predawn morning and permeated the entire city. On one of the city streets walked a singular person, a police constable. Officer Frost had always suffered from asthma as a child, and the filthy smog only made him regret enlisting as a law enforcement officer. The officer meandered his way down the cobblestone road, counting the hours before his shift ended.

Not more than a block away, he saw what he thought to be a lovely couple engaging in a romantic interlude. *But at four o'clock in the morning?* the constable thought. As romantic as it was to see the two men embrace each other in the cold, the streets were not safe at this hour, even if the two men looked capable of defending themselves from any attack.

The constable cut through the smog and reached out to break them apart when he shockingly realized that one of the young men appeared lifeless and was simply being held up by the other. The murderer, now no longer able to hide his ghastly deed, forcefully threw the dead boy into the arms of the officer. The constable, startled by the sight of the dead body, stood frozen in complete shock. The murderer frantically ran into the darkened streets and was successful in evading his custody.

The constable had never seen a dead body, much less held one in his arms. This victim was only seventeen years old.

Chapter Fifty-nine

Sébastien had been sitting quietly in his study for several hours, reading his prized possession of the first edition of *Die Leiden des jungen Werthers*, when he decided that he had read enough and was about to turn in for the night. He closed the book, and from the corner of his eye, he was suddenly stunned by the sight of the bloodstained presence of James St. John-Smythe.

"You are covered with blood!" Sébastien yelled. "You fool! How did you get out of your room?" Seeing the blood on James's clothing only made him more enraged. "You couldn't even control your insatiable appetite long enough to take your prey to your hideout, could you?" The old man flew from his chair, grabbed James by his arms, and pushed him against the solid oak bookshelf, knocking many of the antiquated books onto the floor. Realizing his anger, the old man released his grip.

James was trembling in fear. "My hideout? How did you—"

"Enough! We need to get you out of these clothes before the authorities discover your actions."

"I left the body behind—and there was a witness." James was shaking uncontrollably.

"A *witness?*" the elder man in black exclaimed.

"Yes," James stammered. "A British bobby."

"Bloody hell!"

James was trembling to the point where he was convulsing. "I'm scared."

"I'll handle it," Ducard said as he entered the room, demonstrating that he was clearly in control. "We are going to have to change plans."

"What do you mean?" James asked, trembling as he stood idly by.

"We will have to make your *presentation* sooner than expected."

Chapter Sixty

Insp. Michael Llewelyn had been an inspector with Scotland Yard for over two decades, half of that time with the homicide division, and he was nowhere near retirement. He was now at the scene of the latest murder, gazing at the dead body surrounded by a team of officers and crime technicians. This was the same area where the English bobby had, only hours before, encountered what he thought was one couple in the midst of an affectionate embrace. Now there were only the brutalized remains of another hapless victim of the serial killer.

Inspector Llewelyn immediately took control of the crime scene. His voice commanded respect as he spoke to the group of four inspectors. "Do we have a description of the perpetrator?"

"Only that the killer wore a hat and a long denim jacket," said Insp. Mathew Phillips, one of the younger detectives. Phillips was Llewelyn's most reliable junior partner.

"So you are saying we have no description."

"Correct," Phillips was embarrassed to say.

"Do we have anything at all?" Llewelyn had crouched to get a better view of the body.

Phillips lowered himself. "It appears to be the work of the Sinner, and the killer is becoming more brazen."

"What makes you say that?"

"He's never left any of the other bodies out in the open like this. He was clearly sending a message."

"Not likely," Inspector Llewelyn disagreed as he stood upright. "The others were tortured, sodomized, and then desecrated. If anything, he has become reckless, probably because of alcohol and/or drugs." Llewelyn pointed to the victim's arm. "The wristband establishes that it's very likely that this victim met his killer in a bar. He was caught by surprise. He wasn't able to finish his *work*, if you will. I suggest we check CCTV of every bar within a five-mile radius. I also think we'd best be suited to focus on placing undercover officers in all the bars in the area and to focus on highly inebriated subjects. His work was unfinished. He is unsatisfied, and so he will be seeking to consummate his pleasure. But this recklessness could be our best lead."

The inspector gazed toward the eastern horizon. It was dawn, and the sun was about to rise. Llewelyn shook his head in frustration. To his disgust, he saw a group of vans pulling up.

"Oh no, not the press!" he exclaimed.

He motioned for Inspector Phillips to stay behind and secure the crime scene while he walked toward the reporters as they hurried to set up their cameras. Llewelyn hated talking to the press more than anything, but preserving the integrity of his investigation was paramount to anything else. He was about to approach one of the reporters when suddenly, a microphone was thrust into his face.

"Inspector, could please tell us the identity of the victim?" asked a reporter.

"Do you have any idea as to who the murderer may be?" asked another.

"Please," pleaded the inspector, "allow me to speak. This is obviously the early stages of our investigation. We cannot say anything other than that Scotland Yard will pull all its resources in keeping our community safe. I ask that everyone stay vigilant and notify the police if you see anything unusual. Thank you, and that is all for now."

On that note, Llewelyn returned to his crime scene, leaving behind the screams of the reporters.

Llewelyn soon rejoined Inspector Phillips and the others. He knew that this was going to be a long day and that the Sinner was most certainly one of his most difficult cases in his career. As he contemplated his next move, Llewelyn stared down at the lifeless boy, and he knew that that ghastly image would haunt him forever.

*   *   *

Throughout London, people were staring, shocked, at their television screens, terrified at the notion that there was a killer loose on the streets. However, there was one person who was overjoyed as he watched Llewelyn speak: James St. John-Smythe. He felt challenged by the inspector. He felt compelled to reach out to him.

Chapter Sixty=one

The detectives of the Homicide Bureau of Scotland Yard had been working full-time since the discovery of the first victim. It had been six long months, and they were no closer to identifying the killer than they had been on the first day. Each team of detectives covered a different aspect of the investigation. One team handled all the tips and followed up on every lead; another team was responsible for supervising the forensics, trying to match up any fingerprint and DNA found at the scenes of each crime. The remaining team conducted field interviews of each and every citizen (especially all known registered sex offenders) living in the surrounding areas where every victim was found. Supervising them all was Inspector Llewelyn.

Each detective was expected to pull twelve to sixteen hours a day but were not shamed for going home to rest for a few hours. Llewelyn never went home, for he had no home, and that was no secret to the other detectives. Llewelyn had been married four times. Each marriage irretrievably broke because of his unbridled commitment to his job. Because of his well-earned reputation for hard work, he was given special permission to sleep in one of the empty offices that was modified by adding a bathroom with a shower. Llewelyn lived and breathed homicide investigations and would not have any other job. He turned down his last two promotions because it would have consigned him behind a desk. He was happy being an inspector.

At this moment, Llewelyn was painstakingly setting up a war room in the conference room adjacent to his office where his team of detectives could meet on a daily basis. He refused any assistance so that his investigators could stay on task; he would go about it alone. Photocopies of every single report and supplement lay across the floor as he contemplated how best to organize them. No lead or tip was too frivolous, and every field interview must contain a piece of the very large and complex puzzle. He just needed the time to put it all together. *If only there were more hours to the day.*

He sat on the floor and was about to reread each report from the beginning when Inspector Phillips walked into the room.

"Inspector," his junior detective said softly. "Sorry to disturb, but there is a call for you."

Llewelyn looked at the phone on his desk. "I didn't hear my phone ring."

"No, sir. It apparently came in on the main switchboard."

"*Switchboard?* Is it another tip? Direct it to that unit."

"Sir, the caller asked for you personally."

Llewelyn was intrigued. He walked over to the desk and asked that the call be diverted to his extension. The phone rang, and he picked it up.

"Hello, this is Inspector Llewelyn speaking."

There was silence on the other hand.

"Hello?" he repeated.

His patience growing thin, Llewelyn was about to hang up when he heard a raspy voice coming from the other end. "Inspector? Inspector Llewelyn?"

"Yes, this is he."

"I want you to know that I saw you give your impromptu press conference. Very well done."

"Identify yourself," Llewelyn demanded.

"Let's just say I am going to be keeping you quite busy for a while."

"Is this the man who calls himself the Sinner?"

"Inspector, you do me great honor." The caller sounded pleased.

With that confirmation, Inspector Llewelyn gave Phillips a series of hand signals to get the rest of the crew and then put the call on speaker. While the voice resonated on the speaker, the entire team of detectives were listening and frantically taking notes.

"Can *everyone* hear me okay?" The caller noticed the change in background noise.

"What do you mean?" Llewelyn feigned ignorance. "It's only you and I—"

"Ahhh, Inspector, please do not insult me . . . ever again," the voice said sternly.

The very sound of his shrewd voice coming out of the speakers sent chills up the arms of everyone listening.

"My apologies," Llewelyn said. The inspector then pointed to one of his technicians to begin the trace of the call.

I'm on it, the technician mouthed as he nodded.

"Sir, when can we meet?" the inspector asked.

"Wouldn't you like that? But I can tell you the answer. *Never.* You will never have the occasion to meet me, but I have seen you."

The inspector listened carefully, trying to make out any distinctive features of his voice. There was no mechanical distortion, but the caller clearly was disguising his true voice.

"If we cannot meet, then what can I do to convince you to put an end to the madness?"

The caller laughed. "My good sir, I will never stop."

"Then why are you calling?"

"Because I wanted you to get to know me."

"Can you at least tell me why you are doing this?"

"Ah, the best way to answer that is with scripture." The caller paused and took in a deep breath. "'I do not understand what I do. For what I want to do, I do not do, but what I hate, I do. And if I do what I do not want to do, I agree that the law is good. As it is, it is no longer I myself who do it, but it is sin living in me. For I know that good itself does not dwell in me—that is, in my sinful nature. For I have the desire to do what is good, but I cannot carry it out. For I do not do the good I want to do but the evil I do not want to do—this, I keep on doing. Now if I do what I do not want to do, it is no longer I who do it, but it is sin living in me that does it.'"

"I never went to catechism school," said the inspector. "I don't know the Bible."

"Romans 7:15–20."

"Nope. Doesn't ring a bell," Llewelyn said smugly.

"It's too bad," the caller said. "Maybe *you* should be called the Sinner."

"Why don't you just tell me who you are?" Llewelyn's anger gave his game away.

"My, my, Inspector. Such a temper. I thought we could become friends."

"Then why the charade?" said the inspector, no longer disguising his temper.

"This is not a game, Inspector." The caller had also revealed his anger. "This is life and death."

"Then why are you calling me?"

"Because I am trying to taunt you. I will continue to kill, and you will never find me. Do you remember the letter I wrote to the press about being compared to *Jack the Ripper?*"

Annoyed, Llewelyn mumbled something incoherent. He received a hand signal from his technician to keep the caller talking. "Yes, I remember," said Llewelyn.

"Well, maybe I was a little rough on the press. Perhaps I'll apologize to them later, but I was a little honored by the comparison. Did you know that Hitler was conceived the night of Mary Ann Nichols's death? A sacrifice was made by one murder in honor of another—"

"My apologies, but you are rambling." Llewelyn could no longer hide his impatience. "You are making no sense. What do you want from us?"

"I want you to fear me!" The voice was angry. The caller was breathing heavily. "I was trying to engage in small talk, and now you have offended me. You will no longer hear from me, and whatever hopes you may have had in catching me are now gone. I bid you all a good night."

The line went dead. The entire team of detectives looked at Llewelyn with disapproval. He made no apologies.

"Did you get a trace?" he said, turning to the technician.

"No," the technician said, disappointed. "There wasn't enough time."

"I doubt we would have had a successful trace. This man sounded too sophisticated. He most assuredly would have a device to block our tracers. We will have to find him with good old-fashioned detective work." Llewelyn returned to his war room, leaving the crew to their tasks.

Chapter Sixty-two

The streets of London had been quiet for three weeks. The citizens of London were beginning to feel unconcerned about the killer among them. During those weeks, the denizens were distracted from the horror of the Sinner by the emergence of a new celebrity: a dashing young man who stood over six feet tall, with fair skin, blond hair, and piercing green eyes. The media would come to call him a "rising star" and "the world's most eligible bachelor."

Nobody knew where James St. John-Smythe came from, only that he suddenly appeared at many of the world's greatest social events. He was first noticed at the Cannes Film Festival in France and then seen at the Milan Fashion Week in Italy and later at many other events in New York, Chicago, and Los Angeles.

James St. John-Smythe eventually made his debut on every existing social media outlet, quickly amassing over a million followers. His loyal fan base followed his every move. People all over the world were so smitten with this new celebrity that they all but forgot the troubles of the world. There was no more fear of wars, terrorists such as Yousef, or serial killers. For a total of three months, this new celebrity consumed the airwaves with headlines such as "Who is he?" "Where did he come from?" "Who is he dating now?" "Who is he wearing?"

The only thing the world knew was that his name was James St. John-Smythe, but one Monday morning the news headlines promised that within five days, the world would come to truly know who this mysterious man really was. During those ensuing days, all the new outlets were promoting what was promised to be a history-making, worldwide event.

Chapter Sixty-three

The BBC television crew had spent three hours preparing the library/study of the enormous mansion known as Wyndham Court. The world-renowned station had, for weeks, been promoting a once-in-a-lifetime exclusive interview. The subject of the interview was the elder man in black, who was using his nom de guerre, Jean-Jacque Ducard.

The female reporter glared at her compact mirror for one last long minute. *God, I'm gorgeous*, she said to herself ever so proudly. If she could kiss herself, she would have. She closed the compact shut at the sound of a door. The door to the study was held open by a large ominous man dressed in black. Another MIB walked through and visually scanned the room. Several more MIBs walked in, and each man covered the various areas of the room. Finally, the prize interviewee himself, Ducard, walked into the room.

The reporter immediately gawked at the men, noticing that they were dressed in the same uniquely fitted dark suits, white cuff-linked shirts, and black ties. However, there was something about Mr. Ducard, something so distinguishing and elegant that only served to set him apart from the other men. Despite his advanced age, she found Ducard to be beguiling. He had this air of superiority that she found to be so attractive. For the first time in her long and illustrious career, she was nervous—and visibly so, partly because it was predicted that her program was to be one of the highest rated programs in the world, partly because of this man.

"H-hello, I'm Felicity Kruger," she muttered, her hands trembling, so she chose not to shake his hand for fear he might notice.

She was in awe at his stature. He stood tall and proud and seemingly had the appearance of a man virile and youthful. For a man of his age, this was a masterful trick.

"I know who you are." Ducard spoke with confidence. "It is my pleasure to meet you."

His British accent was clearly the product of the finest university, and his voice was so mesmerizing that she now suddenly felt compelled to raise her hand. He shook it firmly.

"Mr. Ducard, I cannot tell you what an honor it is to finally meet with you. My producer and I spent months trying to secure this interview, and I . . . I'm quite honestly in shock that I'm finally here with you."

Ducard motioned to the couch. "Please sit."

"Yes, thank you. We go live in about twenty minutes. I think my producer explained to you that the first few minutes or so, we will be airing a prerecorded segment that I recorded yesterday. Once that is over, the director will cue us when we are live. We will go on with our interview without breaking for several minutes. Then we will hear from some commentators, who will be appearing remotely, and then finally close with a prerecorded comment that I also filmed yesterday. After that, we will be out of your way."

"Please take your time."

"T-thank you." She smiled.

There was an awkward moment of silence. She spent it staring into his blue eyes. Eventually, the director gave Felicity the one-minute sign. Ducard and Felicity sat back and waited until the opening theme to her show began to play. On a video screen situated a few feet away, they could see the opening to her show. Within seconds, a montage of still and video images of James St. John-Smythe appeared on the screen; these were random shots of James as he gallivanted around the world. A moment or two into the footage, Felicity's voiceover started.

"James St. John-Smythe—even his name evokes an aura of mystery, a name as mysterious as the man himself. This man virtually came out of nowhere, appearing in the limelight for the first time only a few months ago. He was first spotted at a Parisian nightclub with an entourage of over twenty men, where he spent over tens of thousands of pounds in food and drinks. He quickly made the French papers. The next night, he was seen at another Parisian club spending twice as much. The paparazzi didn't know who he was but soon began to follow him as he partied throughout Europe. He was photographed in bars and clubs in Rome, Barcelona, Munich, and London, spending exorbitant amounts of money. Everyone had been craving to know as much as they can about him. After an impromptu encounter outside a London bar, yours truly was finally able to put a name to his lovely face. *James St. John-Smythe.* And even though the world has now come to know his name, they still do not know anything about his origin or the source of his wealth. He has established himself as the world's most eligible bachelor. It was discovered that he attended Fettes College and then studied at St. John's College and at the University of Oxford, graduating with a second-class honors BA in jurisprudence. He joined a prestigious international law firm, focusing on international human rights law, logging countless hours of pro bono work. St. John-Smythe made his first 'professional' appearance as a UNICEF spokesperson for youth and then went on to become a UNICEF goodwill ambassador. He also would serve as a special advisor for global youth issues. He would go on to write several essays, op-eds, and other pieces for periodicals all over the world. And as a tribute to all his good work, he has been awarded several humanitarian awards and honorary doctorates by several universities and has been nominated for the Nobel Peace Prize. He has led an impressive life indeed—and all at the very tender age of thirty-two."

The monitor then displayed a prerecorded video of Felicity sitting in a studio. "Tonight we are going to interview the man behind the curtain, as it were. The man behind this young man's rise to glory, the source of his wealth—Jean-Jacques Ducard."

Ducard watched as the television monitor switched to show images of him that had been surreptitiously taken throughout the last several days as he ventured into the London town and dined at the finest restaurants. He listened as the prerecorded voice of Felicity Kruger continued.

"Mr. Ducard is somewhat of an enigma himself. All that we know of this mysterious benefactor is that he is a European aristocrat living on the rich estate of Wyndham Court. And tonight, for the first time, I will interview Mr. Ducard in the hopes of unveiling the mystery of James St. John-Smythe."

The director then gave the signal that they were about to go live. Felicity looked at the camera. Her nervousness was all but gone as her professionalism took over. A mere moment passed, and she was now reporting live.

"We are here live at one of the beautiful palatial mansions here in Windlesham, England, and with me is international philanthropist and business financier Jean-Jacques Ducard, who is here to present what promises to be an earth-shattering story of perhaps biblical proportions. For weeks, advanced press releases and leaks have revealed that this man, James St. John-Smythe, will be the center of what will most certainly be the most controversial story of the century. Specifically, Mr. Ducard will proffer that St. John-Smythe is a royal member of the Merovingian dynasty. For those of you who are not familiar with the legend, several books have hypothesized that a bloodline from Jesus and Mary Magdalene eventually became the Merovingian dynasty. You heard me correctly—an heir to Jesus Christ." She paused for effect and then turned to Ducard. "I'd like to start off by asking—are you a member of that secret society known as the Priory of Sion?"

Ducard chuckled. "Heavens, no. The priory has had a long and illustrious history but only in works of fiction. My organization dates back to the First Crusade, starting with the creation of the Knights Templar, and is a fraternal organization made up of descendants from *the* original Knights Templar. We are not part of *that* fictional group, but we are sworn to identify and protect the descendants of Jesus."

"This is remarkable!" she exclaimed. "Descendants of Jesus! That *is* the stuff of movies."

"Not really," Ducard continued. "This is not a new concept. As early as the thirteenth century, a Cistercian monk claimed this same belief as part of the Catharist belief that the earthly Jesus Christ had a relationship with Mary Magdalene. In 1886, a book called *Les Evangiles sans Dieu* described the historical Jesus as having married Mary Magdalene and that both had traveled to the south of France, where they had a son. In the 1970s, a Kashmiri man came forward and claimed to be a Kashmiri descendant of Jesus."

At that moment, for the world to see, the television prompter presented a graphical chart that had been previously provided by Ducard to the producers. The chart was animated and displayed an extensive genealogical tree that appeared to extend back nearly two thousand years.

Ducard pointed to the chart. "For many generations, my organization has painstakingly examined centuries of birth records to compile this family tree. As the audience at home can see, the pedigree chart establishes and confirms that Jesus and Mary Magdalene are the ancestors of all the European royal families of the Common Era. As a result, we have been able to trace a direct bloodline from Jesus and Mary Magdalene and its relationship with the Merovingians as well as with their modern descendants—the House of Habsburg, the Grand Ducal Family of Luxembourg, the Clan Sinclair, the House of Stuart, the House of Cavendish, the House of Bourbon, the House of Orléans, as well as numerous other noble families."

The animated chart spanned through various lineages and countless families before culminating in one very familiar name.

"And as you can see, while there may be thousands of descendants, Mr. St. John-Smythe is the most recently discovered heir. It took us many decades to find his parents, only to discover that they were killed in a tragic accident. We found James St. John-Smythe in a foster home being raised by a kind but poor family. Our fraternal organization took him in under our supervision, and we raised him the best that we could. We paid for his finest education and groomed him to be the best of the best."

"And why has your organization taken the time to compile these charts and look for him?" Felicity asked.

"It has always been our belief that the direct descendant of Jesus will eventually emerge as a great man, a great monarch who will govern a holy European empire. And we believe that man to be James St. John-Smythe.”

“Are you suggesting that James will be interpreted as a mystical second coming of Christ?

Ducard smiled. “Good lord, not at all. Those are matters of faith. I’m just here to tell you that Mr. St. John-Smythe will be a very important man. As you know, he has already been involved in philanthropy, raising millions for charity and donating his own time and money toward helping the less fortunate. What we are saying is that he will continue doing all that—and more.”

“So when will he make his formal introduction?” Felicity asked.

“Soon. Very soon. He is currently on a goodwill trip to Angola, opening up a new school and a hospital, and will return shortly.”

“This is an incredible revelation.” Felicity was genuinely astonished. She then turned to face the camera and the countless viewers watching all over the world. “I cannot thank you enough for being on our show, and I’m sure I speak for the entire world when I say we are looking forward to officially meeting this young man. Now we have appearing remotely two guests who would like to share their thoughts on this subject.”

She turned to face the live video feed of two men who were appearing via split screen from two different locations: a Catholic priest from Rome and a Baptist minister from Galveston, Texas.

“We have Fr. O’Farrill, official spokesperson for the Roman Catholic Church, and Rev. Tom Martin of the Family Worship Council appearing on your screens. Welcome to the show, gentlemen. Fr. O’Farrill, let’s start off with your thoughts.”

From the Vatican, the priest could be seen shaking his head in disbelief. He was clearly angry. “No mainstream Christian denomination has ever adhered to a *Jesus bloodline hypothesis* as a dogma or as an object of religious devotion. We strictly maintain that Jesus is God incarnate and was perpetually celibate, continent, and chaste. Make no mistake. Jesus died, was resurrected, ascended to heaven, and will eventually return to Earth, thereby making all this, Jesus bloodline hypothesis and related messianic expectations, impossible—”

The Protestant evangelical minister, speaking from his home office, interrupted the priest, pointing his finger as if it were in Ducard's face. "What this man is spewing is blasphemous. He shouldn't be allowed to speak such vile things on the world stage. If both Mr. *Du-card* and this St. John-Smythe are going to continue spreading these immoral and sacrilegious lies, then they're to be condemned as heretics, and they should both be destroyed."

"*Destroyed?*" Felicity repeated, surprised. "Surely, you cannot be serious."

"My dear," the minister responded, "I have never been more serious. We believe that the Antichrist, prophesied in the Book of Revelation, plans to present himself as a descendant from the Davidic line to bolster his false claim that he is the Jewish Messiah. If this man is going to come forward and make such a claim, then yes, he must be destroyed!"

There was shock on Felicity's face. From his home office in Texas, the minister suddenly rose to his feet and shouted obscenities at Ducard, vowing to have his army of Christian soldiers hunt down both him and St. John-Smythe until they were dead. All the uncensored threats were aired on live television.

The director cut off the minister's audio and irately screamed into Felicity's earpiece, "Get ready to cut back to you!"

Felicity acknowledged the command and turned to face where Ducard had been sitting, but the old man had long since been gone, scurried away by his team of men. The room was empty and silent. Felicity was speechless.

After eight years of broadcast service, Felicity had never been so embarrassed. The director ordered her to announce a commercial break, but when the camera went off, the entire show had now been preempted by an infomercial hosted by a silly old man selling a juicer that was guaranteed to extend one's life. Felicity could hear the commercial playing from her earpiece. Both she and her producer stared at each other. They did not know what to do or what to say, but when they saw the team of darkly clad men march back in, they knew one thing for sure—they had to leave.

Chapter Sixty-four

"I did not authorize this press conference!" There was violence in Sébastien's words. "Moreover, the council did not authorize this! We were not ready for the presentment!"

During the tirade by the Texas minister, the contingent of men had stealthily moved Ducard to the library, where he was confronted by his brother.

"Actually," Ducard replied, "the council did approve of it."

"They did?" Sébastien was bewildered. "When?"

"A week ago."

"Why wasn't I informed?"

"Let's just say we knew what your position was going to be," Ducard commented. "Besides, we needed you to focus on handling some of James's *indiscretions.*"

Sébastien was livid. "This is intolerable! I don't support this! There was much more work to do, and we still haven't dealt with cleaning up *his* mess." He paused long enough to retrieve a newspaper article lying on the arm of a chair. "Have you read *this?*"

The headline read, *The Sinner Strikes Again.* Ducard ripped the paper from Sébastien's hands and discarded it into a waste basket. Sébastien was taken aback at Ducard's lack of concern.

"Where is James, by the way?" Sébastien wondered.

"Like I said in the interview, I have him doing some charity work in Angola—far away from his usual penchant for young lads. And don't worry. I've had his secret passage hidden within his closet sealed off. He shan't be sneaking out again."

Removing the article from the trash, Sébastien asked, "And what are you doing about *this* mess?"

"I've taken care of that," Ducard said quite confidently, almost too much so. "The police won't get too far in their investigation."

"How, may I ask?"

Ducard casually walked to the bar and served himself a healthy pour of vintage scotch: Macallan "M" single-malt. He turned to his brother and said, "That is my concern. You have other pressing matters to attend."

Sébastien was bewildered. "What could be more pressing?"

Ducard finished his drink in one large gulp. He poured himself another. "It appears that your failed little experiment from ages past has potentially come back to haunt us."

"What do you mean?"

"A few days ago, our spyware has detected that someone in Italy has been using a hotel internet searching for information on your failed refuge."

"*Refuge?* You don't mean the orph—" Sébastien stammered and was deeply confounded. "Certainly not *the* orphanage."

Ducard replaced his glass. "Yes, that misguided plan of yours. The one that ended in complete failure."

"That cannot be." Sébastien was in awe. "That was over thirty years ago." Sébastien turned to the other MIBs. "Pull the video from the hotel cameras and find out who it is."

"We have." Ducard removed a packet of blurry photographs and showed them to Sébastien.

Sébastien strained his eyes to make out the face on the image. It was a hazy photograph, but he ventured to guess it was the image of an American, perhaps of Jewish descent.

"His name is Seth Jacobson. He's a lawyer from America." Ducard started again. "We're checking the hotels now. We'll have his exact location in a matter of time. That little *project* from thirty years ago was *your* idea. This will be *your* mess to clean up." He threw the photographs at his brother's feet.

Sébastien was perplexed as he looked down at the ground. "It can't be. No one would know about *that*."

"Don't you think it too much of a coincidence that an American would be searching for information on *that* orphanage?"

Sébastien's silence was enough of acquiescence.

Ducard went on. "I'm afraid that *your* secret project is on the verge of being revealed."

*   *   *

At that very moment, hundreds of miles away, an American lawyer was running scared in the heart of Europe.

Chapter Sixty-five

At Scotland Yard, Inspector Llewelyn and his team of detectives were in his makeshift war room, staring at the wall covered with pictures of the various crime scenes and of the many young victims. It was way past the midnight hour, and they each felt that nothing had been accomplished, that they were no closer to uncovering the identity of the savage killer.

Llewelyn stood staring at the wall and proceeded to talk to his team, with them at his back. "It's clear that he murdered most of these victims at a secret location, had his way with them, and disposed of them where they could be found. If you look at the spots where the victims were located, they are only within a half-mile radius of one another." He paused long enough to draw a circle on the map pinned next to the photos. "That means, more than likely, that his secret location is within this parameter."

Phillips, his junior detective, chimed in. "That could mean his secret location is in any one of the many apartments, vacant buildings, and warehouses that are in that area. Locating it would be a daunting task."

"Precisely," Llewelyn responded. He lit a cigarette and directed his attention to another detective. "What about the videos I asked for?"

"Nothing. All the cameras from the various crime scenes have been reviewed, and nothing was captured."

Llewelyn angrily threw his cigarette to the ground. "Bloody hell!" He turned back to the map, scratching his head. He reached for another cigarette.

"I'm curious about this last crime scene. The officer came across the murderer mere moments after the victim had been killed. Now why wouldn't the killer wait to get his victim to his secret location?" Phillips asked.

"He is becoming more brazen, obviously," Llewelyn offered. "This is what serial killers do. His psychosis is pushing him to be more daring. He is searching for a feeling. He now feels the urge to do his deed as soon as possible. He won't stop until he dies or we catch him." Llewelyn examined the map even more closely. "Now we know that the victim was last seen in the gay bar an hour before his murder. And so assuming the victim encountered his killer within the bar and agreed to engage in sexual relations, where would they go? Outside?"

"I've never encountered that," the patrolman answered. "Those patrons are very sophisticated, upper-middle class, mostly. They would go to a more intimate location."

"I see." Llewelyn suddenly sounded more optimistic, so much so that the room of officers welcomed the change in his tone. "That would mean that he would have expected to go to his private flat. And so since they were walking in an easterly direction, maybe the flat would be within walking distance in that same direction. His urge prevented them from getting there—but maybe."

The men watched as Llewelyn drew a straight line toward the eastern section of the map.

"Well done, Detective," said a gruff voice coming from the rear of the room.

The voice belonged to Master Sergeant Downing. The officers rose to their feet out of respect.

"You have effectively narrowed down the area within a few apartment buildings."

Llewelyn acknowledged the compliment but was too tired to reply. Just then, a phone rang. The room went completely silent. Phillips answered it and listened intently to the caller. Within moments, the junior detective hung up the phone. He had a grim look on his face.

"Inspector, I regret to inform you, but there has been another killing."

Chapter Sixty-six

When Colin McDowell woke up in that strange and isolated room, he had no memory of how he had gotten there. His last memory was of being in a dance bar, dancing with some stranger. The stranger appeared vaguely familiar, even though he wore a wig covered by a knit hat. The two had danced for a couple of hours and shared a drink. Then he found himself naked on a steel cot with his arms chained to the headboard.

From the other room, he heard the muffled screams of another boy. Colin got scared. He tried to free himself from the shackles to the point where he bled from his wrists, yet he continued to struggle. The sudden silence of the young boy in the next room had given Colin a sudden surge of adrenaline. Colin focused his energy on the metal headboard. He was able to break one of the metal pipes. With that, he removed the handcuff from the metal and was free to make his escape.

He tiptoed across the room in hopes of not drawing the attention of his kidnapper. The only sound that came from the other room was grunts from the assailant. Colin imagined the horror that had been committed upon the victim. As Colin tried to walk quietly across, a floorboard creaked. That caused the assailant to stop his ecstatic moaning. Colin knew he only had a matter of minutes to escape. He was about to open the front door when his attacker came up from behind him and placed him in a bear hug. Colin struggled for his life. He jerked his head back and headbutted the attacker.

In that one moment, Colin was able to burst through the door, and he made his way down what seemed to be an endless flight of stairs. He somehow ended up on the street. Colin was dismayed that it was predawn and that the streets were empty. Colin screamed, but no one there heard him. He stood there in the middle of the street, naked, and begged for help, but he was all alone. The night was silent except for the faint footsteps of his attacker. The man no longer wore the hat or the wig, and it was only then that Colin recognized who his killer was.

Chapter Sixty-seven

The parade of police cars careened through the winding streets of London with lights and sirens brightening the predawn. The vehicles stopped in tandem at a side street already crowded with a mass of people. Llewelyn and his partner forced their way through the crowd to find the latest victim. The nude body had been horribly mutilated. Llewelyn and Phillips stood over the young man. They watched as an assistant coroner examined the body.

The coroner looked up at Llewelyn. "Inspector, I would surmise that he's only been dead for less than an hour."

"Who found him?" Llewelyn asked.

A rookie officer replied, "A vagrant actually discovered the body, but I was the first to arrive."

"Has he been identified?" Llewelyn turned to Phillips.

"Preliminarily," Phillips replied, looking at his notepad. "En route to here, I was told that forensics thinks he's a young man named McDowell. Colin McDowell."

Llewelyn began writing down his own notes. "Why?"

Phillips answered quickly. "His friends noticed that one minute, he was seen dancing with a man, and then . . . he was gone. They immediately sensed danger because he never did that kind of thing and reported his absence to management. After a bit of convincing, the manager, in turn, called law enforcement. The patrolmen were on their way to the club when the vagrant came across the body. The officers were diverted to this location."

"Did the vagrant see anyone?" Llewelyn asked.

"No."

Just then, Llewelyn noticed an officer racing toward him.

"Sir," he gasped, struggling for breath, "a resident just reported that she thought she heard a young man screaming from that area down the street." He pointed down the street he had just come from. "She thought she was dreaming until she saw the police arrive."

A rush of euphoria reenergized Llewelyn. "We may have just received the break we've been looking for. Thank you, Officer."

Llewelyn sprinted across the road, leading his army of police officers to the area of the buildings with a velocity that most of the men had not achieved in many years. They stopped before a series of seemingly abandoned buildings. It was apparent to Llewelyn that the buildings were originally part of a business complex, long since closed down.

The inspector stood there silently as he caught his breath, studying all the buildings. There was a total of five buildings; each was four stories tall. Most of the windows had been boarded up, and the doors were chained shut. However, there was one window on the top floor whose glass was intact, and a dim light could be seen reflecting from within.

Without saying a word, Llewelyn made his way to the second building. The front of the building had every appearance of being a defunct building, but still, Llewelyn's instinct told him that this was nothing more than a facade. He placed his hands on the board affixed to the front door and noticed that it had been loosely placed there. Llewelyn cast aside the board, and his face beamed as he was now able to gain access.

Llewelyn led his team into the building. They all marveled that despite the structure having the outward appearance of a derelict building, the interior had been completely refurbished. Inside, it was a renovated condominium with two apartments on each floor, but the place was apparently vacant.

Still short of breath, Llewelyn dreaded the idea of having to scale the stairs, but his instinct told him that what he was looking for would be on the fourth floor. As he stepped forward, he suddenly noticed a trail of blood. Fearful of contaminating the crime scene, Llewelyn beckoned his team back and made the trek on his own. He perilously climbed the stairs, carefully avoiding the blood.

The stairwell was dimly lit by a single lightbulb on the ceiling. He made his way to the top floor and noticed a door slightly ajar. From where he stood, he craned his neck to look inside the room. He nudged the door wide enough to slide through. The apartment was fully furnished and untouched; with the exception of the trail of blood, there was no evidence of violence. Llewelyn followed the blood trail to the only bedroom in the far end. Curiously, the trail ended at the closet. *Perhaps this is where the victim had been before he was discovered*, he thought.

He peered into the closet to notice nothing but an unexpected array of men's clothing. Llewelyn heard what he thought to be a sound coming from behind the closet wall. He stepped back, startled, and contemplated retreating for the other officers. Within moments, the rattling behind the wall ceased. Whoever or whatever had been behind the wall was now gone.

Llewelyn raced down the stairs to the streets and ordered his team to set up a perimeter. "Hurry!" Llewelyn barked. "He's exiting the building!"

The men stepped outside to find the city block covered with curious spectators. If the killer had, in fact, escaped the building, the officers knew that it would be near impossible to find him among the crowd. To Llewelyn's frustration, the officers gave up their search. The number of spectators was too massive. He ordered his team to enter the building.

Within the hour, a group of evidence technicians secured the area with crime scene tape and began their analysis. Llewelyn returned to the bedroom closet and placed his gloved hands on what turned out to be a false wall. He pushed hard enough that the wall slid open. He instinctively swiped his hand against the inner wall to find a light switch. Llewelyn turned on the switch to see a small room that was not only the size of a solitary confinement jail cell but also designed to resemble one. Llewelyn and the others were sickened by the rancid smell emanating from the bloodstained walls and floors and the fragments of bone, fecal matter, and body parts strewn throughout.

The walls were made of large masonry blocks, and a metal cot had been attached to the far wall. It had been drenched with blood. On the concrete floor, there were metal shackles welded to the ground; large chunks of skin were still attached to the metal, evidence of the fierce struggle a poor soul had to endure to free himself. Llewelyn then noticed a surgical instrument table, made of stainless steel, that had been propped against the nearest wall. The table carried on it an array of bloodied surgical instruments whose only purpose had to be to inflict pain and suffering.

Llewelyn searched for what had to be another trap door that allowed the killer to flee. As he expected, underneath the cot, the inspector found an escape hatch that revealed a makeshift chute with a wooden ladder that led all the way down to the basement, more than four stories below. Llewelyn deduced that down in the basement was another door that opened to the adjacent streets. Llewelyn furled his brow in frustration.

"Contact the crime scene techs," Llewelyn said, looking back at Phillips. "I want this crime scene secured and all the blood carefully collected. Order DNA scans immediately. Get me the owner of these buildings and anyone even remotely connected to it. I want this killer identified within the next hour."

Phillips and the others dutifully obeyed. As he faced the crowd of spectators, Llewelyn thought of individually detaining each person in the hopes that the killer would be among them. He thought against it, knowing that the killer would be long gone. He was wrong in his belief.

*   *   *

From across the street, James St. John-Smythe was among the crowd of spectators, disguised in a wig and glasses, cursing his own existence, and as the sun began to rise, James faded with the night.

Chapter Sixty-eight

In the dark recesses of Wyndham Court, James St. John-Smythe had secluded himself in his room. He lay in a curled, fetal position on his bed. He had been crying. He was terrified. He was whispering a prayer of forgiveness. He had never been more afraid of Ducard and Sébastien. He knew what they were capable of doing.

James had only just returned from his goodwill trip to South Africa the night before. He had been ordered to stay in his room. *Your presentment is drawing nigh*, the elders reminded him, *and the event could not be compromised.* Under no circumstances was he to leave, but James's urges continued to control him. He snuck out of his room by climbing out of the window and took one of the many junk cars he had parked, hidden, a mile away from the home. He drove his way to London and made his way to the nightclub, and that was where he had met Colin.

James managed to seduce the young man, bought him a drink, and slipped a bit of Rohypnol in the cocktail. James escorted Colin to his car, where he drove his victim to the abandoned buildings that served as James's hideaway. He carried his prey up the stairs and into his private torture chamber. Inside the room was another young man who had already been there for a week, chained to the metal bed. That young man was weak from several days of no nourishment because of

James's trip—not that he would have fed him much away. He removed the chained victim from his shackles and replaced him with Colin.

James took a pair of scissors and cut the clothes off Colin. He left him there naked, knowing Colin would be asleep for another hour, giving James time to have his way with the first young man. However, James's frolic only lasted a few minutes when heard the noise from the other room. Colin was trying to escape. James encountered his prey in the middle of the street, and the view of the young man standing there naked made him desire to conduct his dastardly deed right on the road. The danger of killing the lad out in the open gave James more of a thrill. After killing the young man, James continued to desecrate his lifeless body. A police siren in the distance scared James into returning to his car. He was in such haste that he carelessly left the body behind and made his way back to his home on the richly estate. Two hours later, James snuck into his room and prayed himself to sleep.

Chapter Sixty-nine

James was startled from his light slumber as the two elders burst into his room.

"They have found your private flat! It is only a matter of time before they find you!" Sébastien said as he rushed to assault the petulant heir to the purported throne of Jesus but was forcibly stopped by Ducard.

"Enough! Unhand him! He cannot have a mark on his body for the presentment," Ducard demanded.

"The council still has intentions of proceeding with the presentment?"

"Yes, we do," Ducard said ever so casually. "In three days."

Sébastien was in disbelief. "And when the authorities come and arrest him in the middle of everything?"

"They won't. They cannot trace the buildings to him in any way."

Sébastien had never been so irate. "But that won't stop them from continuing in their investigation!"

"Their investigation will be quashed very soon." Ducard reached over to grab Sébastien's hand and gently released his brother's grip on James. "Now please be so kind as to let him go. We do not want to place any marks on his face."

"You assured me of that days ago! The hunt for James continues!" Sébastien exclaimed.

"In due time, my brother. In due time."

Sébastien released his grip and stormed out of the room. James's body relaxed as he was let go; he straightened his shirt and smirked.

Chapter Seventy

Llewelyn and his team of detectives had been carefully examining every minute area of the abandoned apartment. The detectives were exhausted, having worked for the last twenty hours. Llewelyn displayed no sign of tiredness as he diligently oversaw the entire process. He paused as a young female officer approached him with a fair-haired man dressed in a dark suit.

The young officer appeared anxious as she was hesitant to speak. "Inspector Llewelyn, excuse the interruption, but I have been asked to introduce you to Detective Fairfield."

"*Detective Fairfield?*" Llewelyn reacted indignantly, surprised.

Fairfield responded gracefully and held out his hand. "Yes, sir, at your service."

"I know all the detectives in London." Llewelyn stared the young man up and down. "I don't know you."

The young officer was startled by Inspector Llewelyn's rudeness and took that as her cue to leave the two men.

Having been rejected the courtesy of a simple handshake, Fairfield lowered his hand and removed a cigarette from his breast pocket. "Actually, I've been transferred from Sandford and have only just been promoted. The chief inspector thought it best if I learned from you."

Inspector Llewelyn rudely took the cigarette from Fairfield's mouth and placed it in his breast pocket. "There's no smoking in my crime scene." He then proceeded to stare at the stranger. "I wish I had been notified of this. I have no time to train a rookie."

"It was at the chief inspector's insistence," Fairfield commented.

Llewelyn said resignedly, "You can observe, but please do not interfere with my investigation."

"Understood." Fairfield stepped back as Phillips approached Inspector Llewelyn.

"Inspector, we have the labs working on the DNA, and they should have the results within hours," Phillips said proudly with a smile to his face.

Llewelyn, on the other hand, was not so happy. "What about the fingerprints and the ownership documents? I want to know who owns these buildings."

Phillips was reluctant to reply. "The prints are not back from the technician, and property records are not open yet."

"I don't care that the offices are not open yet. Get them now—"

"Forgive my intrusion," Fairfield brazenly interrupted, "but the ownership records are bound to be in a straw owner's name. That may not get us anywhere. I can start a trace on the true owner."

Llewelyn stared at the young man. "Fairfield? Your name is Fairfield, correct?"

"Yes, Fairfield, Edward Fairfield."

"I said *don't interfere*."

"I'm not trying to. I want to help," Fairfield said defensively. "I have an uncle who works at a title company that can assist us with the documents. Besides, I have been sent here to learn."

"Learn by watching and by minding your place," Llewelyn said, poking the junior detective in the chest.

Llewelyn paused and watched as the crime scene photographer took extensive photographs of the bloodied area. The images of the remains of the young lads were forever ingrained in his mind. It was at that moment that the impact of this event took its toll on Llewelyn. Llewelyn pounded his fist into his open hand. He had never been so angry. It was at that moment that he made the commitment to capture the killer—even if it cost him his life.

The silence of the moment was broken as news alerts were sounding on the phone of every officer and crime scene technician present. Llewelyn dismissed the tone of his own phone and was annoyed that his entire team stopped what they were doing to read the news. The alert had nothing to do with the murders but instead was about the announcement of the worldwide event that would come to be known as *the presentment.*

Chapter Seventy-one

Nearly a billion viewers from all over the world were glued to their television screens; those people who could not afford television sets found themselves huddled next to masses of people sharing a screen on street blocks and storefronts. Large outdoor events were held where thousands could see the grand occasion on large screens and monitors.

The biggest event was held in the heart of Times Square, where over two million people were crammed throughout the city blocks to watch from the various billboard screens. They were going to be part of history, an event so momentous that it was going to change the world, but it was an event so controversial that it was marred by protestors scattered throughout the globe. The protestors though were greatly outnumbered by the curious and the true believers; this was what they had been waiting for all their lives.

The masses had spent weeks in anticipation of this momentous event. Those who had come to see the event in public arenas spent several days and nights waiting to be let in. Finally, the event was going to take place that evening.

Chapter Seventy-two

The courtyard at Wyndham Court was brimming with some of the wealthiest and most exclusive invitees, all representing the highest classes of society from all over the world—kings, queens, presidents, and prime ministers—along with the wealthiest of the 1 percent. The media was there as well. Every major news network from every country had their cameras focused on the elites as they were dropped off by their personal chauffeurs. The motorcade of the most expensive cars and limousines extended for miles. It took several hours for every guest to be dropped off and escorted into the mansion. The media was forced to be camped several yards off the property and had to use large camera cranes with telescopic lenses to film the event. There was only one news reporter who was allowed an intimate view of the event from the mansion itself: Felicity Kruger.

Felicity was surprised to have received the call from Ducard himself; she was certain that after her botched interview, her career was over, but instead, quite the opposite happened. The backlash from the initial interview sent the ratings skyrocketing. The interview catapulted her career, and the follow-up news coverage gave the elders the attention that they needed to propel James's stardom.

*   *   *

Felicity Kruger had been at Wyndham Court since the night before, having been given a special suite within the palatial mansion for herself and one for each of her crew. The night before the event, she dined with Ducard in a banquet hall, while her crew ate in a smaller dining room. Felicity and Ducard sat on opposite ends of a large table made of pure mahogany as they were catered to by several servants.

A private chef flown in from France made the very special meal for them both: an array of dishes filled with coq au vin, braised in red wine, lardons, and mushrooms; escargots de Bourgogne topped with parsley butter; and a platter of ortolan bunting. This entire meal was coupled with two bottles of Cheval Blanc 1947 Saint-Émilion.

She was not allowed to ask of Ducard any questions, but by the end of the meal, he knew everything about her. Because of a mixture of wine and Ducard's charm, she desired to make love to him. She had been seduced.

He was the oldest man she had ever made love to, but in the throes of passion, he was her very best. There was no stopping him that night; he lasted until dawn. Even that morning, she was still feeling the ecstasy of the previous night. She had dozed off for what she thought was a moment but awoke six hours later to the sound of a servant bringing her brunch in bed.

She looked at her watch and realized that she had just enough time to eat, shower, and get dressed. After that night, the only other time she would see Ducard would be from afar as he stood next to James St. John-Smythe. She soon realized why she had been awarded this exclusive opportunity, but in many ways, it was well worth the price.

*   *   *

At eight o'clock that night, Felicity stood on the grounds of Wyndham Court, underneath the second-story balcony of the mansion. She had her microphone at hand, and the camera was on her face.

"Reporting from Wyndham Court, we bring you live coverage of the ceremonial 'coronation' of James St. John-Smythe as the latest monarch of the Merovingian dynasty. In just a few moments, the heir himself will appear on the balcony above me and formally accept the title. It is ceremonial in the sense that the coronation does not come with any real power, but the reason it is very significant is because as of today, James St. John-Smythe will be the ceremonial leader of the descendants of Christ."

To her surprise, James did not appear on the balcony as expected, but instead, he was paraded through the crowd of people standing on the grounds, reminiscent of Jesus's triumphal entry into Jerusalem. The camera panned back to her as she continued.

"The 'coronation' is meant to mimic the coronation of kings and queens as celebrated in countless other countries, including this one." She paused long enough as the camera panned across the large crowd of people. "And as you can see from the public masses present, they revel in it as if it were the real thing."

Appearing on countless screens around the world, a graphic featured the same virtual genealogical tree shown during Ducard's interview.

Felicity continued, "Originally, the Merovingians were a Salian Frankish dynasty that came to rule the Franks in a region known as Francia in the middle of the fifth century. Their rule lasted about three hundred years, ending in 752 AD, when Pope Zachary formally deposed their last king, Childeric III. However, the Merovingians kept a secret very close to their heart. The Merovingians believed themselves to be descended from Jesus. They carried this secret with them for generations until rumors turned into legend, which turned into books and then into movies. With time, many came to accept this family as the descendants of Christ. That is why on this day, James St. John-Smythe's coronation will have a profound effect on those countless millions of believers who are confident that he is one of the descendants of Jesus who will serve as their temporal leader. Our interview with Mr. Ducard several days ago revealed that their genealogists painstakingly confirmed that St. John-Smythe is, in fact, a member of this royal family. Even though Mr. Ducard's organization identified a myriad of descendants, James was chosen from the countless candidates to be their leader. St. John-Smythe promises to be a beacon for the lost masses seeking guidance in this grief-stricken world."

Felicity paused as James made his way past the crowd and entered the house. Within a few moments, James stepped onto the second-story balcony, dressed regally, and approached the podium before him.

Ducard and Sébastien stood by him on each side. The audiences both there at Wyndham Court and throughout the world screamed and cheered in admiration.

"As the ceremony is about to end, we now turn to hear James's remarks," Felicity said as the cameras focused on James.

James waited several moments to let the sound of the cheers drown out before he could speak. He adjusted the microphone. There was no written speech, no notes; it was oration spoken from the heart, which, as intended, added to its authenticity. The crowds went silent.

"I am at a loss for words at how honored I am to be chosen as the vicar for the man who begot our most remarkable bloodline. When I was a child, before my mother died, she used to tell me how she dreamed of me speaking in front of large crowds of people and how I would be an important person for the people. Well, today is the day that my mother dreamed of. I have been blessed with riches beyond my or her wildest dreams. Yet I promise not to use this treasure to enrich myself but to use that fortune to spread the hope of good will and peace to all men.

"To those of you who are perhaps wary of my family lineage, I say unto you—have no fear. I am no substitute or replacement for my ancestor who changed the course of history. I do say to you that I will do everything in my power to be a new disciple, to be the thirteenth apostle. Jesus taught us, 'And the seed whose fruit is righteousness is sown in peace by those who make peace.' With that mindset, it is my intention to travel and spread the hope of peace. It is my hope that within my generation, there will be no more wars, no more terrorists, and no more suffering.

"Do not be deceived. I will bring forth more than just *words*. I will bring action. During my visits, I plan on forging basic plans to bring the change the world wants. I will contribute to and seek the contributions of the world's richest people to set up foundations that will place money in the poorest sections of the world to rebuild their towns, build new schools, and create access to food and water so that in time, there will be no more hunger, no more homelessness, and no more poverty."

The world that was watching erupted into a loud and unified cheer.

St. John-Smythe continued speaking for twenty minutes over the loud roar of the crowd. He paused now and then to let the cheers subside. Near the end, he stared into the camera and said to the world, "*His* peace . . . My peace, I give unto you. Let not your heart be troubled. And be not afraid."

Once again, the world delighted in unison. As James finished his speech, he waved to the crowd and majestically entered the residence.

Felicity resumed her coverage. "As you can see from the large crowds throughout the world and from the sound of the cheers, St. John-Smythe has already amassed a legion of supporters. He also has an array of international diplomats looking to meet with him. He's already scheduled to give a speech at the United Nations next week and then has one scheduled before the Council on Foreign Relations the week after that. In the coming months, he also plans to meet with various heads of state, including Pres. Nicolas Adams of the United States, and the pope himself is willing to give him an audience. His mission is to spread goodwill and work with the leaders of the world to implement his plan of bringing prosperity into this world. There is no doubt that this young man is going to play an important role in history."

Felicity signed off and then marveled at the spectacle around her. She gazed up at the balcony, hoping to catch one last sight of Ducard, but he had retreated into the mansion with James. Felicity would never see Ducard again.

Chapter Seventy-three

"James," his mother would whisper in his ear, "I see great things for you. I see you standing in front of many people. You are giving a great speech. Millions of people will adore you. They will love you."

This divination, his mother would say to her son as she tucked him in every night. There was not a single day that she did not dote on her son—that is, until she and his father died in the accident.

James's parents were simple folks, not particularly well-off; his father was a factory worker and his mother a nurse. Their impoverishment would later strike James as odd when he would come to find out that he was the unrefuted heir to the throne of Jesus. He later discovered that other members of the royal bloodline came from wealth but were too old or too feeble to take on the great responsibility of being the temporal vicar. He rationalized that his birth into poverty made him a better candidate for the role.

While his parents were devout Catholics—churchgoing, simple folks—there was a dark side to his family. His parents were drunks who enjoyed getting inebriated every night before bed. They also enjoyed being violent with each other. His parents were equals when it came to the physical attacks. No one would ever get the better of the other—unless they turned their violence to James.

James knew not to interrupt their drinking and fighting, but fate would draw their eyes, and he would unwittingly be the victim of their wrath. James took his beatings well; it was a routine and dark aspect to his family life. As a young boy, James would take out his anger by hurting the random stray cats he would find wandering in his neighborhood. His rage would range from beatings to outright mutilations. After each violent outburst, he would pray to God for forgiveness, and with every absolution from God, he would go back to hurting. By the time he was ten years old, he found himself aroused by his mutilations. He eventually found pleasure in masturbating before the ghastly remains.

James's biggest trauma came when his mother caught him pleasuring himself in the backyard of their family home. His mother was outraged and forced him to recite the prayers of the rosary—and then she beat him into unconsciousness. James would later wake up to find his mother fondling him. This had not been the first time she touched him. This would be their little secret. After she would pleasure her son, she would cuddle with him and stroke his fine hair.

"James," she whispered, "I see great things for you. I see you standing in front of many people. You are giving a great speech. Millions of people will adore you. They will love you."

James would smile and go back to sleep.

He dared not tell his father, lest he risk another round of beatings. In the few rare instances that his parents were not fighting, he was happy. All he ever wanted was his parents to be happy as well.

*   *   *

James would never forget the last time he saw his parents. It was a Sunday afternoon in the town of Lewisham, and James had just turned eleven years old. Sundays were days of rest. There was mass and Sunday brunch, but there was no going out. Sunday was about resting and getting ready for the new week, but that night was different.

A much younger Ducard and Sébastien made a surprise visit to their home. James had seen them once or twice before, but it was always a brief visit just before his mother would tuck him in.

"James, I have always told you that I see great things for you. I see you standing before a large crowd. You are giving a great speech.

Millions of people will adore you. They will love you," she repeated as she formally introduced James to these two men. "These men will help you achieve that greatness."

James recalled the moment Ducard and Sébastien suddenly appeared at their doorsteps, dressed immaculately in black, and life miraculously got better for his parents. His family did not become rich overnight, but suddenly, money was no longer an issue for his blue-collar family. The two men left no doubt that it was all to benefit James, and even though he was a child, it only emboldened his ego.

The last time he saw his parents, they kissed him goodbye and left to go on holiday. The kindly men, Ducard and Sébastien, would keep him company until they returned. His parents never came back. The next morning, he was told by Sébastien that his parents had been killed in an airplane crash. James handled the news relatively well for a child, but inside, he was destroyed. He was initially placed in a foster home, but it was one that was financed and controlled by the elders, and unbeknownst to the children, it was one of countless other homes, boarding schools, and facilities scattered throughout the world that housed other potential heirs to the royal bloodline. They were all to be meticulously groomed, and ultimately, the best of the lot was to be selected.

Within a year, the other children in the foster home despised James's arrogance, and they, rightfully, perceived him as a threat. He was physically bullied by the other boys, and then one day he fought back. James severely beat one of the boys to death, and to his astonishment, he enjoyed seeing the boy writhe in pain, struggling to breathe. James was not present when the boy died, but the notion that the boy had died brought him great pleasure. He masturbated to that mental image.

The administrators of the home gave up on the boy, and to the dismay of the elders, James was placed in juvenile detention. (That aspect of James's life was kept hidden from the public.). Whilst in detention, James grew even more violent. He started experimenting in sex with boys and girls, but it was not about sexual gratification but more a form of foreplay before violence. As James grew, he craved the satisfaction that came from the physical violence; the sex was more of an afterthought.

Of all the potential heirs, James was one of a handful of candidates from throughout the world whom the elders thought were pure enough to take on the role of temporal vicar. At the time, they were willing to overlook his degeneracy. When the foster homes and juvenile system decided that they could no longer care for him, the elders took it upon themselves to take him and do their best to train and educate him for his potential new role as the world's savior. It was Ducard and Sébastien who paid for his finest education and groomed him for this role. Other elders throughout the world had their own candidates, and soon, the collective council of elders would have to vote on the best choice. Throughout James's young adulthood, he was becoming the leading favorite—until the elders learned of his first victim.

Chapter Seventy-four

Jean-Jacques Ducard and Ariel Sébastien were both born in France, just months apart in 1924, Ducard in Neuilly-sur-Seine and Sébastien in Saint-Cloud. They had never met during the majority of their lives, but they were told of each other, and they knew that they shared a common goal.

The two men were born into wealth but had no real family. They were reared by an array of brethren, men in black who trained the two men into a life of loyalty and secrecy. When they each reached the age of reason, they were finally told of the importance they had been born into. They were told that they were given the solemn duty to protect the holy bloodline, the heir of Jesus. They were part of "the brotherhood."

The organization had no real name, and none of the members knew from whence it came—only that it had always existed. The brotherhood's sacred texts were the stuff of legend and fantasy in that they boasted their lineage to the twelve kings of the lost continent of Atlantis, the pharaohs of ancient Egypt, the Babylonians, the kings of the legendary civilization of Thule, and the emperors of Rome. Their sacred goal was to "immanentize the eschaton"—to bring about the final, heaven-like stage of history. By the time of the Roman Empire, the brotherhood's members had expanded to the entire world and infiltrated every aspect of commerce and government of every nation in the world, but the brotherhood, in some respects, felt useless to its members. The state of the world was one of chaos and turmoil. The world and its people were in need of a savior, a redeemer, but there was no savior to be found. The brotherhood could do nothing but seek and wait.

Four hundred years before the beginning of the Common Era, the prophets foretold of the birth of a savior who would lead mankind into the final stage of heaven. For many centuries, the brotherhood awaited the birth of this redeemer. The brotherhood's texts revealed that the original men in black were three sages who had been guided by a heavenly body that appeared over the Judean night sky that led them to a stable where they greeted the infant savior as he entered the world. The three sages were the elder representatives of the worldwide brotherhood who had pledged their fealty to the savior—and ultimately to his heirs.

The sages kept their watchful eye over the child, but when a spiteful vassal of the Roman Empire had his own prophets previously warn him of the impending birth of a threat to his kingdom, the vassal ordered the death of all male infants born at the time of the appearance of the heavenly body. As a result, the three sages safely escorted the redeemer and his family into Egypt. They continued their vigil of the child until the boy grew into a man.

As a young adult, their redeemer gradually accumulated a large following of poor, sick, and disenfranchised people. The redeemer taught them of love and hope. As the young savior's popularity grew, so did the dangers to his life. He was soon surrounded by twelve of the best of the brotherhood's strongest and fiercest protectors. For three years, the twelve protectors guided the redeemer throughout Judea, Samaria, and Galilee, dutifully protecting him from his enemies—but among them was a traitor.

After nearly thirty millennia of undying allegiance, the brotherhood was caught off guard by the betrayal, a betrayal brought on by greed. In a garden at the foot of the Mount of Olives, the devoted disciples were overcome by the temple guards and a maddening mob; their redeemer had been arrested. It was the first time that the brotherhood had failed, and sadly, it would not be their last.

They stood silent as their leader was tried and sentenced to be crucified. They hid among the crowd as their master made his way down a way of suffering and sobbed as a kindly handmaiden provided the man a veil to wipe the blood from his face. One of the original men in black would take that veil, and it would later become a *vera icon*. The disciples watched in horror as the Romans tied their redeemer to a tree and saw him suffer for several hours until the Romans pierced his side with a spear.

One of the men in black would recover the discarded spear and take it for safekeeping, but in time, that weapon would fall in and out of the hands of vile and power-hungry men. Nearly two thousand years later, one such vile man would start a world war in the hopes of acquiring the spear. Not long after that, a military general participated in that same war with the same intent. The folly of trying to possess the spear would cause their death. In time, the spear would be lost to history.

When their redeemer died on that tree, the world shook, and the traitor's life was forfeited, as demanded by their sacred oath. The savior was left by the Romans to rot on the tree, but the erstwhile protectors would not let that happen. One of the elders from Arimathie paid for a private tomb. The redeemer was taken to the tomb, and within three days, his body was gone.

As a result of the redeemer's death and disappearance, his followers grew exponentially. Despite the mysterious absence of the redeemer's body, his disciples continued to mourn; they felt that the very reason for their existence had ceased. Then the favorite of the redeemer appeared before the disciples as they soothed their mourning in an upper room of their secret location. She was pregnant with a child, and the child had to have been the redeemer's. In that instant, the brotherhood realized their new cause—they would be protectors of the lineage.

From that moment on, a new brotherhood had arisen. From generation to generation, the brotherhood grew, as did the multitude of the redeemer's descendants. As the centuries went by, the brotherhood continued to permeate every aspect of society, and they continued to control the world, all for the benefit of the heirs.

* * *

When Ducard and Sébastien were in their early twenties, they were inducted into the modern-day version of the brotherhood. They had come to learn that they could trace their own ancestors to the Knights Templar. Ducard and Sébastien were only two of hundreds of thousands of the brotherhood scattered throughout the world, each with the same goal. Their mandate was to identify and protect the heirs.

With time, the brothers felt that the world was becoming morally corrupt; the world needed its redeemer to return. They would spend the majority of their adulthood painstakingly tracing every genealogical chart and search among the multitude of heirs who would fit the role perfectly. In the 1940s, they identified a Spaniard, but his unexpected death from cancer caused the brotherhood to look for other candidates. Later in the 1950s, they found an American, but his affection for heroin made him an unlikely candidate. In the 1960s, they found a Frenchman, but he was killed in Vietnam.

By this time, Ducard and Sébastien had grown restless and doubted they would ever find anyone suitable for this solemn duty. None of the then current heirs met their very high standards, and they were resigned to giving up on their goal—that is, until Sébastien, being the voracious reader that he was, came across books written by Alvin Toffler, Aldous Huxley, and Ira Levin. That, in turn, led him to privately commission the brilliant minds of molecular biologists James Dewey Watson and Francis Harry Compton Crick and chemist Rosalind Franklin to draft a treatise on a private research project. These scientists were sworn to secrecy and paid handsomely to remain that way. Sébastien presented the wildly innovative idea to Ducard and handed him the results of the commissioned research. Ducard was not impressed.

"This is the stuff of science fiction," Ducard criticized, but Sébastien nonetheless convinced the brotherhood to support and finance the new plan.

Desperate for success, Sébastien spent the next three years implementing his newly developed operation. The plan involved searching for the perfect relic, which could only be found in the most secretive recesses of the Catholic Church. Sébastien indirectly convinced a Catholic scientist to develop a project that would give them access to the important relic to affirm and validate their faith.

That man was Mathew Allison. With Sébastien's influence, he was able to stealthily use Mathew Allison and his team of scientists to accomplish the brotherhood's private plan. However, notwithstanding the brotherhood's overwhelming strength and power, they were not entirely invincible to the stubborn old princes within the church.

The reigning pope at the time had heard rumors of a secret cabal that had secretly pervaded the church, and the Holy Father was concerned that this experiment had evil intentions. The pope would not have any of that. The Holy Father instructed his staff to put an end to the experiment and ordered that the American scientists be restricted from entering the Vatican.

"But I gave them my word," Padre Silvio pleaded with the pope.

"And that is of no importance to me," the Pope replied. "I have no obligation to keep your word. Send them home."

Padre Silvio bowed his head in remorse, but he had never had any intention of obeying that order. Padre Silvio served a higher purpose. He bade the pope good night and injected him with syringe filled with a poisonous toxin that mimicked a heart attack. John Paul I died on September 29, 1978, and his body was interred in the Vatican Grottoes. A new pope was elected—a member of the brotherhood.

Padre Silvio gave the brotherhood access to the holy relic. Mark Connolly, the lonely American, would use his training and education to obtain exactly what was needed to put the plan into effect. Within a few years, the plan would end in absolute failure, and an intentionally set fire would bring that disastrous chapter to a close, but the screams of a badly burned woman carrying a precious bundle within her arms—and the wails of a deranged patient—would bring that horrifying incident back into the light.

Fiorello.

Chapter Seventy-five

After the debacle that was the failed experiment, the brothers spent a decade going back to their original objective and once again painstakingly sought out the perfect candidate. They came across James St. John-Smythe when he was a toddler but nearly dismissed him because of his impoverished background. However, his lineage was soon confirmed by way of his mother. His mother had no idea. The brotherhood resumed their focus on the young lad; they would rehabilitate his image. James had always been told that his parents died in a plane crash, but the reality was that they were paid off—two million pounds in return for their son. They were instructed to go on holiday and to never return. They could never see their son again.

The elders spent their vast resources educating James and the countless other heirs, providing them with the best of everything. When many of the candidates entered their teens, the time had come for the collective brotherhood to choose from the innumerable descendants scattered throughout the world. After weeks of heated debate, the council overwhelmingly chose James St. John-Smythe to be their new redeemer; many of the council dissented. As a result, Ducard and Sébastien dedicated their lives to grooming James, preparing him for his presentment, and now they were coming to the sad realization that because of James's predilections for sex and death, all their efforts were for naught.

Chapter Seventy-six

Inside his private room at Wyndham Court, James was in the midst of a painful spell of dry heaves brought on by the back pages of the local newspaper. In it was the revelation that the secret hideout of the feared serial killer, the Sinner, had been discovered. It was only a matter of time before the killer would be apprehended, promised the case lead's investigator, Inspector Llewelyn.

James began to fear that maybe his phone call to Llewelyn had given the detective a clue that would lead to his capture. James was fearful that his transgressions had caught up with him, but his fear was not directed at the punishment he would face by law enforcement; instead, he could only think what the elders would do if they chose to eliminate him. Not even the fact that he was about to be presented to the world brought him any sense of security. It was the fear of the unimaginable that made him sick, the fear that he would not be able to kill again that made him even sicker. His travel itinerary for the next several weeks, he knew, was designed to keep him from satisfying his lust.

Chapter Seventy-seven

Inspector Llewelyn sat behind his desk at Scotland Yard, surrounded by his team of detectives. Having no desk, Detective Fairfield was forced to stand in the back of the room. He watched as Llewelyn continued reading from the file folder he had been holding in his hands.

Llewelyn removed a three-page document and perused all the pages. He looked up disapprovingly from the folder and said to the others, "This document has the results of the DNA and fingerprint analysis. Many of the samples have been matched to some of the victims, while others are still unknown." Llewelyn stood on his feet. "I want forensics to continue searching and comparing these choices with known samples from our databases. I also want them run against anyone who has ever been associated with that building." He removed a single page document from the folder. "I also have a list of people who witnessed activity around that building. This list includes everyone from the postal carriers to the old folks who walk their dogs. I will be personally interviewing these witnesses while the rest of you continue to sweep the neighborhood for more clues." Llewelyn was about to continue when his chief stormed into the room.

"Llewelyn, please step into my office." With the same swiftness as when he had arrived, he walked out of the room without bothering to see if Llewelyn had heard him.

Llewelyn dutifully followed his supervisor down the long hallway, without a single word being exchanged between the two. Within moments, Llewelyn was inside the chief's office. The chief peered over his reading glasses, glaring at Llewelyn with a look of disappointment. Llewelyn calmly responded by closing the office door. He was respectful of his supervisor but was not intimidated by the chief's demeanor. Llewelyn stood firm as he stared at his superior.

After several moments of silence, Llewelyn was the first to speak. "Chief, couldn't this have waited? We were about to go back and canvass the neighborhood."

"That's why I interrupted you," the chief said. "I just received a call from the brass. We need all available officers to provide escort and protection for St. John-Smythe."

"St. John—who?"

"Where have you been?" the chief asked, surprised. "He's this new diplomat—royalty of sorts—and he needs all the protection we can provide while he's traveling throughout the world for the next few weeks. I need you to release your team—"

Llewelyn stepped up in protest. "A *few weeks?* I cannot afford to cease my investigation for a single minute, much less a few weeks."

The chief rose from his own chair and pointed right at Llewelyn. "You don't have any say in his matter. In fact, you personally may have to provide protective detail."

"Me? Who gave you this directive and when?" Llewelyn asked defiantly.

"I did." The chief paused for effect. "Just now. Now go do your job before I relieve you of your duties."

Llewelyn angrily stormed out the door. Within moments, he would make the heartbreaking announcement to his team of devoted men and women that all their hard work on the search for the serial killer would be suspended indefinitely. After the announcement, Llewelyn grabbed an armful of his files and stormed out of the building.

Detective Fairfield stared out of Llewelyn's office window, ominously silent, watching Llewelyn as he walked to his car.

Chapter Seventy-eight

James St. John-Smythe had been standing naked in the middle of his hotel suite, staring out of his corner windows, one window overlooking Columbus Circle, the other Central Park. He had just arrived in New York that afternoon. He was scheduled to make an appearance before the United Nations as a guest speaker on world hunger at ten o'clock the next morning; he had plenty of time to enjoy his first visit in New York.

It was nearly 11:00 p.m. He looked out each window and saw the multitude of people down below, all of whom were oblivious to the man staring at them, unaware to the evil desires he wished upon them. He was getting aroused at the idea of walking the streets, but he knew he would have a difficult time escaping his security detail. He stepped closer to one of the windows, fantasizing that everyone could see his naked body. He could no longer contain himself. James put on some running gear and raced past his detail standing guard at the door.

"Sir," one of the security men said, trying to stop him, "you cannot leave—"

"I'm only going jogging," James quickly said, rushing past them, listening as they frantically spoke into their radios.

James took the elevator down to the lobby and went running along Central Park West toward Eighth Avenue. James knew that his security detail was not prepared for a late-night jog, but what he did not count on was that there had been a separate detail, in four separate vehicles, ready to follow him at a moment's notice.

James continued his brisk pace, searching for what could be his prey, but the streets of Manhattan were vastly different from the red-light districts of London. He longed for the Central Park of the past that he had read so much about, where gay lovers could meet for anonymous sex. As he made his way down the avenue, he envied all the gay partners publicly and proudly expressing their affection. Sadly, there was no one there for him; he was determined to find someone.

A little less than an hour later, he found himself at Washington Square Park. He stopped to catch his breath. It was almost midnight, and yet there were people everywhere. He walked around and scoured the area for anyone who piqued his interest. Standing underneath the arch was a group of street dancers entertaining a group of tourists. The impressive dance routine lasted fifteen minutes and ended with a round of applause. The four dancers collected their belongings and split the small collection of money among them. They split about eight dollars each and said their goodbyes.

One of the young men, a Latino who had to be no older than sixteen, went his own way. James caught up with the young man and offered him a twenty-dollar bill. The boy was startled.

"I didn't mean to scare you," James said, thrusting the money into the teen's hand. "I meant to give you this earlier, but you guys had left so quickly. You guys were great."

The kid stuffed the money into this pocket. "T-thanks."

"How long have you been dancing?"

"I really have to go home," the boy said nervously.

"Oh, yes, of course. I just wanted to let you know that I am a Broadway producer, and I think you would be perfect for this show I am putting together."

With that, the kid's eyes grew wide.

"Really?" the kid asked with eager anticipation.

"Absolutely," James replied. "Your act was lovely."

"What about my friends? What did you think of them? Is there room for them too?"

"Certainly." James smiled. "I can audition them tomorrow."

The kid smiled back. "I've dreamed of being a Broadway dancer since I was little."

James continued, "Why don't we find a place to talk about your role? A coffee shop or something?"

"We can come to my house. I live in Brooklyn. You can meet my mom. We can take the subway—"

"I was thinking of something a little . . . closer."

"I don't . . . I don't know. I really need to get home—"

"That's disappointing," James interrupted. "I really need to make a decision right away. If you can't make a commitment tonight, then I'll have to find someone else. Perhaps one of your friends."

"No, that's fine. We can do it tonight."

"Great," James said joyfully. "Let's walk this way. There must be a place we can discuss this in private."

As they proceeded to walk, a large black sedan pulled alongside them. James's primary security detail came out of the passenger's side.

"Sir, you are needed back at your room," the large burly man said.

This new security detail was made up mostly of men he did not recognize. They were part of Llewelyn's investigative unit who had been reassigned.

James was outraged. "Please do not interrupt me!"

The boy was frightened by the outburst.

A man in black whom James recognized stepped out, holding a cell phone in his hand. The MIB then shoved the phone toward James. "Mr. Ducard insists that you go back—immediately."

Now it was James who was scared. James turned his back to the boy and entered the limousine. The men immediately drove away. The frightened boy ran all the way home.

*   *   *

James listened to the chiding from Ducard as the elder screamed from the cell phone. He said nothing in response and sat quietly as he was driven to his hotel room.

*   *   *

Ducard disconnected the phone and turned to a disapproving Sébastien. "I don't want to hear you complain," Ducard said to his fellow elder. "It's under control."

"*Under control?* May I ask how?" Sébastien asked.

"Danger was diverted in New York. Tomorrow he'll appear before the United Nations and give his speech. After that, he is scheduled to meet the president. At that time, there will be an incident that will make sure James is never suspected of these acts."

Sébastien did not need to hear of the details.

Chapter Seventy-nine

The president walked down the steps of the White House and gave a warm greeting to the "ambassador of the world"—James St. John-Smythe. The two men stood on the steps for several minutes and posed for the nonstop array of photographs. They then proceeded inside and continued the endless multitude of picture taking.

After the photo op ended, the two men spoke for nearly an hour and shared their common desire to end world hunger and poverty. The president congratulated James for his speech before the U.N. – literally representatives from all over the world celebrated his presence. He was given a standing ovation. Much like his presentation before the U.N., James not only promised the president to commit to donating millions of his own wealth toward the various charitable organizations that would assist them in achieving their common goal but also promised to raise millions more from his wealthy associates. The president, in turn, gave his assurance that he would convince Congress to do the same. The president commented that this most recent war on terrorism only served to temporarily halt his commitment to end poverty. The two men struck a new friendship, and after their meeting, they both went outside for another round of photographs.

The whole world watched and cheered at their meeting; together, the two men brought a new sense of hope to the disenfranchised. The better part of the world felt safe once again. However, at the very moment of the meeting, fear rained down on the city of London; a church's cleaning lady was being held at knifepoint.

Chapter Eighty

Inspector Llewelyn had been sitting in his Scotland Yard office for the last several hours, lamenting to himself at how empty his squad room was now that his entire team of police officers had been consigned to protecting a privileged billionaire. He refused to join in on the security detail—the only time he ever refused an order. Instead, Llewelyn spent that time at his office. The door to his office was slowly opened, and on the other side was Phillips, his trusted partner, accompanied by Detective Fairfield.

"Inspector," Phillips said, "the chief has called, inquiring about you. You haven't been answering your phone."

"I turned it off."

"The chief's upset that you didn't fly out with the detail last night," Fairfield added intrusively.

"His 'Royal Highness' was in good hands in New York." Llewelyn was condescending in his response. "You and your men were more than capable to babysit him."

"The chief inspector wants you to call him," his partner said.

Llewelyn did not react.

"Have you been here all night?" Fairfield asked.

Llewelyn was becoming increasingly annoyed. "I'm not stopping until we catch this killer."

"But weren't you told to stop by the chief?" Fairfield dared to ask.

Before Llewelyn could reply, a junior detective stepped into the office and handed Llewelyn a computer printout. The young detective appeared excited and stood before Llewelyn. "Detective, as you recall, one of the witnesses recalled seeing a large black vehicle, perhaps a limousine, near one of the early murders. Per your request, I ran a trace on all limousines and luxury cars rented or owned within a twenty-mile radius."

Llewelyn took the document. The other men watched intently as Llewelyn looked at the list.

"It might narrow your search if you exclude all government vehicles," Fairfield interrupted.

"Why do you say that?" Llewelyn was annoyed but welcomed the suggestion.

Fairfield continued, "No government-issued limousine or car would be involved in such a crime."

Llewelyn handed the printout to his partner. "Maybe he's right. Track down the vehicles owned or rented by civilians only."

"What about these witnesses who identified the vehicles?" Fairfield inquired. "When can we interview them?"

"*We?*" Llewelyn said with a sardonic smile. "No, sir. You're here to watch and learn. And besides, we were told to stop the investigation."

"True," Fairfield said, "but I intend to follow your lead."

Llewelyn smiled and continued to review the list until he spotted a car with the initials "ACC" next to it. Llewelyn showed the list to the junior detective. "What are these initials?"

The junior detective was quick to respond. "That means this car, which was a limousine, is no longer in commission. It was involved in an accident. In fact, a fatality."

Llewelyn looked confused.

The junior detective continued. "'ACC.' That stands for accident, and if you read on, it tells you that there is a code for a fatality."

"Who died?" Llewelyn inquired. "When?"

"When I cross-referenced it to the accident report by matching the agency report number, it listed the decedents as the driver and two passengers."

Llewelyn rose from his chair. "What was the date of the accident?"

"Let's see . . ." The junior detective searched. "The twelfth of Octob—"

Llewelyn was overly excited and grabbed his coat. "That was the night of one of the murders. Where is that limousine now?"

"It should be in the impound. The fatality was ruled an accident. The car is probably on its way to be demolished."

Llewelyn immediately rushed out the door. The other men hastily followed.

Llewelyn turned on his phone and dialed a number. "Forensics?" he demanded. "Get me a forensic examiner to meet me at the impoundment—*now!*" He disconnected the call and dialed a second number. "Impound? Cease all demolishment immediately! I said *immediately!*"

Within a matter of minutes, Llewelyn arrived at the impound lot, where he was greeted by the desk clerk. Llewelyn ignored the clerk and stormed into the lot in search of the car. He located what was left of the vehicle, which was a wrecked pile of steel, badly damaged by fire. The forensic examiner arrived soon after.

"I want every inch dusted," Llewelyn demanded.

"But sir," the forensic examiner said, "the fire -?"

Llewelyn gave the examiner a stern look.

The technician went to work as Llewelyn stood watch. Several hours went by until the technician concluded his testing. "It was a task but I've been able to lift several useful prints from the rear passenger seat," he reported to Llewelyn. "I've also taken the liberty of swabbing for DNA samples."

"Run them all," Llewelyn ordered. "Call me as soon as you finish." He turned to his other officers. "Gather as many of the men off from detail and meet me at the 'war room.'"

It took no more than five minutes for the homicide detectives, including Fairfield, to gather inside the war room. They all stood in silence as Llewelyn walked in and watched as he taped two of the sketch artist's portraits onto the blackboard that was situated in the center of the room. The sketch was of a fair-skinned white male with blue eyes.

Llewelyn faced the crowd. "Ladies and gentlemen, these are artist's renditions of the prime suspect of the homicides. One was identified by an elderly man walking his dog and the other by a neighbor. We have a preliminary report that indicates that the fingerprints and the DNA match the fingerprints found in the torture room located in the apartment. We have found that the apartment was rented by a false name and that the flat was paid in cash, all in one lump sum. The limousine was also purchased by an unknown male, also in cash. However, both sellers have indicated that the buyer resembles the man in these pictures. So the question is this—who has the resources to not only pay cash for the apartment but also pay for the limo?" Llewelyn turned to Inspector Phillips. "I want you to run these renditions on the facial recognition program. But I also want you to try to cross-reference these faces to any affluent living within a ten-mile radius. I want this guy identified by tonight."

The group began to disperse when a frantic call came over all the officers' radios.

"Attention all units! Attention all units!" the dispatched announced.

The entire room came to a sudden halt.

"Suspected killer spotted in the area of Thayer and George Streets," the dispatcher continued.

"*St. James's Church!*" Llewelyn exclaimed.

Not a single word was uttered as the entire squad followed Llewelyn to the parking lot. The scores of detectives got into their cars and sped off down the street. The evening sky was brightened by the litany of red and blue emergency lights, and the cacophony of sirens drowned out the sounds of the night.

"Units on scene . . . Progress report!" Llewelyn barked over the police radio as he raced through the city.

"We have a suspect barricaded within the church. He has a hostage. He's threatening to kill her," the voice responded.

"How did the situation commence?"

"A pedestrian discovered a dead body, and the suspect was hovering over him. Upon being seen, the suspect ran into the church. Inside was a cleaning lady, and he took her hostage."

"Describe the deceased," Llewelyn requested.

"White male. Fatal stab wounds to the chest and neck."

"Any signs of sexual trauma?"

"Forensics has not yet arrived, but it does not appear so."

"Do not engage the suspect!" Llewelyn ordered. "I'm on my way!"

Llewelyn accelerated as fast as he could, in complete disregard for safety. Within minutes, he reached his destination. He parked half a meter away from the police barricade. He flashed his badge to a patrolman standing vigil and was let through. He keenly spotted the team of snipers perched on the rooftop of the building across the street as he made his way toward the elite armed response team—the SCO19. The team leader was dressed like the others—full protective gear, covered from head to toe, with his face covered by a black mask—and he stood in the way of Llewelyn.

"Stop there, sir." The team leader placed his hand on Llewelyn's chest. "This is a hostage situation. This is under my authority."

Llewelyn removed the hand. "This is my investigation. My authority supersedes yours."

"Not under a hostage situation."

The two men squared off until Phillips intervened.

Phillips spoke personally to the SCO19 leader. They were classmates from the academy. "Let him through, Martin."

Martin removed his mask and greeted his friend. "Bloody hell, Phillips. You know this isn't authorized."

"Please," Phillips pleaded. "Inspector Llewelyn has sacrificed so much to track this bloke, and he deserves a chance to put this to rest."

"I don't know, Phillips." Martin was scratching his head.

"We all know how this is going to end, and when it does, the inspector will never have the chance to face this madman again."

"Goddammit, Phillips." Martin relented and signaled his men to let Llewelyn through. "You have five minutes."

Llewelyn paced himself slowly toward the church, stopping short of the entrance. He could feel the snipers' sights on his back. He took a deep breath and entered through the doorway. Llewelyn felt a sense of certain doom as he stepped into what he thought would be the gateway to eternity.

Chapter Eighty-one

Standing before the church's altar, a tall and lanky man was holding a knife to the throat of a frightened woman. The man was trembling, his hostage even more so. Llewelyn held his hands up to show he was unarmed.

"D-don't come any further!" the man said, his voice shaking.

"Who are you?" Llewelyn asked, stepping ever so closely.

"I-I'm the S-sinner. I'm the man r-responsible for all this mayhem."

The detective gazed at the knife in the man's right hand and immediately knew that this man was not the killer. Still, he wanted to be sure. "Do you know who I am?"

"Yeah, you're a cop."

"What's my name?"

"I-I don't know you . . ."

Llewelyn paused and lowered his head in disappointment. He turned and stepped out of the church. Walking past the SCO19 team leader, Llewelyn said to him, "That's not our man. Take him out."

Martin immediately spoke into his radio. "Fire at will!"

Within the seconds, the expert marksman fired a single shot that narrowly missed the hostage but successfully penetrated the skull of the faux killer.

Llewelyn spoke out to his men, who were faithfully waiting just outside the police cordon. "He wasn't the killer. We head back and pick up where we left off."

As expected, the detectives obeyed their directive.

Detective Phillips approached his partner with a concerned look. "How can you be certain?" Phillips asked.

"This man was right-handed. The wounds on our victims are consistent with a left-handed killer, and this man lacked the confidence our killer possesses. Plus, he didn't know me. We resume our investigation."

* * *

During the entire breathtaking scenario, the media—and the entire world—were watching from afar. The spectators watched as Llewelyn approached the ersatz killer. Nothing could be heard between the two men, but the meeting lasted no more than two minutes.

Viewers saw as the inspector left the meeting with a look of disappointment. He was not more than a meter away when trained snipers shot a bullet in the killer's head. The city of London was celebrating.

* * *

At Wyndham Court, the two elders were watching the events from a large screen. They smirked at the apparent assassination of the killer.

"It is done," said Ducard with a cynical smile.

"That inspector Llewelyn will never believe that they got the true killer," Sébastien retorted.

"It makes no difference. The public will think so. That'll suffice for now."

Sébastien shook his head in disagreement. "That'll only last until James returns from his trip."

"We just need to try harder in keeping him under control."

"*We?*" asked Sébastien.

"Yes, this is a collective effort," replied Ducard.

"If it were up to me," Sébastien quipped, "I would have James eliminated."

"If we don't successfully *present* James," Ducard said back, "you and I will be eliminated."

Book Three

Chapter Eighty-two

Present Day
Southern Italy

The small tour bus carefully traversed the narrow road in the medieval and scenic town of Santo Stefano di Sessanio in the province of L'Aquila, Italy. Seth Jacobson was among the many tourists, enjoying the view of the fifteenth-century stone houses. When a misplaced rusty nail penetrated the right front tire, the tour bus became an eyesore on the beautiful scenery. The group of fifteen foreign tourists was invited to disembark the bus while the tire was replaced. Seth Jacobson was the only American. He decided to remain on the bus and read from an English newspaper. The headlining story was that of the rampant serial killer menacing the streets of London—the Sinner. The next big headline was that of Yousef.

So much evil. So much hatred, Seth thought. Disgusted by what he read, he put the paper away. He reached into his back pocket and removed a small photo of his lovelorn partner. He tearfully reflected on how the breakup had caused him to quit his job. He needed to get away; he chose Italy. The sad part was that the trip had been a gift from his partner's parents. This was to be their trip. This was to be their honeymoon.

Now Seth was alone. Not even the scenic view of the Italian countryside brought him any comfort. As far as he was concerned, he could stay sitting on that bus for the rest of his life.

Chapter Eighty-three

Seth was born to be a doctor, according to his parents. That was soon abandoned for a career in jurisprudence. He would be the first lawyer in the family, a small concession to the family legacy. Seth's parents felt that there were not enough good Jewish schools in Tampa, so they decided to send him to Jesuit High School, a Catholic all-male high school. The school had been established in 1899 and was known for producing many of the city's elite. Sadly for Seth, being the only Jew in the school was hard enough on the adolescent, but being the only gay made his life even more miserable.

For four long and arduous years Seth fought so hard to fit in, but most of his classmates made his high school experience unbearable. There was never any physical violence, but the mental anguish the other boys put him through made him contemplate suicide on many occasions. Nonetheless, he endured. His only solace was in photography. He did not care if he ever made a penny in taking pictures; he just loved the process.

Throughout his time in high school, Seth was withdrawn from his friends and, more importantly, from his family. When he graduated, he immediately moved away to Tallahassee, Florida, and attended Florida State University. He majored in political science, and under what he felt to be insurmountable pressure, he applied to law schools. Seth made the mistake of moving back to the Tampa Bay area, close to his family, and opted to attend Stetson University College of Law. His family was content—for now.

His parents praised him for his choice of career and were using their connections to line up a clerkship with a U.S. district court judge and with a position in a prestigious law firm somewhere on the other side. Instead, Seth chose to work for the public defender's clinic. As if that alone was not enough disappointment to his family, Seth's revelation that he was gay sent them into a semi-mild state of despair. Seth did not care too much because now he was finally free to live his life.

At Stetson, he met a twenty-six-year-old third-year law student.

His name was Justin Marcus. Like Seth, Justin's parents were Jews, and his parents were doctors but were much more progressive and supportive of their son. Justin was Seth's student advisor, and they both were members of the Lambda Legal Society, which was made up of gay and lesbian students. The two became involved in a relationship, but their romance was very rocky from beginning to end. Justin was much more career oriented and had his sights on a big law firm in New York. Seth had no desire to live in the Big Apple. Seth wanted a simple, quiet life.

The couple fought often, and one year after Justin graduated, Justin had already moved to a small apartment in Chelsea, Manhattan, right across from the Chelsea Market. They had a long-distance relationship during Seth's final year in law school. At Seth's graduation, Justin proposed to him just after Seth had received his diploma. It came as a surprise to the entire audience—especially to Seth. The entire arena stood in cheers. No one from Seth's family attended his graduation, and Justin's proposal brought a glimmer of happiness to what was a very somber occasion.

Justin convinced Seth to fly up to New York after graduation with the promise that he would love the big city life. The plan was for Seth to stay there for two weeks before he would return to make the final arrangements for the final move. Justin's parents met them at

LaGuardia and surprised them with a future trip to Europe. They drove into Manhattan and settled into Justin's apartment.

That first night, Justin announced to his family that he had just been hired as an associate in one of the largest civil litigation firms in the city. Justin and his family were ecstatic. They spoke of attending big social events, such as the annual Met Gala and other high-society gatherings. It was at that moment that Seth came to the stark realization that he did not want to be married to Justin. They were worlds apart in their dreams and goals, but Seth kept those feelings to himself, even though he thought he was long done with keeping secrets.

Those first few days, Justin proudly introduced Seth to all his colleagues, and they were at dinner gatherings every night. By the next week, the two began to fight, and they barely spoke for the rest of his stay. There was no doubt of Justin's love for Seth, but his career was more important than anything at that moment. Justin dropped him off at the airport and promised to see him within a week; they would get away for a weekend and prepare for the wedding. Within a day of returning to Tampa, Seth called Justin and broke off the wedding. Justin's parents flew down to meet with Seth in a vain attempt to salvage the relationship.

"He has never been happier than when he was with you," they told him. "And we love you too."

Seth kept quiet, and that said enough. They cried together and said their goodbyes, but before they left, Justin's parents handed him his future flight to Europe. It was their gift to him, and he gladly accepted. He would later regret that decision.

*   *   *

It was after his run-in with the magistrate and the mysterious Jane Doe that Seth decided that he was going to quit his job. He just had to summon the courage to actually do it.

Seth had to mentally force himself into his supervisor Cynthia Stein's office. He always marveled at the various newspaper clippings, plaques, and other awards hanging on the wall that she had earned throughout her illustrious career. There was one article among all the others that always caught his eye. It was an article of her involvement in the infamous Isaiah House trial and its earth-shattering verdict. The article was titled "The Verdict — Veritas et Justicia." He never read it but always told himself he would.

Cynthia sensed his distress. "What's going on?"

"I'm just not happy being a lawyer anymore."

"Why?"

"I'm just not able to help people the way I believe they should be helped. Plus, I have this love of photography gnawing at me."

"I understand. I became a lawyer because I wanted to help people. It is tough," Cynthia said, reclining in her chair.

"Yeah," Seth responded.

"But the difference between us is that you didn't want to become a lawyer. You may have wanted to help people but not by being a lawyer."

"But how the hell am I supposed to help people by being a photographer?"

"Maybe your lot in life is not to help people. We can't all be saviors."

"Maybe. How am I to survive by being a photographer?"

"The same way I was able to survive by being a public defender. By being really good at what you love."

They both laughed.

"It's settled then. I'll leave in about a week." Seth was relieved.

"You'll always have a place here if you want to come back."

Seth smiled politely, knowing that he would never want to come back.

*   *   *

A week later, Seth left everything behind and walked out of the public defender's office. Leaving that building had been like a huge boulder was lifted from his shoulders, but despite that sense of relief, Seth could not erase from his mind Jane Doe's badly scarred face and her haunting word: *Fiorello.*

Chapter Eighty-four

Seth awoke from his daze to see the bus driver hovering over him.

"My apologies, my esteemed American guest, but it will take at least an hour to fix the bus," the driver said in his broken English, pointing to Seth's camera. "I suggest that you feel free to walk and take pictures."

Seth reluctantly accepted the invitation and casually exited the bus. He refused to follow his fellow stranded tourists and instead decided to go about his separate way. Seth was both pensive and somber as he meandered aimlessly down the narrow streets. In his melancholy state, he had not realized that he had walked several meters away from the bus. He was impressed by the rustic surroundings and quickly recalled that he had his camera hanging from his neck. He freely photographed the surrounding area and became lost in the moment. He felt alive again.

Seth randomly photographed the scenery, rotating himself 360 degrees, taking pictures of the entire area. Through the camera lens, he glimpsed an antique shop. Interested, he walked toward the store. He photographed the exterior and the surrounding area for several minutes. Eventually, he stepped into the small shop. He gave a polite smile at the shopkeeper. Seth strolled deeper into the store, admiring the various trinkets scattered throughout. He continued to take pictures of the various items, and from the corner of his eye, he spotted a vintage picture. The image was a black-and-white photograph of a handful of nuns surrounded by a group of children. The group was standing before a small building that had the appearance of a school. As an amateur photographer, Seth enjoyed the photograph for its simplicity and its tone.

Seth summoned the shopkeeper and pointed at the photograph. "I like this picture," Seth continued. "Where is this place?"

The shopkeeper replied in broken English, "I . . . sorry . . . I no understand."

"Where is this?" Seth then tried to speak in Italian. "Dove?"

"Ah." The shopkeeper finally understood. "Orfanotrofio Fiorello."

"Orfa . . . What? What did you say?" Seth said, shocked.

"Orfanotrofio Fiorello," the shopkeeper repeated.

Orfanotrofio Fiorello. Those were Jane Doe's exact words.

"Where is that?" Seth repeated. "Dove? Where?"

"Napoli."

"Na-po-li? Naple . . . Naples! Naples?"

"Si," the shopkeeper said gleefully.

Seth removed a wad of American dollars and bought the photograph. He walked out to find that the bus driver had been searching for him. The bus's tire had been fixed. Seth sat quietly in his seat, staring carefully at the picture, studying every person on the image. He was certain that he recognized one of the faces.

Chapter Eighty-five

The hotel Casale Signorini was on a hilltop garden outside of L'Aquila, and Seth had chosen it for its scenic overlook, but he was instead spending his time in the business office, using the hotel computer. He spent hours using search engines, researching "Orfanotrofio Fiorello," finding nothing. Feeling frustrated, he asked the concierge to charter him a car to Naples.

* * *

At that very moment, one of the many MIB operatives monitoring the internet from a secret location received an alert that one of the many keywords that he was directed to look for had been engaged.

* * *

A local resident, a cousin of the concierge, agreed to take Seth on his journey in return for the promise of three hundred euros. The 180-kilometer journey took over two hours to make, but for Seth, it seemed an eternity. They stopped at a small village just outside of Scampia.

Using the driver as an interpreter, Seth and his guide wandered through the village, painstakingly showing the various townspeople the photograph. Person after person, the simple folks knew nothing about the picture. After several hours of fruitless responses, Seth had resigned himself to the sad reality that he would never decipher the riddle behind the Italian word *Fiorello* and the photograph.

As his Italian driver quietly escorted his newfound friend to his vehicle, they spotted an elderly lady marching quietly along the street. In each hand, she was carrying two heavy bags filled with fruits and vegetables. The driver motioned for Seth to stay behind as he approached the elderly lady. She clenched her bags tightly and had to be put at ease. The driver spoke to her in her native dialect and showed her the photograph.

The old lady frowned and uttered quietly, "Orfanotrofio Fiorello."

Even from where Seth stood, he could clearly hear the old lady's words. He ran toward the elderly woman. "Please ask her to repeat herself," Seth pleaded.

"Orfanotrofio Fiorello," the old lady repeated. "En Pozzuoli."

"Pozzuoli?" the driver repeated.

"Si, Pozzuoli—"

Seth interrupted. "Ask her about the picture. Who are these people?"

The old lady recounted the tale in her native language.

The driver struggled to quickly translate; he had difficulty in keeping up. "*Fiorello.* It means little flower. She says it was an orphanage that had been around for many decades. It was the gem of her little town. The children were the heart of the city. The nuns provided care for the children. But about thirty years ago, the place grew darker . . . colder. Everything was behind closed doors. They stopped allowing visitors, and no new orphans were allowed. The people soon began to talk when the orphanage brought in a new group of nuns. The nuns were seldom seen and were never allowed outside the doors."

"When she says the people were 'talking,' what were they saying?" Seth asked.

"She says that it is almost sacrilegious to repeat—"

"Please tell me," Seth begged.

The old lady crossed herself.

The interpretation continued.

"Some would say that the nuns were brought there because . . . because they had broken their vows of chastity."

"You mean they had sex?"

"No, not just sex. She means that the rumors were that these women were pregnant. Breaking your vow of celibacy is a serious sin in the eyes of the church," the driver continued.

"Did the nuns ever give birth to the children?"

"No one knows for certain, but rumor had it that some of the nuns delivered stillborn children or babies with defects or abnormalities. She says that once the nuns started arriving, the orphanage was closed to everyone."

"Why would the church do that?" Seth was intrigued.

"Well, she says that it was rumored that the nuns were sent to the orphanage to hide them in disgrace from the church. The nuns were sent there as a form of punishment."

"*Punishment?*" Seth inquired.

Now both the driver and the old lady crossed themselves.

"Yes. Then God imposed the worst punishment of all. The entire orphanage went ablaze. Some say that is why most, if not all of them, died in the fire. It is said that God imposed the final judgment."

"*Fire?*" Seth said to himself. "Tell me more about the fire."

"The people cannot remember how it happened. All she knows is that nearly all the children and nuns died."

"But not all of them?"

The old lady started crying, and the driver continued.

"Since no one knew how many of the disgraced nuns were placed there, the true body count is unknown. But legend has it that two nuns did manage to escape the fire, each carrying one child in their arms."

"Do we know if these were their own children or some of the orphans?" Seth asked.

"She can only guess. But she can say that as a mother herself, if she were in the middle of a fire, her first instinct would be to save her own child. These women disappeared and were never seen again, so no one truly knows."

"That sounds right," Seth agreed. "And I plan on finding out what happened to them. Thank you so much for your time."

Seth offered his driver an additional five hundred euros to take him to Pozzuoli. Seth spent the entire drive staring at the picture. He was so distracted by the mystery surrounding the orphanage that he was ignoring the beautiful Italian landscape.

They arrived at the peninsular town around midnight, and Seth was fortunate enough to find a vacant room. His driver was lucky enough to have a distant cousin with whom he could stay the night. Seth spent another sleepless night searching the internet, looking for any clues. His persistence only continued to alert the MIBs to his presence.

Seth found it particularly odd that the internet would be completely void of any information on the orphanage. Quicker than he would have liked, he saw the morning sun shine through his window.

Fatigue was starting to set in, but Seth pressed on. He found his driver drinking an espresso in the hotel lobby. The driver had the same ragged look on his face, but the promise of additional euros made it worthy of the driver's time. He smiled when he saw Seth approach him.

"Good morning," said the driver. "I am ready when you are."

Seth smiled back. "I'm ready now."

The two men drove around the Pozzuoli countryside, with the driver following a handwritten map he had gotten from his cousin. The brief jaunt took them to a vacant lot. Although the terrain was barren, there were scant remnants of what had to have been the orphanage.

Seth exited the car and looked upon the area disapprovingly. Because the town was in the center of a volcanic caldera, the smell of sulfur was repugnant, and the cool breeze from the neighboring gulf irritated him. He compared the area to the photograph. There was no doubt that it was the same place. Seth looked around and observed a passerby, a man who had to be in his eighties. He appeared to be out and about for a stroll.

Seth turned to the driver. "Would you please translate for me?"

"Of course," the driver said, greeting the old man.

"Ask him if he knows what happened here."

The old man surprised everyone by answering in English. "I speak English."

"It is my pleasure to meet you." Seth shook the old man's hand. "Are you familiar with the orphanage that used to be here?"

"Yes, I was." The old man removed his hat and wiped the sweat from his brow. "I have lived here all my life."

"Is it true this place was cursed?"

"Cursed? Good lord, no. What occurred here was done at the hands of man."

"What happened?"

"It was the cold of night, and most of the townspeople were locked away for the night. The fire started in two places—one in the sleeping quarters of the nuns and the other in the nursery. The parish priest awoke from his own slumber and tried to open the door to each room, but they had been dead-bolted from the inside. He pounded on the door, begging them to open it. The priest could hear the screams coming from the inside and could hear an infant's wailing. He imagined that the pain they endured had to be unbearable. The nuns must have been confused, struggling to breathe, and could not reach the door. The flames reached the ceiling and engulfed the rest of the church. The fumes made it impossible for him to breathe and the darkness of the smoke impossible for him to see. The priest had no choice but to run for his own safety. Within moments, the entire structure had been incinerated."

Seth had been troubled by the story. "Is it possible that any of them survived?"

"*Impossibile.* Impossible. The townspeople came out of their homes, and we valiantly tried to put out the fire. No one made it out alive except the priest, who had to live with that guilt for the rest of his life." The old man composed himself. "We recovered as many of the remains as we could. There was no way anybody could have survived."

"The babies?"

"That was the most anguishing thing about the entire event. The poor infants. They were already ill, and to suffer even more . . ."

Seth noticed the old man had tears in his eyes. "It must have been so difficult."

"It was, but with the grace of God, the people of this town endured."

"Thank you for your assistance," he said, shaking the old man's hand.

Seth was about to turn and leave, but the old man would not release his grip.

The old man whispered his warning. "I recommend that you do not pursue this matter. What happened here at Fiorello may not have been a curse from God, but it was definitely *evil*."

Seth was shaken. The old man finally released his grip.

*   *   *

Seth left Pozzuoli not knowing any more information to the mystery of the word *Fiorello* than he did when he had first arrived. He knew it was time to leave and go back to the one person who could possibly help him solve this enigma. He would be forced to go to the same person who had opened the mystery door: Jane Doe.

Chapter Eighty-six

The very day Seth's plane landed at Tampa International Airport, he hailed a taxi and directed the driver to take him to the hospital. Despite his intense exhaustion from the marathon-length flight, Seth scurried down the hospital halls. He was approached by the same concerned nurse as before.

The nurse, startled by his appearance, placed her hand on his chest. She stopped him from entering the mental ward. "Mr. Jacobson, what are you doing here? You can't go in there. You don't work for the state anymore."

"Look, please let me in," Seth beckoned. "I know that I lied to you by not doing anything to help Jane Doe, but I'm ready to help her."

"It's too late," the nurse replied.

Seth was startled. "Too late? You don't mean——"

"No, not like that," the nurse answered. "She's still alive. She's just too far gone."

Seth removed a manila folder from within his jacket. With both his hands, he placed it before her. "But I have something that I think can help her." He barged past her and tried to make his way into the ward.

"You can't. You are not allowed," the nurse insisted.

Seth pulled out the content of the manila folder and showed it to her. "Please!"

The nurse looked at the photograph and relented. She led Seth to the elevator at the end of the hallway. She pressed the bottommost button, and they both stood silent as the elevator led them to the basement.

"The basement? Why?" he murmured.

The elevator door opened, and she led him out. "It's no longer a basement. It's where we keep our . . . our less desirous patients."

Seth was shocked at the rancid smell that permeated throughout the long corridor. The elongated corridor was lined up with patients lying motionless, strapped to their gurneys. The groans from all the patients were harmonious in that they were consistent from every single patient.

As Seth passed each invalid, he struggled to refrain from vomiting from both the putrid smell and the ghastly sight. His fear that one may reach out and grab him forced him to keep a safe distance. He struggled to see despite the dim lighting and had hoped to cast his eyes on the one and only face he could welcome.

Finally, near the end of the hallway was the elderly woman with her scars, the elderly woman who had been treated as if she had no value to her life, not even worthy of a real name. Seth noticed she had tears in her eyes. She was uttering the same haunting word: *Fiorello.*

Seth took out the photograph of the nuns and the children standing before the orphanage and held it before her. "Do you recognize this picture?" Seth asked her. "Please look at it."

The old lady struggled to open her eyes. Once she did, the tears continued to flow. Her hands trembled as she reached out for it. She had no strength to grasp it. It fell to the floor. Seth retrieved it and held it before her.

"Please," he beckoned.

"F-Fiorello?" she whispered. "Fiorello . . ."

The nurse was shocked at how responsive the patient had become, but that soon changed as Jane Doe began to sob inconsolably.

The nurse bellowed, "Pease stop it! You are making it worse!"

"Si. Fiorello, m-mio . . . mio figlio," the patient whispered.

Seth stood in awe. He was in shock. He tried to soothe her by caressing her head.

"I need to sedate her." The nurse was about to turn but was held back by Seth.

"Wait," he said. "I need her lucid."

The nurse stood still, on the verge of shock herself. "What happened? What did she say?"

"My Italian is rusty, but she identified the orphanage in the picture. And from the little Italian I do understand, I think she said, 'My son.'"

Chapter Eighty-seven

Seth and the nurse each looked at Jane Doe's distorted state.

"You've known her longer than anybody." Seth asked, "Does she have a son?"

"I've been her nurse since she was brought in from the homeless shelter as a drunken derelict and suicide risk," the nurse stammered. "But that was so many years ago, and I've never known her to have any family."

Seth continued to stare at the patient, almost lovingly. He started to sympathize for her in a way he would never have allowed himself to feel for any client. He continued to console her by caressing her hand. "Did she ever speak in English?"

"Not really, but she would at least try, but ever since the doctors increased her medication—well, she is so heavily sedated that she only mumbles."

Seth released her hand and rushed out the door.

"Mr. Jacobson, where are you going?" the nurse asked.

"I'm going to keep a promise that I should have kept a long time ago."

Chapter Eighty-eight

"Let me get this straight," the magistrate barked from behind the front door to his house. He was in his pajamas. "You're no longer working for the public defender's office, but you are filing this emergency motion for relief to cease medicating Jane Doe, who is no longer one of your clients."

"I may have resigned, but I'm still a licensed attorney." Seth was defiant. "And I'm only looking for relief for twenty-four hours. That's it. Twenty-four hours, and then you could go back to doping her all over again."

"What's your basis?"

"It's all set out in the motion. I have come across newly discovered information that leads me to believe that if I can get her off the medication, I can get her to tell me where she's from, who she is, and whether or not she has any family."

"Yes, but you are not telling me the basis for your belief." The magistrate handed him back the brief. "You've given me no indication of where you came across this 'newly discovered' information."

"If I had the time to go into that much detail, I wouldn't have styled it as an 'emergency motion.'" Seth's tone was sardonic and offended the magistrate.

"Look, Seth—"

"It's Mr. Jacobson," Seth retorted. "I hated it when my mom would say, 'Look, Seth.'"

The magistrate gulped as he swallowed his pride. "Mr. Jacobson, why don't you go back on your sabbatical and continue your new hobby of photography?"

"It wasn't a sabbatical. It was more of a permanent vacation."

"Whatever. Just leave the practice of law to someone who actually cares."

"*Someone who actually cares.*" Seth chuckled. "You know what? That's fair. I did stop caring a long time ago. Let me tell you about the practice of law. What goes on in that makeshift courthouse at the hospital is not the practice of law. It's a travesty of justice that has gone unchecked for decades. If it hadn't been for budget restraints at the public defender's office, I would have filed writs of habeas corpus in federal court for every single involuntary placement order you've signed. I think enough of those orders of placement would have had you indicted for civil rights violations. And I've seen what you have stored in the basement of that hospital. Don't make me open up that can of worms."

The magistrate was visibly startled as he came out from behind the door. "Why you arrogant little—I'll have your job!"

"Remember, I'm on sabbatical. I have no job for you to take." Seth humbled himself. "Please. All I need is twenty-four hours with her."

The startled magistrate took his still-shaking hands and ripped the paper from Seth's hand. He half-heartedly scribbled his signature on the order. "Twenty-four hours and not a second more. Do you understand?"

Seth glanced down at the paper, making sure it was all in order, and raced out to his car.

Chapter Eighty=nine

Seth slowly peeked into the private hospital room he had secured for his client. He was hopeful that he would not have woken her from her slumber, but to his surprise, she was awake. The badly scarred woman had been off her medication for over twenty hours and had not been this lucid in decades. She was tired of sleeping. She looked up at Seth's face and smiled.

Seth gently pressed his hand against hers. "Hello. I'm Seth."

"M-my name is Teresa," the older lady replied with her broken English. Her throat was dry.

Seth offered her a drink of water.

"My name is Teresa Aprile," she said in between swallows. "How did you know about Fiorello?"

"I really don't know much about Fiorello." He felt comfortable enough to sit alongside her on her bed. "But I would really like to know. It was all you talked about for the last several years. Tell me about your scars, about the fire, about your son."

Teresa sobbed. "It's so painful to recall, but I will tell you what I do know." Teresa closed her eyes as she recalled her past. "I was born and raised in a small town outside of Rome, the youngest of eight children. We were four boys and four girls. All but one sister joined the convent, and two of my brothers became priests. Since I was a child, I knew I was being called to become a nun. I was a devout Catholic and faithful to the church. I joined the convent at thirteen, and because of my father's connections, I was promised an assignment at the Vatican itself. Three years later, I began having problems common only to girls and was taken to the hospital, where I had minor surgery. A few days later, I was released from the hospital, but I didn't feel any better. I became sicker and started vomiting daily. One night I was rushed to the hospital, fearing the worst. Instead . . . I was told that I was pregnant." Her tears flowed uncontrollably.

Seth stuttered through his astonishment. "Who . . . Who was the father?"

"You don't understand." She was indignant. "I was chaste."

"Had . . . Had you been r-raped?"

"No, I have always been chaste. I have never been with a man."

"Then how?"

"I don't know—"

Seth jumped to his feet. "That's crazy. It's unbelievable."

"That is what my parents said." Teresa could not contain her emotions and struggled to speak. "In fact, my whole family disowned me."

"I-I just don't believe it."

"None of my family or my friends would believe it. I couldn't believe it myself. I was so very young that I thought it to be a miracle."

Seth noticed her emotional state and felt remorse for his outburst.

Teresa continued, "And certainly, the church didn't believe it either. I was given two choices—leave the church or be banished to Fiorello, where I would give birth and then give up the baby for adoption."

"That is unconscionable."

"I wish it had been a cruel joke. But what was even stranger was that I wasn't the only sister banished there. We were a total of five nuns. There were five of us from all over Europe."

"Five?"

"Yes, we all shared the same experience."

"You are not saying—"

"Yes, they—we all claimed the same miracle."

"Miracle? *Immaculate conception?*"

"We were all young and naive. More importantly, we were faithful. We accepted banishment and kept silent. We accepted 'responsibility' for our sin, and we were willing to give up our children with the promise that we would be able to restore our honor."

The room was now silent as Seth stood there, incredulous. There was something about the way Teresa looked that made him believe her.

"Why would you bear responsibility? *Responsibility* for what? You did nothing wrong."

Teresa continued to sob. "Like I said, we were naive, and we felt that we had to take responsibility for . . . for our *condition*."

Seth removed the picture of the nuns and placed it before her. "Tell me what happened with the children."

He noticed her hesitation, and she became more visibly uncomfortable. This time, he held her hand.

"As our bellies grew, the sisters grew closer. We had a unique bond. We felt God had chosen this for us. But things became ominous. Strange men in dark suits came to the orphanage quite frequently. These men met secretly with our mother superior behind closed doors. Since we could not leave the grounds, the strange men brought these . . . these foreign doctors to the orphanage."

"Foreign doctors?" Seth asked.

"Yes, they had strong European accents. Since we were not allowed to leave the orphanage, not even to go to the hospital, these men in dark suits brought in these special doctors to the orphanage. These doctors came in quite regularly to check up on us. But despite the presence of these men, the five of us were all excited about the births of th-these beautiful creations. That is, until the first of the five delivered. We were all there when the first nun delivered, but her baby boy was stillborn. But more disturbing was that the baby had all these deformities. The b-baby had m-missing limbs and . . . his organs were outside of h-his body. It was a blessing that the baby died. His mother bled to death shortly after."

Teresa reached for another cup of water, and Seth helped her drink from it.

She continued, "Two months later, the second nun delivered a boy. That baby survived but was missing its foot and ears and had other health issues. That baby died a few weeks later. Four months after that, I was the third to deliver. I had t—" Teresa momentarily paused as a nurse came into the room and began to check her vital signs. "My child was born partially blind, and his legs were deformed. But he was my son, and I was blessed to have had him. The doctors said that my son would also have cognitive problems. I was determined to stay with my child for as long as I could. A month after my delivery, the fourth nun delivered her boy, and that baby had also had severe health issues. That mother also died at childbirth. The other nuns and I continued to care for that baby."

There was a sense of eeriness that clouded the room. Seth felt compelled to look over his shoulder and stared at the nurse.

He thought, *Why is this nurse taking so long? Where is the regular nurse?* When the nurse finally finished her duties, he followed the nurse to the door and closed it behind her. Seth was sure the rest of the hospital staff were listening in on their conversation.

Teresa was slightly relieved that the door was closed and that they were alone. "The last nun's child was the closest to a healthy child to be born. His mother's name was Maria-Elena. She was a nun from Spain who became one of my closest friends. The doctors took extra care of her, and she spent the entire pregnancy bedridden. Her delivery was the only one we were not allowed to attend. It was behind closed doors. When they brought out the baby, I was overjoyed. Even the doctors seemed elated—that is, until the doctors noticed that one leg was shorter than the other. The child was otherwise healthy and normal. But as I held my own infant in my arms, I noticed that the doctors had the same look on their faces that they had with every other child—a look of . . . disappointment. Maria-Elena spent the recovery confined to her bed. We were not allowed into her private room."

Seth held his hands to his head and manically paced across the room. "This is so insane—so unbelievable."

Teresa continued, "The doctors left the orphanage with that last delivery and never came back . . . but the men in black suits were still coming. They became more secretive. Mother Superior was suddenly transferred and never replaced. We were pretty much left to fend for ourselves."

Seth noticed that she was now shaking uncontrollably.

"We all felt something sinister was about to happen," Teresa continued. "That last nun, Maria-Elena, had always been headstrong. We could hear her protest that she wanted to leave the room. And then one night she was gone. She had escaped with her son without any advance warning to any of us. She did not even tell me. I never saw her again.

"A week later, I woke up to the fire. I had fallen asleep in the nursery, and the room had already been engulfed. I ran to the door, but it had been locked, but no matter how hard I tried, the door wouldn't unlock. The nursery was also filled with the town's orphans . . ." Teresa began to shake uncontrollably. "T-there were a total of eight other children of different ages. I had to make a choice . . . I had to make a choice!"

Seth tried to console her with an embrace.

"I was desperate to survive, and out of sheer adrenaline, I took a chair and shattered one of the windows. I grabbed my child and barely made it through the window. The flames and the smoke were too great for me to go back in. I had to watch them die. I ran into the woods as far as I could until I passed out with my child in my arms. We were the only two to survive. The screams of the other children still haunt me."

"Do you know how all this could have happened?"

"I know that the fire had to have been deliberately set. Looking back, in the days leading up to the fire, I could tell by the looks of the men in black suits that they knew in advance that something like this would happen to us. No one was supposed to have survived that fire."

"But what about the babies? How were they even conceived?"

"I-I do not know. But I know that these men were somehow responsible for our pregnancies and that whatever it is that they did to us—whatever it was that they had planned for us—was a complete failure."

Seth caressed her face. "And your scars?"

She closed her eyes at his touch. "The fire nearly consumed me."

"Where did you go?"

"I was scared for my life. I felt I had nowhere to go. My son and I slept in the streets for days. I treated my own wounds, stealing food whenever I could. I had disguised myself as a gypsy. I could barely keep us both alive. After about a week, I traveled to Rome and took my baby to one of my sisters. Despite my apparent shame, I knew I could count on her to see to it that the baby would be protected. I fled to America alone, making my way to New York. Somehow I managed to make my way here, Florida. After many years of depression, I suffered a breakdown and tried to kill myself. I don't even remember how I ended up in the hospital. It's been too many years . . ."

She struggled to get up. Seth eased her back into bed.

"I need to go back. I need to find my son. He has to be alive," she said desperately.

"I can help you get back to Italy. Your passport may still be around, perhaps here in storage. If not, we can contact your embassy." Seth paused to think about his words. "Going to the consulate, however, might bring some attention to you, to us. Do you . . . Do you think that the people responsible for all this are still out there?"

"I don't know about the men dressed in black," Teresa whimpered. "But I saw one of the children. It was on the news. I saw him on TV." She pointed to the television hanging across from her bed.

Seth looked up at it and came to the realization that it had been on the entire time. It had been on mute.

"I saw one of the children," she said. "He is a grown man now, but it was the same face. It was one of them. One of the babies must have survived."

The room was now silent.

Chapter Ninety

It was past three o'clock in the morning, and except for the skeleton crew of nurses, cleaning crew, and snoring patients, the hospital was virtually silent. The sound of Seth and his newfound friend easily rose above this quiet. He had been practically interrogating her for several hours, but neither showed any sign of exhaustion.

"How do you know it was him?" Seth asked.

Teresa was hesitant to answer but struggled through it. "You must first understand that despite all their imperfections, the babies shared the same angelic features. They could pass for brothers. One night, in my hospital bed, I was watching the news, and they aired a story on that man who is always on all the news channels. I have always dreamed about what my baby would look like as a young man, and that man looked a lot like what my son would have looked like. I may have been in a daze from all the medication, but I know what I saw. It was that image on the television screen that got me to say 'Fiorello' after all those years of silence."

Seth scratched his head in confusion. "What are you trying to say?"

"Please bear with me," Teresa continued. "In one of the stories, there was a still photograph of the man, and behind him was a woman whom I recognized. It was his mother. I know it was her."

Seth was not sure if the weakness he felt in his legs was from sleep deprivation or from the anxiety of what he was hearing. "Who? Who are you talking about now?"

"Maria-Elena! I'm talking about Maria-Elena. She's still alive—and her son. I saw her and her son on television."

Seth was perplexed. "You saw this Maria-Elena on TV? What do you mean you saw her? How?"

Teresa frantically pointed to the television. "I saw Maria-Elena and her son on the news. They are both still alive!"

"How did you see them on the television?" Seth asked emphatically. "Who are you talking about?"

"I don't know *his* name, but I swear I saw him on the news. He has been on the television for the last several months. Even while I was drugged, I could recognize him."

Seth was even more perplexed. *Who could she be talking about?*

"And if Maria-Elena and her son are still alive, then my son must also be alive. I'm going to go back to Italy. I need to find my son." Teresa was hysterical.

"But wait. You can't leave. You're committed to the hospital," Seth pleaded.

"I don't want to get you into any further trouble, but I have to leave," Teresa said emphatically.

Seth was nervously sweating. "None of this makes sense. I'm tempted to go with you, but I'm maxed out on my credit cards and—"

Teresa took his hands in hers and calmed him down. "You have done more than enough. I can't ask you to do that."

"I can't let you go alone." Seth stood upright. "I'm going with you."

"I cannot ask you to do this," she said graciously.

"But you have no money and no resources to get back to Italy."

"I will find a way. If it gets me back to my son." Teresa was tearful.

"I'll get you the money."

"You would help me with that?" she asked.

"Yes, I can borrow the money," he said. "But you'll have to let me go with you."

Teresa appeared relieved. "I cannot thank you enough."

"First, we have to dig up your passport. Where would it be?"

"I haven't seen my personal belongings since they removed me from my room."

"I think I know where your items might be." Seth took a hard swallow. "The basement."

Chapter Ninety-one

Seth took advantage of the late hour and returned to the same basement where Teresa had been confined. He walked past the nurse's station—there was no one attending to it—and made his way to the place he believed might be the storage room. As he made his way down the corridor, he was still repulsed by the sight of the deranged patients. The flickering light made it hard for him to see.

He found the storage room at the end of the passage. Inside the makeshift closet was a cluttered mess of miscellaneous items, some strewn throughout the room and others placed in large garbage bags. He looked at each item scattered on the floor, finding nothing. He then turned his attention to the various bags. Every bag was tied in a simple knot, each with a paper tag taped to it with a handwritten name scribbled on it. He perused through each tag, finding eight with the name Jane Doe.

Seth easily untied each bag and looked through the first four of the bags, and luckily for him, he did not have to go beyond the fifth bag. Seth rummaged through a pile of old clothes, paperwork from the various Baker Act proceedings, and some old maps until he found what he had been looking for—Teresa's passport, long forgotten, seemingly found among her personal belongings at the time she had been discovered wandering the streets in her depressed state all those years ago.

He read through it and was impressed with the picture of her younger self. The passport was dated, but a trip to the Italian consulate in Miami would have that fixed. He dreaded the idea of the trip to Europe, but he knew it needed to be done to decipher the riddle that was Fiorello.

Chapter Ninety-two

Seth took some of Teresa's old clothes from the closet and gave it to her to put on. Once dressed, Seth and Teresa snuck out of the hospital room, and in the predawn hours, they took his car and drove down to Miami.

*   *   *

The next morning, a group of doctors and nurses came into Jane Doe's room to administer the heavy dose of medication to sedate her. The temporary injunction granted by the magistrate had expired.

Leading the way was the kindly nurse who had first convinced Seth to look after Jane Doe. She opened the door for the team, and they found the room to be empty. The doctors were aghast and stormed out of the room. The nurse stayed behind and smiled.

Chapter Ninety-three

Rome, Italy

The immigration inspector carefully examined Teresa's passport for what seemed like an hour. Her Italian passport was old but, thanks to the Italian consulate, still valid. The inspector handed the passport back to Teresa and allowed both her and Seth to continue forward. The pair held onto their breath as they made their way out of the airport terminal and toward the exit. They hailed a taxi and entered a small car. As the car sped off, Seth gazed out the rear window, looking for any sign of anyone following them.

"I can't believe we made it this far," Seth said as he finally breathed out a sigh of relief.

"We were lucky to not have been discovered," Teresa said in agreement.

"Where do we go from here?" Seth asked, still looking over his shoulder.

She turned to the taxi driver and said, "Tivoli."

Seth asked, "What are we going to do once we get there?"

"Sit back," she said. "Rest . . . for we have a long journey ahead of us."

The taxi driver made his way toward his destination and turned on his radio. As the driver turned the radio dial, the news of global turmoil permeated each station. Seth understood enough Italian to be disturbed by the news: the threat of terrorism was on the rise, and a serial killer was running rampant in England. Seth was too restless to sleep. He silently watched the landscape until they reached their destination.

Chapter Ninety-four

Tivoli, Italy

The small villa was modest in its appearance, but it was obvious to Seth that it held sentimental value to Teresa. She struggled to get out of the vehicle as her emotions overcame her. She stepped onto the gravel and walked toward the place that was once her childhood home.

"It . . . It's been so long." She cried. "It's been so very long."

"Where are we?" Seth asked.

"This was our family home," she replied. "This is where my parents raised me and my siblings. I know my sister would have never abandoned this place, and I know she would have never abandoned my son. I hope she has found it in her heart to forgive me—"

"*Forgive?*" Seth said, perplexed. "But you've done nothing wrong."

Teresa smiled and walked to the door. She softly knocked and waited with bated breath. There was silence from within. *Has our home been abandoned?* She knocked again, this time a little harder, a little more desperately.

Seth, gazing at her from behind, sensed her agony. He extended his arms to console her and lead her away, but before he could, he heard a noise from behind the door. The door slowly opened, and standing behind it was an elderly woman dressed in a traditional Catholic habit.

"T-Teresa?" the elderly woman from within the home asked with a look of instant recognition.

Teresa fell into her sister's arms and sobbed inconsolably. "Lucia, my beautiful sister!"

The two sisters then held each other at arm's length, long enough to gaze at each other's faces. They both cried and returned to each other's arms.

"Teresa, I'm so sorry. I feared you were dead."

"*You* are sorry?" Teresa was bewildered.

"Yes," Lucia replied, "for having doubted you. I'm so sorry."

Teresa continued to weep. She struggled to speak through her tears. "Where is my son?"

"He's not here. But he's okay."

"Where is he? I want to see my son!" Teresa became hysterical.

Lucia gazed at Seth and beckoned them both inside. "I promise that I'll take you to him, but please, both of you, come inside before you're seen."

Seth followed the sisters into the home, where they made their brief introductions.

Once he was settled in, Seth asked, "Seen? Seen by whom?"

Lucia stood in the middle of her small living room. "I will try to answer all your questions. But let me explain. Teresa, when you showed up with the baby, I was angry at you. I didn't know what to believe. I was ashamed. But still, I took your baby. I couldn't punish the baby for your sins."

"But I—" Teresa tried to respond.

"Let me finish," Lucia interrupted. "Not long after I took your baby, these strange men dressed in black suits came here looking for you and the baby. I hid the baby well. They went looking for you with our other siblings as well. Our siblings thought you dead, and for your safety, you had to stay dead. For many months after you had left me the baby, I knew that I was being watched. Wherever I went, I knew that I was being followed. I kept the baby hidden until I could get him to the hospital. I told no one. These men in black didn't count on me to be a liar. They believed you and the others were dead from the fire. After several years, they stopped coming by, and they ceased following me. I did well in hiding the baby, first from shame and then out of fear. I feared our lives were in danger. Finally, after never seeing you again, I thought you had, in fact, died."

"Where is my son now?" Teresa pleaded earnestly.

Lucia hesitated. "I . . . I took him to a sanitarium."

Teresa was crying. "*A sanitarium?*"

"He needed special care that I couldn't provide," Lucia explained. "But it's one run by the church. I know the caretakers there. I trust them with his well-being. And I visit him every day. He is fine. He has flourished. He's partially blind, but you wouldn't tell. He has difficulty walking, but he can manage. I have been a volunteer at the hospital for decades. It gives me a reason to visit and be with him."

"You still see him?" Teresa was overjoyed. "Can he speak?"

"Yes, with difficulty. He asks for you every day."

Teresa was in tears. "He . . . He asks for me?"

"Yes." Lucia smiled. "You will see him soon."

"Take me to him," Teresa said gleefully.

"I think it's best you go alone."

Teresa turned to face the door. "Then show me where he is."

Lucia stood between her sister and the door. "You will see your son. But the hospital is not open to visitors right now. Besides, it is best that you *not* go now—if you've been followed."

"Followed?" Teresa asked.

Lucia seemingly ignored the question. "In the abundance of caution, you must spend the night at our brother's apartment."

"Our brother?" Teresa inquired. "Armando? Is he still alive?"

Visibly distressed, Lucia sat on a nearby sofa chair. "No, he passed away eight years ago. But I've been keeping his home. Go rest there tonight, and you will see your son soon."

"But I want to see—"

Seth grabbed Teresa by the hand. "She's right. We don't know what we are dealing with. If everything you have experienced is any indication, these people are dangerous."

"Okay," Teresa said reluctantly. "But we need to go see my son first thing in the morning."

Lucia agreed, and the two sisters embraced. Seth stepped outside to allow the sisters make up for lost time. He wandered about for several hours until the sisters emerged from the home. Their faces were stained with the tears of mixed emotion—joy and heartbreak.

"I have Armando's old car parked in the back. Please take it to his apartment. The keys are in the glove box," Lucia offered. "I think you should minimize your contact with any strangers."

Seth hugged Lucia in gratitude. "That is a good idea." He proceeded to run to the back of the house, where he would find a vehicle covered in tarp.

Lucia handed her sister a piece of paper. "Armando's apartment and the name and address of the hospital are on that piece of paper. Go to the hospital tomorrow morning."

Once again, Teresa broke down in tears. The sisters held each other one last time.

"Thank you for your love of my son," Teresa said sobbingly.

"He is beautiful. You will see."

They were soon distracted by the sound of a rusty old Fiat Spider that Seth drove from the rear of the villa. He left the engine idle as he patiently waited for the sisters to say their final goodbyes. Teresa then sat in the passenger side, and Seth drove off down the road.

Chapter Ninety-five

Rome, Italy

After an hour's drive down Via E80 to Via Nomentana, Seth and Teresa made their way to Armando's apartment in Rome. The home was a small one-room apartment decorated with Catholic imagery and icons. It had not been lived in for years. It smelled of mold. Teresa tidied up the place a bit and then took her leave to sleep in the only bedroom.

Seth said his good night and made his bed on the small sofa chair. After several weeks of sleeplessness, he fell asleep easily. Teresa, on the other hand, was restless. She sat on her brother's old bed and stared out the window. The streets were eerily quiet, and it brought some sense of peace to her mind, but all she could think about was seeing her son.

* * *

The following morning, Teresa and Seth took the Fiat to the Ospedali Salvator Mundi. Lucia had explained to Teresa that the basement below the hospital housed the city's oldest existing sanitarium, and it was only accessible by way of an unassuming door at the end of the long hallway on the first level. Only volunteers were allowed entry into the asylum, and those volunteers were mostly priests and nuns. As a result, Teresa was wearing her sister's habit, and Seth was dressed like a priest, a leftover from Armando's wardrobe. Once the couple made their way past the front desk, they both exhaled a sigh of relief. The two scurried down the hallway and entered the stairwell leading down to the sanitarium.

Seth noticed Teresa's distressed look. He placed his hand on her shoulder. "Are you okay?"

"N-no, I'm not," she struggled to answer. "I'm bothered by the fact that my son and I had to endure the same fate of being confined to a mental hospital."

At the bottom of the stairwell, there was one final door that, once opened, revealed a common area, a recreation room of sorts, filled with children's toys and a television. Scattered throughout the room were several mentally impaired young men, many of whom were confined to wheelchairs. Teresa took some comfort in feeling that this place had been treating her son more humanely.

Seth wandered about, looking at each young man carefully. "There are so many of them. How will we know your son?"

"I will know," Teresa said with an air of confidence.

She walked directly to one particular invalid sitting in a wheelchair. While the other young men were staring at the singular television, this one young man was staring at three beautiful paintings that Seth recognized from his art classes: a painting by Eugène Delacroix, *Entrèe des Croisès a Constantinople*, another by Jacopo Il Giovane, *The Siege of Constantinople*, and the last by Gustave Doré, *Dandolo Preaching the Crusade*. Each of these paintings had the same striking theme.

Teresa caressed the young man's head and approached his ear. "Joshua. Joshua, it's me," she whispered.

Joshua reacted instantly. "M-m-mama. M-mama."

Teresa was grief-stricken at the extent of her son's disability. The young man could only move with great difficulty. She went to hug him, and it pained him to do the same. They were both filled with emotion and began to cry. They stared at each other's eyes. The young man seemed concerned over her scars. She placed her son's hands on her wounds as if to let him know that she was okay. They stared at each other for several moments and rested their foreheads against each other.

The vision brought Seth to tears. The man, with his long hair and beard, resembled an image Seth had seen in the newspapers and television news so many times before, but he could not quite place a name to the image. He stepped out of the room to give the mother and child time to reunite.

Chapter Ninety-six

Seth had momentarily dozed off on a wooden chair when he suddenly felt Teresa's hand on his shoulder. Seth glanced at his watch—six hours had passed.

"Joshua's asleep," Teresa said silently. "It's time we get some rest."

After a brief ride, the two made it back to the apartment, but the drive was not without tension. Seth was certain that one of the many black sedans he had spotted traveling along the same roadways was following them. The fact that many of those black vehicles would eventually veer off in different directions did not serve to assuage his paranoia. Seth had never been so afraid.

*   *   *

That night, Seth's earlier slumber made it easy for him to forsake the luxury of going to sleep, and he opted instead to sit on the living room sofa; a sense of foreboding kept him awake all night.

He turned on the television to watch the news, and the image of Yousef was playing on every news channel. He studied closely the terrorist's facial features. *The resemblance is uncanny! How can it be?*

The image of Yousef only brought Seth consternation. He switched off the television. He stared out the window and trembled at every sound.

*　*　*

Had Seth known that his and Teresa's every move had been monitored by the MIBs since they first arrived in Europe and that one of the several black sedans that had been following them was parked outside the home, only a few yards away, it would have killed him.

*　*　*

Just before the sun rose, Seth finally succumbed to exhaustion, but the rumblings of Teresa as she awoke from her own slumber woke him right back up. He rose from the couch to greet her; he was pleased to see her smile. Seth could sense her gratitude.

A knock on the front door caused Seth to feel that sense of dread once again. Seth was pleasantly surprised to see that it was Lucia on the other side.

"Good morning," Lucia said gleefully.

Teresa rushed to hug her sister. "You were right," Teresa said with great pride. "He's beautiful."

Lucia smiled.

"Thank you for taking care of him all these years."

"Of course. It was my pleasure." Lucia quickly turned serious. "What are your plans?"

"I don't know," Teresa replied, "but I cannot leave him alone."

"What if your lives are still in danger?" Lucia asked.

"I have thought of that for all these decades. But I refuse to abandon him one minute longer."

"At a minimum, you can do what I have been doing for the last several years, which is to volunteer at the hospital and spend your time with him there."

"He's in good health. I know that he has been well taken care of, but I would like to bring him home with me." Teresa was overwhelmed with emotion.

Lucia was equally emotional. "That would be lovely once we know that you are both safe. Why don't we make a meal and have dinner with him tonight? The hospital will allow me to bring him here for a few hours at least."

"That is a wonderful idea," Teresa said gleefully.

Teresa was about to gather her things when Lucia stopped her.

"Let me be the one to go to the market," Lucia insisted. "I know my way around, and I don't feel comfortable with you walking around alone just yet."

Teresa agreed. Lucia retrieved two empty bags from within a kitchen cabinet, and she casually headed toward the front door. Seth had said nothing, not wanting to intrude; his expression of gratitude said enough. Teresa kissed her sister and smiled. Lucia walked out the door.

Teresa sat next to Seth and clasped his hand. "I wanted to thank you for bringing me here." Teresa cracked a smile, which was more of a grin, but it was more than she had done in a long time. "I have waited so long for this moment. I will be forever in your debt."

Seth smiled back at her.

"I've decided to stay," Teresa said to him. "But I think you should leave. You've done more than enough. I think there is nothing left for you to do to help."

Seth shook his head in disagreement. "But what about the people who did this to you? I came here to solve that mystery. Wouldn't you want to know how and why this happened? I can help you with that—"

Teresa was surprisingly overwhelmed with joy. "I have my son now, and that is all I care about. I don't know if I want to know how or why this happened, but I do know it gave me my son. I would think that those people are long gone now, and it's best that we move forward."

"I don't think it will be that easy." Seth hesitated. "I've been up all night thinking about something you said. You said that you thought you had seen Maria-Elena on television."

Teresa nodded.

"I don't know how to say this, but your son resembles that . . . that terrorist. Does that sound crazy?"

"*Terrorist?*" Teresa asked emphatically.

"The man you saw on TV, remember? He's a terrorist," Seth repeated excitedly.

"Yes, I did see a man," Teresa agreed. "At first, I thought I was insane, and then I thought it was the medication, but I'm certain of what I saw on television. And I don't want to believe it."

"I don't want to believe it either. But I think you are correct. Which means I can't leave now." Seth was adamant.

"If that terrorist is . . ." She struggled to say the words. "If that terrorist is Maria-Elena's child . . . But that cannot be my concern. My place is here with my son." Teresa kissed Seth on his forehead. "Thank you for all your help. I owe you my life. Tonight we eat together."

Seth was too exhausted to argue and decided to appease her. "I'm going to pack my stuff and make arrangements to get back to the United States. I can leave as early as tomorrow, I think."

The two hugged ever so tightly, hoping that this ordeal was over.

*   *   *

The same black sedan that had been following Seth and Teresa was now following a new target: Lucia Aprile. The occupants in the car watched as Lucia made her way to the market.

Chapter Ninety-seven

The corner market was filled with its array of usual customers—the elder villagers, the parish priests and nuns, and the various local citizens. Lucia walked over to the vegetable stand and carefully selected the ripest tomatoes, the most verdant green peppers, and the largest cloves of garlic. Lucia loved the aroma of garlic. She also bought six of the largest loaves of bread. She paid for the items and, with the help of the vendor, stuffed her two bags and began her journey home.

As Lucia Aprile traversed the cobblestone streets, she remembered the many times she had made the same trip growing up. Before her parents had bought the villa in the countryside, they lived in the home that would become Armando's. Lucia's mother entrusted her to make the trip daily to the very same corner market to buy the necessary ingredients for the night's supper. Lucia had always wanted to be a nun because that was what her parents had wanted her to be. She wanted nothing more than to please her parents. She made a commitment to never marry because she was going to care for her parents for the rest of their lives. Her parents had a perfect marriage with the perfect family. The love and commitment her family had for one another was sincere. The majority of her siblings joined the clergy and the sisterhood for the very same reason—to keep the family united.

Her parents died at a ripe old age, and the siblings bonded more than ever—that is, until Teresa wrote to the family that she was pregnant. The family was outraged and embarrassed. Each sibling wrote to her, expressing their disappointment and utter disgust. They thanked God that their parents had died and told her that they never wanted to see her again. When the church banished her to Fiorello, the family was relieved.

Several months would pass, and the letters from Teresa eventually stopped. She was as good as dead to them. Lucia was the only sibling who mourned her sister's loss; she struggled with the grief. However, when the news of the fire reached their town, the Aprile family regretted their actions and words. They begged for God's forgiveness. From that moment on, the family was never the same again. Lucia sank deeper into depression and contemplated suicide. Lucia took a leave of absence from the sisterhood and isolated herself from her family and the world.

After several months, Lucia Aprile's life returned to some semblance of normalcy—that is, until one late night, when she heard an unexpected knock on her door.

Chapter Ninety-eight

Lucia could barely hear the rasping on the door. For a moment, she thought it was the wind. She awoke from her wine-induced slumber, stumbled toward the door, opened it, and could not believe her eyes. *I must be hallucinating*, she thought.

Standing outside the doorway was Teresa, holding a baby, swaddled in a filthy rag. Teresa was covered in filth and reeked of garbage. The scars on her face startled Lucia.

Lucia held her breath and then started to scream. "But you are supposed to be dead! They said you died in the fire!"

"Please," Teresa pleaded, "help my baby."

"You disgraced the family."

"No, I did not . . . Please help. If not for me, for the baby."

Lucia looked down at the baby, and despite his grimy appearance, his face was that of an angel. Lucia started to cry. She took the baby into her arms and placed a gentle kiss on his head. She gazed up at her sister and tentatively touched her sister's scars.

Lucia gasped in horror. "Come inside."

Lucia carefully placed the baby in the center of a bed, took her sister by the hand, and led her into a bathroom. Lucia took peroxide from the medicine cabinet and poured it over a hand towel. She carefully dabbed the rag over her sister's face and watched as Teresa grimaced in silence. Despite the excruciating pain, she only whimpered once.

"Teresa, what happened to you?" Lucia said as she placed her sister's head softly on her shoulder.

Teresa sobbed. "I cannot even begin to explain how any of this happened, but a terrible thing happened to us. I do know that my life is in danger. My baby's life is in danger."

"Let us go to the police——"

"No, I cannot trust anyone but you."

"*Me?* But I abandoned you. I let you die. *We* let you die."

The sisters began to cry. Teresa stepped toward the bed and reached for her baby.

"I'm *dead*, and I must remain *dead*," she said, handing the baby to Lucia. "Please take the baby and care for him. I cannot provide for him. I'm a constant risk to his safety."

Lucia comforted the crying baby. "I will take care of him. Where will you go?"

"I don't know."

"Can you at least bathe and rest for the night?"

"No, it is better that I remain this way. I blend in better with the night."

Lucia removed some money from a dresser drawer and handed it to Teresa. Teresa kissed the baby. The two sisters said goodbye, and Lucia watched as Teresa disappeared into the darkness.

"Wait!" Lucia cried out. "What is the baby's name?"

"Joshua," said Teresa's voice as she faded into the shadows of the night.

That first night with the baby was an eventful one. Lucia had no experience in raising a child, and she struggled in feeding the infant and changing its diapers. The baby was visibly deformed, and she could tell that it was mentally underdeveloped, but still, the baby was alive, and she would keep it alive. For the next six months, there was no sleep.

Eventually, both of them settled into a routine and a bit of normalcy. Lucia had grown to love the child, and it was now a part of her life. She could not imagine life without Joshua.

Life was perfect until that second mysterious knock on the door.

Chapter Ninety-nine

Once again, it was in the middle of the night, but this time, Lucia was more prepared to handle any surprise. She looked through the window and saw four men dressed in black suits. Instinct told her that these were the men who had placed Teresa's life in danger. She looked back to see that the baby was sound asleep on her bed but had become restless at the sound of a knock on the door. She did not want to open the door but knew that the men would not leave. She held her breath and opened the door.

Standing before her were Ducard and Sébastien, although she never got to know their names. They matched the description of the men who had been haunting the nuns at the orphanage. They made every effort to appear harmless but did not smile. Two other men behind them stood silent and acted as sentries. In the background, she noticed several more of the men in black standing next to a black sedan.

Ducard removed his sunglasses, and with a lukewarm smirk, he greeted Lucia. "Good evening. We are sorry to bother you so late in the evening, but we are here by directive of the church. We have been asked to investigate the death of your sister."

Lucia stood there, silent. She desperately tried to disguise her fear.

"May we come in?" Ducard said, more of a demand than a request.

Lucia hesitated and casually glanced over her shoulder to see that the door to her bedroom was slightly ajar but closed enough to keep the baby from the men's view. "Please do come in."

She invited the men in. She immediately led them toward the kitchen table. She was the only one who sat.

Ducard continued, "Signorina Lucia, pardon our intrusion, but we need to ask you if you know anything about the death of your sister."

Lucia began to cry. Her tears were sincere. "I know nothing of her death."

"When was the last time you saw your sister?"

"It's been years. I cannot even recall the last time I saw her."

"Are you saying that you have not seen her at all?" Sébastien interjected. He was visibly distrustful.

"Y-yes. Years. Not since . . ." She suddenly realized that she was about to say too much. "Not since our parents died."

"Why would you stop talking to her?" Ducard asked.

"It has been too long to remember." She feigned ignorance.

"Please try to recall!" Sébastien demanded, raising his voice.

Lucia was fearful that his booming voice would awaken the baby, and so she quickly rose to her feet. "With all due respect, I do not feel comfortable answering these questions right now. It is late. Would you prefer if I make an official statement at your office? Is it at the Vatican?"

Sébastien quickly realized that they were in danger of being exposed, and so he led Ducard out the door. "Our apologies," Sébastien said. "It is late, and we are eager to find the cause of the fire that led to your sister's death."

"My siblings and I would appreciate that."

Ducard smiled. "Yes, your siblings. We will be visiting them soon."

"I pray that it will not be at this late hour?" she remarked.

"Not at all," Ducard quipped as he exited out the door. Halfway to his sedan, he stopped and turned around. "And do please let us know if you hear anything—or from anyone."

"Of course. But how would I get a hold of you?" Lucia asked.

With a cynical grin, he said, "We will be in touch with you."

Lucia closed the door and held her breath in fear. Moments later, Joshua would cry out in hunger. She rushed to the baby, and they both cried themselves to sleep.

The next day, she received a call from her siblings, who told her of the same eerie visit. Even though they knew nothing of Teresa's resurgence, their shame of Teresa caused them to not acknowledge her pregnancy.

Several days would pass before Lucia drummed up enough courage to take the child to a safer place. She knew that she could not risk keeping the baby at home. Lucia waited for Joshua to fall asleep and gently placed him in one of her shopping bags. Lucia donned one of her nun's habits for the first time in years and walked over to her usual market, where she bought some various fruits and vegetables. She stuffed them in her bag, careful not to hurt the hidden infant. After a few moments, she could feel the baby become restless, and she made her way to the hospital.

*   *   *

Two of the men in black watched from afar in their sedan. After watching her make the usual trek for two straight weeks, they ceased their surveillance of her before she left for the hospital.

*   *   *

At the hospital, as Lucia returned with baby Joshua, the staff greeted Lucia, and they welcomed her back. She had once been a volunteer there, and they always needed help. She went straight to the infant ward, which housed several babies suffering from birth defects. She found an empty crib and placed the baby inside. She took a paper placard and handwrote the baby's name: "Joshua." She placed the card on the crib. The hospital staff were so overwhelmed with the various patients that they did notice the new arrival for quite some time.

*   *   *

The men in black would sporadically return several more times over the course of the next three years under the guise that they were still investigating the fire. Lucia felt secure that the fact that these men were still taking the time to interview her meant that they had no knowledge of Joshua. She knew that the baby would be safe. Little did she know that after a brief break, the men in black would resume their search for that child.

For nearly three decades, Lucia would care for and nurture the baby into adulthood. With great effort, she taught the nearly blind baby to speak and eventually walk with the assistance of a cane or a walker, but he would never be well enough to leave the confines of the hospital. Lucia spent years showing him pictures of Teresa and sharing with him stories of what a wonderful woman she was. Lucia made it a point to let him know that she was out there somewhere.

Joshua grew to love his mother, and there were many restless moments when he was in solitude that he would cry out for his mama. Lucia would sometimes join him in his grief, wondering where in the world her dear sister Teresa was.

*   *   *

As the years passed by, one by one, Lucia's siblings would die of old age and disease, and in the end, she and Joshua were all who were left of her family, and as she grew older, she very seldom left his side. The fear and dread that these men in black would return never subsided. She personally never felt safe again.

Now, decades later, as she walked home from the market, she saw the black sedan and came to the sad realization that these evil men in black had come back into her life.

Chapter One Hundred

Seth was responsible for reuniting Teresa's family, but it was his own actions that would bring their eventual downfall.

The men in black had been monitoring Seth's movements ever since he first researched the words "orfanotrofio" and "Fiorello" on the internet. Over the course of the last several years, the MIBs' spyware had infiltrated nearly every major search engine in the world. The instant Seth began his search of those two obscure words, alerts were sent to the operatives, and they began their hunt for the person behind the keyboard. The alert first came from someone doing research from a public library in Tampa, Florida, but the MIB monitors were unable to identify their subject. It was not until Seth landed in Europe and resumed his search that the MIBs were able to learn Seth's full name through the customs office. From the moment on, the hunt was on.

Over Ducard's objection, Sébastien ordered his men to simply monitor and trace their steps to see what it was that Seth was pursuing. They were not to engage the targets or hurt them in any way until they knew everything about the American's motives. Sébastien had a deep desire that Seth's interest in Fiorello was the ratification of a long-lost cause from so many years ago.

Chapter One Hundred One

As Lucia crossed the street, she spotted the black luxury sedan parked a few yards away. Sensing danger, she began to walk faster and decided to walk past the apartment. The car began to follow her.

"Oh no . . . *Teresa*," Lucia said to herself. Even in this most dire situation, she could only think of her sister.

Lucia made a decision to head toward a neighboring apartment, three blocks down. She hoped to somehow warn Teresa. As she continued her brisk pace, she spotted Seth walking on the other side of the street. Seth caught a glimpse of Lucia. He was about to wave at her, but he could tell by her expression that something was wrong.

She signaled him with her eyes. *Walk away! Don't come near me!* To her relief, Seth kept on walking. The sedan kept following her. In a valiant attempt to distract her pursuers from her sister, Lucia decided to change her course of travel and approached the sedan head on.

The driver spoke into the microphone hidden within his shirtsleeve. "She's engaging us. She's coming right toward us."

Another voice responded through his earpiece. "Can you abort?"

"Negative," the driver, dressed in black, replied. "We've been compromised. If she was going to lead us to anyone, she certainly won't do it now."

"Then we have no choice," the voice said gravely. "She cannot be in a position to recognize you. Eliminate her."

The driver assented and suddenly accelerated his car toward Lucia. Lucia stood there defiantly and prayed for her sister's safety.

The driver smashed into Lucia. Her body was dragged for several feet. She died instantly. The driver sped off.

Seth witnessed the entire event from across the street; it took everything in his willpower not to scream out loud. He struggled to maintain his composure. Of all the witnesses to the murder, he was the only one who did not come to her aid. He did not want to compromise Teresa's safety; besides, he knew it was too late.

Crowds of screaming people rushed to her body as he instead made every attempt to casually walk away. Seth turned a corner, and once he knew that he was alone, he fell to the ground and broke down in tears. He lay there, weeping, in a state of shock. He finally caught his breath and struggled to stand on his feet. He knew he had to warn Teresa, but he was too scared to move. He collapsed back onto his knees.

Chapter One Hundred Two

Seth waited until nightfall, hiding in the darkness of the buildings, and watched as the paramedics carried Lucia's remains away. The spectators gradually dispersed, exposing the bloodstained streets. Even then, he waited another hour before venturing out of the shadows.

He roamed aimlessly, gathering his senses and then making his way to his destination—Teresa's apartment. He carefully looked around before entering the home. To his surprise, it was eerily vacant.

"My god!" he screamed. "Teresa! Teresa!"

Did they kill her too? he thought. In a state of panic, he rushed out the door and headed to the only place he could think of where Teresa might be.

Chapter One Hundred Three

Teresa had been joyfully in the kitchen preparing for Lucia's eventual return and happily anticipated the time she would spend with her sister. It had been many years since she last cooked, but being in the kitchen and cooking for her large family as a young girl was one of her happiest moments. It was all coming back to her. Seth had offered to help, but after she refused, he stepped outside to catch some fresh air.

Teresa began removing the utensils needed when she heard what she thought was the sound of a distant scream. She stood there, frozen, her heart skipping a beat. She closed her eyes and said a prayer. She opened her eyes at the sound of another scream. Tears began to stream down her face. Teresa knew something must have happened to her Lucia; her sister had already taken too long to return from the market.

At that moment, she could only think of her beloved son. She exited the door and ran toward the hospital. As she ran, she could hear the sirens approaching what could only be the tragedy that had befallen her sister.

Chapter One Hundred Four

After a thirty-minute walk, Seth made his way to the Ospedali Salvator Mundi. He raced straight to the mental ward and found Teresa right where he had expected to find her, sitting quietly next to her son. Teresa looked at Seth and knew instantly that he had witnessed death. Seth's face was swollen from crying, the tears still streaming from his eyes. His grimace said it all, confirming her worst fear.

"No, not Lucia!" Teresa bellowed.

Saved from having to say the words, he opted to instead warn her of the impending doom. "Teresa, *they* are here."

"Who?"

"It has to be the same men who are behind *this*," he replied, pointing to her son, Joshua. "They found your sister Lucia—"

Hearing Lucia's name moved Teresa to tears. "Please, dear God!"

"We have to leave now before *they* find you here."

"*But where would we go?*" Teresa screamed.

"We need to find Maria-Elena."

"Maria-Elena?" Teresa said, perplexed. "But why?"

"Since this ordeal began," he said, caressing her scars, "you have been plagued by pain and death. What makes you think it'll stop?"

Teresa felt the scars on her own face. "How can Maria-Elena help us?"

Seth continued. "If it is true that Maria-Elena is still alive, then she might know who is behind this, maybe put a stop to this before harm comes to you—or your son."

"I wouldn't know where to begin. Maria-Elena could be anywhere in the world. If she is the mother of that terrorist, she could be hiding in the Middle East."

The thought of traveling to the Middle East frightened Seth. "What about her family? Could we track her down through her family in Spain?"

Teresa pondered the thought. "I suppose, if they're still alive. She told me that her family owned a small farm outside of Seville. We could start there."

"Let's go then," Seth said excitedly.

Teresa angrily shook her head. "I am not leaving my son. If my life is in danger, then so is my son's."

"We cannot be traveling throughout Europe pushing him around in a wheelchair."

Teresa was defensive. "He has great difficulty walking, but he can walk short distances. We can get to a train and take the bus from there."

"Are you serious?"

"Yes, I think so."

"Then let's go. But we must hurry."

Seth assisted Teresa with her son, and they secretly wandered out of the hospital. Teresa and Joshua hid in an alley, while Seth hailed a taxicab. He motioned the driver to wait, and he scurried back to retrieve his companions. Joshua was a greater burden than Seth expected because the young man struggled to walk with his cane. After an arduous process, the three made their way into the vehicle. Teresa spoke to the driver in Italian, and he proceeded to speed through the streets of Rome.

Teresa saw the spot where her sister had died. She did not say anything; she mourned her sister in silence.

Chapter One Hundred Five

Sébastien was livid; he had just been notified of the woman's death. "I ordered them not to be touched, and instead, she was terminated by being run over in the middle of the street in broad daylight!" He turned to Ducard. "I thought we only hired professionals!"

"I'm not excusing their actions, but they were caught by surprise by her brazen behavior," Ducard replied. "She came right at them. I would have done the same."

"They couldn't have been more discreet?" Sébastien asked impatiently. "The spyware traced the computer within a few miles of the residence. With just a little more patience, we would have located the American. She was our best lead. And now he is lost to us again."

Ducard found himself a seat. "I'm not worried. It is only a matter of time before that stupid American will activate the spyware again."

Chapter One Hundred Six

The taxi traveled for over an hour until it made it to its destination: the Roma Termini. Once again, they struggled to get Joshua out of the vehicle and into the lobby of the station. Teresa bought three tickets to Spain.

The train had just made its last call when the three boarded the train and made their way to their seats. Joshua was overjoyed by the experience of being on a train. He managed to tell his mother that he had seen trains on television but had never ridden one. Teresa embraced her son and encouraged him to look out the window. Seth had no energy to smile but was moved with compassion by the genuine display of curiosity.

"I really hope that we find the people whom we are looking for." Teresa looked worried. "Do you really think Maria-Elena can help us find these people or why they did this to us?"

"We have no choice but to try," Seth said. "I hope Seville is a good start."

"Her family in Seville was the only family she had. We have to pray that her relatives will lead us to her and that she will lead us to whoever is behind this."

Seth paused momentarily. He looked aghast.

"What is it?" Teresa asked.

"Something just occurred to me. What if *they* are looking for her too? What if *they* are there waiting for us?"

"We have to confront this to end it once and for all." Teresa appeared more confident. "You know that they have waited over thirty years to track me down. They won't stop hunting us down. You saw what *they* did to my sister. They are going to try to kill us one way or another."

Seth eased himself back and watched as Teresa closed her eyes in prayer. She soon fell asleep. Joshua remained awake and sat motionless. Seth had momentarily dozed off but was suddenly brought back to reality by the touch of Joshua's hands. The two men stared at each other, and for the first time, Seth saw the humanity in Joshua's eyes.

Chapter One Hundred Seven

Seville, Spain

On the plain of the River Guadalquivir lies the two-thousand-year-old city of Seville. Seth was impressed with the city's maze of narrow twisting streets and its homes modeled after the Moorish style. The pleasing odor of freshly cooked paella filled the air, but Seth had no time to enjoy it. After the three disembarked from the train and cautiously made their way across Constitución Avenue, they made their way toward the Cathedral of Saint Mary. Teresa approached an elderly fruit vendor on a corner.

"Good morning. I am looking for the family of Maria-Elena de la Cuesta." Her Spanish was flawless.

"Maria-Elena de la Cuesta?" the vendor replied in his Andalusian accent. "Ah, that is a name I have not heard in many, many years. She was the poor nun disgraced and sent to exile in Rome?"

"Yes, that is the one. Her family owned a farm here many years ago. Are they still alive?"

"Oh, yes. Her father is quite old and sick, but her mother passed. Others live there as well. They still own the small farm. It is a few miles south from here."

"Thank you so very much." Teresa kissed the vendor farewell on each cheek.

The vendor stopped her before she could leave. "I see that your young man is sickly. Let my grandchild drive you to the farm." The old man pointed to his teenage grandson, who had been unloading fruits from the trunk of his small car.

"I cannot tell you how grateful we would be." Teresa smiled.

The old man gave his grandson instructions, to which the young boy dutifully agreed. The three passengers fit snugly into the car and were taken down a rocky road. Seth could not help but look to see if any cars were following them. Thankfully, they were the only ones on the road.

Chapter One Hundred Eight

Seth must have dozed off because the next thing he realized was that the young man had parked his car alongside the dirt road beside a wooden fence that surrounded a small brick frame house situated on a hectare of land. Before the passengers could even exit the car, an ornery old man who appeared to be in his late nineties exited his home, pointing his cane at the young driver.

"Mateo," he said to the young man, yelling in Spanish, "who are these people? Why did you bring them here?"

Teresa exited the car and approached the fence line.

The old man turned his attention to her. "What are you doing here? Get off my land!"

"My name is Teresa Aprile." Teresa clasped her hands as if in prayer, pleading for the old man's attention. "I was a nun with your daughter, Maria-Elena. We were friends a very long time ago."

"Don't mention that name to me! That name means nothing to me!" The old man was irate.

Teresa pleaded, "I beg of you, listen. We mean her no harm. Our lives are in danger, and we need her help."

"I said get off my land!"

Teresa carefully removed Joshua from the car and led him to the old man. "I am only trying to protect my son. I was there when she gave birth to her son, and I'll do anything to protect our children."

The old man paused as if he recognized Joshua, but the man was too irate and grimaced in pain as he tried to motion to Teresa to go away; he clearly suffered from arthritis.

"Let them in," said a calm voice from within the residence.

Teresa was taken aback as she saw Maria-Elena step out of the doorway. Seth gasped in shock, his heart racing a million beats a second. His suspicions were confirmed; Maria-Elena was Yousef's mother - *Aamilah.*

Chapter One Hundred Nine

Maria-Elena gracefully walked over to Joshua and gently embraced him. She was in awe at the resemblance to her own son. She caressed his face and gently kissed his forehead.

"It has been so long since I saw you," she said to Joshua, speaking in flawless Italian. "You had just been born, and now look at the handsome man you have become."

Maria-Elena then turned to Teresa, and they fell into each other's arms. They wept and dried the tears from each other's faces.

After several endearing moments, Teresa and Maria-Elena made their way into the home. The two sat at the kitchen table, while the others waited in the small family room. The old man grumbled something in Spanish and wandered into his bedroom. Maria-Elena wore a dark Spanish gown with a black mantilla covering her head. The two women sat across from each other on the table and caressed each other's hands.

"I have not seen you since before I fled," Maria-Elena whispered, caressing Teresa's scarred face.

They spoke in English for Seth's benefit as he listened from the family room.

"Why did you leave us?" Teresa asked.

"I knew that something was wrong with the way those men in black took an interest in us as we carried our children. It was clear that they were only interested in the outcome. But as we each gave birth to our sickly babies their disappointment was frighteningly obvious. After the last of the babies were born, they could not disguise their disgust. At that very moment, I knew our lives were in danger. I had to leave. I could not leave my baby there."

"Where did you go?" Teresa wondered.

"I'm sure like you, I wandered the world, seeking refuge. I only felt safe in the Middle East. I changed my name to Aamilah and learned Arabic. I met an older cleric, Mustafa, who shared with me his religion and taught me how to be at peace. He was like a father to my son." Maria-Elena became somber.

"What is wrong?" Teresa asked earnestly.

"Mustafa was murdered by the Westerners. My son lost a great role model and lost his best friend."

Teresa held her sister's hands even more tightly. "I am sorry for your pain."

Maria-Elena caught her breath. "No, I am sorry for your pain. I should not have fled that night. But I trusted my instincts and escaped into the night, and I have always regretted that I didn't stop to wake you or the others. I thought . . . I honestly thought that I would run and send for you and the others later. But I did not expect the fire. I am so sorry . . ."

The two sisters consoled each other.

Teresa whimpered, and her voice was strained as she spoke. "Have you ever wondered why *this* happened to us?"

"All I've ever wondered is *how* this could have happened to us." Maria-Elena's voice was equally frail.

"No, I mean *why?* Why *us?*" Teresa corrected.

"We were young. We were naive. We were obedient." Maria-Elena then threw a question at Teresa. "But have you never stopped to think *how* this happened to us?"

Teresa did not hesitate in answering, "I have no doubt that we were each blessed with gifts from God. We were chaste, virtuous, and loyal to God."

"A *gift?*" Maria-Elena said irately. "Look at your son, Joshua. Think about the other babies that suffered or the ones that didn't survive."

"Things like illness and death happen every day, and that has never caused us to waver in our faith," Teresa replied.

"I no longer have faith," Maria-Elena said, rising from her chair. "I have seen so much hate, violence, and death. I have witnessed the killing and maiming of women and children, death at the hands of strangers, death for no reason at all."

It was at that moment that Teresa began to cry, but hers were not tears of sorrow; ironically, they were tears of joy. "I have witnessed the miracle of life from where there should be no life. I have not seen my child in decades, but he is here with me now. And while I do know that there is an evil that has been hunting us down, together, we could all put an end to this violence."

Maria-Elena removed her hands from Teresa's and looked at her sister with a sad expression. "Do you know who my son is?"

It was here that Seth came in from the living room and interrupted. "I know. I know who your son is, and with his resources, maybe he can help us—"

Maria-Elena shook her head. "He has his own calling. He cannot help us in this endeavor."

"We cannot go on running for the rest of our lives," Seth said. "I would hope that you could at least try."

"I'm afraid that my son won't be alive much longer. His destiny has him on a path which he will not survive."

"Maybe our meeting was meant to be," Seth said angrily. "Maybe 'God' put us together to prevent your son from engaging in whatever it is that will destroy him."

"I wish that were so." Maria-Elena lowered her head, removing her mantilla.

"Can you at least ask him?" Teresa asked.

"My very call to him could place his life in jeopardy," Maria-Elena protested. "And our lives as well."

Teresa was trembling. "All our lives are in danger. Thirty years ago, a fire killed our sisters and their children, and I still carry the scars from that fire. And my sister Lucia was crushed by a car. I know that these people will not stop until they kill me and my son. This call could save *your* own son's life."

Maria-Elena could see the agony in Teresa's face. "You . . . Your sister? Killed?"

"Yes, they killed Lucia in plain daylight, and I know that they will not stop looking for us."

Maria-Elena rose to her feet and stood there, agonizing over the choice she was about to make. She replaced the mantilla over her head and entered another room. Within moments, she returned with a satellite phone and spoke into it. "Hello, son. I have an urgent need to see you."

Both Teresa and Seth marveled at Maria-Elena's Arabic dialect.

"I know, but it is an emergency . . . Yes, I am here . . . Yes, I can travel there. It will take a day or two, but I can make it. Thank you, my son." Maria-Elena disconnected the call, looked at her companions, and said, "My son has agreed to meet with us. If you are still intent on doing this, we must leave as soon as possible."

Chapter One Hundred Ten

Maria-Elena was trembling. "He will meet with us. We have to leave in the morning."

Seth became anxious and was almost too afraid to ask the following question. "Um, where are we going?"

"At this point, I cannot say. My son spoke to me in code. We will have to travel discreetly."

"Thank you." Teresa was relieved beyond expression.

Maria-Elena turned to Seth. "I hope you were right about getting my son involved. Now we must rest."

Seth had been impatiently circling the room. He suddenly stopped and took Teresa to the side. "I don't know if we did the right thing. Her son is a terrorist. He is the most hunted man on the planet. Did we do the right thing?"

Teresa was surprisingly defensive. "He is no more dangerous than the men who are after us. We have no choice."

Seth could not shake the gnawing feeling that perhaps they had made the worst mistake of their lives.

*   *   *

The MIBs listened intently to the call and made arrangements to have a team follow Seth and the others to the train station. The destination was London, England.

Chapter One Hundred Eleven

The train from Spain to London arrived at nine forty in the evening. Shortly after disembarking, Seth hailed a taxi, where the driver listened intently to the directions given by Maria-Elena. Within thirty minutes, the taxi pulled into the southern town of Croydon. The driver continued to follow Maria-Elena's directions, and they soon stopped at an old, dilapidated building. It was there that the driver dropped them off.

*   *   *

Not more than a kilometer away, a team of MIBs watched from afar, setting their plan in motion.

One of the operatives spoke into his communicator. "Targets are in sight. We are a go."

"Do not—I repeat—do *not* engage them until I give the order," Sébastien demanded from his study at Wyndham Court. "Any insubordination will be dealt with personally by me."

Chapter One Hundred Twelve

One of the four miracles attributed to Saint Mungo was putting out a fire in a monastery while he slept, sometime in the sixth century. He was one of the many saints the nuns at Fiorello prayed to for help—but to no avail. Still, Teresa and Maria-Elena thought it to be a miracle that the now abandoned homeless shelter where they had sought refuge in the London borough of Croydon would be named after the venerated man.

Inside the homeless shelter, Seth was disgusted by the scent that permeated throughout the dilapidated four-story apartment that had been converted into a shelter. The building was vacant, and Maria-Elena led the others into a small bedroom on the third floor. Seth helped Joshua to a mat on the floor that would serve as his bed while the two sisters spoke.

"We will stay here until my son makes contact with me."

Seth noticed that Joshua was shivering; he politely interrupted the sisters. "Excuse me, but Joshua is becoming ill."

"It is the bad weather and lack of sleep," Teresa said, rushing to her son's aid. She was visibly distressed. "We cannot go any further. I trust that your son can help us in some way. My son needs medical attention."

"I am hopeful for all our sakes. I'll get some medication for your son. I will seek a pharmacy," Maria-Elena volunteered.

"I'll go with you. It isn't safe alone out there." Seth's voice was shaky.

"Maria-Elena, I thank you with all my heart," Teresa said lovingly.

Seth led Maria-Elena to the elevator down to the ground floor. The two stepped out into the night, not realizing that danger lurked nearby.

*   *   *

Ducard waited for Sébastien to take leave for the evening before calling one of the MIBs doing surveillance. "I want a status report," Ducard demanded.

"There is a total of four. Two females and two males," said the field agent.

"Describe the women."

"Both middle-aged. European. Perhaps Spanish or Italian."

"And the males?"

"One is the American lawyer."

"And the other?" asked Ducard.

"Tall, lanky, early thirties, long black hair. Severely disabled."

Ducard was incredulous. "Where are they now?"

"One of the women and the lawyer exited the building. Destination unknown."

"The invalid?"

"Still inside the building," the voice replied from the radio.

"Supersede all orders. Kill the invalid."

The man on the radio had been disciplined in the art of blind obedience and knew not to question the superseding directive.

*   *   *

While Seth and Maria-Elena were descending in the elevator, an MIB broke the lock to the back door of the dilapidated building and made his way up the stairwell to the third floor.

Inside the bedroom, Teresa cradled Joshua in her arms. "My baby," Teresa whispered, "you are burning up. I'm going to get some water for you."

Joshua whimpered, beckoning his mother to stay. She caressed his hand, reassuring him that he would be safe. She slowly removed her hand from his grip and exited the room.

The hallways were eerily silent. There was no one around. She made her way down the hallway in the hopes of finding a kitchen or a bathroom faucet. Not finding one, she elected to enter the stairwell, intending to look one flight below. Once inside the stairwell, she could hear footsteps coming up the flight of stairs.

Teresa's heart fluttered, and she immediately panicked. Her instinct told her something was wrong; she wanted so desperately to run, but she could not leave her son alone. She reversed her course and ran up the stairs and back into the room. She found her son on the floor where she had left him and struggled while lifting him onto his feet. Teresa scurried him out the door and walked him toward the elevator. The scared woman then heard the footsteps come out of the stairwell and into the hallway.

She knew that running away together would be useless and far too dangerous, and so she turned to her son and whispered into his ear, "Joshua, my son, listen to me. You have to go. Run. Find Seth and Maria-Elena. Run for help."

"Mama . . . Mama?" Joshua was trembling. He struggled to walk as his mother helped him into the elevator.

"I know, baby. I know. I've only just found you. We have no time. Run, baby, run."

The two entered what Teresa knew would be their last embrace. They were both in tears. She pushed her son into the elevator, leaving her alone. She raced back into her room and awaited her fate.

The MIB quietly made his way down the hall, stopping just outside the room. He pressed his ear to the door and placed his gloved hand next to the knob, confirming that it was locked. He removed a lockpick from his breast pocket and easily unlocked the door. After a brief moment to remove a gun, he violently swung the door open, finding the room empty. Hearing movement behind him, he turned to watch the door close behind him; his target had been hiding, pressed against the wall adjacent to the door.

The MIB jerked the door open to see Teresa running down the hallway. She headed into the stairwell as the MIB gave chase. She decided to take the one route that would keep her attacker away from her son, and that was *up* the stairs. Teresa was making her way to the roof.

The man grimaced as he briefly lost sight of her, but within moments, he managed to see her run toward the rooftop door. The MIB stopped running, and he gracefully walked up the flight of stairs. As he approached the top of the stairs, he paused upon reaching the door. He quietly replaced his gun and removed a syringe from the same breast pocket.

On the rooftop, just on the other side of the door, Teresa stood silent, pressed against a wall, in a state of shock. She had never felt so frightened as she stood alone on the rooftop. She heard rumblings coming from the other side of the door. Teresa ever so silently stepped backward toward the edge of the rooftop. She gazed downward and saw the ground below her. She heard the sound of gravel and saw that the MIB was now in front of her.

The MIB stood menacingly before her, and yet Teresa caught a brief glimpse of distress in the eyes of the man. Teresa was convinced that the MIB recognized that if she jumped off the roof, it would bring unnecessary attention to them. She thought it just might give her loved ones just enough time to get away.

The MIB replaced the syringe in his pocket and showed her his empty hands in a feeble attempt to assuage her. He treaded gently toward her. "Where is the boy?" asked the menace.

Teresa chose to ignore him. She reached into her dress pocket and, with her left hand, removed an object. Teresa held the object firmly in her hand. She closed her eyes and softly said a prayer. Teresa opened them to see the man upon her. Before he could grasp her, she leapt to her death. Her scream was silenced when she struck the ground.

The MIB sighed in disappointment and calmly made his way down the stairwell.

Chapter One Hundred Thirteen

Joshua struggled to make his way out of the building. He usually relied on his cane, but the stress of the situation gave him the strength to move forward without it. He was partially blind, but the bright streetlights gave him enough guidance to wander far away from the building. He was unsuitably dressed for the cold of the night in the same T-shirt, jeans, and sandals he wore since leaving Spain.

Joshua braced his hand against the wall and winced in agony as he limped ahead. His fever was rising, and he was shivering. The streets were silent, with a smattering of pedestrians scattered throughout. Joshua was nothing more than an inebriate to these random folks and was literally ignored. With every shadow that passed, Joshua yearned it to be his mama.

Chapter One Hundred Fourteen

Moments before Teresa's demise, Seth and Maria-Elena were returning from their brief mission. They had found a pharmacy, but without a prescription, the pharmacist refused to give them any antibiotic and instead offered them paracetamol. They purchased a small bottle and made haste out of the store.

They were less than a meter away when they heard the screams of Teresa as she fell from the building. They glanced at each other and rushed toward the shelter. Seth was weak-kneed. For him, this was all too eerily similar. He saw Teresa's lifeless body and pushed Maria-Elena aside.

"Oh my god!" Seth screamed. "They killed her."

Maria-Elena cried out, "No, please, God, no!"

In spite of the shock, Seth realized the danger, covered her mouth, and pushed her to the side of the building. "She just fell to her death," Seth whispered. "That means her killer is still around."

They both remained silent for what seemed an eternity. The streets were quiet. No one was rushing to Teresa's aid.

"We have to help her," Maria-Elena said in a soft voice.

"*They* are still out there," Seth reminded her.

Maria-Elena was about to break loose of Seth's grip when she heard a noise come from the building across the street—it was Joshua. Joshua was crouched, straddling his knees, sitting in a corner.

"Joshua!" they both shouted.

"You go to Joshua," Seth suggested. "I'll see to Teresa."

Maria-Elena scurried across the street, where she found Joshua now lying on the floor. He was in fetal position; he was trembling from both a fever and fear. She lifted Joshua into her arms.

He gazed up at Maria-Elena and must have thought her to be his mother. "Mama. Mama."

Across the street from them both, Seth walked in the shadow of the building in an attempt to avoid being seen. He then slowly walked over to Teresa as he looked around for signs of danger. She appeared completely broken, bones shattered; she was having difficulty breathing. Seth was careful not to touch her.

Teresa struggled to speak. "M-my . . . my son . . . J-Josh . . . Joshua."

Seth gently caressed her face. "Quiet. Just rest. We will get you help."

"P-p-please . . . p-protect . . . m-my s-sons . . . sons . . ."

"I will. I promise I will protect Joshua."

"N-no . . . J-Joshua . . . n-not . . . no . . ." She was slowly fading away. She slowly lifted her left hand and placed the object she had been holding into his hands. Seth took the object without looking at it.

"Please don't talk." Seth was trying to comfort her while being ill at ease out in the open.

"M-my . . . oth-other . . . I-I had . . . t-to . . ."

"You had to . . . what? Is there a prayer you want me to say?" Seth asked but soon realized that she was gone.

Seth began to cry, and fearing for his life, he began to run across the street to join the other two. A small crowd was beginning to form. The sounds of sirens came from the distance. Seth could hear Joshua bellow from the distance.

"Mama! Mama!"

Seth panicked and instinctively looked around. He ran to Maria-Elena. "We have to leave. We aren't safe. *They* are out there watching us." Seth was exasperated.

Maria-Elena agreed, and they both struggled to lift the sickly and distraught Joshua to his feet. They painstakingly made their way down the street. All the while, Seth scanned the street in a paranoid daze.

Unbeknownst to them, the same MIB who had caused Teresa's death had been watching out of sight from an adjacent building. He calmly stepped into the cover of darkness.

Chapter One Hundred Fifteen

The three made their way down the street as the MIB stalked them silently from a distance. Growing weary from carrying Joshua, Seth and Maria-Elena stopped at a café for a brief respite. They begged the owner to let them stay as he complained that he was about to close up for the night. Maria-Elena identified herself as a nun caring for an invalid, and the owner reluctantly agreed. The owner offered them water and went about his business, cleaning up the restaurant, while the trio rested at a table near the entrance.

Maria-Elena placed the medicine into Joshua's mouth and assisted him with the water. Joshua relaxed his head on her shoulder. The three sat quietly while an old television sitting on the bar played in the background.

Seth was the first to break their silence. "I won't lie to you," Seth said to Maria-Elena. "I'm afraid."

"I am as well," Maria-Elena replied. "There's an evil out there that is far more powerful than we ever imagined."

"Do you have any idea who or *what* is behind this?" Seth was compelled to ask.

Maria-Elena sighed. "For over thirty years, I have asked the same question. I do not know. But I can only blame it on the church."

"*The church?*" Seth gasped. "You mean *the* Catholic Church?"

"Who else could've been behind impregnating us against our will and then sending us to the same orphanage as banishment? And who else would have the power to destroy that place by trying to burn all of us?"

Seth was perplexed. "How could all of you be impregnated without knowing?"

Maria-Elena was quick to respond. "I remember realizing that the one thing my fellow sisters and I had in common was that we had all been seen by the same team of doctors in Rome. Normally, nuns from the various convents in Europe were sent to local doctors for their regular checkups. But not us. Even though we were from separate convents from all over Europe, *we* were sent to one doctor in Rome. I remembered that he was not Italian and would only speak English. It was immediately after our initial visits that we all got pregnant. Not only did we get pregnant at the same time, but also, we were banished to Fiorello together."

Seth was even more confused than ever. "But why?"

"As I mentioned, I do not understand it myself."

"I may not be a Christian, but I cannot believe the church would be so callous."

"Really?" Maria-Elena spat. "Do I need to remind you of what we did during the Inquisition, what we did to the Moors during the Crusades, or what has been done to countless others in the name of the church?" She paused long enough to comfort Joshua. "That night, as the fire raged, killing my sisters and all those innocent children, I swore I would never trust the church again. When I ran for my life with my child in my arms, I swore I would never practice my faith again. I found a new faith, one based on peace."

"I think you and I both know that it has never really been the *religion* that has caused the pain but the so-called practitioners," Seth said apologetically.

Maria-Elena regained her composure. "We must go. We've been here too long. We mustn't stay in one place. We must move around."

Seth agreed. He assisted Joshua to his feet. They thanked the café owner and went out the door. Before they could step outside the café, the television hanging above the bar was playing the breaking news that Yousef had been assassinated.

Maria-Elena started at the television in shock but did not scream out.

Seth looked at her. "Maria-Elena, I-I am so sorry."

She sobbed silently. "My son was a brave man. He knew the dangers that he was facing."

"Maria-Elena," Seth said gently, "I know that now is not the time to mention this, but where do we go from here?"

She quietly hugged Joshua and did not respond.

Seth followed her as she stepped onto the street. Seth gently grabbed her arm and led her away from the streetlights. "Maria-Elena, stop for a minute. Please listen to me."

The firm grip of his hands quickly brought her to reality.

"Where do we go from here?" Seth asked again. "*They* are still out here. Is there another shelter we can find?"

"I don't know of any," Maria-Elena said. "And I cannot communicate with my son—"

"But we cannot stay here on the streets." Seth gave Joshua a concerned look. "Joshua needs medical attention. We can only give him so much of that medicine."

She gazed at Joshua, and the look on the young man's face brought her back to reality. "What if we went back to the shelter?"

Seth was amazed at her question. "That's crazy."

"I know it is, but right now, there is nowhere else to go."

"But to go back to the shelter?"

"Right now, the shelter is a crime scene. The police will be there for several more hours. If we can sneak back in somehow, we would be safe—for a while, at least."

Seth had nothing to say.

"It's our only option," she continued.

Seth relented and agreed. They took Joshua by the hand and made their way back toward the shelter.

As they got closer to the shelter, they could see the squadron of police cars surrounding the area. The crime scene technicians were on scene, photographing the area; Teresa's body was still there. Joshua was about to scream out, but Maria-Elena soothed him before he could utter a word.

"Let's make it to the back of the building," she said, taking the lead.

They were in the adjacent building and saw that the rear of the shelter was clear. They walked toward the back and noticed that the back door was still ajar from when the MIB had broken into it. There was no police presence inside the building, and all indications were that the police were treating the incident as a suicide. If any of the investigators had been on the roof, they were long gone.

They walked in through the back door and could see the flurry of activity just outside the front window. They were careful not to be seen. Maria-Elena chose a room nearest the front door. They kept the lights off so that they could focus on the police presence outside.

"Keep him quiet," she said to Seth as she gently closed the curtains to the front window. As she peered out the window, she could see the technicians carry Teresa's lifeless body into the ambulance. Maria-Elena collapsed onto her knees and started to wail. "So much death!"

Seth crawled over to her and took her into his arms. "Maria-Elena, you must be calm. You must be strong for Joshua. If the police hear you, then they will certainly take us into custody, and we will have no guarantees that they can protect us."

Maria-Elena buried her head into Seth's shoulder and continued to sob. He sat on the floor, motionless, and held her in the same position for several hours. He studied the silhouettes of the people on the other side of the curtains and knew it was only a matter of time before the police would be gone—and then they would be on their own.

Chapter One Hundred Sixteen

It had to be way past 3:00 a.m., and Seth's head had been pounding from the lack of sleep and from the enormous amount of stress. Both Maria-Elena and Joshua were now curled on the floor, fast asleep. An hour had passed since the police left the area. He looked out in between the curtains and saw nothing but quiet streets. The few streetlights that were operable barely illuminated the area. Despite seeing nothing, he knew that *they* were out there—watching.

Seth returned to his corner of the room. He reached into his pocket, looking for his cell phone, when he felt an object that he did not recognize. It was the item that Teresa had handed to him before she died. Seth removed the item and saw that it was a pendant with a drawing of two men. The men in the drawings were painted wearing medieval clothing, with golden halos above their head. The pendant was clearly meant to be a Catholic icon. He smiled, knowing it must have had sentimental value to Teresa.

Seth turned it over, and the following words were inscribed on the back: Santi Cosma e Damiano. He was curious as to the pendant's meaning. He reached into his pocket again and removed his phone. He accessed the internet and typed in the exact words as he copied them from the inscription. After a few moments, a series of links came up.

Seth chose from the first one and read aloud from the description. "Saints Cosmas and Damian . . . two Arab physicians . . . brothers . . . patron saints of physicians . . . and twins . . . Christian martyrs."

Seth continued to smile. Holding the pendant close to his heart, he thought of Teresa. He placed the charm in his pocket for safekeeping.

Suddenly, he thought he saw movement coming from outside, and he crawled his way over to the window. He only managed to get his right eye to look in between the space of the curtains. The streets seemed darker than before, but he was certain he could see movement in the night. Seth was getting anxious.

I can't take this anymore . . . What do they want from us?

Seth stared out the window for several more minutes. He fretted over not knowing how these mysterious forces were able to trace their every moment. He quickly looked down at his phone and suddenly realized that he must have left an obvious trail through his use of the internet.

Seth got up from the floor and quietly stepped out of the room, gently closing the door behind him. He walked into the main room and gazed out the main window. He was tired of running. He was tired of being afraid. Instead, he would confront them and hope to appeal to their sense of decency. *Decency? Who am I kidding? These guys are killers. But we can't keep on running. Let's get this over with.*

He grabbed his phone and began to search the internet. He typed in the words *orfanotrofio* and *Fiorello*. Strangely, the links that he had been able to previously pull up were no longer there. He typed in the name Pozzuoli, the city where the school had once stood, and a string of links came up. He clicked on the top result, which was an "official" website for the seaside town, and within that page, he found another search bar. He placed his finger within that search bar and typed the familiar words. *Orfanotrofio Fiorello.* Seth paused. He hesitated but then hit Enter.

To his surprise, a brief blurb came up about how the old school was once housed in that town—but nothing about its sordid history. His sixth sense caused him to look outside the window. It was still the middle of the night, and the streets were empty. Seeing nothing, he returned to his phone, closing the article and then clicking onto the next link in line, continuing the same pattern for every other link after that until he reached the end. Seth was exhausted and did not know what more he could do.

He looked out the window for what he thought would be the last time, his eyes straining to see through the darkness. This time, there was something out there. The headlights of a black car came suddenly on. Seth's heart began racing. He watched as the lights from a second car came on. It was apparent to him that the MIBs were narrowing in on his location. Seth was going to make their job easier.

Within the search bar of his phone, he typed in the name of the school again but followed it with the following message: "Call. Me." Once again, he paused but for a much longer time. Then he hit Enter.

A third set of lights came on, and now the cars were literally parked in front of his building.

He typed the words once again. "Call. Me."

* * *

In a remote monitoring room, an MIB operative picked up the message: "Call. Me." He immediately messaged his superior, who, in turn, contacted Sébastien. Within moments and to all the other operatives' surprise, Sébastien was standing behind them. Sébastien was intrigued, and he gave a signal of approval.

* * *

Several agonizing moments passed, and suddenly, Seth's phone rang. It was from a blocked number.

Seth slowly answered, "H-hello?"

There was silence on the other end.

Seth continued to speak. "My . . . My name is Seth. I'm sure you know this already, but I am an American."

Still more silence.

He continued as he looked out the window, "I don't—I mean, I can't even begin to understand what is going on, but what I can tell you is that whatever it is that you did, it worked." Seth continued to speak as he made his way toward the door. "I don't know if you have had the chance to meet this young man, but he is—rather, *they* . . . they are remarkable."

Seth approached the front door and peered out the small window frame. The black sedans were just a few feet away. The headlights made it difficult for him to see inside any of the vehicles.

"Whatever it is that you did, it worked. These men are real. They're human. They're alive. They are alive."

Seth nervously took in a deep breath of air and cautiously opened the door. He stepped out into the night. He stared out at each car as they idled, squinting at the sight of each of the bright headlights.

"So please, I beg of you, let them live. They are alive. *It* worked. Whatever it is you were doing, it worked."

Miles away, on the other end of the phone, through the wire intercept, Sébastien heard the plea for mercy. The elder could not see Seth but could hear the desperation. Sébastien glanced at one of his men, and with a single look, the other man knew what Sébastien wanted. The dutiful MIB spoke into his radio, speaking into the earpiece of each of the three drivers.

Seth stood there quietly, lowering his cell phone to his side. It was useless, he thought. He wandered into the street, straightened his back, and held his head up. He closed his eyes, waiting for the inevitable. He heard the sound of the cars as each car drove in reverse. Within no time, the cars were gone. Seth stood there alone, in disbelief.

Chapter One Hundred Seventeen

Maria-Elena could hear all the commotion made by Seth, and it woke her up from her slumber. She called for him from the front door. "Seth, are you okay? What are you doing outside?"

Seth was still in shock, and it took him a moment to respond. "Yes," he said. "I'm fine."

"What are you doing here?" she asked. "What is going on?"

"I really don't know, but I think we are safe . . . for now? I hope."

She motioned at him. "Come inside."

"I will," he said, distressed. "I just need a moment to calm my nerves."

Maria-Elena stepped out of the room to reach out for Seth. She took him by his hand. "Come inside, please."

From the corner of her eye, she could see that Joshua had also awoken. He was standing by the door. Joshua painstakingly made his way toward the other two.

The screeching sound of a braking car startled Seth from his state of shock. The sound came from a large van. The vehicle stopped just short of Seth. Two men exited the van, armed with automatic rifles pointed directly at Seth and Maria-Elena.

Seth was in a renewed state of disbelief. "But I thought—"

The sight of the AK-47 thrust before his face cut Seth short. The men placed pillow sheets over the heads of Seth and his companions, and they were forced into the van. Once the hostages were secured inside, the van sped away. A lone sentry MIB watched from the distance as it all unfolded with a puzzled look on his face.

Chapter One Hundred Eighteen

"You aborted the mission to kill them?" Ducard reacted in outrage.

"Yes," Sébastien replied, almost joyfully. "I spoke to the American. He said that our experiment worked. Don't you understand? It worked."

"You spoke to the American?"

"Actually, he spoke . . and I listened. The American confirmed that he is in the company of one of the *survivors*. At a minimum, we must meet this subject. There may still be hope. Hope for humanity."

"You are a fool!" Ducard spewed. "All reports are that this young man is blind and can barely walk! He is a failure! Your plan was a failure!"

Sébastien was equally aggressive. "Before you act impulsively, let's examine the evidence. We know from our operatives that they traced the American and his female companion from Italy to Spain. While in Spain, they met with another woman who appeared to be dressed in Middle Eastern attire."

"This other woman, from Spain—how old is she?" Ducard inquired.

"She appears to be the same age as the Italian woman."

"Do you think one of these two women is a survivor of the fire?" asked Ducard.

Sébastien was slow to respond. "The remains were so badly charred we had a difficult time in getting an accurate body count. However, surveillance reveals that one of the women, the Italian, is badly scarred."

Ducard was visibly frustrated. "Consistent with a fire."

"Correct."

Ducard gazed at his brother and knew that he had more bad tidings. "What? What is it?"

"We had our operatives go back to Pozzuoli and interview some of the villagers who were old enough to recall the fire. There were earlier recounts that one mother and her child had left the orphanage . . . *before* the fire."

"*Before* the fire?" Ducard exclaimed.

"Correct."

"The Spanish woman!"

"Yes," Sébastien answered.

"That would mean . . . Good lord!" shouted Ducard. "That would mean that in addition to these two mothers, there could be a total of *two* offspring out there."

Sébastien said excitedly, "Yes, the invalid and one other offspring."

Ducard was in disbelief.

"Actually, there is one more thing."

Ducard was visibly impatient. "What now?"

"After the call with the American, I went back and reread all the medical records, looking for any clues, and I came across a possible discrepancy."

Ducard frowned. "What is the discrepancy?"

"It is hard to tell because one of the doctors we had employed made an unreadable notation as to one of the deliveries, and because we quickly *terminated* all the doctors, we could not ask him to read his handwritten notes."

"*What is the discrepancy?*" Ducard repeated angrily.

"It appears from the nearly indecipherable notes that one of the mothers had . . . *twins*."

"*Twins?* That would mean that there are *three* failed test subjects!" Ducard screamed angrily. "Issue the order! I want them all terminated!"

Sébastien stood defiant. "Not until I can locate and personally examine these three subjects."

"Sébastien." Ducard stood in his brother's face. "Do not make me go to the council. You have made an oath of obedience. The council has ruled, and you *will* obey."

"What would you have me do?" Sébastien said reluctantly.

"Now that we have distracted the public on this . . . serial killer nonsense, we can focus on preparing Master James for his final duty."

"So soon?"

"Yes. By this time next month, he will be meeting with the heads of the Greek Orthodox, the Coptic, and the Catholic Churches. He will finally unite all the Latin and Eastern Rite Churches and be ordained the temporal *and* spiritual leader of them all. And then within two months, he will return to address the United Nations and petition the members to begin the process of forming a united world government."

"He's not ready—"

"We cannot wait any longer. The world cannot wait any longer." Ducard turned to leave and issued one final directive. "Find that third offspring and kill them all."

Book Four

Chapter One Hundred Nineteen

Reporters and their news cameras had surrounded Scotland Yard. They were scrambling, hoping to interview the chief inspector. Llewelyn had just returned from his encounter at St. James's Church and observed from his car as his chief, no doubt, was taking credit for the killing. Llewelyn had a foul taste in his mouth; he had nothing but disdain for the press, unlike the chief inspector, who reveled in their presence. He exited his car and casually walked over toward his office.

"I had my men working hard in twenty-four shifts, and under my supervision, we were—"

The chief inspector was cut short as the swarm of cameramen moved to follow Llewelyn as he walked past them. The chief was perturbed.

"Inspector Llewelyn!" they shouted as they ran to catch up to him. "Inspector, would you like to say a few words?" they continued to ask as he ignored them. "Inspector? Inspector?"

"No comment," Llewelyn muttered before stopping in his tracks. He turned to face the cameras. "I do have one thing to say. The killer is still out there. And none of us are safe until he is caught. And now let me pass so that my men and I can continue our work." He briskly walked past the swarm of reporters as he rushed into the building.

The cameras then turned their attention to the chief inspector. The hue on the chief's face was bright red; he had never been so humiliated. He was agitated by the presence of all the microphones thrust in his face.

"Any follow-up, Chief Inspector?" the reporters asked.

"No comment." The chief inspector walked away.

Chapter One Hundred Twenty

As Llewelyn walked down the hallway of Scotland Yard leading to his office, he felt the stares of his fellow officers. They had been watching what occurred outside on their televisions as it unfolded live. They stood along the hallway, keeping their silence.

"What are you standing around for? Get back to work!" Llewelyn demanded.

Their absence of sound was deafening. He knew the cause of their silence. He stepped into his war room and was shocked as he saw two other detectives taking the room apart. Llewelyn violently ripped the documents from the men's hands. He grabbed each man one at a time and pushed them out the door. As expected, he saw the chief inspector angrily make his way down the hall. The chief was livid as he entered the war room. He slammed the door shut and turned his wrath toward Llewelyn.

"How dare you undermine my authority? You know damn well that this case was closed the minute that man was killed!"

Llewelyn chuckled as he replied, "And you know very damn well that that man was not the killer."

"You can't possibly know that. And at a very minimum, you don't say that to the public!"

"The public has every right to know the truth," Llewelyn said emphatically.

"I'll say it again. The investigation is over, and your involvement is over. That's an order. We have our killer." The chief raced out of the door.

Llewelyn stood at his door and yelled out to his chief, "That man was not the killer! The Sinner is still out there, and if we hesitate or delay our investigation for even one minute, it'll be that much harder to catch him! Blood will be on your hands!"

The chief turned to Llewelyn and said, "It's over. And you are on holiday until further notice." With that, the chief walked away.

Llewelyn was much too disciplined to fight back, but for the first time in his long career, he felt dejected.

Chapter One Hundred Twenty-one

Inspector Llewelyn had fallen asleep at his desk. After his confrontation with the chief, Llewelyn had returned to his office to resume the investigation. It was a quarter past two in the morning.

He jolted awake. The seven minutes of slumber were the only respite he had received in days. He wiped the corners of his eyes. Through the haze, he saw Fairfield hovering over him.

"Inspector, you've been up for several days. Call it a night and get some rest."

"Perhaps you're right. I'm so exhausted that I cannot even see straight," Llewelyn was too tired to fight. He sluggishly walked out of his office.

Fairfield stayed behind. He watched as the fatigued Llewelyn quietly walked toward the elevator. Fairfield waited several moments to make sure Llewelyn was gone. Once assured, he began to peruse through Llewelyn's case files scattered throughout the man's desk. Fairfield was startled by a booming voice; it belonged to Llewelyn.

"As I'm walking out, I'm thinking to myself, 'You and I have both been up all night, but why isn't he exhausted? Why isn't he walking me out?'"

Fairfield stammered. "I am exhausted. I just want to learn as much as I can."

"And you thought it appropriate to go through the very files I explicitly wanted no one to touch. Now put that file down." Llewelyn approached him angrily. "Who sent you?"

"I-I don't understand the question."

"I have been an inspector for over twenty years, and everything about you reeks of corruption. Your 'transfer' to this case was approved by our superiors, but there's nothing to confirm that. I've looked for the paperwork, and it doesn't exist. I'll ask again. *Who sent you?*"

Fairfield ignored the question and attempted to walk out of the room.

Llewelyn blocked his path and grabbed the younger man by the coat, pushing him violently against the wall. "Who sent you? Are you here to sabotage the case? Who are you protecting?"

The two men struggled with each other. Llewelyn underestimated the younger man's prowess, but Fairfield was no match for Llewelyn's experience. Llewelyn successfully catapulted his opponent out the door.

"Don't wander too far," Llewelyn warned. "As soon I discover who is behind you, you will all be arrested."

Fairfield wiped the sweat off his brow. He replaced his look of surprise with a menacing smirk. "You don't know what you're facing. We're very powerful and very resourceful. We have our operatives deeply embedded into all aspects of society, in every government. We're all over the world. You'll never arrest me because you'll never see me again. But we will be watching you." Fairfield walked away, seemingly disappearing into the night.

Chapter One Hundred Twenty-two

Rome, Italy
The Vatican

The international media was in frenzy as they amassed outside Vatican City. A special conclave of the heads of the Eastern, Coptic, and Latin Rite Churches, along with their respective bishops and cardinals, had been dispatched to Rome to meet with the pope to discuss the impact James St. John-Smythe was having on Christendom. The cameras filmed a sea of red, purple, and black robes as the church leaders arrived one by one. It took several hours for the men to make their way inside the Vatican.

The church princes filed their way into the Sistine Chapel. The doors to the chapel were bolted shut. The frescoes of Michelangelo looked down menacingly at them all. There were over nine hundred men crammed into the rectangular building, and the loud grumblings were only exaggerated by the echoes of the large room. The murmuring suddenly grew silent as the Holy Father himself walked in. The men bowed in respect.

The pope was in his late eighties and needed assistance to enter the room and to be seated. He was hunched over from decades of kneeling in prayer. He was an Italian and a true man of faith, and because of his age, he was not one easily motivated by external influences; still, the ever-growing popularity of St. John-Smythe and the declining membership of the Catholic body pushed the need for drastic change.

Emissaries to St. John-Smythe had reached out to the church leaders for a meeting on how to unite the church into one body. The pope could no longer ignore the cries from both within and outside the church. All the church leaders took up most of the nave in the Sacre Gotte, lining up as far back as the vestibule. The pope was escorted by two priests to stand before them all.

"My brothers." The pope's voice was frail and could barely be heard as he spoke from the center of the papal center. "A new era has dawned upon us. A new voice has arisen. A new shepherd to our sheep. Perhaps it is time to allow this new voice to speak for us."

The room broke into a vociferous frenzy as there were some cheers of agreement but many more shouts of protests.

"Please let me finish," the old man said as he painfully raised his hand. "Our church has been mired in controversy, and our flock has been losing the faith. The number of qualified priests is dwindling. The church is dying."

"And you propose to replace us with this . . . this *charlatan?*" screamed one of the Coptic bishops.

"No, not at all," answered the pope. "I am suggesting that we simply agree to meet with him and form an informal alliance. An alliance with James St. John-Smythe as our ambassador to the world. Nothing more."

"But what of his falsehood of being born of the bloodline of Jesus?" screamed a Greek bishop.

"We cannot allow such heresy to continue to be espoused," a Polish cardinal demanded.

The pope sighed. "We could always waste our energy renewing our dispute of the epistles banned by the bishops of Nicene that are locked away in our Vatican Library, but instead, I remind you that our beliefs are the foundation of our faith, and nothing—and no one—can ever change that bedrock. The sad reality is that our latest and younger flock have been so poisoned by books and movies that they have strayed from our traditional beliefs. Gentlemen, we are at the crossroads of a new era. We either bring our people back into our fold or fade away like a distant memory."

The pope's pleas for unity were sincere, and many of the princes were eager to unify the church, but there were still many more who dissented. Still, hidden among them were agents of the brotherhood who were able to persuade those dissenters. After several hours of debate, there were no more murmurs or protests. There were only reluctant nods of agreement.

* * *

The crowd outside the Vatican had grown silent and was waiting with bated breath. After the two-hour meeting, a Vatican spokesperson came out and announced the dramatic news. In two weeks, the collective heads of the church would be meeting with James St. John-Smythe and make the earth-shattering announcement that St. John-Smythe would unite the world's Christian churches as their temporal leader.

* * *

James had been watching the newscast in his suite at Wyndham Court. He began to smile; his urges were beginning to rise. He got on his knees and began to pray. He prayed that God would give him the strength to resist his temptation—at least until after his meeting with the church. He was so close to achieving his lifelong dream.

Chapter One Hundred Twenty-three

Hours following his fateful encounter with Fairfield, Inspector Llewelyn watched as the sun rose from his office window. He watched as the swarm of police officers were returning to begin a new shift. He wandered throughout the halls of the police station, mindful of all the eyes that were upon him and leery of them all. He made his way into the war room and replaced one solitary document on the bulletin board. The need to study the sketch of the suspect momentarily overwhelmed him. Llewelyn turned his attention to the photographs of the mangled limousine and of the private apartment-turned-torture-chamber with the pricey collectibles.

"Expensive car. Pricy taste. Cash at hand," he muttered to himself. "Who could have that kind of *power and resource?*" he said, mimicking Fairfield's last words to him.

Llewelyn then turned to his laptop and conducted an impromptu internet search. Upon seeing the results, he drafted a quick email and made a call into his phone.

"Prepare me a search warrant," he said to the person on the other end. "I want it to encompass DNA and fingerprints. I want it executed in two hours. I'm sending it to you now."

Moments later, just as he expected, his chief burst into the room.

"What in bloody hell do you think you are doing?" the chief yelled, throwing a document at him. "I never authorized this search warrant."

"That was quick." Llewelyn smirked. "I've never had to get your approval before."

"For something like *this*, you do. I'm cancelling it now."

"Fine. I'll just go get what I need myself." Llewelyn turned toward the door.

"Don't you dare! If you leave this office, you will be terminated!"

Llewelyn ignored the threat and pressed forward on his mission. The chief inspector stood before the doorframe. His demeanor was calmer, and yet Llewelyn sensed fear in him.

"Llewelyn," the chief stammered, "why are you doing this? Do you understand what's at stake here?"

"What's at stake is that there's a killer out there on the loose, and he needs to be apprehended." Llewelyn stood before his superior ever so gallantly.

"P-please don't do this." The chief inspector, at that moment, seemed to be on the verge of a nervous breakdown. "What's at stake is my life and the lives of my wife and children."

Llewelyn was taken aback. "Chief, what have you gotten yourself into?"

"I have no time to explain, but if you proceed with your course of action, I'll be forced to take whatever action is necessary to protect my family." The chief was trembling.

Llewelyn was emotionless. "I regret that there will be consequences for *your* actions, but that was your choice and your choice alone. You can always join me."

"I-I cannot."

"Then I wish you the best, and do what you must, but I will arrest . . . James St. John-Smythe."

With that, Llewelyn raced out of his office.

The chief inspector made one last beckoning. "Llewelyn! Please don't do this! Llewelyn! Come back here!"

The chief inspector's pleas went unheeded.

Chapter One Hundred Twenty-four

Llewelyn sped his vehicle toward Wyndham Court. During the entire drive, Llewelyn could not help but think of the amount of pressure that must have been placed upon his chief inspector. His chief had always been a man of dignity, a man of loyalty, a man of fellowship, but during their confrontation, the chief was as weak and timid as a child. At that instant, Llewelyn truly felt a sense of sympathy for his old friend. However, Llewelyn was a man of honor too; his oath of loyalty to the police force and to his community demanded that he fulfill his duty.

The trip to Wyndham Court took longer than he had expected. Traffic was unusually heavy for this afternoon hour. Llewelyn did not recall so much construction work on this stretch of highway. He would later kick himself for not noticing that despite the heavy use of cones and barricades, there were no workers on the road. It would eventually make sense to him that these obstacles were nothing more than a ruse to buy the killer more time.

When he finally arrived at Wyndham Court, a blockade of police cars prevented him from taking his car any farther than the edge of the front gate. A team of his fellow officers approached his window.

"Inspector, I am sorry, but we cannot allow you to pass," said one of the young officers.

"Officer, you've known me for a very long time, and I've known you to be a dedicated officer. If you don't let me pass, you are letting a killer go free."

The young officer hesitated, but after several agonizing moments, he reluctantly let Llewelyn pass. Llewelyn exited the car and angrily paced toward the front door of the mansion, where he was met by the elderly Ducard.

"Inspector Llewelyn, how may I be of service to you?"

"I'm here to affect the arrest of James St. John-Smythe."

"I'm sure that there is some misunderstanding—" said the old man.

"Bring him to me now, or I will arrest you for obstruction."

"Young man, if you only knew—"

"I've already been threatened, and I won't be dissuaded from fulfilling my duties. I will not be intimidated. Comply with my order or . . ." Llewelyn took out his cell phone and held it to Ducard's face. "With one phone call, I will hold a news conference outside your gates."

The elderly man was visibly angry but was moved by the danger of unwanted exposure. There was still time to control the situation, the elder thought as he turned to a manservant standing behind him. "Thompson, please summon Master St. John-Smythe. Tell him he has an unexpected but most welcome guest."

The manservant dutifully obeyed and ran up the elegant staircase, but within moments, he returned alone. "Master, I regret to inform you that the young master James is not in his room."

The elderly man had a legitimate look of surprise on his face.

"It looks like your master is going to save me the trouble of having to secure an arrest warrant," Llewelyn said contently before turning to leave.

The elderly man raced into the house and turned to the team of heavily armed MIBs who had been waiting and watching in the dark. "Find that bastard now before he ruins it all to bloody hell!"

Chapter One Hundred Twenty-five

James St. John-Smythe had finished his prayers and managed to walk out of the house through a window in the servants' quarters. His prayers had not been good enough. He could not resist his temptation. He craved the taste of blood.

James wandered for an hour through the back roads and came upon an elderly woman walking toward his car. He greeted the gentle lady before casually slicing her throat with a pocketknife. He took her keys and stuffed her in the trunk. He made his way to the nearest town.

* * *

Sébastien was enraged. He confronted his brother in the study. "Brother, we have been at odds for many years now. You are my elder, and I have been nothing more than obedient, but James has been nothing more than a liability. He must be taken before the council."

Ducard responded solemnly, "Yes, my brother. *We* must both go before the council."

Sébastien frowned in disappointment. The two brothers exited the study and began their hunt for James.

Chapter One Hundred Twenty-six

After leaving Wyndham Court, Llewelyn proceeded to drive around, wandering aimlessly, hoping to find his prey. He put out an APB for James, expecting that the chief inspector would order his men to half-heartedly obey it. Not long after the sun had begun to set, Llewelyn made his way to the clubs that the victims frequented. He parked his car on a side street and meandered about the area. He roamed the streets, painstakingly looking for St. John-Smythe. Llewelyn was not going to stop until he found the killer that night. He silently made a vow; either he or James St. John-Smythe would be dead by night's end.

As the moments turned into hours, Llewelyn began to feel a sense of dread that he would not find this maniac before the next unfortunate person fell victim to James's vicious attack.

Unbeknownst to Llewelyn, James was just a street block away, on the prowl, looking for his next victim.

Chapter One Hundred Twenty-seven

It did not take James very long to wander within the shadows and encounter a young prostitute. The young man was easily swayed by James's charm and wit and the flash of money. They engaged in small talk for a few minutes before James led him to a darkened corner. James could no longer resist his primal urge and began to strangle his young victim.

The lad violently resisted and tried to run, but James's brutal strength was overwhelming. The firm grasp around his neck prevented him from screaming out. The violence grew more intense as James began to beat the young man. Fortunately for the victim, another wayward youth observed the struggle and began to scream out for help.

A small crowd started to approach them, and a frightened James ran away. Seeing the running figure, a group of boys gave chase. The would-be killer desperately ran down the street but was suddenly blocked by a police cruiser. Inside the cruiser were Fairfield and the chief inspector. They exited the vehicle and greeted James.

"Stop," the chief inspector ordered. "You are safe with us."

James was in a state of dismay.

Fairfield took James's hand. "You're among *brothers*. Your safety is assured, but we must leave now."

James hesitated too long, and the crowd of people that had been forming in the distance was approaching.

"Get in the car now!" Fairfield barked.

James was pushed into the car by the chief as the crowd neared. The chief was careful to cover his sire's face. Fairfield, displaying his badge, held them all off and ordered them to back away.

"The suspect is in custody, good folks. You may all disperse now," Fairfield said convincingly.

The crowd cheered in unison as they slowly began to disperse. Before Fairfield could reenter his car, he witnessed Llewelyn arrive on the scene. Fairfield quickly blocked his way.

Llewelyn made every effort to force his way to apprehend James. "Let me through!" Llewelyn demanded of Fairfield.

The chief stepped away from St. John-Smythe and confronted Llewelyn by grabbing his arm. "We have this under control."

"Let me go!" Llewelyn demanded.

"Stop now, or I'll have you arrested," said the chief as both he and Fairfield displayed the firearms hidden within their jackets.

Llewelyn, realizing his actions would be futile, relented and backed away. The chief and Fairfield reentered the cruiser, and Llewelyn watched in anger as the cruiser drove away. James and his two companions remained silent as the sirens cleared the police car's path.

Chapter One Hundred Twenty-eight

James St. John-Smythe smirked from the back seat as the police cruiser made its way through the traffic. He motioned to Fairfield, sitting next to him, to remove the handcuffs from his wrists. Fairfield feigned distraction and ignored him.

James turned his attention to the chief inspector. "Excuse me, Chief. Would you kindly tell your officer to remove these . . . these shackles?"

The chief looked back at James and gave him a look of disappointment. "In due time."

"Excuse me?" James said in disbelief. "I insist that you unbind me now."

For the next several minutes, James's demands were ignored as the police vehicle continued its journey.

The chief inspector continued to drive listening to the police dispatcher cancel the APB for the suspected killer. But as the police cruiser made its way through the streets of London, a new radio announcement was being disseminated alerting all law enforcement officers to be on high alert for any suspicious activity related to a terrorist attack. The chief inspector turned off his radio; his focus was to deliver James St. John-Smythe to his masters and was hopeful that by doing so, he would spare his own life. At that moment, the chief inspector could care less if terrorists destroyed the world.

Chapter One Hundred Twenty-nine

SOCOM
MacDill Air Force Base
Tampa, Florida

Billy Assad had not slept in weeks; he was physically drained. He walked into the break room after a brief nap and poured himself a pot of coffee as a young FBI analyst approached him.

"Sir, we've picked up more intel," said the twenty-four-year-old recent Quantico graduate. She spoke with an Indiana twang.

"What now?" he said as he followed her to a makeshift war room.

The war room was filled with bulletin boards placed throughout, each laden with photographs and charts, and there was a large map of the United States attached to the main wall, covered with tacks. The conference table sat in the middle of the room, cluttered with documents.

"So what's the latest?" Billy asked

"We're picking up more and more chatter."

Billy Assad took a sip of the bitter coffee. He disgustedly threw out the contents of his mug into a nearby trash can. "What is the chatter revealing?"

"It appears that they are starting to get organized."

"Any specific details?"

"There is a lot of discussion of organizing a major strike."

"Good lord!" Billy exclaimed. "Any idea as to when or where?"

"No," the analyst replied. "It's all sporadic. Random, even."

"Any details at all?"

"The closest we can decipher is on New Year's Eve."

"New Year's Eve?" Billy said, surprised. "New Year's Eve is four days away." Billy was visibly anxious. "Anything more specific, like *what* is going to happen?"

"Negative."

"HUMINT, intercepts, anything?"

"Nothing," she responded. "Sorry, sir."

"It's not your fault." He started to stare at the map. "It could be anywhere or . . . *everywhere*. We need to contact the field offices in every major city. I'll need all the local law enforcement on high alert. I need all those cells monitored and surveilled from here until then."

"We have already alerted the field offices, INTERPOL, as well as law enforcement agencies in every major European city." She proudly said.

"Good," he replied, as they both continued to stare at the map.

"Sir," the analyst interrupted. "There's something about that map that has always bothered me."

"What's that?" Billy asked.

She pointed to various designations on the map. "These thumbtacks represent each attack on U.S. soil. You tasked me with making sense of these 'coordinated' attacks, especially if they were tied in with the chatter, the intel, and the video messages."

"Correct," he mused. "And you've uncovered what?"

"Well, that's it. *Nothing.* I haven't been able to uncover anything. It's like there's no pattern. It's all too random."

"Random?" he questioned.

"All too random. Not very organized."

Billy gazed at the map. "I think you're correct!" he exclaimed.

He scurried to the master control room, where he approached General Norton. The general peered at Billy with his familiar scowl.

"Where have you been?" the general asked.

"Working hard, sir," Billy responded.

"Hmph."

"General, it's possible that there is no coordination at all. These attacks on American soil could all be random, independent, and solitary acts."

"Nonsense." The general pointed to an onscreen image of the United States that highlighted the various American attacks. "All *this*—random? Impossible."

"I'm not saying I agree. I'm just saying that—"

"Stop wasting your time on useless theories!" the general barked. "Tell me something concrete."

"Yes, sir," Billy said dutifully. "The cells plan on striking on New Year's Eve."

"What? And where?" the general demanded to know.

Billy sighed. "Well, we don't know—*yet*."

"Then get back to work." The general returned to his duties.

Billy Assad turned to the analyst. "Tell the other analysts that I want those video messages broken down to every minute detail. I want the chatter transcribed and every informant brought in. We have little time to spare." Before the analyst could walk away, Billy stopped her. "I want all the field offices in Philadelphia, LA, Chicago, and every other major city to have their agents coordinate with local law enforcement and to scour their respective cities and find me something. Get the national guard involved and on standby too." He walked out of the room.

"Where are you going?" the general demanded to know.

"I'm going to the one place that is certain to be attacked—New York."

Chapter One Hundred Thirty

New York, New York
December 26

Samina Pal had dreamed of being a doctor, and after meeting Billy in the hallways of Franklin Delano Roosevelt High School, she knew at that very moment that her life would never be the same. She spoke of changing her dreams. She spoke of marriage and of family, but Billy would not have her change her plans, not even for him. That made her love him even more.

Billy courted her throughout high school, and they started dating in college. Samina attended medical school, and Billy pursued his degree in criminology while working as a detective with the NYPD. He pursued his career all while supporting hers. Once Samina had completed her residency, they agreed to start a family. By their second child, she had started her own family medical clinic.

Twenty years after meeting, life was good but not perfect for Samina. It was now Saturday morning, and with her kids still in bed, she decided to cook them breakfast. She did not hear the door open and see her husband walk in. She first noticed him when he was standing beside her in the kitchen.

"Honey!" she exclaimed with glee, rushing into his arms. "When did you come into town?"

"I flew in this morning. I needed to see you and the kids."

"Wonderful! How long will you be in town?" she said, sitting him down at the kitchen table.

"Not sure, but I'll be working straight through New Year's Eve."

He looked exhausted to her.

"I understand," she said with a sad voice. "We know how busy you are. We were kind of hoping that you would be here for Christmas."

"I needed to see you, even if it was for a few hours." His voice shook. "I don't know how much longer this operation will last."

"How is it going?"

Billy rubbed his temples. "Not sure. We have all this information but all leading to nothing. It feels like the world is on the brink of collapse, on the verge of something huge, but none of us can figure out *what* is going to happen or *when* it's going to happen."

Samina was scared. "What do you mean? Is something going to happen, honey?"

"That's just the point. I don't know. None of us do."

"What does your heart tell you?" Samina asked.

"It's almost like *we* want something bad to happen. It's like *we* thrive on fear. *We* thrive on finding something, anything, that can cause us to react."

"But why would we want that?"

"We fear what we don't know. We hate what we don't like, and it's so much easier to get rid of it." Billy, noticing his wife was trembling, reached out to comfort her.

"Is that what this is all about?" she pleaded.

"God, I hope not. I've been analyzing domestic and foreign intelligence for so long that I've never had any reason to doubt it before."

"I don't understand," she said, grasping her husband's hands.

"I don't pretend to understand it either. But it seems like our government and the governments around the world are content in making enemies of anyone whom we don't agree with."

"For what reason?"

"To justify killing our enemies," Billy said remorsefully.

"What do you mean?" Samina was confused.

"Our government spends billions of dollars annually in building our military might to fight off terrorists who live in tents and caves. These terrorists virtually have no chance of reaching our soil with the limited resources that they have."

She asked, "But what about 9/11?"

"That was a lapse of security more than anything," Billy replied. "We've literally ensured that that can never happen again. But instead of investing in these Third World countries, in rebuilding them and educating their people, in an attempt to prevent this from happening again, we're bombing them back to the Dark Ages, and as a result, we are creating more terrorists."

"Are we that shallow?" she inquired. "Do we really not care?"

"Trust me," he said. "I didn't want to believe it either. For every bomb we drop, for every civilian, woman, and child we kill, there is a sibling, a daughter, a son left behind, dealing with the grief, and eventually, that grief turns into anger and sometimes revenge."

Samina reached out to her husband. She spoke softly. "But how do you explain the radicalization of our own Americans?"

"Our people are watching as we engage in this behavior, and that flies in the face of all that we were taught to believe in."

"How do you mean?"

"We teach our children that we are the greatest country in the world and that we can achieve our dreams with a little hard work and perseverance. But instead, our children see how hard our parents work to be able to barely pay the rent, the food, and the car payment. Millions of Americans struggle to put food on their tables, and nearly half a million people live without shelter. And while our politicians either promise to improve the situation to get them elected or praise vast improvements 'achieved' to get them reelected, in reality, nothing actually changes. As a result, our children watch as their parents suffer, never gaining any stride. The kids become resentful, angry, and some look for someone who can make a real change."

"But we have one of the most compassionate governments in history. Our president has done more to reach out to minorities and foreign leaders than any other president," Samina said almost angrily.

"There's no question that we believe our president is a good man with good intentions, but his actions, at a minimum, show otherwise. Through his drone operations, he has killed nearly a hundred civilians in the first four years of his administration. And that doesn't count the bombing of the Doctors Without Borders trauma center in Kunduz, Afghanistan, where forty-two people were killed and thirty were injured."

"But that was accidental," Samina defended.

"That may very well be, but the MSF declared it a breach of international humanitarian law and a war crime. And those watching it from here thought the same thing. And this coming from a Nobel Peace Prize winner."

"Isn't that what Yousef is espousing?" Samina asked.

"That's exactly what he's preaching. And the people are listening. They are starting to wake up and realize that our country may not be any better than 'those' other countries. I'm surprised that it took me this long to realize that."

Samina was trembling in fear. "I never realized how volatile it all is."

"That's why Yousef is so dangerous," Billy asserted. "He appeals to those who feel that they are disenfranchised and oppressed."

"Is he really organizing American cells to strike out?"

"That's what our intelligence is saying," he answered. "But . . ."

"But what?" she asked.

"This is the same intelligence that told us that the autistic Abshir Abdulmaid was a threat to national security from his small apartment in Brooklyn or that told us that the three Time Square bombers were about to wreak havoc in New York City. We were wrong about them, and maybe we are wrong about Yousef."

"So what are you going to do?"

"Do what I always do."

"What is that?" she asked.

"Be a good soldier and do as I'm told."

Chapter One Hundred Thirty-one

December 28

There was a new agent using Billy Assad's old office at the FBI headquarters in Manhattan. Billy walked into the room and introduced himself.

The junior agent was embarrassed and immediately apologized. "Sir, I'm so sorry. We have run out of space, and I had nowhere else to go."

Billy smiled at the junior agent. "No need to apologize."

"Let me move my things out of here."

Billy waved him down. "No, stay. I've got some things to do. I'll let you know if I need it."

Billy's visit with his family made him even more anxious than ever before. His team's inability to provide any specific details about the imminent attack made Billy extremely concerned over the safety of his own family. The stress was almost unbearable. He had no time to sit around and administrate behind his desk. He decided it was time to act. Just outside his former office, he greeted his old assistant.

"Welcome back, Mr. Assad." She smiled as she pulled out a notepad.

He gave her a brief smile and dispensed with the usual pleasantry. "I need you to please set up an office-wide meeting in the briefing room."

Surprised at his brashness, she immediately sent an office-wide email. Billy Assad walked out of the room and made his way to what would be the biggest fight of his career.

Chapter One Hundred Thirty-two

December 28

New Year's Eve was only three days away, and with a sense of urgency, Billy Assad stepped into the briefing room and faced his team of old and very new faces.

"This is it, folks," he addressed the agents in the crowded room. "As you know, there are legal ways to obtain a wiretap on U.S. citizens. We can seek a warrant under Title III of the U.S. criminal code by showing a federal court that there is probable cause to believe the target has engaged or is engaging in criminal activity. On the other hand, the standard for electronic surveillance for foreign intelligence purposes is lower."

A rookie agent raised her hand. "Why is that? I never understood the distinction."

Billy was visibly perturbed. "I don't have time to rehash your training at Quantico, but to answer your question, in the event that a judge happens to ask you the same question, the answer is as follows. When it comes to national security, our Fourth Amendment rights are balanced against the government's interest in protecting the country."

The rookie agent had more questions but dared not to ask.

Billy resumed his presentation. "I want affidavits prepared of all suspected terrorist cells on our lists and submitted to the Foreign Intelligence Surveillance Court in four hours. I don't need novel-length affidavits. I just need enough probable cause to show the FISC that we have cause to conduct electronic surveillance on these 'agents of a foreign power.'" Billy ignored the murmur among the crowd of agents. "I have read every single 302 written by our field agents, and I think we have enough intel to show that our targets are knowingly engaging in clandestine intelligence activities."

The agents took their copious notes.

"A few months back," Billy said, "I learned a valuable lesson with a suspected Ethiopian target who wasn't a target at all. But we learned from that mistake, and we have followed the Attorney General Guidelines to every detail. Our threat assessments are based on the chatter, human intel, and informants. This was enough to open our investigation on these FISA subjects, and with the collective information, we should have more than enough probable cause for the surveillance. I want both search and arrest warrants. So start typing and let's go!"

The team of agents went to their stations and began their arduous task. They painstakingly spent the next few hours drafting their individual affidavits. The documents were each read and approved by Billy, and within moments of their reading, the agents were on their way to the FISC judges. Within hours, the wiretaps went up.

There were a total of eighteen targets, random people from different ethnicities and religions scattered throughout New York City. Despite their diversity, they all had two things in common: their anger at America and their high regard for Yousef.

Within hours, the dedicated agents listened intently to every phone call and monitored every social media post and chat. Anyone of those targets remotely construed as "engaging in clandestine intelligence activities" on behalf of Yousef was documented. With each phone call, search warrants and arrest warrants were simultaneously prepared. There was no time to waste. Soon, FBI agents around the country were following suit.

*   *   *

Agents throughout the country were working tirelessly as they continued their electronic surveillance. With each call, spin-off wiretaps were requested as additional targets were identified. In New York City alone, there were over forty total targets. Additional agents were brought in from neighboring cities, and local law enforcement officers were asked to join in.

The field agents were tasked with conducting twenty-four-hour visual surveillance on the various targets' homes and places of employment. The agents were ready to move in at a moment's notice.

It was clear to the agents that with every conversation, the targets were feeling inspired. They were still dealing with the pangs of Yousef's death but were hopeful that there was one last lingering message yet to be revealed. Yousef's disciples were ready to strike on command.

With each passing hour, the chatter and discussions from across the nation were becoming increasingly intense. Surveillance teams on the ground were painstakingly following many of the targets as they went from location to location. They were followed to church gatherings, mosques, and visits with other like-minded individuals. There was not enough time or manpower to follow them everywhere they went. The agents were feeling overwhelmed and were getting anxious; they could sense something was about to happen.

Chapter One Hundred Thirty-three

December 29

It was 9:45 p.m., and Billy Assad was still reviewing the volumes of reports from the field agents. New Year's Eve was slightly more than two days away, and he could not afford to make a mistake. Despite the ever-increasing tension, there was nothing definitive to act upon. Billy retrieved his desk phone and called one of his analysts, the one with the Indiana twang. The phone did not even ring from Billy's end before it was answered.

"Hello?"

"Yes, it's me. I need you to go back and review all of Yousef's videotapes again."

"Do you mean the most recent ones?" the analyst asked.

"No," he corrected. "All of them."

"Wouldn't it make sense to review the ones leading up to now?"

"No, we can't afford to miss a beat. I want them all reviewed—again. We have to be missing something."

Her voice sounded stressed. "We don't have enough time or people to accomplish that."

"Well, then find the time!"

Billy had never raised his voice in his entire career, but on this night, stress and exhaustion had set in, and Billy could not contain himself. He had the images of his wife and kids on his mind, and he did not want to lose them because of his negligence.

He picked up the phone again and made another call. This time, it was to the FBI director in Washington, D.C. The two men spoke for over twenty minutes. What Billy had to say piqued the director's interest. At the end of the conversation, Billy had the authorization to put into action a plan that just might save many families, including his own.

Billy made one final call to his assistant. "I need you to set up a video conference with all of the SACs in the country. All of them."

Chapter One Hundred Thirty-four

December 30

The conference room to the New York FBI headquarters was filled with all the chiefs and supervisory agents. On video screens against the wall were most of the SACs from throughout the country. Those who were not present had not yet been located, but Billy Assad did not want to wait for them. It was 1:50 a.m., and Billy was starting his emergency meeting.

"I appreciate your attendance at the last minute. I've read all our field reports, and I think we can agree that we all have the same sense of urgency. But time is almost up. The analysts across the board agree that the cells plan on striking at midnight on New Year's Eve. We need to act preemptively. I'm suggesting that we convert all our affidavits in support of the wiretaps, supplement them with what we have uncovered in the last twenty-four hours . . . and convert them into search warrants."

The agents both in that room and abroad were uneasy. There was a universal uneasiness that permeated across the airwaves.

Billy Assad continued, "You heard me correctly. I am convinced that there is enough probable cause to search these residences and businesses and stop any one of these groups before they can act."

"*Groups?*" asked a SAC from San Francisco.

"We here at the NOLA office don't have enough to prove that they are, in fact, a 'group,' much less a 'cell,'" said another SAC from New Orleans.

"That's not the standard the courts will be concerned with," Billy struck back. "Is there probable cause to believe that these people are threats to our national security, and is there probable cause to believe that they are in possession of evidence of a crime? That is the question that will be asked, and our answer has to be a resounding yes."

The room grumbled even louder.

"I have a question that nobody has asked," commented the same SAC from San Francisco. "Have the director and the AG approved this course of action?"

"I wouldn't be wasting your time setting up this conference otherwise."

The room went silent.

"The AG is expecting search warrants to be executed by six o'clock tomorrow morning." Billy's directive went against everything he ever stood for, but all he could think about was his family.

"Six o'clock? That's less than five hours away!" a SAC from Albuquerque shouted from his office, nearly two thousand miles away.

"Then don't waste any more time talking to me." Billy shut off all the screens and walked out of the room.

Chapter One Hundred Thirty-five

December 30

At approximately 6:20 a.m. Eastern Time, teams of FBI agents throughout the country executed volumes of search warrants. This operation took place in nearly every major city. As each search warrant was executed, modest homes in the suburbs were torn apart, apartments in the cities rummaged, and businesses disrupted as the agents ripped through these premises in search of evidence. At each location, the agents spent hours searching and seizing any piece of evidence remotely linked to an act of terrorism. Computer monitors, laptops, iPads, and every imaginable piece of computer equipment was seized and triaged by computer forensic experts.

Families were separated and detained, left to stand in the cold of the predawn hours while the search continued. Many of the women and children were crying as they wondered what was going on. The agents remained stoic as they continued in their mission, none of them saying a word as their targets demanded answers.

The entire operation ended nearly simultaneously. There was a total of seventy-nine arrests throughout the country but mostly for resisting arrest and the possession of controlled substances. Not a single person was arrested for conspiracy to commit terrorism against the United States.

Protestors throughout the country were screaming of governmental abuse and violations of privacy rights, due process, and equal protection. Political pundits took to the airwaves to give their opinion on the matter. Surprisingly, there was vast political support for the day's events—all in the name of national security. The biggest opponent of the obvious civil rights violations was the man who had spearheaded it all, Billy Assad, and it tore him up inside that he had to take such extraordinary actions, but all he could think about was his family.

*   *   *

At the end of the long day, Billy sat back in his chair and read every dismal report. He watched the television interview of his FBI director as the director gave a positive spin as to how the day's operation, dubbed Operation Silent Running, had led to multiple arrests of suspected terrorists, which most likely saved countless Americans lives. Within a minute after the press conference ended, Billy's phone rang.

"Hello, Director," Billy said with trepidation. He closed his eyes, expecting the reaming of his career.

"On behalf of the FBI, I want to congratulate you," the director said, to Billy's surprise. "You have done a wonderful job. The attorney general and, more importantly, the president of the United States are extremely pleased with your work. You should've been here at the press conference."

"I, uh, I had work to do."

"Always working!" The director laughed. "Well, the public at large feels very safe. A job well done."

Billy dropped the phone, and for the first time in several weeks, he felt at ease. *Maybe it was for the greater good. Maybe we did save lives.* He rested his head on the chair and closed his eyes. To his surprise, he dozed off.

The ringing tone of his phone woke him up. Billy rubbed his eyes and shook his head to wake up. He took a deep breath, waited a moment, and then reached to answer the phone.

"This is Assad."

"Mr. Assad." It was the voice of his analyst from Indiana calling from SOCOM.

"Yes?" Recognizing the stress in her voice, Billy was concerned. "What's going on?"

"Sir, General Norton asked me to call you."

Billy was becoming frustrated. "What is going on?"

"CIA is reporting that Yousef is still alive. He's been spotted in Europe."

Billy was stunned. "Dear lord."

"There's more, sir."

"What else?"

"Yousef has released a new video."

Chapter One Hundred Thirty-six

Yemen

By the time of Yousef's assassination, his camp had already been reduced to a skeleton crew. News of his death caused many of his followers to flee, and there were only a handful of loyalists who chose to remain behind. These few men felt they had a mission to fulfill.

One loyalist was sixteen-year-old Asiel. Asiel had been orphaned by a drone strike a month before he had joined the cause. Yousef had recognized the pain in the young boy's eyes; it was the same look Yousef had when he had lost his uncle Mustafa. At first, Yousef took the boy in to serve as an errand boy, but in the end, he saw something in the young man that mimicked Yousef's own life, and perhaps the boy's life would match his own destiny. However, for now, Asiel and the others were awaiting word from someone, anyone, who would tell them what to do next.

Five men sat in Yousef's main tent, crouched on the floor, staring at one another. The others were only slightly older than Asiel. He mysteriously felt ill and told the others that he was going to grab some fresh air. He stepped outside and breathed in the humid air. Asiel felt no better. He craned his neck and gazed into the blue sky. He thought he saw a glimmer above. The sun was in his eyes. He was uneasy and began to wander in the hopes of getting a better view. The entire area was quiet. There was not a sound coming from anywhere.

Asiel continued his trek, making his way over a dune, and still, he saw nothing. He returned his gaze toward the tent to realize he was several hundred yards away. Suddenly, he became nauseous as fear overtook him. He looked above again and sensed danger. He screamed out, but the others could not hear him. As he began to run toward the camp, a missile strike from the stealth drone above destroyed the remnants of the camp in a hellfire blaze. Asiel sobbed as he saw his friends burn to death.

Once again, the death of his loved ones came from America's hands. He was now the last of Yousef's loyalists. He felt that something greater had saved him and that perhaps he was spared for a reason. Maybe one day he would be as important and as influential as Yousef.

*   *   *

At SOCOM, General Norton celebrated the successful strike. He turned to face the men and women of the command center. He had a big smile on his face.

"Give yourself a round of applause, folks," the general ordered.

The room cheered.

The general continued his rally. "With that blast, we saw the end of Yousef's regime."

The general had never been so wrong in his life. Moments after Asiel's life had been spared by fate or perhaps by destiny, Asiel accessed his satellite phone and made a call. Within moments, on the other end of the call was a familiar voice.

Chapter One Hundred Thirty=seven

December 31

Nearly every major law enforcement agency in the country had converged in Times Square: the NYPD, the national guard, homeland security, the MTA, and the FBI. Collectively, they all agreed that the New Year's event would go as planned but with the tightest security New York had ever seen. The areas between Herald Square and Columbus Circle were completely barricaded. Twenty-four hours before the expected ball drop, law enforcement began limiting access to Times Square, starting at Forty-Third Street and Broadway. Additional roadblocks were placed south to Thirty-Eighth Street and as far north as Fifty-Ninth Street.

Billy witnessed the gridlock caused by the roadblocks all the way from his office window in Lower Manhattan. It was 7:20 p.m., and the taillights and headlights of the sea of cars lit up the night. He continued to stare out the window, and he was frantically racking his brain. *There must be more that I can do.*

He felt helpless standing there in his office. He could not wait anymore. Billy raced out the door and hailed a taxi to take him to Times Square. As a result of the heightened security, traffic was so severely backed up that it took Billy's taxi over an hour just to travel a mile.

Billy frantically looked at his watch. It was 9:50 p.m. He opted to race out of the taxi and run by foot.

Chapter One Hundred Thirty-eight

In the outskirts of London, two armed men stood guard outside an abandoned warehouse. They ignored the muted racket coming from inside.

*   *   *

The pillowcase over Seth's head stifled his breath. He was bound to a chair, his hands tied behind his back. Despite the covering over his head, he could hear the groans coming from Joshua. Seth could imagine that Joshua must have also been bound and gagged.

The pillowcase was violently yanked from over his head. He could see that they were inside a barren warehouse. Somebody was standing before him.

"Before you die, tell me—why are you here?" asked a mysterious voice.

The glare from the light bulb above the voice created a dark, shadowy figure. The shadow moved forward, blocking the brightness, revealing Yousef's stark countenance.

Seth gasped, amazed at the uncanny resemblance to Joshua. "You're alive? We were told you were assassinated."

Assassinated. As Yousef heard the words come out of the American's mouth, he was replaying the events before his purported assassination.

He thought about all the times that his imam had persuaded him to continue his endeavors, followed by all the mysterious phone calls. Yousef suddenly realized that his imam was much too eager for him to leave. He sensed that there was danger and would not risk leaving in one of the caravan of cars. He called for his imam.

The imam came in as beckoned. "My son, you must leave now."

"I need you to do something for me."

"Of course, my son."

"I need you to limp your way into any one of those cars and drive away."

"What?" The imam was perplexed. "Why would you want me to leave?"

"Because the second I drive away in one of those cars, I will be assassinated."

"I-I don't understand—"

"Yes, you do," Yousef responded. "If you don't get in that car, I will have my men kill you. If there is nothing to fear, then nothing will happen to you."

"But, my son—"

"You have thirty seconds to get in one of those cars."

The imam trembled in fear and proceeded to walk to a car.

"No, limp," Yousef demanded.

The imam feigned a limp and hopped into one of the cars. Yousef waved from within the tent and gave the driver a heartfelt smile. He bade his men farewell. The car drove off into eternity.

Yousef now hovered over the American. "Why are you here?" Yousef repeated angrily.

"I-I'm not here to interfere. I'm not an agent—I mean, I'm not a government agent. I simply wanted to help—help a . . . a friend." Seth was too frightened to be coherent.

Yousef got into his face. "What did you and that woman want with my mother?"

Seth glanced over to Joshua, who was still moaning in pain. "If you remove that man's blindfold, you'll see why I'm here."

"I have no time for this." Yousef signaled to his men. "Kill them. Kill them both."

"Wait!" Seth begged. "Please wait. This man is your brother."

Yousef stood silent for a moment. "What are you talking about?"

"Just remove the goddamn blindfold!" Seth said with surprisingly a lot of command.

Yousef stepped over to Joshua and angrily removed the pillowcase. He was stunned by the sight of his doppelgänger. His loyal aides were equally shocked.

"What trickery is this?"

"I don't know," Seth replied. "That's what I'm trying to find out."

Yousef stepped back. "This is another American trick. Kill them both!"

As his men were about to move in, Yousef's mother walked into the room from a side door.

"Stop!" Maria-Elena screamed. "I told you he would be telling the truth. Seth is innocent in all this."

"Mother," Yousef said, whispering to her, "I asked you to wait in the other room."

"My son, forgive me and please hear me out," Maria-Elena pleaded. "You always knew I was a Spaniard by birth, but we stopped talking about that when you became a young man. I never told you this, but I had been a nun since my teenage years. Several of my fellow sisters, including myself, were impregnated without our consent—without our knowledge."

Yousef had a look of despair. Maria-Elena looked over at Seth.

"I—" Seth interrupted Maria-Elena. "*We* later surmised that your mother and the others must have been part of some . . . some form of experiment."

Maria-Elena continued, "My sisters and I—we were selected for reasons that I cannot imagine. After we discovered that we were pregnant, we were banished to a convent in Italy—Fiorello, 'little flower.' After nine months, several of us gave birth to baby boys . . .

and you were one of them." Maria-Elena then turned to caress the whimpering Joshua. "This young man was one of them too."

"Is he truly my brother?" Yousef asked.

"I did not give birth to him, but all the children must have had the same donor. Many of them were sickly, like Joshua, all except you."

Yousef pointed to his frail leg. "But I was born defective."

"True, but you were perfect in every other way."

"What happened to the other children?" Yousef asked.

"I grew so leery of all the unusual activity surrounding the births that I fled our home. I fled as far away as I could to protect you. I fled to the Middle East and raised you in our new home. The others died in a fire set by those who caused this. Only you and Joshua survived." Maria-Elena grabbed her son's hands. "You must not harm them. They are not here to hurt you."

"I don't understand . . ." Yousef was filled with emotion.

"I gave up trying to understand," his mother said. "You were a blessing to me, and I've cherished every moment with you. You were a blessing from God. I cannot tell you what to do with your destiny. But I know in my heart you were given to me for a reason."

Yousef broke away from his mom and kneeled before Joshua. He caressed his brother's face. Joshua reacted as if he recognized him.

Yousef beckoned to two of his four men. "Release them." He then turned his attention to Seth. "Do you have any more thoughts on all this?"

Seth stammered. "I-I have p-put a lot of thought to this. But it's all a theory."

"Share it with me," Yousef said politely but ever so directly.

In his mind's eye, Seth imagined his theory as he uttered it. "You have a group of young, virtuous, and chaste nuns who all went to the same doctors for regular checkups. These doctors all work for the same sinister . . . cabal, devising some sort of mysterious plan. As a result, these nuns just happen to become pregnant. They each carry a male child. It was known that the church would protect its reputation by hiding *the sisters* in that orphanage, away from any embarrassing exposure. In fact, during my research, I came across the story of a church in Ireland that was run by the Bon Secours Sisters, and that was purported to have the remains of eight hundred children in unmarked graves. Thousands of unmarried pregnant women, including rape victims, were sent to that church to give birth—"

Maria-Elena interrupted. "But how? None of us were raped or were promiscuous."

"It's obvious," Seth continued. "This was no random miracle. It's all artificial insemination. You were all chosen by design. That's why you were all sent to the same orphanage. And while you were all living there, this cabal continued to monitor your pregnancies. One by one, each of your pregnancies came out terribly wrong. With the near exception of one—Yousef's. Even now, you walk with a slight limp based on your minor birth defect. It's a slight defect, but it must have been enough to cause great consternation. Whatever the true mission may have been, it had to have been deemed a complete and utter failure. The strange men left, never to be seen again. Maria-Elena's premonition leads her to flee and take her baby away. Not long after, there's a mysterious fire that kills nearly everyone. Killing off witnesses and destroying evidence. Decades go by, and no one is the wiser until I come across Teresa in a mental hospital in the United States."

Maria-Elena was pacing the room nervously. "Artificially inseminated? For what reason?"

"That's what's so crazy. I don't really know . . . I have my suspicions, but . . . it is clear that you each had the same donor."

"The same donor?" Maria-Elena was furious. "How can you know that?"

Seth answered, "You said it yourself. All the babies looked the same, and the resemblance between Yousef and Joshua is incredible."

"Tell me about this *donor*," Maria-Elena said, curious. "Tell me what you are thinking."

Seth had a look of embarrassment, but he pressed on. "With all this crazy talk about this guy – James St. John-Smythe – in England claiming to be a descendent of Christ, it just made me think how desperate people are for a savior. What if . . ." Seth hesitated. "It's just too crazy to even say out loud."

Yousef spoke. "Please go on."

"What if *they*, this cabal, selected the nuns in an attempt to replicate the immaculate conception?"

"*What?*" Maria-Elena and Yousef both said simultaneously.

"I know it sounds absurd. But wouldn't it make sense to pick virgin nuns in the hopes of recreating the immaculate conception? All in the hopes of 'resurrecting' Jesus Christ?"

Maria-Elena shook her head in disagreement. "That would be blasphemous."

Seth's head was throbbing; he began to rub his temple. "I can't even think straight. I'm so exhausted. Just ignore me."

Yousef stared at Joshua and gave him a warm smile. He looked back at Seth and commented, "That would mean that the people behind St. John-Smythe or any one of the reputed descendants of Christ had to be the sperm donor."

"I thought of that," Seth responded quickly. "But none of you look like St. John-Smythe. You both have strong, dark, Mediterranean features. A stark contrast to St. John-Smythe's white, European features. No, for this to work, it would have to be a perfect duplicate. A clone."

"A *clone?*" Yousef exclaimed. "That is scientifically impossible."

"As far as you and I know, it is."

"Where would they get the DNA from?" Yousef joined his mother in pacing around the room. "This is crazy!"

"I'm not sure." Seth envisioned countless possibilities. "Legend has it that the Spear of Destiny was used to pierce the side of Jesus. The spear is rumored to be housed in a museum in Vienna. These men could have accessed that. Or they could have located the Sudarium of Oviedo, the reputed cloth that was used to cover Jesus's face after his death. If there is anything that would have his DNA, it would be that item."

In his mind's eye, Seth envisioned a young scientist stealing a sample of blood from an object. In his vision, the scientist was handing over the sample to the men in black. Seth suddenly had a disturbing vision of the young scientist dying. *They would dare not risk leaving behind any witnesses.*

Seth composed himself and continued, "There's also the Veil of Veronica, rumored to be at Saint Peter's Basilica, but no one really knows if it is the 'real' veil." He paused and then muttered, "Oh, and how could I forget the Shro—"

Before Seth could complete his thought, he was interrupted by the ringing tone from Yousef's satellite phone. Yousef stepped aside and spoke softly into it. It was Asiel.

"Are you okay?" Yousef asked as he heard his young acolyte near death. "You must be careful, but it is vital that you listen to me very carefully . . ."

He walked away from everyone's earshot and muttered some instructions. Within moments, he canceled the call.

"Soon, they will know I'm alive," Yousef said, returning to the others. "With this call, they will have tracked me here. I must leave."

"Wait!" Seth said, blocking his path. "If this is true, you and Joshua were meant to be something great, a part of something greater, something . . . You just can't leave."

The room went quiet.

"I . . . I . . . dr-dream . . . dream . . . of . . . a h-horse and a man . . ." Joshua whispered, breaking the silence.

Yousef looked at Joshua in bewilderment. "What did you say?"

"I . . . I dream of a . . . horse . . . a horse."

"*A horse?*" Yousef said excitedly. "You dream of a horse? Are you riding the horse? Are you dressed like . . . like . . . like a king or a prince . . . or a knight?"

"A . . . king . . . a knight . . . riding a horse," Joshua replied.

"What are you two talking about?" Seth asked.

"I have this same recurring dream," Yousef answered. "But it can't possibly mean anything."

Seth was excited. "It must mean something if you are both having the same dream."

"In my dream," Yousef began to explain, "there is a knight, riding a horse, being chased by his enemies. He's carrying something, something valuable or precious. With each dream, he gets closer to his destination. A castle or a palace or something in the distance. But he never seems to make it."

"The Christian Crusades?" Seth pondered. "It must represent—"

"The dream represents the oppression, the pain, and the killing the Christians have inflicted on what they deemed as heretics. I have been here far too long. It is time for me to leave. Do not attempt to follow me. It is too dangerous. The Americans have already killed one of my decoys and destroyed most of my camp. Wait for several hours after we leave. Then you go your own way."

Yousef took his mother by the hand and turned to leave—but not before he was embraced by Joshua.

Yousef gently pulled away. "I cannot take you with me. It is too dangerous for you. Farewell."

"We cannot take Joshua with us?" Maria-Elena pleaded.

"No," Yousef replied. "It's too dangerous for us alone. His life is more at risk with me than it is if we leave him. Please. We must leave."

"Please," she begged. "I promised his mother—"

Yousef softly interrupted his mother as he gently caressed her face. "You know I am right. He will not be safe with us."

Streams of tears flowed from Maria-Elena's eyes as she nodded. She rushed to embrace Joshua. "Joshua, please be careful," Maria-Elena said tearfully. "Listen to Seth. He's a good man. He will take care of you."

Joshua cried and held onto her arm firmly. Maria-Elena slowly removed his grip and walked away. Seth held Joshua back, and the sickly man began to cry.

Chapter One Hundred Thirty-nine

SOCOM
December 31
10:15 p.m.

General Norton was starting to show signs of exhaustion, exhaustion not just from this recent operation but also from decades of traveling the world, hunting down enemies to his country. His fatigue had become obvious to his team; it must have been weeks since they last saw him take leave to go to sleep, but no one dared to say anything.

The general stood stoic as he watched the various monitors before him, each displaying images of a different part of the country and of the world. The general's concentration was broken as Billy Assad's young analyst came in, holding two files.

"General, I have the reports as requested by Mr. Assad."

"What reports?" the general demanded to know.

The young analyst handed him the first of the two binders. "This one has the complete summary of Yousef's videos, breaking each and

BRYANT R. CAMARENO

every one down frame by frame. Our final analysis is that we still cannot decipher his secret messages. We have studied every gesture, every eye blink, every color scheme in the background, and we still have nothing."

"What about the other report?" the general asked as he removed the binder from her hands. This binder was larger and contained hundreds of pages.

"This is the summary of the most recent chatter from all the wiretaps we have pending."

The general flipped through the first twenty pages. "Tell me we at least have some intel from all this."

She stuttered as she looked the general in the eye. "The only thing we have is that all the chatter seems to confirm that something is going to happen on New Year's Eve."

The general looked at the atomic clock on the wall. "Dammit! That's only a few hours away. Do we have a location?"

"No," she replied. "The chatter is from all over the country. This incident could happen anywhere—or everywhere . . ."

The general slid the binder across the desk. He glanced at the screens before him. He then scanned around the room and noticed that someone was conspicuously absent. "Where the hell is Mr. Assad anyway?"

"He flew to New York, remember? He was going to check in on his family and see if there was any intel from the New York office."

"New York?" the general repeated as he looked at the series of monitors focusing in on Times Square.

He watched as the scores of NYPD officers and city workers worked hard setting up the barricades in preparation for the monumental event: the ball drop. The event was hours away, and the masses of people were reaching over a million.

The general felt uneasy. "God, not New York. Get me Assad on the phone—now!"

Within moments, one of the analysts was overheard speaking with a fellow field agent over the phone. The words overheard brought all work to a stop. The general himself turned to the CIA analyst, waiting to hear the news. It took several minutes before the CIA analyst terminated the call.

The general looked at that man, curious. "Do you have something to share with us?"

The CIA analyst fumbled with his words. "This . . . This can't be right."

"*What can't be right?*" the general shouted.

"One of our field ops picked up a signal on one of the phones that we're monitoring."

The general was losing his patience. "Whose phone?"

"You-Yousef. We intercepted one of Yousef's calls. They believe he's still alive."

There were gasps of shock throughout the room.

Chapter One Hundred Forty

New York, New York
December 31
10:45 p.m.

Billy raced down Seventh Avenue, running through the crowds of people, glaring at every neon sign throughout his peripheral vision. He was desperately looking for any type of clue as to the impending doom—anywhere and everywhere. He stopped to catch his breath, and then his phone rang. It was General Norton.

"Mr. Assad!" the general barked.

Billy could tell that he was on speaker, and he sensed the general's tension.

"Bad news."

"What is it?" Billy said impatiently, stopping in the middle of the street. The crowd was annoyed that Billy was standing in their way. He had no problem ignoring them.

"We picked up Yousef on his phone. He's still alive."

Billy was terrified by the news. He pressed forward on his quest, picking up his pace, and was soon running. "Where is he now?"

"It looks like he's heading to London. How soon can you get there?"

"I can't do it, General. The attack will take place here, in New York, and I'm going to find that cell."

"Mr. Assad," his junior analyst said, speaking into the speaker, "you don't know if it's New York. It could be anywhere in the world—"

"She's right," the general interrupted. "That's why you need to fly to London. If he's caught, I need you there to interrogate him."

"The attack could be everywhere,' Billy responded. "Yousef has followers all over the world. He has cells here in New York."

The general looked up at the screens displaying New York's busy streets. He felt what Billy did; the city was in danger. "Do you have anything that confirms New York City?"

Billy responded in between breaths, "Aside from the numerous arrests, no. But our agents our interrogating each suspect intensively. We hope to have something soon."

"We need something, anything, fast, or we're going to have to take Yousef out," the general added.

"What do you mean?"

"One of our drones is zeroing in on him now."

"Drone? Why a drone?" Billy Assad inquired. His voice came in muffled from the speaker on the desk.

"If we can't get any information from these cells, then we will have no choice but to eliminate him. We can't risk Yousef giving the command to start the attack."

"But a drone? In London?"

"Yousef would see military forces coming a mile away," the general replied. "A drone will hit him before he knows it."

Intrigued, Billy Assad followed up with another question. "Have the British authorities been informed?"

"Yes, we have. They have agreed. We are all on the same side here on this war on terrorism." The general turned his attention to another speaker. "Langley, status of that drone?" General Norton asked.

"ETA to London in fifteen minutes," said the voice.

"What about British civilian casualties? Can't we use an EMP?" Billy asked earnestly.

"We can't get one loaded in time. Yousef is located at an abandoned industrial park. It's after hours. If there are any civilian casualties, it'll be nominal," the general said casually. "Langley? Keep me posted."

"ETA in ten minutes," said the voice from Langley.

"Billy, you've got fifteen minutes to get me something."

More death, more destruction. Billy Assad felt sick to his stomach.

Chapter One Hundred Forty-one

James St. John-Smythe's voice was sore from yelling. By the time the police vehicle stopped, he had nothing left but a rasp. He glanced up to see that they had arrived at a private airport. He had never been to this one before, but he was certain he recognized the sole jet stationed on the runway. It was one of the elders' many private planes.

Fairfield and the chief inspector said nothing as they pulled up next to the plane. Two men in black opened the door and signaled James to get out.

"Thank goodness," James said to the men. "I must protest how these two officers have treated me. I really would like—"

The men in black were so forceful in escorting James that he was stunned to silence. James became ill as he approached the plane. As the men sat him in the front seat, James noticed that inside the plane, there were two pilots and his two man-handlers. James glanced outside the window and watched as Fairfield stood behind the chief inspector and placed a gun to his head. The chief inspector appeared resigned as to what his fate was going to be. Fairfield pulled the trigger, and the chief fell to the ground. James was surprisingly moved by the execution.

Just before the plane taxied down the runaway, James could see Fairfield drag the dead man's body into the car. He knew that both the body and the car would soon be lost to all eternity. It was at that moment that James feared that he would meet the same fate.

Chapter One Hundred Forty-two

The jet flew for about an hour. The two men sat behind James, ever so vigilant and equally silent. James peered out the window and saw the most verdant island he had ever seen. The island appeared to be deserted. He surmised that they were somewhere off the coast of Scotland. His heart started racing as the jet descended onto a singular runway.

Moments after landing, the two men in black grabbed James by each arm, and he was forced off the plane. The plane wasted no time in taking off again, leaving the three men standing alone on a barren stretch of asphalt.

After twenty minutes, James heard the engine of a car and saw that it belonged to black sedan. The sedan was driving on a makeshift road made of sand and gravel. It stopped just short of them. The three men entered the back seat, James noticing that the driver was even more menacing than his two companions.

The car made its way down the makeshift road, passing rolling hills and swampy moors. The journey lasted for almost an hour. Finally, through the front windshield, James could see a palatial mansion situated in the heart of a steep-sided valley, surrounded by two large cliffs, both of which provided just enough coverage to prevent the large home from being observed from above. The mansion was three times as large as Wyndham Court.

Several armed men in black lined the dirt road on each side. The black car drove right past them. Night was about to fall, and the fog was beginning to rise from the ground. The sedan stopped at a large wrought-iron gate. A singular camera moved and zoomed in on the driver. The driver gestured, and the gate opened.

On the other side of the gate was a long stretch of cobblestone road. At the far end of the road was the ultimate destination: the palatial residence.

Standing outside the residence was a legion of more men dressed in black. Two of his companions violently forced James out of the car. James was no longer smirking; he was terrified. James grew faint and fell to his knees. The two men heaved him up by each arm and carried him up the stairs into the house. The legion of men had led the way.

He was carried across the room toward two large doors that were guarded by four men. Two of those men opened the large heavy doors to reveal a vast ceremonial hall. The large group of men walked in, and the doors were closed behind them. Within a few moments, James was dragged into the center of the ceremonial hall. Surrounding him were over a hundred men, all wearing black hooded robes.

Chapter One Hundred Forty-three

London, England

Yousef, with his mother by his side, exited the abandoned building. His loyal men followed closely behind him. They discreetly made their way out of the building toward the van parked out front. He held his mother's hands as if to reassure her.

Maria-Elena smiled at her son. She had not seen him so happy in such a long time. She was confident that his "reunion" with Joshua must have given him a new sense of hope.

As they paced closer to the van, Yousef breathed out a sigh of relief, knowing that he was on his way to freedom.

* * *

Miles above them, a military drone watched them from afar. The drone pilot focused in on the van and awaited his command.

Chapter One Hundred Forty-four

The ceremonial hall was breathtaking in that it was two stories high, with a stone marble floor and a series of columns that rivaled those at the Temple of Horus in Edfu. The columns were covered with ancient hieroglyphics and otherworldly symbols. The hall was filled with over a hundred black-robed men scattered throughout the room, many of whom were watching from the balcony of the second level. Standing in the center was the grandmaster, wearing a red robe.

James was dragged into the semicircle of spectators and placed before the grandmaster. Of all the men before him, James only recognized Ducard and Sébastien. He was suddenly blindfolded and stripped naked. Ominous music began to play in the background. The group of men placed ceramic masks over their faces, and then there was silence.

A moment later, the grandmaster spoke. "You were chosen from His countless descendants to lead the way for the lost masses. We were tolerant and perhaps ignorant of your indiscretions, but they can no longer be ignored. You have been a disgrace to your lineage, and we will no longer tolerate your failures. The penalty is death. Your only consolation will be that your death will be revealed to be heroic. No one will know of the true cause of your demise, but it won't be long before you are forgotten from memory."

James tried to act brave, but his frail voice gave him away. "You dare not touch me. I am the rightful heir. You cater to me."

"Such a lost soul," the grandmaster said. "Pity."

James was led to a plastic tarp placed on the floor. He was pushed down to the ground.

"No, wait! Please! Give me one more chance!"

A large, masked executioner stood behind James. He took a large blade and slit his throat. The waterfall of blood exiting his neck afforded James a quick death. His corpse was carried away, and his body was placed in a gold-laden box. A team of custodial workers rushed into the hall, diligently wrapped up the plastic sheet and cleaned up the pool of blood.

The grandmaster then turned to Ducard and Sébastien. The circle of men removed the robes from the two brothers.

"The council of elders has voted on your fate as well. You were both tasked with bringing this objective to life, and you have failed in every way imaginable. You were the appointed guardians for the heir, and you were negligent in your duties. There can be no other punishment than death. Your death will be swift and private. However, your loyalty will not go unrecognized, and your families will be provided for. They will not suffer because of your ineptitude. We have been brothers for a long time, and you will both be missed. A new heir is being sought, and new guardians will be appointed. Any last words?"

Sébastien spoke out proudly. "I honorably served my fellow brethren and this council," he said solemnly. "I will gladly give up my life for the benefit of our cause."

Ducard remained silent, and both men were led away for a more private and honorable death.

The grandmaster removed his robe and handed it to his dutiful manservant. He then turned to his council of elders.

"Instruct our people to publish a story recounting James's heroic death feeding the hungry in Sudan. Waste no time in finding a suitable heir. And I want the American and those with him dead. I want all traces of *that* failed experiment eliminated."

In no time, loyal MIBs stationed within London received the call to resume their search of Seth and his companions. Despite the stand-down alert that had been given by Sébastien, a two-man team had been watching Seth from afar. The men in black had followed Seth and his companions as they had been kidnapped and taken to the abandoned warehouse.

The darkly clad men were now standing outside, watching as Yousef escorted his mother into the van. They realized that Seth and Joshua were staying behind; the warehouse would be the perfect place to dispose of the last remaining threats to the brotherhood.

Chapter One Hundred Forty-five

Maria-Elena, experiencing an eerie premonition, suddenly stopped walking and turned to her son. She had a change of heart and was visibly distressed. "Yousef, we cannot leave without Joshua. I understand that you're not safe staying here, but I cannot leave without him."

"Me? *We* are not safe," Yousef responded. "We're both in danger."

"My life has been in danger since the moment we escaped the orphanage. I've been looking over my shoulder your entire life, and I've endured a lifetime of sleepless nights. I'm not afraid to die, but I cannot leave Joshua alone."

Yousef could not stand to see his mother in pain but was reluctant to change his mind. "We cannot take him with us. He will be more at risk with me."

"I know that, and I know that he will only slow you down. He's my sister's son, and I have to care for him."

"Mother, I don't have time to argue. We must leave now.'

As the two continued to bicker, the drone grew closer to its target.

*   *   *

"Target on sight," said the voice from Langley.

General Norton scowled. "Target confirmed?"

"Target confirmed," said one of the analysts in the room.

On the large screen above them, the people in the room could see the heat imaging of Yousef and his men.

"Mr. Assad, do you have anything for me at all from out there in New York?"

Billy Assad had still been listening from his end. "The field agents across the country are reporting back that their interrogations aren't getting any results."

The general lowered his head. "Then we have no choice." He turned his attention to the large screen bearing the image of their intended target. "Eliminate the target," the general ordered.

At that moment, Maria-Elena's image was zoomed in on the screen.

"Wait a minute," said the drone pilot from his control booth in Nevada. "That looks like a female."

"Shit," the general cursed. "That must be his mother."

"What are my orders?" asked the drone operator.

There was no response from SOCOM. They were all holding their breaths.

"What are my orders, sir?" the drone operator asked again.

For the first time in the general's illustrious career, he was dumbfounded. He looked back at his JAG officer. The JAG officer was also bewildered.

Time seemed to stand still. Soon, a decision would be made that would destroy the lives of the very people who could unlock the mystery of Fiorello.

Chapter One Hundred Forty-six

Maria-Elena could tell by the tone in Yousef's voice that no matter how much she protested, her son would not be leaving without her. She allowed him to grab her and did not resist as he escorted her into the van. Yousef and his mother sat in the back seat, and he ordered the driver to speed away.

Yousef spoke into his satellite phone. "Release the videos."

*   *   *

Nearly four thousand miles away, standing outside a cave in the most barren desert in Yemen, Asiel, the sole remaining aide to Yousef's cause, received the call from his master. During their last conversation, Asiel had been given directions to the hidden cave, where Yousef kept a separate batch of videos and computer equipment that would serve as backup in case of loss.

The young man disconnected the call and stepped into the cave. Placed atop a small wooden table was a laptop. The loyal aide typed in the nine-character password he had committed to memory and located the file. Moments before Yousef went on his journey to reunite with his mother, the young man had helped his master record one last video.

The young man became emotional as he recounted what everyone knew would be Yousef's most powerful message. Somehow the two of them knew that this would be Yousef's last. The entire presentation only lasted ten minutes, but it would resonate with anyone who watched it. Yousef knew that this last video would have an impact on anyone who believed that the world needed to change and that Yousef was the one who could bring about that change.

The young man clicked on that last video and began to upload it on various social media platforms. Within minutes, his mission was complete.

He took great joy in seeing the number of views that the video was receiving. In only a few minutes, the video registered over ten thousand hits, but that was only a fraction of the total number of views it would receive. In only an hour, it would receive nearly three million views.

*   *   *

Among those millions of viewers, some were from America. A firefighter at Engine 17 in Detroit, Michigan, watched the video on his laptop. A taxi driver parked alongside North State Street, adjacent to the Chicago Theater, watched it play on his cell phone. An NYPD officer saw it on the news. The video played on the computers, laptops, and cell phones of civil servants and military officers throughout the country. The message to them was all too clear: terror was to strike at midnight, December 31.

Chapter One Hundred Forty-seven

December 31
11:47 p.m.

"General." The voice of a CIA analyst from Langley broke the silence. "This may be our last chance. We are minutes away from the midnight hour. We must strike now."

The general gave another glance to his JAG officer. He then spoke to the drone pilot. "Captain, what say you?"

Miles away in Nevada, the drone pilot looked at the copilot sitting next to him. They were both perplexed, but the captain answered the general in a way that he thought his commander would want to hear.

"Sir, I think the casualties would be nominal. At most, it's one civilian."

The general was impressed with the exactness of the response, but he was not so sure. He took another look at the JAG officer.

The Harvard Law graduate was proud of his career. He enlisted in the army when he was eighteen, served five years with distinction, and took his GI Bill to pay for his college, and then he went to law school. Like many proud patriots, he reenlisted after 9/11 and went to JAG school. He rose to the rank of major and was handpicked to attend the U.S. Army War College.

As a born-again Christian, the veteran JAG officer struggled with the concept of war. He was pro-life, and certainly, one could not be pro-life and yet be pro-war. However, after he had read Saint Augustine's principle of just-war theory, he was convinced that some wars and the deaths associated with them were not only justified but also God sanctioned. Still, at this very moment, Yousef's mother was not on any kill list and was clearly a civilian.

The deaths of civilians are only justified when they are unavoidable victims of a military attack on a strategic target. The JAG officer recalled his teacher's lecture from War College. Still, the JAG officer was worried about the legal consequences of her possible death. The JAG officer was not ready to make that call.

Chapter One Hundred Forty-eight

The attorney general was terrified of the idea of celebrating New Year's Eve out in the public and instead decided to stay at his private residence in Spokane, Washington, and watch the events from there. His phone rang, and he knew it could only be trouble. It was General Norton.

"General, it must be important if you are calling me at home."

"It is, sir. We have a situation."

"What is it? Speak." The AG was growing impatient.

"We have a clear shot of Yousef," the general explained, "but he's in the company of a female. We think it's his mother."

"What does the JAG say?"

"He wants your input," the general said through the phone.

The AG contemplated his next words. After a brief pause, he said rhetorically, "If we wait, what happens to Yousef? He disappears, and we pray that we can find him again?"

"Correct," the general answered.

"Is it just the one civilian?" the AG asked.

"And three militant combatants. There may be other civilians inside a warehouse a few yards away. Minimal risk to them."

"Are you certain that if we don't strike now, the target is lost again?"

"Yes, sir," the general said without hesitation.

"Then you have my approval." The AG disconnected the call and returned to his family.

The CIA in Langley, the pilot in Nevada, and the JAG at SOCOM heard the response. The general gave the JAG officer one last look. The JAG officer reluctantly held his thumb up.

Chapter One Hundred Forty-nine

Seth was desperately trying to comfort the inconsolable Joshua, who had been yearning for his mother, but somehow he knew that she was out of his life once again. Joshua was now asking for Maria-Elena.

"Please be quiet," Seth pleaded, fearful of any potential danger the young man's voice might attract.

"M-Ma-Mari . . . L-Lena . . ." The young man struggled to say her name.

"Maria-Elena is gone." Seth became despondent. "Lucia is gone . . . and your mama, Teresa, is gone."

Joshua was heading out the door. "N-no, Ma-Mari . . . Lena—"

Seth grabbed him by the arm but was careful not to harm him. "Please be quiet. Please."

Joshua disobeyed and pressed forward. Seth relented and let him loose.

Chapter One Hundred Fifty

As the van inched forward, Yousef gazed out the rear window and saw Joshua struggling as he made his way out of the building. Seth was walking out behind him, attempting to slow him down. Yousef saw the look of sadness on Joshua's face.

At that same moment, the drone pilot zeroed in on Yousef's van, awaiting orders to fire.

Yousef wanted to ignore his brother, Joshua, but could not resist looking back. Suddenly, Yousef saw a dark vehicle drive up, stopping half a meter away from the warehouse. Five armed MIBs were racing toward Joshua. Alarmed, Yousef ordered the driver to stop, but the driver was shocked by the appearance of the black sedan and continued forward.

Fearing that the men in black were American agents, Yousef bellowed a warning to Seth and Joshua to go back inside. The MIBs grew menacingly closer and were in arm's reach of Joshua. Before the car could accelerate, Yousef slid the door open and jumped out of the car, rolling onto the street. Maria-Elena screamed in horror. Slightly bruised, Yousef jumped to his feet and made his way toward Joshua.

At that very moment, in SOCOM, General Norton issued his command. "Fire!"

Within an instant, the drone pilot in Nevada launched the missile toward the van.

Chapter One Hundred Fifty-one

As Billy continued to race down the parade of people, he was replaying in his head every frame of every video released by Yousef, replaying every sound bite, every hand gesture, and every color scheme of every background he could remember.

Billy stopped in the midst of the maddening crowd to catch his breath and called his analyst. "Any update on the analysis of the videos?"

"Nothing," said the junior analyst.

Billy hung up the receiver before she could say more. He spoke into his radio. "All units, please check in."

One by one, each field agent from every major city throughout the country replied in the same way: *Nothing.*

* * *

At the same time, every recipient of Yousef's latest message was making their final preparations—including the contingent of his followers participating in the revelry in Times Square.

Chapter One Hundred Fifty-two

Moments after Yousef jumped out of the van, the drone launched its missile, destroying the car. Maria-Elena was killed in the fiery destruction.

The destructive explosion and the damaging shrapnel propelled the brothers, Yousef and Joshua, into the air and against the wall of the warehouse. They both fell hard against the ground. The effects of the explosion badly damaged the surrounding structures and ripped the MIBs into shreds. Joshua was clinging to life. Yousef was mortally wounded. Both brothers lay next to each other, dying. The force had knocked Seth into unconsciousness.

The explosion caught the attention of everyone nearby, and soon, law enforcement, paramedics, and reporters were making their way to the scene.

Chapter One Hundred Fifty-three

Seth awoke from his injury. His head was throbbing, his vision blurred. He managed to prop himself against a wall and watched as Yousef struggled to caress the face of Joshua. Seth began to cry.

Yousef rolled over onto his side and found that his phone was still in his hand. He painstakingly brought it to his face and pressed the speaker button.

Chapter One Hundred Fifty-four

As the fire began to quell, British forces surrounded the two brothers. A crowd also started to gather, many of whom were streaming with their phones. In addition, the media was starting to arrive. The British police pointed their guns at Yousef, mistaking his satellite phone for a weapon.

"Drop it now!" the men commanded. "Drop it, or we will shoot you!"

Yousef ignored their commands and placed the phone to his mouth. The officers gave no other warning and fired two shots into his body.

His sheer will to live was overwhelming. He would not die—not yet. Yousef placed the phone to his mouth and spoke.

Chapter One Hundred Fifty-five

Television screens all over the world carried the streams of Yousef's actions. Hidden among the spectators throughout the country were Yousef's loyalists, each carrying their own personalized form of weapon, waiting to execute their final plan, willing to die for Yousef's cause.

The innocent bystanders abroad held their breath as they witnessed on the various television screens and monitors what could only be Yousef's attempt to give his final command—a command that could only mean certain doom and destruction. One screen in particular was in Times Square.

*   *   *

11:58 p.m.

Billy Assad resumed his race through the mass of people down Seventh Avenue, displaying his badge and announcing himself as FBI. He scanned the crowd, looking for anything, anyone who might be considered suspicious. He was making his way to the digital billboard that spanned the entire block from Forty-Fifth Street to Forty-Sixty Street on Broadway.

His heart was beating hard against his chest. Stuck behind a large crowd on Thirty-Ninth Street, Billy stopped to catch his breath. His legs were throbbing; his head was bursting. He knew that the clock would be striking at midnight, and he was hoping that it was not too late. He did the only thing he knew he could do, and that was to pray.

Chapter One Hundred Fifty-six

Yousef's voice was raspy and low. He could barely be heard.

"Tell . . . Tell . . . them . . . to . . . t-to . . . stop. Tell . . . Tell . . . them . . . to . . . stop . . . stop . . . the . . . attack . . . stop . . . the . . . attack . . ."

Yousef's final message was quickly televised around the globe. The news outlets proudly announced the apparent assassination of Yousef, ignoring his final words, but the whole world was watching. Yousef's message was replayed over and over. His command quickly spread around the world.

Yousef's followers heeded his last message. Those who had been planning individual attacks all went about their way and hid among the crowds of people, believing Yousef had changed the world.

Disaster was diverted.

Chapter One Hundred Fifty-seven

London, England

Propped up against a wall, Seth was nursing his injuries. He was watching as the two brothers writhed in pain. *It's over. It is finally over. With their deaths, this horrific nightmare would be finally over.* This was the only thought that brought Seth comfort.

At that moment, Seth noticed that Joshua was grasping for his mother's charm, which had been ripped from his hands during the explosion. Seth crawled over to Joshua and smiled as he gave the pendant to the dying man. Teresa's dying words suddenly flooded Seth's mind.

"*P-p-please . . . p-protect . . . m-my s-sons . . . sons . . .*"

Seth was upset at himself because he had failed to protect her *sons*. Clearly, Teresa had met Yousef and Joshua.

"*N-no . . . J-Joshua . . . n-not . . . no . . .*"

He shed a tear as he recalled the moment Teresa had given him the pendant.

"*M-my . . . oth-other . . . I-I had . . . t-t—*"

"*You had to . . . what?*" he had asked her before she passed away.

"*I had to . . .*" These were the same words Teresa had said to him when they first spoke at the hospital in Tampa. "*I had to . . .*" she had said. "*I had to make a choice,*" she would say later, recounting her failed attempt to save all the babies. *Or was it?* he thought.

"*I had two. My other—I had two . . .*"

Seth was startled back to reality as the British forces carried him away from the area.

"No, wait . . ." Seth resisted their aid, not wanting to leave Joshua behind.

Seth relented and was handed over to a team of paramedics, who quickly treated him for his injuries. He looked back at the brothers one last time. Tears streamed down his face; he was relieved as he watched each of the two brothers take their last breath.

*   *   *

Yousef dropped the phone as he prepared to die. He glanced over at Joshua and reached out for him. Yousef gazed at Joshua and smiled. The brothers embraced and comforted themselves to the end. As Yousef lay dying, he dreamt his dream that one final time.

Chapter One Hundred Fifty-eight

In his final vision, Yousef's dream was more detailed. Sharply, he saw the same Crusader riding his horse across the desert sand. To his surprise, he could see that the young knight resembled both himself *and* Joshua.

Had I been wrong in thinking the knight was the enemy? Yousef pondered. *Was my imam wrong this entire time? Or was I being misled?*

Strangely, Yousef had a sense of relief that the knight was about to complete his long and arduous journey. The knight was wounded and exhausted. His destination was a castle in the distance, only a league away.

The steed suddenly collapsed under its own weight, thrusting the knight forward, causing him to crash onto the desert sand. The knight lay there, motionless, winded, holding tightly onto the satchel with his left hand. He lifted his head to see his enemies gaining ground. They were almost upon him. With great difficulty, he stood upright and unsheathed his sword with his right hand.

The knight turned to face the castle and painfully resumed his journey on foot, firmly grasping the satchel with one hand and his sword in the other. He was only able to take a few steps before collapsing again. The valiant knight prayed for forgiveness and began to cry. He passed out from the sheer pain.

Moments later, the knight was awoken by the rich general, who had been poking him with his sword. Annoyed, the good knight pushed the sword away and reached for his own sword. It was no longer at his side. It was in the hand of one of the many knights hovering over him.

The army of knights surrounded him and began to laugh as the knight slowly got on his feet. He proudly faced the rich general.

The general reached down for the satchel, but the good knight slapped his hand away. The general, in turn, struck his fist across the knight's face. The knight fell onto his knees as the others continued to laugh.

The general attempted again to reach for the satchel, and again, the good knight slapped his hand away. The general responded with a more violent blow to the head, but this time, it was the good knight who was laughing. The others stopped their snickering. The good knight raised his hand as if to ask for permission to rise. The rich general assented. The good knight stood up proud and upright, satchel held tightly in his grasp.

The rich general gave the good knight a nod as a semblance of respect. The general then plunged his sword deep into the good knight's chest. The knight felt no pain as he fought hard to breathe, but still, he refused to let the satchel go. As the knight's muscles began to relax from the mortal wound, the satchel slowly dropped from his hand and fell open as it touched the ground. The team of greedy knights gazed at the relic in complete awe.

The good knight dared not look at the holy item, feeling that he was no longer worthy of such an honor. The knight fell backward, landing on top of the relic, and stared into the sky.

At that very moment, Yousef opened his own eyes and stared into the sky. In his mind's eye, Yousef recognized the item inside the satchel; it was the shroud of Jesus of Nazareth.

Yousef closed his eyes one final time and realized his true destiny. He was martyred, and terrorism was diverted.

Both the good knight and Yousef took their last breaths as the army of greedy knights surrounded the shroud. Out of apparent respect for their former brother-knight, they waited for him to die before seizing the item.

Yousef's final vision was that of the sweat from the knight's brow sliding down his forehead mixing with the blood oozing from the gash across the bridge of his nose, finally merging with the tears streaming down his cheek. Yousef watched as the combined blood, sweat, and tears of the young Crusader dripped from the face of the good knight and fell onto the shroud.

Chapter One Hundred Fifty-nine

11:59 p.m.

Billy Assad stopped in his tracks and stared at the masses of people around him. He watched as the crowd glared at the big screen. Billy watched as the screen displayed images of the spectators from all over the world. There was an air of solemnity. Billy noticed that the crowd around him seemed to admire the dying man.

Maybe the death of Yousef was bringing the world together, in unison and perhaps in peace, if for just this one night, he thought.

He made a call to his FBI analyst. "Have all the interviews of the arrestees been completed?"

"Yes," the analyst responded.

"Have any of our agents confirmed that any of them were actually part of a cell?"

"Negative, sir. I mean, no, not yet."

Billy paused before replying. "And you won't—*ever.*"

"What do you mean?" the analyst asked.

Billy looked around at all the faces as they gawked in awe. "We spent weeks if not months looking for a direct connection between Yousef and these attackers when there was none. There were no secret or subliminal messages. There were no real cells. Yousef was simply a messenger carrying a message, a message that resonated with every disgruntled or disenfranchised person in this world. They acted on their own."

"So there is no danger?" the FBI analyst asked.

"No, there still is," Billy said cautiously. "The danger is still out there. They're out there somewhere—but acting independently."

"But Yousef's final words were to *stop* the attack."

"I know, but if they're acting independently, they can still lash out on their own. But for now, I think we're safe." He disconnected the call, leaving her with more questions than answers.

Billy Assad stared at the Times Square ball as it reached its destination. His ears were deafened by the cheers of celebration, the revelry, the bringing in of the new year. There was a combined sense of joy, a promise of peace and prosperity—even if for one night.

Mahmoud "Billy" Assad made his own personal resolution in that fresh new year. He would drop the moniker Billy. He would go by his given name: Mahmoud. He would no longer ignore his Muslim heritage.

Mahmoud Assad was pleasantly shocked and in disbelief. He looked at his watch to confirm that it was now thirty-five seconds into the new year, and with every passing second, it brought a smile to his face because in that satisfying passage of time, he believed that God had answered his prayers.

Epilogue I

Eaton College
Eton, Berkshire

A line of thirteen-year-old boys made their way into their respective classrooms to begin their studies for the day, led by a headmaster. A caravan of five black sedans drove their way onto the school grounds. The cars parked outside the school gates, and a large-framed man dressed in black proceeded to the car behind him. He reached for the door handle and was motioned to wait by a man inside.

"One moment," the grandmaster commanded.

The burly man dutifully obeyed.

"Are you sure this candidate is of the bloodline?" the grandmaster asked the man seated to his left.

"Yes," said the elder next to him. "We have painstakingly reviewed his pedigree over the course of the last seven to eight years."

"Very well. I hope so—for your sake."

The grandmaster, followed by four of his men, made his way to the provost's office.

"Welcome, my lord," the provost said gleefully. "We have been waiting for you."

"Where is the boy?" the grandmaster asked, wasting no time.

"Come this way," the provost said, beckoning him to follow. The provost continued to speak as he led the men to a classroom at the end of the hall. "This young man has already excelled in English, the arts, and mathematics. He is an excellent choice, an excellent choice indeed."

The grandmaster looked into the rectangular door window, peering into the classroom of boys. "Which one is he?"

The provost gazed into the window and pointed to a young boy sitting in the third chair of the last row. "There. That one. The one with the blond hair and blue eyes."

The grandmaster seemed displeased. "Summon him here."

The provost trembled as he entered the classroom. The grandmaster watched as the provost spoke to the professor. The professor, in turn, spoke to the young boy. The boy had a startled look on his face as he was led out of the classroom.

The provost gladly introduced him to the grandmaster. "Young man, let me introduce you to a very important man."

"It is a pleasure to meet you, good sir."

The grandmaster smiled. "What is your name, young man?"

"My name is Willem. Willem D'Arcy."

The grandmaster lifted Willem D'Arcy's chin up. "Young man, this is an important day for you and a lot of people throughout the world. I see great things for you. I see you standing in front of many people. You are giving a great speech. Millions of people will adore you. They will love you."

Epilogue II

Lay-Saint-Christophe, France

Far away, a young man resembling Yousef and Joshua sat on the cold, hard floor of the now-abandoned Sanatorium Lay-Saint-Christophe, cradling his head in his hands, crying out for his mama. Inside one of his hands, the young man was clutching tightly the pendant of Santi Cosma e Damiano—the patron saints of twins.

The End

2 1982 02943 1750

CPSIA information can be obtained
at www.ICGtesting.com
Printed in the USA
LVHW091119200222
711543LV00030B/25

9 781664 150515